In Search of Walid Masoud

Middle East Literature in Translation
Michael Beard and Adnan Haydar, *Series Editors*

In Search of
WALID MASOUD

a novel

JABRA IBRAHIM JABRA

Translated from the Arabic by
Roger Allen *and* Adnan Haydar

SYRACUSE UNIVERSITY PRESS

English translation copyright © 2000 by Syracuse University Press
Syracuse, New York 13244-5160

All Rights Reserved

First Edition 2000
00 01 02 03 04 05   6 5 4 3 2 1

This book was originally published in Arabic as *'al-Bahth an Walīd Mas'ūd* in 1978 by Dār al-Ādāb, Beirut.

The translators would like to acknowledge the contribution of Dr. Salma Jayyusi (director of the Project for the Translation of Arabic [PROTA]) and Christopher Tingley to the process of editing and translating the text. They also wish to express their gratitude to Jabra Ibrahim Jabra's heirs for their courtesy in making their father's work available.

The paper used in this publication meets the minimum requirements of American National Standard for Information Sciences—Permanence of Paper for Printed Library Materials, ANSI Z39.48-1984.∞™

Library of Congress Cataloging-in-Publication Data
Jabra, Jabra Ibrahim.
   [Bahth 'an Walid Mas'ud. English]
   In search of Walid Masoud : a novel / by Jabra Ibrahim Jabra ; translated from the Arabic by Roger Allen and Adnan Haydar.
   p. cm.—(Middle East literature in translation)
ISBN 0-8156-0646-X (alk. paper)
I. Allen, Roger M. A. II. Haydar, Adnan. III. Title. IV. Series.
PJ7840.A322 B3413 2000
892.7'36—dc21   00-028493

Manufactured in the United States of America

For her, who saw what she saw of life
And kept up the struggle, with characteristic pride

... oh, why
have to be human, and, shunning Destiny,
long for Destiny?...
  Not because happiness really
Exists, that premature profit of imminent loss...
...
But because being here amounts to so much, because all
This Here and Now, so fleeting, seems to require us and strangely
Concerns us...
  ... Once and no more. And we, too,
Once. And never again. But this
having been once, though only once,
having been once on earth—can it ever be cancelled?

Rilke, *The Ninth Elegy*
(quoted here in English from translation by J. B. Leishman and Stephen Spender)

Jabra Ibrahim Jabra, one of Palestine's most distinguished authors, was born in Bethlehem in 1920. He left Palestine after 1948 and settled in Iraq, where he eventually took up citizenship. Originally published in 1978, *In Search of Walid Masoud* is one of his two major novels. His other major novel, *The Ship* (1973), has also been translated into English by Adnan Haydar and Roger Allen. Jabra's published collections of prose poetry include *Tammuz in the City* (1959) and *The Agony of the Sun* (1981). He wrote volumes of literary criticism on contemporary Arabic poetry, including *Freedom and Chaos* (1960) and *The Closed Orbit* (1964). Jabra translated several English works into Arabic, the most notable of which is James Frazer's *The Golden Bough*, which was published in English as *Adonis, A Study in Ancient Oriental Myths and Religions* (1957). In 1987, he published *The First Well*, an autobiographical accound of his childhood in Palestine. Jabra was the 1990 recipient of both the Sultan Uweis Prize for Literary Criticism and the Jerusalem medal for literary achievement. Jabra Ibrahim Jabra died in 1994.

Roger Allen is professor of Arabic language and literature at the University of Pennsylvania. He is author of *The Arabic Literary Heritage* (1998), *The Arab Novel: An Historical and Critical Introduction* (1995), *A Period of Time* (1992), and *Modern Arabic Literature* (1987). He has also translated many modern Arabic authors, including Najib Mahfouz, Abd al-Rahman Munif, and, with Adnan Haydar, Jabra Ibrahim Jabra (*The Ship*).

Adnan Haydar is director of the Arabic program and professor of Arabic and comparative literature at the University of Arkansas, where he also directed the King Fahd Middle East Studies Program from 1993 to 1999. He has coauthored and coedited five books, including *Naguib Mahfouz: From Regional Fame to Global Recognition*, and published numerous translations and interpretations of poetry and fiction, including Khalil Hawi's *Naked in Exile* and Jabra Ibrahim Jabra's celebrated novel *The Ship*.

Contents

1. Dr. Jawad Husni Inherits a Heavy Legacy / 1

2. Dr. Jawad Husni Starts the Search, Partly Guided by the Perspective of Kazim Ismail and Ibrahim al-Hajj Nawfal / 25

3. Issa Nasser Witnesses the Death of Masoud Farhan, Having Known Him for Part of His Life / 65

4. Walid Masoud Remembers the Hermits in a Distant Cave / 83

5. Dr. Tariq Raouf Contemplates Capricorn / 101

6. Walid Masoud Writes the First Pages of His Autobiography / 130

7. Maryam al-Saffar Hangs On to a Rock Deep Inside Her / 145

8. Walid Masoud Passes Through Rain that Keeps Recurring / 180

9. Wisal Raouf Reveals Her Secrets / 189

10. Marwan Walid Attacks Umm al-Ayn with His Colleagues / 224

11. Ibrahim al-Hajj Nawfal Reveals Secrets Till Dawn / 230

12. Dr. Jawad Husni Promises More / 276

In Search of Walid Masoud

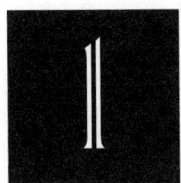

Dr. Jawad Husni Inherits a Heavy Legacy

"If only there were an elixir for the memory, something that could bring events back in the order they happened, one by one, then turn them into words that would cascade out onto paper!"

Perhaps I might, at this point, resort to these words Walid Masoud so often repeated in his last months. However much we fight against it, we remain the playthings of our memories. We are, at one and the same time, their products and their victims. Rightly or wrongly, they obsess us, sweetening the bitterness, deluding us and consuming our souls with sighs. How are we to capture these inverted dreams that both freeze the past and release it—these images scattered, at times, like clouds over the expanses of the mind, like precious diamonds compressed within the folds of the soul?

When young we're ashamed of slipping back into our memories because present and future are more important, more momentous. But as the years go by, the sense of shame grows less, not because present and future have lost their importance and weight, but because we can only live through most of the experiences they bring by harking back to our old ones, both pleasurable and painful, to those experiences that become, at once, ever more glowing and ever more blurred in the mind. So come now, patience, perseverance, words, help me to shed some light on them, and force them into intelligible lines.

Intelligible lines, did I say? Each line represents a year, a month, or at least a day; and how can a line like that be intelligible when every word in it is tied to separate strings reaching back into the vast expanses of the self, which are so filled with the pegs of tents pitched and struck down by the hundreds?

My knowledge of Walid Masoud was profound, not only in terms of time and place, but in terms of the complex human dimension that linked him so subtly with the lives of dozens of men and women. He reacted to those men and women more violently than I did; his relationships with them flared up and cooled off with an instinctive spontaneity, and it was my job to soften the effects of this with what he always called my genius for preventing the clash of opposites, for fusing opposites even, without causing harm to anyone, or at least not to other people. He often accused me of not owing allegiance to anyone, since I was capable of maintaining allegiance to all these people, who would be attracted to a particular person, then repelled by conflicting magnetic forces, whereas I would remain in the middle, with the thin strand between me and each one of them unbroken.

Then again, this may have been an illusion on my part. Perhaps I was holding the strands of various relationships and friendships in my hand, and though I still held on to the near ends, the far end had slipped off and gotten lost. Still, I behaved as if all the strands were connected, as if each person, in spite of everything, remained loyal to me. I don't deny that I was shocked, from time to time, to find the other person behaving as though he'd never known me or broken bread with me, or as though I'd nursed a grudge against him that he felt he should return. In my experience, there were only a few people like that, most of them probably unimportant anyway; yet, when I discovered this quality in someone I liked, I felt bitterly disappointed, and it left a deep wound inside me. Something like this happened to me once or twice with Walid himself, but I endured the disappointment and the wound in silence till he came back to me with a laugh and embraced me—I forgave him everything, even his tendency to sudden reserve. I used to think up excuses that never occurred even to him, or which he might have rejected. In the last few years, as a wealth of new lines developed around his eyes and mouth, I watched him and worried about him. Twenty years I had known him, with earth turning to gold in his hands; and I saw him reject all that, while his whole being began to show something like fissures in a rock, as though some internal chemical reaction was being reflected in his voice, his words, his eyes.

Walid was always searching for the balance he had talked about all his life, and had never found. *Balance*, he used to say, is a rough general term we use. In a world of terror, murder, hunger, and hatred, how can you find your inner psychological balance—or whatever you want to call it—without feeling you're standing on the far fringe of humanity? How can you be humane yet transcend the problems of humanity? This idea of balance was a mirage, of course, alluring but incapable of deceiving for long. Yet, Walid never despaired, or perhaps I refused to believe despair could take hold of him. He used to go through some intense crises; he'd blaspheme, block his ears, declare life was in the grip of evil, and burn in anger for days on end. If he'd gone no further than that, there would have been nothing very remarkable about him. After all, people sit in cafés and say things like that, and they meet in houses and reach the same conclusion—it happens all the time these days. The important thing was that Walid's crises never brought him to that apathy toward life and its ups and downs, that apathy that is just one facet of the unspoken despair most people actually live day after day. That's not to deny, of course, that optimism can be shallow and paltry, too. "Optimism about what, exactly?"

The fact is that self-examination of this sort never stopped Walid for long. University students may indulge in pessimism and optimism, curse and become enraged, and imagine there's some great alternative they can discover. That's their right, their duty even. But Walid had been through it all many years before, and he was done with it.

So what was left? Balance. And how could he achieve it? At what point on the shuddering zigzag line could he set it, when his whole world was slippery and shaky, with endless ups and downs that defeated mind and logic alike? At times he used to say that if he'd lived in an earlier age, he might have talked about the possibility of finding balance in art and religion, of finding union with beauty, for example, in the manner of ancient Sufis: unification with beauty by worshiping it. That, he said, was a laughable idea. He'd never even worshiped in a religious sense. Should he burn incense? Or write poems he'd never recite to anyone, to be read at dawn like litanies? Should he embrace a beautiful woman, stroke her flesh lustfully to a climax, and pretend he worshiped her? And after that, what? Yet, after challenging everything so passionately, after battling and pounding his fists and risking everything, he would say that in the end beauty was the most important thing of all, and contemplating beauty was akin to the Sufis' contemplation of the essence of God. Amid the turmoil was a calm voice; in the thick of contradictions, a tangible hidden harmony; and between the poles of attraction and repulsion, a deep still point: the eye of the storm, a rapture no words could define in a world of inanity and hidden fear.

"When I was young," he said, "and I saw for the first time the way people sometimes speak and then look around worried as if someone has heard them, I was really alarmed. Are we to be afraid of other people knowing what we say? And as the years went by, the furtive, scared looks and the anxious questions were repeated so often they became the normal thing. Terror became part of our lives, and we learned to live with it and get around it as best as we could, so that conspiracy was built into the ordinary way we thought. We think like terrified people, like those trying to avoid the evil in others. And then, under the strain of thinking like this, they expect you to be creative, to scatter pearls of originality and dazzle eyes that have been purblind for generations. I shall seek the eye of the storm and rid myself of all this thinking."

That's what he told a newspaper in response to a question from an insistent journalist, a few months before he disappeared. And when the journalist persisted with yet another question, he added: "Please don't talk to me about courage. Courage is a purely personal and private matter. Speaking out is a completely foolish thing to do now, and convinces no one. No one even listens. It's like beating a drum among the deaf. The only courage that deserves to be translated into action is challenging death with raised fists and violence, thereby using death itself to trample down death, as in the death of a freedom fighter, for example. But as for all of you, let me tell you: You're all cowards. Beat your cans and drums at the whale if you like, and hope it coughs up the moon from its throat."

Recently, his tone had become ever more harsh; that much was obvious. I had no doubt about his appetite and lust for life and the future, but I noticed, too, that he'd become more inclined to silence in the face of other people's verbiage, and I started to feel that reaching him, reaching his innermost thoughts and feelings, had become difficult. He was barricading himself behind a concrete wall, as if indulging an addiction to some secret, mysterious drink he refused to share with anyone else.

Walid telephoned me the morning he disappeared. I was in bed when Hala called me to the phone around six o'clock.

"What's up?" I asked, still sleepy.

"Jawad," he said, "I'm going off in my car today."

"Today?" I asked. "Just like that?"

"Yes. I wanted to say good-bye. I'm sorry I woke you up so early. It's just that I wanted to be sure I'd catch you before you left for college."

"When will you be back?"

"Back? I don't know. Take care of my mail as usual, please. I've told Furat, my housekeeper, to give you my letters. I may be away for a while this time."

I didn't ask him where he was going, although I suspected it would most probably be Lebanon and then Italy. He'd done that more than once before and been away a long time. Every year he would renew my power of attorney over a number of his affairs, for fear something might happen to delay his return to Baghdad. This time, though, he actually went away and never returned. His disappearance caused quite a commotion, which I hadn't expected. Some people said he'd emigrated to Canada or Australia; others suggested that he'd been murdered, or that he'd gone back secretly to Occupied Palestine. At any rate, he disappeared. During those last six months, managing his affairs tired me out, because I had to answer many of the letters sent to him, quite apart from the hundreds of questions his disappearance left unanswered. He left his car in the middle of the desert highway to Syria, about fifty miles west of Rutba; he left no word about what happened, but because he loved riddles, he left a tape in his car on which he'd recorded many things. The one thing he hadn't recorded was the one thing everybody was dying to know: where had he gone?

A few weeks later rumors spread that he'd been found murdered in Lebanon; a mutilated corpse no one could identify was found at the foot of Dahr al-Baydar, and some people said it was Walid Masoud's. At that point, I felt he must indeed be dead, and considered my intuition reliable because I'd known him for so long. I saw him in my mind's eye rolling down the rocks in one of the valleys of Lebanon, and I couldn't get him out of my mind for days. Twenty years of friendship fell apart, and I kept searching for the pieces one by one, hoping, by doing this, to find a key to the secret of his disappearance.

All I had were memories and piles of his papers stuffed into large envelopes, and whenever I opened one of them, time seemed to pour down on me from every direction, till I felt I was choking. Then I'd put the papers back in the envelopes and start breathing freely again.

A number of Walid's friends were as shocked as I was. Amer Abd al-Hamid, whom I've never seen mention anybody's death or anybody's marriage, as though people's feelings at vital moments simply didn't concern him, used to imagine—or else I did—that he'd never grieve at anyone's death or departure. Yet, even he was really shaken up by Walid's disappearance. He became a recluse for days, refusing to see anyone, and for weeks, he gave up his big dinner parties that had so enriched our social lives.

Ibrahim al-Hajj Nawfal came by one evening unannounced, his lips trembling with anger; I wasn't sure whether he was going to fly into a temper or burst into tears. He started pounding his fists against the arm of the lounge chair he was sitting in.

"It's impossible!" he kept saying. "Impossible! This is a trick, Jawad; Walid's been the victim of some horrible deception. Please, let me hear the tape he left in the car."

But he was in no condition to listen to anything, not even Walid's voice. When Hala brought us two whiskeys, he gulped his down, got up, grabbed the bottle, and then poured himself more than half a glass.

That evening, Dr. Tariq Raouf telephoned me to ask about the rumors that had started circulating.

"You know, Jawad," he said, "I may have been the last person to see Walid." I was surprised at this, as I didn't think there was any strong bond of friendship between them.

"You actually saw him the night before he left?" I asked. "Did you say good-bye to him?"

"Yes, I did," he replied, his voice sounding strange over the phone. "At Rutba. I was there with Kazim. Didn't Kazim tell you?"

"I haven't seen him since he came back."

"Kazim and I were traveling to Greece in my car. We reached Rutba at midnight. Our passports had been checked—you know that huge, dirty hall, like a cross between a customs office and a café. That was where we saw Walid, with his passport in his hand. We greeted him, then said good-bye. He looked lost even then."

When I turned around to tell Ibrahim what Tariq had said, I saw he'd been straining his ears, listening closely to our conversation.

"I'm going to see Kazim tomorrow," he said, "and find out the details."

What details would Ibrahim learn from a friend who saw Walid for two minutes perhaps, as the two of them were getting into their cars; and all this in the middle of a dark night, at a customs station in the desert? A day or two later I met Kazim myself, and we had a long talk about Walid, but we gleaned nothing new about his disappearance.

I went back to the tape several times, playing it piece by piece and reflecting on every single word. We'd found it in a small red Japanese cassette player, and hadn't paid much attention to it at first. The recorder was lying on the floor of the car, and there was another one installed under the car radio with a music cassette in it that had been played to the end. A small microphone from the red one was tied to the steering wheel, and the record button was depressed, so Walid had clearly been recording as he drove, before whatever happened actually did happen.

When I played the tape, I found that the first part had recorded the music from the other tape in the car's cassette player. It was Henry Purcell's *Harpsichord Suites*, which Walid had recently bought and played a lot. Then came Walid's voice, not always very clear because of the music and the sound of the engine in the background. He was recording as he drove, most probably at tremendous speed. But the words followed naturally, intermittent at times, continuous at others. There was no doubt it was Walid's voice.

The tape surprised me when I first heard it, and hasn't stopped surprising me since. For some reason I can't pin down, I got the impression Walid was out to confuse us all with this "final" tape of his, or maybe he wanted, for the last time, to be frank with all of us, to put his cards on the table, so to speak. Which was the face, and which was the mask? Which one of them had I known for twenty long years that now flew by as though they were just two days? Even if Walid was clearly undergoing some very painful experience, or gripped by a depression that gave a delirious flow to his words, as though they were a kind of defense mechanism he was using to try and save himself, still there were words on the tape that merited serious study. It didn't contain anything that could be described as a defendant's statement, or a "letter to the editor" that someone writes to defend himself against an accusation in a newspaper or a magazine. (In any case, Walid had never done anything like that in his whole life; when someone attacked him, he responded with a silence loaded with contempt.) Walid had chosen to abandon logic, at least on the surface. It's difficult to know precisely what made him record such telling words, on the very day he disappeared.

More than two months later, Amer passed by one evening and asked me to play the tape. "Does he mention any names?" he asked.

"A whole bunch of names," I said.

"People we know? If you don't mind," he went on, "I suggest I invite a number of Walid's friends to my house next Thursday. We'll surprise them all by playing the tape . . ."

"But I don't think you'll find out anything new. Walid doesn't accuse anyone, or expose anyone."

"Do you think the idea would have crossed my mind if there was any chance of exposing somebody?"

I wasn't happy about Amer's plan. He has a certain tendency to play malicious tricks on people without showing any sign of the way he's secretly laughing inside.

"I find Walid's words obscure, desperate, innocent, happy, all at once," he said. "So let's make playing the tape an occasion to talk about a friend we all care about. Anyhow, we'll restrict the group to his closest friends."

After some hesitation, I agreed. But I didn't give Amer the tape; I told him I'd bring it with me. Later, I sat down to transcribe the tape, exactly as I heard it, an uninterrupted, interlocking flow of words. That way I'd be able to read it and study it in every detail. I'd add it to Walid's other papers and books in case it could help me with the study I'd decided to write about him.

• • •

Thursday was a scorching hot day, but night brought with it the promise of a breeze. Amer welcomed us at the door, and Hala warmly embraced his wife, Ann. Then we walked straight to the big garden, through hanging palms, to a cool spot. Close by, a few fountains were shooting jets of water into the air, which then fell like silver beads into a long blue pond, with lights shimmering through the water. Chairs had been arranged, rather unusually, in two small circles in a corner of the garden, which made me suspect there wouldn't be many guests this time.

Fadil, the waiter, gave me a drink and gave Hala some juice. A little later Dr. Tariq Raouf came in with Samira, his wife, and his younger sister Wisal, whom my wife and I didn't know very well. Then Ibrahim Nawfal arrived, followed a little while later by Kazim Ismail. They both looked extremely smart (those poor bachelors!). Ibrahim was obviously delighted to see Maryam al-Saffar come in (he couldn't hide his admiration from anyone). She was accompanied by Jinan al-Thamer and a Palestinian woman I hadn't seen before; Maryam introduced her as Rabah Kamal. The last to arrive were Ihsan Basri and his wife, Nuhad. I didn't know if Amer had already told his guests about what we'd agreed upon, but, at any rate, he'd managed to invite a number of people who hadn't been together under the same roof lately, at his house or anywhere else. With his famous subtlety, he'd made sure of bringing together a group of people who were either interested in what Walid Masoud had to say, or else mentioned in the tape, explicitly or implicitly. Nor did I fail to notice there were slightly more women than men.

Ibrahim wasn't the only one interested in Maryam. I was, too, that evening, because I suspected from the very start that she was none other than the woman named in the tape as "Shahd." I made a point of heading directly for her before she sat next to someone else.

"Doctor Jawad," she asked, starting the conversation, "have you met Rabah? Do you know who introduced me to her?" she continued, when I said I hadn't. "Walid Masoud, in Lebanon, five years ago."

"Unfortunately," Rabah said, "I had to come to Baghdad after... after... Walid left. Wherever I go here, I find people mentioning his name, just the way they used to in Beirut. I had no idea so many people knew him here."

"What? Another woman in Walid's life?" I thought to myself. "Then you knew him?" I asked.

"A little," she said with a certain coyness, failing to hide a strange glow in her eyes. "A long time ago."

"A long time ago?" I said, repeating her words.

"When he was in Jerusalem, in the late forties," she answered. "I was a teenager then."

"Splendid!" I said.

"No," she said, shaking her head, "don't expect me to be a mine of information on him. Maryam said you're writing a book on him. You probably know more about him than I do, even if we go back to those days."

"I want to know more about... his background... his childhood, his father and mother..." I said. There was, I noticed, a tone of eager expectancy to my voice.

"I'm very sorry," she replied with a laugh. "I didn't know him in those very early days."

"Who did then?" I asked desperately.

"A lot of Palestinians knew him," she said. "You know who can tell you about his childhood? A close friend of his family. Quite by chance, I met him a few years ago in Amman. We were furnishing my brother's house. We went to a well-known carpenter there called Issa Nasir; everyone knows his shop. When I discovered he was from Bethlehem, I asked, just as you're asking me now, 'Do you know a man called Walid Masoud?' He was delighted. 'Do you know him?' he asked me. 'He's an old, dear friend,' I replied. 'Fine,' he said. 'I'll arrange a ten percent discount for you, for Walid's sake.'"

"Did he tell you anything about Walid's life?" I asked.

"We didn't go into details," she said, "but he talked more than once about knowing Walid's parents and brothers. Anyway, if he escaped harm during the Black September fighting, he'll still be in Amman, no doubt."

"What's his name again, please?" I asked.

"Issa Nasir."

I took out my notebook and wrote down his name. Then, turning to Maryam, I said, "Do you know about the tape?"

"What tape?" she asked, surprised.

"The one Walid left in his car."

"What about it?"

"He talks about his past, his childhood, and other things."

For all the dim light in the garden, it seemed to me her face had lost color.

"You said, 'and other things'?" she said. "What, for example?"

"His love life."

"His love life? Can I hear it?"

"You will."

At that moment Amer came over and interrupted me; apparently, he couldn't wait till after supper. Apologizing to the two women, he pulled me up by the arm, then took out a pencil from his breast pocket and started tapping his glass.

"Listen, everyone!" he said in a loud voice.

The noise stopped, and all the faces turned toward him.

"Dr. Jawad and I," he said, surveying the guests, "have prepared a little surprise for you. We're sure you'll enjoy it. You've probably heard that on the day he disappeared, Walid Masoud left a tape in his car, on which he recorded some interesting statements that we're sure you'll enjoy listening to. Jawad has the tape, and he's going to tell you all. Please sit down, everyone."

"Please, Jawad," he said, holding my arm, "give us an introduction to the whole thing."

I felt acutely embarrassed; in fact, an unexpected feeling of intense sorrow came over me, and I almost burst into tears.

"Actually," I said, "it's the tape that will tell you everything. Walid recorded it in his car on his last ill-starred trip. If you weren't all friends of his, we wouldn't be wasting your time with it."

At that moment my eyes fell on Wisal Raouf, Dr. Tariq's sister, because she was sitting almost in front of me. I noticed her jaws drop and her eyes widen in a peculiar way. Indeed, it seemed to me that all the faces were registering an unpleasant surprise.

"It goes without saying, of course," I said, hastening to calm their fears, "that Walid speaks well of every one of you. Well, in actual fact he hardly mentions anyone by name, except . . . at any rate . . . would you like to listen, please."

I gave the tape to Amer, who took it to the recorder on a table close by, and put it in. Before pressing the "play" button, he looked around. "Refill your drinks, please," he said. Fadil went around with a trayful of drinks and left. Then Amer played the tape.

The music started, not very clearly, and Amer raised the volume. Then Walid's voice came from the two loudspeakers attached to the stereo: a strange, mechanical voice, familiar to us yet rather unfamiliar, too. Everyone was listening. No one moved. The voice echoed around the garden along with the background hiss and the music, sounding as though it came from some other galaxy, which seemed unconnected with ours at first, but then gradually became somehow more familiar, forging a bond between us and the words:

> A green bookbag olive color full of books copybooks lead pencils and colored pencils school days it's strapped around the neck and bulges under the arm on the waist full of childhood secrets the Exploits of Heroes strange names Hercules Ulysses Achilles Petrocles Priam how does the first hemistich go darkness has run away many thanks be to the one and only God as is most justly due I took the bag emptied it on the windowsill and we went Suleiman and Abd and I jumping down the terraces of the valley to the olive trees olive harvest going on we picked a few strayed olives resting between thorns and slopes and earth or the few left clinging to the high branches shaking nervously the feet secured from long practice and the whole world is full of olive trees stripped and laden hey boys get away from that tree we haven't picked it yet we're only picking the leftovers and the white clouds like lambs grazing in the blue fields of the sky oh John Keats Bright star would I were steadfast as thou art we were just kids I was eight nine ten years old if only I had money Sheikh Salem said with all seriousness I would have paid for his boy's education we eat rice with a piece of meat and the priest in his billowing white beard spread out on his shiny cassock takes out his dentures immerses them in a cup of water and washes them for everyone to see his mouth disappears under his

big mustache I don't want a mustache I told her I'm going to keep on shaving if you grow a mustache she told me a black line over your upper lip as if drawn there in charcoal you'll look like movie stars especially the handsome bad guys who win the money and the women but I love you with or without a mustache she was sunk deep into the armchair her breasts like two ivory spheres and her skirt riding over her thighs collected around her waist her thighs soaking the heat from the slowing burning fire in the big black fireplace in those days we used to go down to the sea and feel icy blasts of the foamy horses sea horses would burst out from the middle of the sea and charge up the beach to dissolve at our feet as we pushed our way through the cool soft sand and her lips cold perfumed crowned with spray and my cheeks in her flowing hair my own hair flying in the wind even though her fingers were entrenched in it we stuck our heads out of the window of the train rumbling roaring and whistling its way over the green fields promise me will you promise that you'll never grow old that you'll never age and I'll promise to stay as you see me now wide-eyed with the same luscious mouth tell me your body will stay like green grass for me to roll in just as I dreamed of you when I listened to music in the school yard I see you sitting under branches weighed down with roses like masses of snow your feet dangling as the olive tree swayed no it wasn't an olive tree I can't forget the olive trees and the red soil and the cold shady caves where we could eat figs and grapes hanging down in huge clusters from the vines and lying like pregnant women on the red soil and the buzzing of bees and hornets we spent the whole day trying to burn the hornet's nest they attacked us and stung me and my face swelled why didn't you cover your face with a screen where on earth could we find a screen in the valley and they were shouting all around us from mountain to mountain even the women were calling out to each other using the air for wireless communication Maryam Maryaaaaaam bring father his lunch a small paper bag with a loaf of flat bread a boiled egg olives and pickled cucumbers and he laughs my father and he says life is like a cucumber my father who before he died was lying on the floor like a huge oak felled by the wind and he knew many stories about acorn bread during the days of the Ottoman War banishment and famine I was born after the famine the road sped away with us we were in a truck and the white road wound through the dust fleeing away from us from me and the hills fleeing away and the stones the stone kilometer landmarks which I learned to read after I grew older and I was able to read the calendar on which 1927 was written April May June and Jasmine and Rayya you longed for Rayya while you got further and further away from her or was I running away from her or was I running away thanks be to the one and only God from her voice her hands her delicate fingers bared like a navel like a cheek's dimple on a smooth belly like a hill on the distant horizon where we see nothing but black birds swooping and vanishing is Paradise there beyond the sky where sky meets horizon and if I were to reach that violet horizon above the blue mountains I would open a window in the sky through which I would enter Paradise O poor ignorant how long will you dream of crossing to other worlds when all you have is this cruel stubborn world you must fight against it I learned this in school when my fingers could hardly hold on to the pen and write and the lines would come crooked not as I wanted them and the pen would not register all the words that flowed from my brain and lips I could almost see them littering the desk and falling around me and I would pick them up again with frozen fingers and the teachers would come and go stomping on the bare floor and they would stand behind us and look at us as we sat there with heads lowered over the paper and I would say to the teacher it's cold and he would smile and say a young man like you complaining about the cold shame on you sir write and so I wrote and we would go out to the snow-covered road Suleiman and Abd and Yusuf and Bishara and Salih and all the neighborhood boys and a soft snowball hits me and I throw it and I hit someone and I make another and it's very cold at first but then I don't feel it anymore I feel warmth in my fingers as the snowballs fly between us scoring hits on faces backs and walls and snow crunching under our feet and I step into pools of melted snow water seeps into my shoes and I feel warm and cold at the same time from the door mother shouts at whom I don't know maybe at me and the sky is blue and the sun is white and cold O for a cup of tea Shahd your name is strange like you I eat you I lick at you like the honey in your name you've been my ideal man for years don't you know or are you deliberately running away from me you've trapped me I shall run away too I shall run away because I always run away until I fall flat on my face I take her serene face in my hands to study her eyes and nose and her delicious cool mouth I won't run away anymore and the next day she ran away and sent me a card from Beirut and I wrote back two or three lines God said let there be love and Heaven and Hell were and one looked like the other and God loved both of them and this is my answer to your old question why is love fraught with sorrow as though it were the beginning of a separation and her long letter reached me I met your son Marwan how beautiful his eyes were gleaming out of his headdress I said to him take me with you and teach me how to shoot a gun love starts and the beginning and the end are repeated on the distant horizon where sky meets earth on clear days when the sun is like falling fire and I'm looking for a shady spot I want to read think cry over sorrows that I know and don't know and I will know them all when separation is complete when loved ones die and the houses are filled with clamor and in the night howls and barks reach us from hill to hill and valley to valley where I lie down on the roof of the old monastery next to the bells embracing a stone which has fallen from its column how beautiful columns are standing or lying on the ground cracked from sun and rain year after year for centuries on end it's the music that I can't do without like a secret addict who can't share with anyone else the contents of his dreams those deceptive horrible delicious dreams and Shahd passes by me in her car she returns to snatch away my security and my peace of mind and threatens not to give them back to me until I pay her a thousand words which she'll put inside her blouse between her breasts I am rich with words for my fortune

> O Sister give me a drink I said
> I'm going south a long long way
> Here drink she said and may it bring
> You cheer for ever and a day

I speak all the languages on earth and Bishara says these are your father's words his stories and poems we're both hiding in the big almond tree that overlooks the new road chewing big green almonds our teeth set on edge at times from the delicious sour taste Maryam is in the vegetable garden feeding the chickens then she looks around lifts her skirt off her small behind and squats against the wall until she hears our giggling then she jumps up frightened and runs away like one of her chickens and she brings me an egg still warm and she says the white hen just laid it I know the white hen she's the companion of the fat red rooster who struts and clucks among his chickens as though he owned all the dunghills in the world but he is at least like Rabab's rooster endowed with a good voice and Maryam outsings him with her shrill powerful voice she claims people can hear her from the top of Mount Khraytoun but there are rarely any people on Mount Khraytoun to hear her calling from Mount Furdays or is it Paradise which I remember the fools' apples that grow on shrubs between the rocks those bright red shiny apples held in the hand they look like gems smooth and red and so tempting but I am afraid to taste them and that madman we saw chained in that dark stone-walled room in Saint George's Monastery how gentle he looked with his long beard and bushy hair then he became wild all of a sudden started screaming and yelling till he collapsed exhausted and I almost died of fear the same kind of fear I felt for Rima maybe he had eaten fools' apples which are found in all the Edens of the world just like Rima did all the way to the old horse-drawn carriage which we rode at noon one day in July on Baghdad roads from Karrada to Waziriyya she sat there at my side clutching in her lap a paper bag full of green apples it was as though her closeness to me aroused mountain coolness and spring breezes and we were worried that the driver would turn around and see us knowing well that we were flirting behind his back as he prodded his horses gently for who would want to rush time or shorten distances when we have enough apples for fifty Eves O sister give me a drink I said but Sahira has no idea about original sin her virginity is in full flower like one of those maddening Baghdad roses her big eyes flash with searing thoughts like the onrush of fire during nights of drought which sometimes seems never-ending and does it end for example at four in the morning when the first tentative chirp is heard from a shy bird in the garden to be repeated again and again and the nightingale's encouraged to slightly vary his song when he's joined by one bird after another until they form a complete orchestra from their trees which begin to wake up with the first rays of dawn how often I've seen those rays changing from brown to gold to blue and then violet as though the world would dissolve its cares in spaces of brilliant colors which presage the rising of the bleeding yellow disc but this isn't quite what I wanted to say I've been through it all thousands of times it no longer surprises me although I'm always apt to have the same surprise as if whenever I hear the same tune I feel the same emotions with all their sharpness and their permanence and their transience like the water of a river racing away while they still swirled around my feet as they dangled from the boat and I'd splash her as she shook her head to get her long hair away from her eyes and she would recite "Margaret are you grieving over Goldengrove unleaving" Shahd are you grieving over the golden groves as they shed their leaves just as you shed your clothes leaf by leaf until the last leaf while sorrow runs streamlike over your face and breasts and stomach and you say this is impossible too much do you find me beautiful as a tree with its leaves shaken off by the wind love to such a tree is sorrow like falling rain and the morning looks strange through the large window like images frozen on a movie screen glowing with yearning mystery desire secrets and pain ah yes Marwan Marwan the pain remains I know I know as in surrealist paintings one tearful mascaraed eye on top of another the rain beats on the windows and flows in streams down the panes the door is open or half-open then closes silently like the door of an ancient prison beyond which volcanoes may erupt and yet you'll have no knowledge of it one cries like a lover unused to crying every tear is like a knife in a wound oh Marwan suddenly the sun fills the world cars honk their horns and rumble noisily through the dust and oh the pain remains even in the distant vistas where the sea and the boats and the fishermen are and the forest and the golden groves shedding their leaves to reveal wild beasts beset by the autumn winds angels are put to flight screaming and oh the pain remains ugh no this is not what I wanted to say let me turn the tape over

Do I want to die too I ask myself but I've known the answer for a long time I don't need to strike a theatrical pose any longer taking in my hands Yorick's skull and other skulls which the grave diggers dig up every second I don't need all of this to remember that all the laughter and beauty will be gobbled up by my lady worm why should I care who gobbles it up after today when the desert road in front of me never ends and I don't want it to end it's more wonderful than all the heads and all the eyes and all the lips put together as Ibrahim used to say when he discovered with a bottle of arrack in his hands that life was a patchwork of dreams and then he would go on not dreams but nightmares because he remembered the woman he'd seen blown to pieces when the bomb exploded for no crime she'd committed he focused his eyes on the glass as the words tumbled out through his rebellious lips we're all bastards he said what about Ophelia I said including Ophelia he answered even though she was more noble than either of us since in a world of villains and traitors she was at least able to commit suicide but life's still more important than her or you or me or more important than lovely heads and big eyes and luscious lips he always contradicted himself and I always regarded myself as being more logical than he was until damn it I don't remember that just like that with a single blow the back was broken logic vanished and the whole world was crushed and came to an end Ibrahim can say what he likes about the importance of life among villains and traitors amid sticky slime and stagnation when Shahd's face is like a jewel like a fools' apple as she offers me her nipples like two harbingers of reward and punishment I gobble them up and go crazy as she lifts her skirt higher and higher to convince me that she has the most beautiful thighs on the banks of the Tigris since Ishtar failed to seduce Gilgamesh and here I am the hairy ape the cry of the primeval forests bursting from my chest to my throat which I transform into words of milk and honey cultured and sweet needing only Mozart to set them to music so that Zerlina can sing them and between her and me is this vast desert and I'm jealous of my own hand for doing what it did and feeling what it felt and I said if only I could put these delicious sensations into a velvet box they'd sparkle like diamonds on a dark night in a world full of beasts crunching pebbles and fiddling with their balls except for Jawad Husni who brings me a new story every day and I know his love is the only love that will not sour but I can't convince him that my sense of balance has been destroyed and been tipped in favor of darkness and beasts what is this maybe it's a hawk no a crow or a kite over the broad valleys between one mountain and another eagles so that no sooner does the sun go down than two or three eagles take off and if they pounce on a bird or an animal no this is certainly a crow I'm sure they're crows summing up the whole of one's life starting from the tales of *Kalila and Dimna* and La Fontaine's *Fables* to the accounts of corpses living or dead which have filled the earth and their stench congests the nostrils of virtuous and evil people alike how do you tell them apart by their noses curved like swords ha ha their ears flattened like trays ha ha their mouths rounded like open manholes here's another crow and yet another one crow after another wherever I look all I see are crows disgusting he's hit the glass what if it broke is it the stench of death carried even by the desert wind like the wind from the swamps she said it in a tone which surprised me you're a wild duck what are you doing among all these birds sitting in the swamps get out of here wild duck run away run away before I at which point I laughed at her poetic flight where shall I run away I said flee wherever your wings take you she replied afterwards she wrote that in a letter in a neat English hand and addressed the envelope to the "wild duck" and from her car she handed me the letter as I stood there on the pavement the car sped off with her yelling run away before it's too late and it was too late it's always too late we always arrive late and flying and wings do us no good the crows invade us in broad daylight and in the dead of night no difference no difference no difference no no no no no no twenty years ago I used to say it with pride ten years before that I used to say it conceitedly and stubbornly but now I say it indifferently although its roots are deep within the heart and the liver and the guts I don't care who hears it the actor's no longer worried about who makes up his audience in fact he's not even worried if there's no audience at all as long as he's at center stage sending his cry into the womb of darkness before the curtain falls and Shahd comes across the Euphrates and across the desert to meet her lover as he hurls words into the womb of darkness which gets pregnant with possibilities and keeps the owls and the crows and the nightingales between her thighs up to the moment of orgasm and death while Ihsan is still arguing with Ibrahim his tongue can barely move in his mouth his hand trembles like Ibrahim's when at the peak of his anger he shouts his eyes filled with tears they're all traitors they're all traitors after that he could only fall back into the abyss of his own reality which is his never-ending nightmare and so to another night and another darkness and another female with pleasure and terror and death between her thighs day after day like some obscene melodrama which has to be acted out ad infinitum and the crows fill the roads nothing but crows loom in the horizon the sun has set and she hasn't arrived yet I have no idea when she will Maryaaaaam bring lunch so I could eat it with Marwan under the big olive tree and sleep on the red soil with my head on a rock I'm going south a long, long way until Shahd arrives and stands over my head and lifts her skirt so I can see everything she has her laughter will cascade upon me like tears for she strides my thoughts like a lustful rider and spurs them in the direction of her whims no no no that's not what I wanted to say even though I did want to say some of it when everything I've already said is merely marginal and the main text is missing so let me try again perhaps using the philosophical method by first defining the question in the hope that Amer would be satisfied and Kazim would not see in it a utopian time bomb let the answer be what it may all the way from Mount Khraytoun to Ayn Sifni where the waters gushed forth and the Flood started and Noah found no one to help him build his Ark and man and everything he made drowned pair by pair oh mother mine how can you possibly save your children this time except with that wonderful pride of yours which you bestowed upon them freely not fearing extravagance since pride was your only dominion and your stubbornness could pulverize rocks dry the seas and fill the mountains with water springs no matter what you said or how you said it and Jawad suppresses his amazement at the large number of women I'd gotten to know in my search for that one woman who might possess my mother's stubbornness and pride and claims he no longer understands me but I'm the one who's never understood anyone even for a single day so let me try to define the question

No sooner had the tape come to an end than I began to feel I'd been crassly stupid in agreeing to Amer's plan to play it publicly that evening. All the women, I noticed, were sobbing and drying their eyes and noses with handkerchiefs. The entire process seemed to me to have embarrassed everyone, whether or not their names were mentioned.

Ibrahim was the first to speak. "Such sadness is terrible," he said. "Walid has mourned himself before anyone else has had the chance. I for one forgive him for what he says about me."

Dr. Tariq, on the other hand, thought differently. "As far as Walid is concerned, this tape is almost a scandal. I wish it hadn't been played like this."

"Why?" asked Amer.

"Because . . . because it's so very personal, so very intimate, full of his own private symbols. Words like these should be listened to by each one of us privately with their author."

"These symbols you mention," commented Kazim Ismail, "don't they deserve some careful, conscious reflection on our part? I always used to say Walid would only ever express himself when he was oblivious to himself, as he was here."

"What's all this talk of symbols?" Maryam asked. "Walid's words are as clear as day. He's crying over his son. He's recalling himself and his son to his mother, the earth he could never stop thinking about."

And then suddenly Jinan's voice rose, loud and tearful. "But who is this Shahd?"

Ibrahim's reply surprised me. "All you women," he said. "You're all Shahd . . . Excuse me, I mean . . . she's the Woman in his life. He kept running away from her and colliding with her on every road he took."

"That's an evasion of the question," Ihsan broke in. "Maybe he had a girlfriend with that name in Lebanon."

"Do we have to know exactly who she is?" Kazim asked. "When someone sums up his entire life, particularly when it concerns his very private life, there's no need to pinpoint identities. In this case, no doubt, they're extremely complex."

"To a certain extent, you're right," Maryam replied. "The strange thing is that my name is mentioned, but it's the name of a little girl he knew a long time ago. Is Margaret, the girl in the verse he quotes, Shahd as well? And who's Sahira? What do you say, Wisal?" she asked, turning to the young woman sitting next to her.

But Wisal said nothing. She merely shook her head. "I don't know any of these people you're talking about," she said in a subdued voice. "I don't know anything."

Dr. Tariq stood up. "There are more important things than all that on the tape," he said. "Walid, as Freud says, suffered from an Oedipal complex . . . Fadil!" He walked toward the waiter who was standing by the bar. "What about this complex?" he asked, addressing the others again.

They all got up one after another. Amer and Ann withdrew to the kitchen through the garden door. Jinan came over to me. "I wish you hadn't played this trick," she whispered. Then she went off to the kitchen, too, to help the hosts bring out the dishes of food and put them on the long table where plates and cutlery had been stacked. Only Wisal remained seated, and when Samira yelled to her to get up and take her plate, I heard her say, "Later. I don't feel like eating now." She stood up and made her way toward the bar, took an empty glass, and then put it down again. As I watched her out of the corner of my eye, she headed toward the fountains, walked through the palm trees, and disappeared into the dark part of the garden where I finally lost sight of her.

I put some food on my plate; then, just at that moment, I saw her coming back and walking straight toward me. Realizing that she wanted to talk to me, I moved toward her. "What were you out to discover tonight, Dr. Jawad?" she asked in a low voice.

"Nothing in particular," I replied with a laugh.

"I don't believe you."

"Then let me say it. We wanted to find out who Shahd is."

"And what will you or Amer achieve if you do find out?"

"Curiosity, Miss Wisal. The suspense is killing us."

"Suppose I told you who Shahd is?"

"Is she one of the women here?"

The others were all busy making comments about the wonderful food for which Ann, or rather her cook, Aydan, was famous. Everybody wanted to forget the subject altogether, or pretended to.

"Suppose I tell you who Shahd is," Wisal repeated. "What will you have discovered?"

"To be frank, I will have discovered how very little I knew about Walid. You're right. Why are we always eager to prove our own ignorance? Let me get you some food."

"No, no, thank you. It looks as if Walid's going to make us all prove our ignorance."

"Did you know him ... well?"

"Me? Hardly at all. How about you?"

I laughed but said nothing.

"What about Amer," she continued, "and my brother Tariq, and Maryam and Jinan and the others?"

"Miss Wisal," I said, "you're very angry, and I don't know why. Or maybe I do."

"No, Dr. Jawad, you don't know. It's not important. I'm angry and that's all there is to it. Part of the reason is that your dear friend Walid Masoud has disappeared without telling us why or where. Strange, isn't it? Did you ever meet his son, Marwan?"

"Only when he was a small child," I replied. "I was a friend of the family then. But I never saw him again after he'd grown up. Did you know that he stayed in Lebanon?"

"Yes, and I met him in Beirut a short while before he fell a martyr."

All of a sudden I felt the earth was splitting open under my feet. I remembered the words of the girl on Walid's tape: "Take me with you and teach me how to shoot . . ." I leaned over to Wisal, my lips almost touching her ear. Her short hair revealed how perfectly formed it was with the diamond earring flashing. "Are you . . . Shahd?" I whispered.

She turned her head violently in my direction. "Are you mad?" she almost screamed. She went quickly to the food table, picked up a plate, and put a piece of meat on it. I stayed where I was, watching her. Till that moment I'd never realized how incredibly beautiful she was. Shahd? Really gorgeous. Sad, and her sadness was unusual, exquisite . . . Should I repeat what Walid had to say about her?

Amer came over to me. "So this is where you are!" he said in a loud, cheerful tone. "I was looking for you." And then in a subdued voice, "Have you discovered anything?"

"Nothing," I replied. "How about you?"

"My brain's not functioning today," he said. "I can't understand a thing. When everyone leaves, I'm going to look at a few books by Freud."

"To find out what the Oedipal complex is?"

"Yes," he replied. "Hey, you haven't had any wine with your food. Never mind! I have another bottle of Beaujolais here. Come now, dinner's nothing without wine. Here!"

He poured me a glass of his best wine.

Dr. Jawad Husni Starts the Search, Partly Guided by the Perspective of Kazim Ismail and Ibrahim al-Hajj Nawfal

If Walid Masoud became wealthy later in life, or at least gave other people that impression, then it was pure coincidence; for money, or more specifically, brokerage, was the profession that imposed itself upon him. The fifteen years he spent working in the Arab Bank acquainted him with the types of monetary movement marked in black and red on colored cards as he sat behind his desk and his telephone. These rates went up and down in accordance with the estimates and plans of minds working together, like some complex, interwoven net surrounding the globe, each mind responding to the other with a skill and cunning technique built up, most probably, by Jewish money lenders through twenty centuries of computation, appraisal, and speculation. These same rates disclosed some of their secrets to Walid in Baghdad in the 1950s, and he found out how to make use of this privileged knowledge in Dubai and Abu Dhabi in the '60s when the sands of the Arabian Gulf poured out their oil to a world thirsty for it.

Yet, some disease he suffered from stopped him from going all the way. He was quite content to make do with less than he could actually make, and he wouldn't follow up the really big deals with all their complex details and ramifications. Walid made a lot of people rich by piling up accounts and shares for them in banks and companies in London, Beirut, Zurich, and New York, but, as far as I know, he made do himself with the little he had transferred to Baghdad or Beirut. It's common knowledge that his friend Amer Abd al-Hamid was one of the people who benefited from dealings between him and a number of sheikhs in Abu Dhabi, Saudi Arabia, and Qatar; Amer himself never denied it and to the end remained more loyal to Walid than he was to any of his brothers or other friends. It was Walid himself who might actually have denied it.

"Amer Abd al-Hamid has a brain like a computer," I often heard him say. "You supply it with information, and it gives you unexpected results, incredibly detailed. He owes everything he has to that intelligence of his; it's made him a part of the technological miracle in a society that can't understand technology."

This statement of Walid's reflects, I'm sure, a basic disposition in his own psyche, which he would never admit. Many people I know regarded him as a wizard with money, someone who'd stop at nothing to get what he wanted. Yet, I still think they were imagining things; in the first place, they never knew him deep down and had searched out only those things in his background that would provide proof of his wizardry; and second, because they were misled by the impression Walid gave, with his travels and his whims and the various rumors that hovered around him, which he made no attempt to deny, that he had the entire world in his pocket. Only a very few people, I think, knew anything about his upbringing and education, and his lifelong struggle to fulfill one or two of his childhood dreams. I would have searched much of this out myself, had it not been for the firm friendship that bound us for so many years, and that was unsullied by either money or self-interest. My relationship with him was a purely intellectual one: I came to admire his writings when I first started to write myself, and went to sit at his feet, to listen and ask questions; and he responded.

When I got my doctorate, our friendship grew much firmer still. I learned details about his life that he talked about with only his closest friends, when he felt completely at ease, and after a while, I found myself joining his intimate group. When Walid introduced me to the group, it was almost as though he wanted me to serve as its chronicler, while realizing, at the same time, that he himself wasn't basically part of it. I'm not sure how far he made himself a part of that society, and

I myself was personally unable to adjust to it, although I did actually become a part. He didn't, though, make a personal issue out of it. As a Palestinian he could always claim he was connected with a society like this, or dissociate himself from it without either difficulty or sense of grief. His real roots were in other hills and valleys that provided him with constant secret sustenance. He never went around maintaining that an essentially bedouin society, an agricultural society at best and in reality a largely intangible one, entered the urban stage only recently, due to historical factors imposed on it by a British mandate over a country that was as much a burden to them just as they were to it. He never went around maintaining that a society of this kind, left to oblivion for more than five centuries had now been set on some solid foundation of civilization, on which further solid structures were being built. And, in the absence of such foundations, he always considered it stupid to imagine the city and its society as being somehow European, springing from the Renaissance, the growth of the bourgeois class and the Industrial Revolution. An uncouth society, dissipated, disturbed, and in flux, bursting in all directions without moving in any particular one—that's the way I pictured things when I was studying it, and that's how Walid unconsciously viewed the situation, too. It was his stubborn idealism, which he abandoned only during his hours of blackest misery, that made him want this society to achieve self-identity through intellect, freedom, and creativity; these, more than any other, were the words that sprang from his lips and pen. Many people regarded this idealism as the weakest aspect of his character, because it amounted to a kind of metaphysics that he had to overcome by using the very rationalism he believed in. He, for his part, couldn't understand the skepticism in other people; to him it implied a pessimism that, in the final analysis, could be used to justify backwardness and cruelty on the part of individual and regime alike.

When, he'd say, we study the various types of industrialization in advanced countries, for example, we find they're like revolutions imposed on those societies from above; they're the work of ruthless minorities who aren't to be swayed from the goals they've set, and regard all obstacles to progress as solvable by technical and rational means. He found this imposed rationalism disturbing, because its advocates chose to view society as being susceptible to rational arrangement through a mixture of acumen and power, and any irrational elements discovered within the societal foundations had to be resolutely mastered and changed in accordance with the needs of the advocates of rationalism themselves. Walid insisted on the usefulness of technology, but questioned how it could possibly succeed in fulfilling its task as long as it was opposed by a basic, nonrational attitude to ideas and things. Technology was a way of treating nature with sheer maximized rationalism, involving a special kind of creativity. How could we create a rationalist posture in a society where the winds of fantasy blow morning and evening, so that it falls easy prey to every kind of rabble-rousing? If we were to believe the principles advanced by the advocates of the technological approach—that man could be either revolutionary or nonrevolutionary—if it was merely a question of degree or timing, with the final result inevitable, then we had to ask, too, what the eventual purpose of all this really was. Was it to achieve material comfort for everyone? If so, fine. But was this enough? And if we agreed that it was, would we achieve the level of civilization we aspire to? Or would it, rather, be a pretext for certain groups to pursue their own particular goals by giving bread for the mouth with one hand and applying a cudgel to the mind with the other, as had happened so many times in the past? The philosophies that argue this point would appear, he said, to have become obscure; they had no confidence in their ability to achieve material comfort while, simultaneously, releasing the human imagination on a course toward all those things that turn life into an adventure, an eruption, a passion. Was there any solution to this dialectical obscurity that endlessly renews itself? And what about those coercive imposed measures? Wouldn't they end up by turning law into a means of terrorizing society rather than organizing it? Didn't they represent an evasion of the more profound ideas humanity aspires to in life, and that people live by consciously or unconsciously? How, then, were we to reconcile what is rational and necessary with what is nonrational and also necessary?

Walid would deal frequently with these issues, for all their inherent contradictions, both in our discussions and in his writings. He was convinced that solutions must, in the final analysis, come from within, from the collective wills that make up the overall identity of the people. As he saw it, the rational facility was a blend of innumerable hues that had to move with absolute freedom, impelled by the ever inscrutable and risky quality of creativity, so that it could carry out its true function in society.

"By virtue of not believing in man, with his rational and creative ambiguities and the sense he has of the need for freedom, you permit yourself to inflict the very worst kinds of terrorism on him under one pretext or another, or else to come to terms with whoever is exerting control over him. The opposite is true, too: to instigate terrorism or to tolerate those who instigate it is proof that you have no faith in mankind, however much you may claim to the contrary." This is a passage from one of his first books, Man and Civilization, and, for all its freshness, it was used by one of our friends as a starting point, when the book came out, for an attack on him in a newspaper, something that shocked and annoyed Walid. This happened in the mid-1950s, and I shall never forget the row over the book, and also over both Walid and Kazim Ismail, who launched the attack.

Kazim had, for some time, been one of Walid's closest friends. In fact, he was the one who originally introduced me to him, and we used to spend evenings at either Kazim's or Walid's house, engaged in long and heated discussions. As far as I was concerned, Kazim wasn't just an old friend of mine; he was also one of my rivals in short-story writing throughout the 1950s, before I finally turned my back on it to take up advanced studies. I found that the scientific study of the various strands of society provided ample compensation for art, as both discovery and pure pleasure.

Walid used to read what we wrote and discuss it with us; and sometimes we'd ask Samira, Kazim's sister, for her judgment, after she returned from studying in the United States. That was how she got to know Walid, a few years before her marriage to Dr. Tariq Raouf. I was aware that Walid, for all his notable success in his brokerage business, was going through a severe psychological crisis at the time, which he rarely discussed with anyone. It was all caused by the mental breakdown suffered by his wife, Rima, or Umm Marwan, as he always called her. That was five or six years after their marriage, and Marwan, as I recall, was no more than three or four years old.

And so Man and Civilization was published; actually, it was no more than a long essay of around 120 pages. It marked the beginning of Walid's disagreement with the world, and, as he himself put it, that was the way it should be—it proved the book wasn't merely another echo of trite current events. He wasn't afraid of disagreeing with the world—quite the contrary. He took a diabolical pleasure in the vast majority of what was written about him, even when he was being attacked. As usual, he never responded to anyone at all.

"I regard attacks on me as being motivated by stupidity or obscenity," he used to say, and "I haven't the slightest intention of squabbling with idiots or foul-mouthed types. As for praise, where it exists, it's usually based on mistaken premises which I find difficult to correct. So let's leave things to pursue their own course. Maybe in twenty years' time people will find out who was right and who was wrong."

Yet, for all this, he was particularly annoyed at Kazim Ismail's attack on him because it came from a man he loved and admired. He felt Kazim's friendship with him should have held him back from writing the kinds of things he wrote in the article. Walid's naïveté about certain basic facts of life was really remarkable given his alleged wizardry when it came to money matters and profit-and-loss markets. Every day he'd discover a new cruelty or meanness or iniquity in people, and it always shocked him! But his reaction in this particular instance was really strange.

I had the details from both Walid and Kazim, each, naturally, giving me a separate account geared to his own point of view. At that time, I thought I might turn the notes I'd collected from their accounts into a publishable story, by simply giving imaginary names to the two main characters. But, when I'd finished writing, I realized I'd told the story exactly as it happened, because I knew so much about them both. Neither of them would have liked it. So I folded it up, put it in one of my old files, and forgot about it.

Today I went back to those papers; and there I found a précis, both symbolic and prophetic, of the character I'd been in contact with for almost twenty years. What's more, the incident itself served to remind me of the ceaseless contradiction between the man's real personality and what was and is still being written about him. I looked through the story again and decided to leave it exactly as it was, except for going through it and changing the fictional names back to the real ones. This made it the exact opposite of what writers of fiction usually claim for their writings, that the events and characters are entirely fictitious—avoiding the possibility that someone will claim he's been slandered on the grounds that he's represented by one of the characters. In this case, my characters are real, and the incident I'm recounting is another small chapter from the life of Walid Masoud; I'm serving as a trustee whose position of responsibility allows him to tell what he knows:

Suddenly he saw him.

No sooner had his car turned off the main street into a narrow side street stretching away into the darkness than his lights picked out a man whose shoulders were hunched in a hopeless way that made his head seem to sink into his back, and whose hands were plunged deep into the pockets of his long raincoat. Even though he hadn't seen him for more than three months, he recognized the man instantly, walking alone there in the midnight rain like something that had crawled out from the world of the dead. As the light fell on him, amid the streaming rain that glistened in the surrounding blackness, the top of his shoulders gleamed, and when his illuminated figure turned round to make way for the car, the two small eyes sunk deep into his face shone through the dark.

The driver stopped the car a short distance away and quickly rolled down the window. "Kazim!" he shouted.

Kazim's head jerked up automatically. His hands sprang from his pockets, and he stretched out his fingers along the side wall. His jaw dropped an inch or so. He let out a frightened grunt of inquiry.

"Kazim!"

Kazim clung to the wall, looking over the top of the gleaming lights to see who was inside the car. "Who is it?" he asked.

The car lurched toward him and then stopped again. The driver opened the door on the right-hand side. "Get in!" he said.

Kazim found himself obeying the command. He got in the car, then recognized the man behind the steering wheel. "Walid!"

he said. "What on earth are you doing here on a foul night like this?" He grabbed hold of the door and slammed it shut.

The man at the wheel drove on. "Your clothes are soaking," he said. "They'll make the seat wet. But never mind! You seem to enjoy sullying everything these days, don't you?"

Kazim's expression showed no sign of gratitude toward his friend. "Why do you impose your generosity on people?" was his grumbling reply.

"Haven't you always sullied everything?" Walid said. "I should have realized that from the very first day I met you. Your greatest pleasure is taking something clean and making it dirty. That's been your way ever since I first met you."

"Is there anything clean in this world that you're afraid for?"

"Where are you going?"

"What a question! Where else on a night like this, except home?"

"We'll be at your house in two minutes."

"Yes. Thank you."

"But you don't really want to go home, do you? You'd rather come with me."

The driver turned around, headed back to the main road, and stepped on the accelerator. Kazim huddled into his corner of the seat, and when Walid snatched a quick glance at him, his head seemed to have disappeared into his chest.

"Yes, you'd rather come with me," Walid repeated. "You've preferred to come with me over the years because I was fond of you. I loved you. Don't you see how dull and barren life is? We used to imagine love could make this yellow, swampy region fertile, just like the rain that's falling now."

The windshield wipers made semicircles as they moved back and forth. The rain glistened as it ran down the glass, illuminated by the streetlights.

"This rain's like tears. And so's love, the love of friends, the love of women, the love of things. A bitter, lustrous pleasure. You've nothing to say, I see. So, Kazim; I always felt you enjoyed soiling things, but I thought there might be one or two things you'd avoid tarnishing with your grubby hands."

"Where are you rushing off to in the rain?" Kazim asked. "It's past midnight."

"Where? To these streets you used to go to in search of a little bit of adventure every night; and then you'd come back to your friends to boast about it and exaggerate it, to tell yet another lie. But I never imagined your biggest lie of all would eventually be used against me of all people."

"I didn't lie about you, Walid. You got angry because I told the truth. Why does the truth make you angry when it's shown to you, and you suddenly realize you're the target of it?"

With the words out, Kazim felt a sensation of profound ease, as though he'd managed to burst a festering ulcer that had been hurting him inside. Deep within one of the recesses of his brain a guffaw was let loose that gave him considerable pleasure, a silent, malicious guffaw—because he'd managed to burst that festering ulcer at last.

"What truth? Are you so utterly naïve now that you believe there's some truth for you to uncover? Is that why you put some foul arrowhead on the tip of this shaft of truth and fired it into the breast of a man who's loved you all these years?"

But Kazim was busy enjoying his profound ease, the guffaw deep inside him. "Call it naïve, if you like," he replied, as the car illuminated everything around it with its streaming light.

"You ignore realities, invent your own fundamental principles, completely vitiate the interpretation by using the logic of hatred and bias, and then you call that intellectual integrity?"

"Huge numbers of people read me; that's enough for me. What I write is read and discussed; it manages to disturb a lot of people. What do realities matter, if the result's the right one? Who's naïve now, Walid? When are you going to grow up?"

"You must have quite a store of hatred in your soul."

"Even hatred's a virtue when you're defending something you believe in."

"But how can you harbor all this hatred and still claim to be defending humanity?"

"It's all a question of definitions. You write with all the zeal of theologians, whereas I, as you know, reject that."

"How many years have we spent arguing with each other? I used to hate to see the contradiction between words and action in your life. I'd see the tears in your eyes as you slaughtered little birds without even looking at what your hands were doing."

"Do you know what your biggest problem is? You're an idealist. You're afraid to look at the sanctifying hand because you're afraid of the result of the struggle."

Walid gripped the steering wheel tightly to conceal his quivering rage. "You're a damned liar," he said, "because there's not a single human value you believe in."

With the guffaw settled deep inside him, Kazim felt no anger. It was as though he'd long been wanting Walid to display this sort of rage. Yet, he also felt a longing for the tea Khayriyya often left on the stove for him. All this cold and rain had given him an addict's thirst. He stared at the lights on the deserted street, but said nothing.

That was the big difference between the two of them: it took a great deal to arouse Kazim, whereas Walid would fly off the handle at the first touch, just like a match. Each complemented the other. If Walid did something he hadn't thought through, Kazim would provide some cold, brilliant logic to help him; and if Kazim was thinking about some matter and his reflection produced an unexpected result, it was Walid who'd be the first to act on the basis of it.

But the difference in their temperaments led, perhaps inevitably, to a difference in social status. In a few years Walid succeeded in reaching a position that his friend Kazim, for all his gifts of insight and logic, had never anticipated. He became one of the directors in the bank where he worked, and, at the same time, his writings began to be received with interest and admiration. It amazed Kazim that Walid was able to combine the quest for necessary material goods with an abstract intellectual search for the rejuvenation of the Arab nation, and, with that peculiarly Palestinian zeal, to examine the entire Arab way of life on every level.

Kazim, on the other hand, had insisted on remaining a lawyer, maintaining that he despised commerce and its ways and that it was risky for an intellectual. "Your skill's inborn," he used to tell

Walid. "You work like a huge windmill. I work like a wristwatch and stick to fine details."

At first Walid saw his friend as an intellectual who set himself above material considerations, so as to look down on life from a clear window whose pane was not, as it were, clouded by the trivia of daily necessity. Kazim, he'd say, observed events and ideas objectively and analyzed them with considerable rigor and concentration, and as such he was one of the guardians of humanity. Yet, deep down, even though he relished Walid's opinion of him, Kazim aspired to be a famous literary figure. His works, he felt, contained a rallying cry to his contemporaries. He was poet, storyteller, and critic all at once, but his poetry gradually grew less after he reached twenty-five, then disappeared completely. Then his stories became fewer and fewer, too. This happened even though both genres were used exclusively as a defense of the little man faced with social oppression at the hands of the bigger man. All that remained was the acid commentator, scrutinizing with a merciless eye and writing his ideas down with a trenchant and bitter pen, bolstered by a wide reading knowledge.

But his writings depended on the whims of time and press, and all that in a country where newspapers and magazines appear and disappear with monstrous regularity. "I've got intellectual congestion," he used to say during particularly fallow seasons, or, "I've written an article, but I refuse to have it published because there's no decent newspaper or periodical around," or "I've finished a story, but I know I won't get it published, so I'll rewrite it."

It wasn't hard for him to rewrite things time after time, not as long as he had an office where he could practice as a lawyer, and as long as he knew there wouldn't be long lines of clients eager to consult him every morning and evening. His time was as empty, as much his own to dispose of, as his office was; and after years of wasted time in his office, he came to feel his gifts had served only to do him harm. People might mention his name as a poet or story writer or critic, but that was all. They never used his writings or the cases he won as a gauge of his success as a lawyer. "You have to remember," he'd often say, "that there's no connection in this country of ours between winning cases and profound thinking or brilliant style, no connection whatsoever."

And so it was that, as he approached thirty-five, his home situation remained the same. He relied to a large degree on what his father, al-Hajj Ismail, made from his leather trade, which he in turn had inherited from his father. His sister Samira, who was his junior by about twelve years, had come from the United States with a master's degree in education. Her salary provided both him and his father with additional help in meeting household expenses, and so he wasn't forced to dismiss Khayriyya and her daughter—they being the only survivors of the poor folks who'd stayed with the family since the old Ottoman times, when his grandfather Haggi Shalabi had been one of the chief merchants in the city.

There were also two spinster aunts in the house who'd sought the protection of his father's roof some forty years earlier. They were both looking for a husband, but the cavalcade of youth had passed them by, and they stayed in the house like two old pieces of furniture that, by force of habit, the family couldn't do without. Nothing new happened in their lives until Kazim's mother died, at which point they told the two children they'd act as mothers to them. Maybe Kazim was so attached to them both because they constantly mentioned how beautiful he was when he was a child. "Kazim! What a handsome boy, just look at his eyes. Big black eyes, chestnut hair, just like strands of silk, cheeks like roses, a tiny nose as delicate as if it had been painted by hand!" But, as Kazim grew up, his features changed gradually and became more angular. A "Baghdad spot" appeared on the tip of his nose and took off a generous slice of his nice skin. His cheeks fattened, and that made his eyes narrow; then his cheeks became lean once more, but his eyes didn't get any wider. All that remained of his youthful good looks was his curly chestnut hair, which he allowed to grow long and made the object of his vanity.

There was one thing Kazim never admitted to anyone, not even to Walid: his feeling of loneliness, a sense that nothing he wrote had fulfilled a single one of his dreams. Whenever he looked into his past, all he saw was a long desert road with a few gaunt palm trees on either side of it; and he'd be walking along it, back and forth, alone. Whenever he saw himself, he was on his own, abandoning his friends, or they were abandoning him; and the spittle would almost burst out onto his lips. As he went back and forth, all he was doing was moving between two points of nothing, of a void that completely swallowed up all the broad expanses.

Whenever he came home late, he'd find his two aunts chatting and arguing. Their high-pitched voices would permeate the atmosphere of every single room in the house. "Maqbula, Hasiba!" he'd shout out, whereupon they'd immediately stop; and a few minutes later he'd hear a hoarse, conciliatory whisper. "Why don't you go to bed?" he'd yell again from his room. And all the while, his sister would be in bed in her room, thumbing through magazines. He'd push the door open a crack and put his head around. "Up late, eh?" he'd say, to which she would respond, "Eh?" without even raising her eyes from the illustrated magazine she was reading.

"Not asleep yet?"

"In a while."

He'd look at the cheap magazine she was reading. "How's knowledge these days? Progressing?"

"What's the matter with you?"

"What a waste of the master's degree!"

He'd shut the door before she could throw the first thing she laid her hands on, and yell "Khayriyya!"

A sound would come from the top of the house, like a startled cat meowing.

"On my way!"

"Anything for dinner?" he'd ask, approaching the source of the meowing.

"One minute, my dear."

This would be followed by a shuffling noise and then the sound of someone coming down the stairs. He'd take off his clothes and get into his pajamas, while Khayriyya got him some food on a tray and put it on the table by his bed. "Is Father at home?" he'd ask.

"The Master hasn't come home yet," she'd meow slowly. "They came for him in a car, and he went with them. He's not back yet. Do you want some tea?"

"Do you have some ready?"

"Yes, I've left the kettle on the stove for you."

Every night she put a kettle of water on low on the stove and left a smaller one by its spout with tea in it, so that the steam would keep brewing the tea till Kazim needed it. He never went without his cup of tea; he had to have it every night before going to sleep.

The smell of dampness inside the car had made him long for this cup of tea. The windows were closed, and there was Walid clasping the steering wheel tight in an attempt to keep his anger under control. For four damned weeks now, this temper had been with him like an attack of illness; it had gotten the better of him. When Kazim said nothing, Walid gave him a quick look and then turned back to concentrate on the slippery road.

"It's not your hatred I hold you responsible for," he said. "You're free to love and hate whatever you like."

"I'm soaked to the skin," Kazim grumbled in response. "Please take me home."

"It's what you did to me personally that I hold against you."

"What's the point of that?" Kazim replied. "Didn't you say there's no such thing as truth?"

"There's something still more important."

"I know what you're going to say. There's trust, love, friendship, virtue of some kind... Well, as far as I'm concerned, I don't accept any of that anymore. The only thing I believe in now is a crazy impulse, sometimes furious, other times subtle. Sometimes it seems like this car of yours, speeding on its way with its two headlights on amid the rain and mud and darkness; and at other times it's like a mouse gnawing the wood on your bed while you're asleep. Car and mouse, they're both real. I recognize both of them. But not virtue and love, or other things of the kind."

"And is that the sum of the truth you've confronted me with?"

"What more do you want? This is the one discovery that makes me unafraid of facing people in the morning. Just imagine, for example, if your father married you off to a girl you'd never seen before. On the first night, you go in to her. She's waiting for you in the dark. You're longing to take her clothes off and feel her nakedness; and when you touch her, all you can feel is a pile of flabby, wrinkled flesh. You pull back with a start and turn the light on to take a look. You were expecting a cascade of roses, and what you find is a heap of flesh and veins. Then what do you do? Do you rush into the streets and sing her praises? I started on my own life, and found it so ugly it shrieks its ugliness to God in heaven . . . Walid, I wish you'd take me home. I'm cold."

Seven years earlier, Kazim had married Majida al-Sabbagh, when she'd graduated from Higher Teachers College. Majida was one of the most beautiful girls in her class, and a reputation for courage was added when she was arrested in her last year and dismissed from college for a while because of her political activities. When Kazim married her, it was like marrying one of his old students. Every word he spoke she considered a pearl to be treasured. She'd read everything he wrote even before she was introduced to him, and then the two names had come together in a Lebanese magazine when one had made some comments about the other that were slightly critical but mostly laudatory. They'd discovered then that they lived in the same part of the Aazamiyya district. When Kazim at last went into her room, after a long and pleasant period of anticipation, he had indeed found the cascade of roses he'd wanted for himself.

But the student didn't long preserve the pearls that fell from the teacher's mouth. When he took her temporarily to live with his family, while a new home was being properly furnished for them, the marriage began to break up. Begun with so much emotional fertility, it ended in drought and divorce, lasting no more than a year. The teacher stayed at home with his family and watched as the young student revolutionary began to organize her own life, then marry again and have two sons. He'd seen her with the boys once, in the Orozdi Bak Store, and gazed at them for a long time. But for her stubbornness and defiance, those could have been his children. He felt the spittle from the depths of his gullet gathering on the tip of his tongue for a spit of outright hatred, but he swallowed it and went out on Rashid Street. The street was clogged with cars, bumper to bumper; they lurched along, accompanied by a great deal of coughing, yelling, and horn blowing, while police whistles made a vain attempt to separate this chain of interlocking wheels. A boy was lying motionless, his chest bare, right across the pavement amid the feet of the crowd of passers-by. You could see his ribs sticking out of his pallid chest. Near him a man sat cross-legged; his eyes were terribly disfigured, and his huge palm was outstretched as he intoned verses from the Quran in a voice that added its discord to the car horns and the cries of roasted-nut and lottery-ticket sellers. Kazim tripped over the foot of the boy spread-eagle on the pavement, and his anger exploded into a curse. All the while, the man was intoning, "Perhaps they will come to know." His ear caught those final words, which went on to echo in his mind, "Perhaps they will come to know... but most people don't know." In the midst of this yelling and laughing stream of humanity he stopped, and his anger exploded again. No, no, they didn't know. Barren years, one after another, a struggle from the very first moment we become aware of life. We study everything, pass judgment on everything, manage everything. But Majida slipped through my grasp. A useless reputation. Perhaps they will come to know. The endless stream of passers-by pressed in on him. It was as though he were that beggar on the pavement, lying there like a meatless bone. And then quite suddenly a hand stretched out from among the masses of hands passing by and grabbed his own.

"Hello, Kazim," a voice said, before he had time to see who it was. Kazim quickly withdrew his hand from the firm, cold grasp. "Mahdi? How are you?"

"Fine, thank you."

"Are you working?"

"Yes, I'm in the machine division, thanks to your friend Abu Marwan."

"Wouldn't it have been better to stay on as an office boy with me?"

"Yes, indeed."

"Fine, Mahdi. Good-bye."

"Good-bye. May God protect you!"

The moment Mahdi had been swept along in the crowd of passers-by, Kazim took a small bottle of cologne from his coat pocket, sprinkled some drops on his hands, and then rubbed them together. Then he put some more drops on them. The scent rose to his nostrils, bringing him a momentary pleasure. He rubbed his hands together again, then suddenly became aware of what he was doing. He put the bottle back in his pocket quickly in case anyone should see that he was disinfecting his hands.

A quarter of an hour later, Kazim was sitting in his office in a building at the beginning of one of the side streets off Rashid Street, sitting at his desk and clasping his pen in his newly scented and disinfected hand. He was about to write an article about Walid Masoud, the author of *Man and Civilization*. His friend, whom he still saw from time to time, though less frequently than in the past, would undoubtedly be expecting him to write something, something supportive of his new work. That was the way Kazim was thinking. But Kazim had decided to send his spittle flowing through the air, even if it fell on his own head later. "I must give a different picture of him than the one he's expecting," he told himself as he clasped the pen to write. "A bourgeois individual who uses humanism as a cover to hide his own class's fears of downfall. He grew up in the lap of luxury, and now he sees civilization through blinkers that make him share the upper class's fear of freedom. He forgets that the need for bread outweighs every other need."

There came, from inside him, that silent, malicious guffaw. "All I have to do is call him bourgeois. That'll bring him down from the little pinnacle he's so fond of sitting on."

"I'm not taking you home."

"I told you, I'm cold."

But Walid kept his foot on the accelerator, his eyes focused on the road that stretched ahead through the sheets of pouring rain. The windshield wipers kept moving back and forth as they pushed the glistening water off to the sides.

"So why don't you describe life as it really is in your writings and make some use of this ugliness you see shrieking out to God in heaven? Or is that what you were trying to do in your article about me?"

"Walid, you've got everything you ever wanted in terms of material gain. Isn't that enough? The very fact you own this car, for example, is symbolic proof you no longer believe in a great deal of what you used to preach in the past, the need for struggle and hardship, and so on."

"So this old wreck of a car's turned into an advertisement for luxury and a renunciation of hardship and struggle and so on? Is that it?"

"Exactly."

"How wretched every value becomes when it's based merely on defeat in life! You grew up in a family with a guaranteed income and a house with plenty of rooms and servants. And you compare yourself with me! Where did I grow up? In one of those palaces you dream about, I suppose?"

"Look at yourself now; that's what's important. Did I make any errors in my description of you?"

"Of course you did, for whatever strange reason—starting with my upbringing and finishing with my writings. You've known me all these years, yet you still know nothing about me and use all these fancy words. Do you imagine people like you can change society, sitting there in your little lair chewing over your petty hatreds and dallying with your succession of failures? How many poor people have you known in your life? How many days have you been hungry or naked?"

"That's all beside the point. Why are you turning the whole thing into a personal issue?"

"That's wonderful! You launch a personal attack on me, and then you object when I ask you about yourself! How many demonstrations have you taken part in? How many bombs have you exploded? How many villages have you visited to study their social conditions? Tell me, how many people do you provide for?"

"That's not important."

"How many people do you provide for? Come on, tell me!"

Kazim shot a venomous look in Walid's direction, but Walid was looking at the road that was meekly submitting to the pounding rain, so that he couldn't see the rancor in his companion's eyes, or the scorn he was striving to suppress.

"Tell me," Walid said again, as Kazim still failed to reply, "how many people do you provide for?"

"I don't take care of anyone, and I don't want to. Your success in business doesn't imply the least success in the ideas of struggle. You deliberately give words a different meaning from the one I intend. I don't support anyone because I've sacrificed everything I hold dear to the cause of the principles I believe in."

Walid shot a swift look in his direction, then let out a loud laugh in his face. "So here we have the martyr of humanity!" he said. "Who are you going to tell that one to? Don't you wonder sometimes—bearing in mind your concern about the truth—if all these fine words you use as a weapon against other people have any real meaning in your own life? You arouse some generous but obscure emotion in people who have met you, and then turn around and dip your fingers in the blood of those who have known and loved you. Wouldn't it be better for you to start with yourself?"

"Listen, Walid," Kazim said, with the first signs of fury in his voice. "I've asked you to take me home."

"Home?" Walid replied in a cold tone that clearly reflected his stubborn resolve. "We're a long way from home."

"Where are you going? This is New Baghdad."

"We're going to Baaquba. This will be the only car on the road."

"Now, in this rain? Have you gone mad? I'm telling you, take me home!"

"Get a grip on yourself, Kazim, as you always have done. Don't be like me. When I get angry, I can't talk; I rush about like a madman. The day I read your article I couldn't believe my eyes. I'm not afraid of anyone attacking me; I'm the huge windmill as you described me. I grind the wheat and chaff together. But your attack hurt me so much because it came from you specifically, you who know better than anyone else the poverty I've suffered and the trials I've had to face. What do you know about struggle, about yelling and standing naked among wolves? For you, words and actions are two separate entities, just as volition and execution are. Your knowledge of life was mere theory right from the start and it's stayed that way. You've never pushed yourself to the stubborn, frightening limits. You've never, for a single day, known hunger or the shiver of cold when winter launches its attack on you and you have only one single threadbare cotton gown that barely covers your private parts."

The car turned off the road toward Baaquba, the piercing headlamps revealing a long, black road, interspersed with gaps of light reflected from the wet ground. To either side there was just pitch darkness. No lights, no houses—just two beams of light extending to infinity. The rain was beating down on the roof of the car, and the pounding was nonstop, like the beaks of thousands of predatory birds.

"For God's sake, slow down!" yelled Kazim. "Are you trying to kill us both?"

He would have liked to push Walid to one side and stop the car by force, but he was afraid any such move would jerk the steering wheel, which, on this slippery road surface, would certainly lead to their deaths. So the car careened on in its stubborn course.

"When you see a drowning man flailing in the water," said Walid, without even looking at Kazim, "you like to stand on his head and lecture at him till he drowns. You've never uttered a word or written a syllable based on a love of anything or a sense of fairness toward anyone. Your words and writings have stemmed solely from a many-sided hatred, from the inconsistencies within yourself, a hatred for everything and everybody. Do you think anything great can ever emerge if it isn't based on love?"

There was nothing Kazim could do; he'd fallen into the trap. He skulked in his seat and once again buried his head in his shoulders, resigning himself to the will of the driver of the car, although he did manage to mutter, "So who's the lecturer now, and who's drowning?"

At this point Kazim suddenly found himself hurled forward as the car skidded violently in a squeal of brakes, and veered to right and left before coming to an abrupt halt in the middle of the road. The headlights looked like a long knife cutting the wasteland of rainy darkness in two.

"You're right," said Walid. "This time, I'm giving the lecture, and you're the drowning man!"

With incredible speed he leaned over to the door handle on the right-hand side where Kazim was sitting, opened the door, and pushed Kazim hard, with steely hands, before Kazim was even aware of what was going on. Kazim fell to the ground on the road with a painful bump. The rain drenched him from all directions, and a river of water flowed under him as well. He saw the door close with a terrible bang and heard Walid saying, "... what cold really means!" Then the car gave a roar and sped away.

Kazim got up at once, although he wasn't steady on his feet. "You bastard," he yelled after the disappearing car. "You pimp! God, I'll kill you, you pimp!"

Then he saw the car stop and turn around. It started coming toward him, its headlights gleaming at him, brutal and mean, as though it was going to wipe him off the face of the earth. He was still yelling. The car sped past him in the other direction with a roar like thunder filling the heavens and making the earth cower.

Darkness and pouring rain, that was all Kazim could see, save for two red beams of light in the distance as the car sped back toward Baghdad. Then they, too, disappeared. Kazim clenched his fists in rage, a vanquished rage; his nails dug into his dirty palms, and a sob coming from deep inside him stuck in his throat. On his face, which was a picture of dejection, the chilling rain mingled with the warm trickle of tears. Nothing was to be seen except the pitch darkness. This bitter, watery mixture landed on his lips and then, making its way between them, settled on his tongue.

That's the way the story I wrote ends; it's called "The Bitter Mixture," and the dramatic situation requires, perhaps, that it should end with such brutality. But honesty demands I should record that it didn't really end that way, or not exactly anyway. Walid really did take his friend Kazim to the road to Baaquba on that foul, wintry night. It was a rough dirt road in those days, and Kazim couldn't find a single tree to shelter him from the pelting rain. And when Walid had pushed him out onto the ground, he really did drive off and leave Kazim to the fury of the heavens, which at that moment was undoubtedly deadly. But Walid had hardly settled alone behind the wheel again before he felt his anger dissipate; the fire that had been raging in his mind suddenly dampened. He felt a strange sensation of sorrow, and, though he did his best to resist, he started to feel sorry for his friend. He couldn't help himself; he stopped the car, turned around, and sped back to where he'd left Kazim.

Kazim saw the car coming and leaped into the middle of the road, waving his arms like a madman; and when the car stopped alongside him, he felt so happy he hardly dared believe his eyes. But when Walid got out and Kazim could see who it was, he moved fearfully back and started running away. But Walid ran up to him with open arms, got hold of him, and gave him a warm hug. Then he started kissing Kazim's cheek, while Kazim tried to hold him off. All the while the rain was pouring down on both of them. "I'm sorry, Kazim," Walid said. "I'm so sorry. I lost all control of myself. Forgive me, Kazim, forgive me." For his part, Kazim stood there shivering but impervious, not knowing how to react. But eventually he, too, relented and calmed down; he embraced Walid, then burst into tears. They went back to the car like two rags soaked in rain and tears. Walid put his foot down on the accelerator, and they drove off.

This time the car didn't go so fast; Walid couldn't have driven like that again, even if he'd wanted to. All the way back they were silent till they got to Kazim's house, both shivering with damp and cold. At the door Kazim hesitated before getting out of the car. "I won't get out," he said, "unless you come into the house as well. We'll drink a cup of tea with some cognac. What do you say?"

"What will they say if they see us soaked to the skin like this at two o'clock in the morning?"

"So what! They're all asleep anyway."

They both got out of the car and went inside, where Kazim found that the heater in his room was on. The water for tea was still on low in the kitchen, and the bottle of Remy Martin cognac, which was Walid's favorite brand, too, was more than half full, just waiting for him in the cupboard. All they had to do was dry themselves as best they could, after which they went on drinking and talking till morning.

"I'm telling you, he was crazy," Kazim said as he described what had happened. "I suddenly found myself in the grip of a man who'd lost his reason. He was driving like a lunatic, but I don't think he was drunk. He was able, the way lunatics occasionally are, to exert an incredible control over everything, over me, the car, and the road. I even ended up thinking the rain itself was all under his control; I'm not kidding!"

It was a strange truce that came about between Kazim and Walid. Kazim isn't a simple man, or someone who'll let his emotions take hold of him in a moment of weakness and make him forget about everything else. He was nurtured on the notion of being skeptical about everything, of boasting that "he always read what had been rubbed out," of insisting that, if we manage to look at the other side of the picture, we can unravel many of the obscurities on the exposed side. We should always look for what's been rubbed out, he'd say, for the other side. This "search" would, though, often go to extremes of rumor and conjecture, and in the end true and false would be so intermingled that it would be impossible to distinguish between the two. Sometimes this would be the source of power in his writing, but equally often it was a sign of its weakness. With Kazim you found yourself in a labyrinth of givens that he imagined he'd fully dealt with, whereas in fact they constituted a haven for his doubts and fancies rather than objective, statistical truth. If you pointed this out to him, he'd say that in the final analysis he relied on a process of making his internal feelings the arbiter between himself and his own soul. Detailed examination of a subject leads to a degree of insight that makes the accuracy or inaccuracy of the minor factual details irrelevant. What matters is the final result.

His views on Walid, whom he had known for some years, are an example of this. I argued with him about them, but without success. As Kazim was beginning to view him at that time, Walid was a scion of an "extinct aristocracy," as he put it, that couldn't forget its past, that was dazed by the world of ordinary people and turned totally inward on itself. All this impelled the members of the group to undertake imaginary acts of chivalry and entertain obscure, elitist visions. Walid tried to conceal this, or suppress it, because it didn't fit the age he was living in. "He wants to be an important part of his time," Kazim said. But deep down, at the level where he communicated with himself, he was holding on tightly to his old aristocratic background.

Kazim used to amuse me with his talk about this kind of "hidden" aristocracy. But he was serious, and explained it to me in great detail. "It's one of the vestiges of the Ottoman period in several Arab countries," he'd say, nervously flicking the ash off his cigarette from time to time. "And even though it's disappeared as a social or political force, it's still active on the inner, psychological level, like some disease that gives someone an internal strength although he's ashamed to mention it. The fact that Walid had a Christian upbringing doesn't in any way lessen the importance of this; in fact, it makes the whole thing more complicated. He gives the appearance of not belonging one hundred percent to any one country or class. These chivalrous feelings of his may well be unconscious as far as he's concerned, now that he's pushed his aristocratic feelings as far from his mind and consciousness as he can; he's suppressed them in much the same way as a child, according to Freud, suppresses sexual urges. They force him to adopt a land and a class, but in an individualist way, or an autocratic way, rather—steeped in romantic dreams of the kind we know so well from our readings on German and Italian nationalism in the last century. The bourgeoisie that continually aspires to occupy the place of the class above it will always adopt the members of the class that's vanished, and incorporate them within itself, because unknown to themselves they'll be serving its goals perfectly. That's the trap Walid's fallen into, and he refuses to believe he's in it."

Khayriyya had put a tray of teacups on the small table, and Samira got up and offered one to me and another to her brother. "Kazim," she said with a laugh as she took the third cup for herself, "if Walid had said the same thing to me about you, I might have believed it, or most of it. But how can you say it about Walid?"

"Do you think you know Walid better than I do?" he replied with a trace of anger in his voice. "What do you know about his life? Have you read his book?"

"Of course I've read his book. But I didn't read it as if I were reading a coffee cup or telling fortunes, the way you do."

Kazim swallowed the remainder of his tea in one gulp and stood up to put it back on the tray. "The trouble with you people," he said, "is that you're too literal in your perceptions. Words are just a collection of lifeless letters, and you make no attempt to go beyond them in your thinking. That's your approach to everything Walid says or writes."

Samira took the empty cup from my hand.

"However brilliant your interpretation may be," I said, "it's totally wide off the mark. Walid's something entirely different from what you're describing. There's something internal, hidden; I agree with you on that. But what is that thing? I don't think you've figured that out yet."

"Whatever the case, Kazim," said Samira, "it certainly isn't the vestiges of some obliterated aristocracy as you imagine. You're being too clever. Walid's lost his roots—you don't have to be a genius to see that—and he's trying to find a country where he can replant them. Without that he can't think, write, or achieve anything. But have you been able to probe his inner soul? I don't think so. What do you know about his life?"

"The things I know about his life are what he's been prepared to tell me, and that isn't very much. Besides, they've been chosen to accord with the image he wants to have of himself and show to others. I need hardly say that sort of image doesn't convince me at all. It's the image Ibrahim al-Hajj Nawfal has of him, though, and makes him extol Walid to the heavens. I saw him coming away from Walid's house yesterday, and he looked as though he'd been on a pilgrimage to a saint's shrine, or met some legendary hero."

"He sees the exact opposite of what you see in Walid's soul. Why shouldn't he be right to the same degree you reckon yourself to be?" Samira asked.

"Why don't we say then," I said, "that the true Walid lies in some middle region between your vision of him and Ibrahim's?"

Kazim gave a laugh and lit another cigarette. "The most courteous of us all, that's you, Jawad!" he said. "You'd like to satisfy both Ibrahim and me. I'm pretty sure, though, that your real views are totally at odds with the opinions of both of us. Tell me now, isn't that the case?"

"Perhaps," I replied. "In any case you know I never make random judgments. In my view every matter has a thousand aspects to it."

"Do you see, Samira?" Kazim said, turning to his sister. "There's the diplomat using smooth words so he doesn't have to reveal his real position."

He looked at me. "A thousand aspects? Just tell me about two of them, and I'll do without the other nine hundred and ninety-eight!"

But before I could respond with some other maneuver, Kazim suddenly raised his hand in the air as though to harvest a thought that had floated down from the ceiling. "Don't you wonder sometimes," he asked, "what the connection is between Walid and Ibrahim?"

"Their personalities are very different," I replied. "But then you should remember they've been detained together more than once in the last year. There must be some common bond linking two such disparate personalities together in spite of their differences."

"You mean the political situation? No, Jawad, there's a more important bond between them. You're not an idiot—I don't have to go into details."

"What do you mean?" I replied, astonished at this totally mysterious comment.

He stubbed out his cigarette in the ashtray. "Why all this naïveté?" he asked, staring at the ash. He looked up at me. "Rima," he went on, "is the whole world to Ibrahim. And you talk about a common bond between two opposites?"

"No, Kazim!" said Samira in something close to a groan.

"Ibrahim admires Umm Marwan's personality, it's true," I said.

"Admires her personality? Just that? What about her beauty? I believe Ibrahim had something to do with her nervous breakdown, or, let's call things by their proper names, her madness."

"Never," I replied. "Impossible!"

"Ibrahim could drive the angels crazy. He has a particular genius that can blend the serious and the farcical, and his emotions are scattered all around him like the leaves of a huge tree on a windy day. I know you don't like hearing this sort of thing."

"Of course I don't like it. I don't know what's the matter with you these days. You keep coming up with these strange ideas."

Samira, too, disagreed with her brother. "A persecution complex: that's what's bothering Kazim," she said, revealing her ability to speak frankly and her tendency to be slightly and delightfully naïve. "And the way he reacts is to knock down his friends and loved ones in this thoughtless fashion."

She turned to look at her brother. "Kazim, my dear brother," she said with a frown, "you shouldn't go on like this. The argument you had with your Aunt Maqbula this morning was inexcusable. You said things to her, and even to me, that I never expected to hear in this house. Why don't you go on a vacation to give your nerves a rest? Go to Lebanon, Jordan, Jerusalem, London. Get out of this environment for a month or two."

"Shall I travel on the money of your deceased?" he asked. "You're talking as though you've come to me from Mars or something!"

This family quarrel made me feel very uneasy, and I was anxious to try to make things easier for Kazim. But I realized in a sudden flash that his experience with Walid on that rainy night had left a deep wound in his self-esteem, that I saw before me an extremely clever man beset by one defeat after another. Samira may have been more right than she realized. Every defeat he suffered added another sense of failure to the overall feeling of downfall that he felt piling up inside him. He'd started to feel persecuted and assumed the only way he could overcome it was to occupy his mind with the destruction of other people. The "Watchman of Humanity" that Walid had once loved so much was no longer a watchman ready to defend humanity; he was defending himself instead. He might continue to claim he was defending the major ideals, but he wouldn't hesitate to plot and cause trouble in the name of that cause. It was just a waste of time, finally, for any one of us to argue with him about anything.

Suddenly, Kazim stood up; he looked very pale, so much so I thought he was about to faint. For two or three seconds he didn't move. Then he sped toward the sitting room door without saying a word or looking at either Samira or me, flung it open, and slammed it behind him. Then we heard him open the front door and close it with a bang. By the time Samira and I had hurried out after him, he was already disappearing in the direction of the main street.

Samira and I stood there by the front gate exchanging worried glances. I was seriously concerned about Kazim now. "Jawad," Samira begged me in a way I hadn't seen before, "please don't leave him. You're his closest friend and ours, too. Don't let him go. Convince him, please. Every time he gets angry, I'm afraid he'll behave like everyone else: go and drink arrack somewhere and then come home in the middle of the night to carry on with his beastly arguments."

I said good-bye to her, then ran to catch up with Kazim. Just as I reached the main street the Aazamiyya–Rashid Street bus was coming to a stop at the bus stop close by, and, seeing Kazim get on, I started running as fast as I could. I made it just as the bus was moving away, and stood there panting by the front seat near Kazim. He showed no surprise and said nothing until the conductor was standing in front of me; then he stretched out his hand with the money and asked for two tickets. By now the bus was crowded. I looked past Kazim through the closed window of the bus. "It's going to rain again," I said.

"We'll all drown," he replied without looking around. "There'll be no escape; either we burn or we drown."

When we got out, he made to go off on his own. "See you tonight at the Sharif and Haddad Restaurant," he said.

I grabbed him by the arm. "No," I insisted. "Stay with me. Let's go to the Roxy Cinema."

"Don't we have enough problems? Do we have to go and watch other people's as well?"

"What problems, man?"

"Okay! After we've seen the film, I'll take you for a quarter of arrack at Sharif and Haddad."

"Here's to after the film, then!"

It was just before four-thirty in the afternoon, and the cinema was a short walk away. For the first time Kazim gave a smile, as he saw a number of young girls going into the cinema lobby. "You old rogue," he said, poking my ribs with his elbow. "You knew all the time school and college girls go to the movies at this time of day. Just wait till I tell Hala you're still fooling around!"

"How do you know," I asked as I was purchasing the tickets, "that I didn't arrange to meet her here?"

"Poor old Jawad! Here he is, engaged, and he can still meet his fiancée only in public places!"

"Don't worry yourself. Maybe we can find you a fiancée, too!"

We made our way between the crowd of people going in and coming out. "A fiancée for me?" Kazim intoned, looking around him. "Isn't that forbidden? They've taken me out of the running, the bastards!"

"Get your hopes up, you old pessimist!" I told him as we went to sit down in the warm, humid theater that echoed to the sound of voices and the sighs of Farid al-Atrash singing. "There are a thousand girls who'd like a look from you."

"Just show me a single girl who's looking at me now or would even want to," he said, looking to right and left. "You've always been such an optimist, Jawad!"

Then the film started.

By the time we left the cinema, Kazim was feeling a bit more cheerful. We saw a number of people we knew and exchanged greetings here and there, and Kazim made some enthusiastic remarks about a girl who was walking silently along with her mother; her hands were thrust deep into the pockets of a splendid long red coat, while her eyes stared off into the distance as though she could see no one around her. "Do you know her?" he asked me. "That's Sawsan Abd al-Hadi. Just get me a girl with that kind of serene beauty and lofty demeanor, and I'll give up ten years of my life. She's a student at the Queen's High School; they say she's a gifted artist as well."

"Well, come to your senses then," I joked, "and let's get you engaged to her."

"Are you crazy? I was only dreaming!"

"Dream on then! Just as Lenin said: Let the masses dream."

"Except that Stalin ignored the directive!"

As he said that, he stopped me; it was as though he'd decided to surprise me with some new statement. "Jawad," he said, "let's go and see Walid."

That really did surprise me, and I hesitated about going along with the idea. "If you just want to start the argument and fighting all over again, then find someone else to go with you."

"No, absolutely not," he replied, pulling me along by the arm. He stopped a taxi, which then hurried us away toward Antar Square, and for some reason or other, the image of Sawsan Abd al-Hadi, with her distant look and her slow, swaying walk, flashed across my mind as we were driven across town in this ancient car. I must ask Hala about her, I thought to myself.

Fortunately, Walid was at home, and he and Rima greeted us in the small book-filled sitting room. Walid seemed to have been writing at the dinner table in a small alcove off the sitting room. There were papers and books strewn over the table, and a solitary cup of coffee could be seen amid the masses of paper. A record still played on the phonograph, and the sound of music filled the house. Little Marwan was also sitting at the table, on a chair with a cushion on top of it, drawing a picture with colored crayons. "Hello, Uncle!" he shouted from his chair.

Walid looked depressed and tired. He lowered the volume on the phonograph, and we all sat down; then Rima went to the kitchen and asked the maid to make some coffee. When she came back, with her tall, slender figure, and her long hair in a disheveled cascade around her face, which was pale in spite of her rosy cheeks, she asked Kazim: "What were you and Walid up to on that long rainy night? Tell me the truth, now! Were you both at your house as Walid claims?"

I saw Walid wink at Kazim and bite his lip. "Yes, we were at my house, of course," Kazim replied.

"Were you really arguing till morning?"

I noticed a frightening light-blue ring around her eyes at this point.

"As usual," replied Kazim with a laugh. "I'm sorry we couldn't let you know. Our telephone was out of order."

"Was your sister, Samira, with you the whole time?"

This question nonplussed him a little. "Samira?" he replied a little tensely. "Good heavens! She's asleep by ten."

Rima sat down and looked at me. "I was scared to death," she said.

"I was afraid they'd arrested him again. Good God, how long will this go on?"

Kazim leaned over to her, cutting me off before I had a chance to respond. "The time will come soon, Umm Marwan," he said, "when this will all be over."

"When are you going to get married?" she asked, popping a surprise question at him.

"Me, get married?" he replied. "Again? Who'd want to go through the whole experience a second time, when he's escaped the first time only by the skin of his teeth?"

"And how about you, Jawad? How are things with Hala?"

"Wonderful. We're going to get married as soon as she graduates this year. Then . . ."

"Then what?"

"Then we'll go to America, so I can study for the doctorate."

She turned around and looked at Walid. "Why don't we go to America, too?" she asked.

"America?" Walid said, shaking his head forcefully. "America's here, Rima, right here."

Her eyes were gleaming in a peculiar way. What, I asked myself, is this frightening, crazy beauty? "This pattern of coming and going, Walid," she said, "arrest, banishment and return—doesn't it wear you out? They're playing cat and mouse with you, darling, and then, one cold night, they'll hack you down."

"Have you forgotten what you told me yesterday?"

"What did I say?"

"You told me, Rima, never to give in."

Rima shuddered and shook her head violently. "You're right," she said, her eyes staring at us. "I'll make him like his father, refusing to give in." Then she looked into my eyes and continued like someone calling for help: "Oh Jawad, I'm tired, so very tired."

She fell silent, the gleam leaving her eyes. Then she stretched out her arms on the armrests of the chair and let her hands dangle like two wilting roses, and at a single stroke she was gone, right there before our very eyes. She looked just like Mary Magdalene in any old picture; her blouse was open enough to show part of her bosom, and her thick, disheveled hair fell over her shoulders as though she were about to use it to wash the feet of a crucified beloved.

When the Palestinian maid brought in the coffee, Rima simply put hers down beside her without taking a single sip. Walid looked worried, and all he could do was look at his wife from time to time. No doubt he was upset that his friends should see her in this state. For my part I was secretly annoyed with Kazim for making this foolish suggestion that we should visit them unannounced, even though we'd done it often enough in the past. I had no idea what he wanted to talk to Walid about. He just stayed where he was, showing no sign of urgency; it was almost as though he wanted to get a really good look at Rima at her very worst. If only I'd gone with him to Sharif and Haddad, I thought, instead of inflicting this unwarranted humiliation on Walid! I was anxious to save the situation in any way possible. I asked Walid about the music that had just come to an end, then about the pieces of paper scattered all over the table. We got up to look at Marwan's drawing and kept on talking. All this time, Rima said nothing; she was there, yet she wasn't there, looking yet seeing and hearing nothing. Walid took me to one side. "Umm Marwan's gone, Jawad," he said. "Gone. I'm going to take her to Bethlehem . . . Maybe to her father's or a sanatorium there. Neither of us can sleep at night now. Dr. Tariq Raouf's on his way to take a look at her."

Now at last Kazim helped out with the conversation. "I'm so sorry, Walid," he stammered. "I shouldn't have insisted we come tonight. I had no idea of all this. I wanted to talk to you about a project for a book, or something of that sort. But this isn't the time. I'm sorry."

Walid seemed unable to concentrate on what he was hearing or saying. "Is it anything urgent?" he managed to say. "I'd be glad to help."

"No, no," Kazim replied, "it's nothing urgent. Is there anything I can do for you?"

"No, no, thank you!"

"I hope you'll have the chance to start reading your newspaper again in three or four days."

"Oh, I read it every day!" Walid replied with a sarcastic laugh. "None of us can do without that marvelous daily sustenance of ours, can we?"

"Come on, Kazim," I said. "It's late."

We went to say good-bye to Rima, and she stood up. I had the feeling, as she stared at us, that she'd forgotten who we were. Even so, she accompanied us to the door with Walid, and he came with us to the gate, apologizing to us just as we were apologizing to him. It was beginning to drizzle slightly, and so we quickened our pace. Just then a car drove past us and stopped. "Where's Mr. Walid Masoud's house, please?" the driver asked.

"You must be Dr. Tariq Raouf," I said. "They're expecting you." We showed him the house.

I wasn't in the least surprised, a few days later, to find an article in the paper written by Kazim Ismail, the import of which was that his review of Walid Masoud's book, Man and Civilization, published a few weeks earlier, had been an attempt at investigating one possible aspect of a most fertile and important subject of study. Today, the article said, he proposed to examine another way of looking at the book, to deal with a particular intellectual dimension it had, the underlying basis of which was its awareness of the trials of humanity in the second half of the twentieth century following the Palestine disaster, along with a daringly forward-looking approach that placed its author in the very forefront of . . . and so on and so on, along the same lines. It wasn't the actual exaggeration that astonished me; what perplexed me was this new evidence of contradiction in Kazim. How had he found it in himself to perform this complete and brazen volte-face? There was no reference to the long-lost aristocracy anymore, or the delusions of chivalry or bourgeois snares. Instead, there was a lot of talk about either/or, freedom or madness, confrontation or suicide. It was as though Kazim were at last confessing that he'd looked over the precipice of a terrifying abyss, and seen not only Walid and Rima Masoud, but also Kazim Ismail himself.

I tried to contact him that day, but he wasn't there; and the following afternoon Samira told me he'd asked her to apologize for him for not being able to see me or contact me before his departure. He'd boarded a plane for Lebanon at nine o'clock that morning. "Ibrahim asked for him several times yesterday, too," she added. "Please don't tell Ibrahim this, but Kazim didn't want to see him and told us to say he was out of the house."

"Kazim's mentally exhausted," I replied. "The trip will be good for him."

"I kept encouraging him. I even bought him the ticket myself. I told him to have a good time in Beirut, in the mountains, wherever he liked, and not to hurry about coming back." She paused for a moment, then whispered, "They say there's another wave of arrests under way."

It was precisely that which led me to go to Ibrahim al-Hajj Nawfal's office that afternoon, to check up on him and on Walid as well. I was sure he'd be in touch with Walid, and I didn't want to cause him any bother by telephoning him or paying him another traumatic visit.

• • •

All that was ten years ago. Ibrahim is still the same; he hasn't changed, and he never will. He was a friend of Kazim's although he was younger, and it was a turbulent, strange friendship, a mixture of love and hatred in unknown amounts. He criticized Kazim a lot, and Kazim wasn't stingy in criticizing Ibrahim either. But when they called a truce, they were like two exotic birds cooing to each other—until one of them ruffled the other's feathers again.

I'd gotten used to all this, yet I never fully understood, through all these years, the real nature of that obscure bond that tied Ibrahim and Walid to each other. Ibrahim hasn't been writing as much recently as he did in the 1950s, but he's kept the trenchant, impulsive personality that crystallized in those early years: that of a man who relished everything and, to achieve his goal, had sold his soul to some devil who'd soon come to claim his due. One wonders whether Ibrahim found in Walid the person whom he really, unconsciously, wanted to be, and whether that's why he clung to him so tenaciously.

Ibrahim, then, is exactly the same as he was: whenever he gets excited or annoyed about something, his voice starts to rise and fall with its own particular rhythm. His tongue moves like a skewer over hot coals, but the fire may remain dormant inside him until he's started drinking; then, when that happens, he starts fooling around with the fire, stirring it up and throwing it around, and if anyone gets burned, too bad! He talks with the voices of angels and devils. He lashes out and slaps everything in sight. At first he'll jeer, and then as the drinking leads him into folly, he'll laugh and then yell. This is his freedom at last, the freedom he's been searching for with such relish. Sometimes he imagines he's breaking down the walls that keep him separated from it. Then, at midnight and in the early morning hours, all this would-be freedom drains away; he makes peace with his companions, and anger changes first to pity, then to sorrow, and last to a profound and miserable depression. He may sigh or sob, and his large black eyes will narrow as a couple of tears well up. Then he'll whisper something that sounds like a hiss, but his lips will be drawn so tight by this final tense breakdown that it's hard to tell what his last words were.

Yet, this description of him from Walid's last tape, which I find myself repeating approximately here, is only part of the truth; it represents Ibrahim as he is today. In the 1950s he'd stay up at the very peak of his anger and not come down. Then, as the years rolled by, his successive experiences began to eat away at him, and this slow but sure process produced the distressing twitch in his hand and that final dissolution of his voice into a profound sensation of loss and tragedy. Back in those days, he was still the young man full of ideas and mental images that you imagined all the dictionaries in the world could never adequately convey. He wanted them to burst out on people, in newspapers, in the streets, with friends, among enemies, in the face of the police, with students, ever since he'd taken part in the demonstrations that followed them throughout the decade.

That's the way he was on that afternoon in 1957. We talked about so many things: the situation in Iraq, Jamal Abd al-Nasser, the Baghdad Pact, Walid and Rima, modern poetry, economic decline ("But my father's still the biggest importer in the country," he said. "Do you need to have a check for fifty thousand dinars cashed on the spot at the bank? Just get my father to sign it!"), the Baghdad Group paintings, the pioneer artists fair, the ball he'd taken his sister Nawal to at Amana Dance Hall, where he saw the most beautiful women in Baghdad; all these myriad subjects formed, during this visit, an incredible soufflé of ideas. Today, though, he was totally preoccupied with the news his friend Dr. Tariq Raouf had confirmed for him that day, namely, that Rima was really very ill. Walid, he said, seemed to be the victim of a set of circumstances made only more complex by a capricious and violent fate that seemed destined to dog him to the bitter end.

We were in his office on the fourth floor, and he was standing with his back to the closed window. Suddenly, he turned around and opened the window to breathe in the city air. He gazed at the dreary succession of dingy roofs. "So help me God!" he said as though he wanted whoever was in the heavens to hear him. "If I hear Walid's been arrested again, I swear I'll go and attack the police station where he's detained with ten bombs in my pocket. Be it on me and my enemies, O Lord!" He turned toward me and looked me straight in the eye. "If only I knew how to get hold of some bombs!"

This picture's remained etched in my mind for many years, and its details come to life again every time I visit him in that room. Over this long period, the room's been transformed into a very elegant office with steel and leather furniture, oil paintings on the walls, and bronze and wood statues that he buys in large numbers from Baghdad artists. The paltry wooden window's been widened and now has an aluminum frame, quite apart from the metal blind that covers it. And no, he doesn't open it now to stare into the distant sky. "The sky's inside me," he said, pounding his chest with his fist. "I'm in a cozy womb here; so what if it's phony? What do you think of this new picture by Sawsan Abd al-Hadi?" He gave a wink and tightened his lips. "She's a womb, too," he added, "just as Walid said one day."

I told him how I'd seen Sawsan for the first time at the Roxy Cinema when she was a student, and what Kazim had said about her then. "Why doesn't he marry her?" he asked. "She may be a widow, but she's still in the prime of her womanhood. Only Kazim, poor chap, isn't in the prime of his manhood."

"How do you know?" I asked with a laugh.

"Let's ask the ladies. They'll know for sure."

Suddenly, he turned and looked earnestly at Sawsan Abd al-Hadi's picture. "Any news about Abu Marwan?" he asked.

"I'm still at a loss," I said, filling my pipe. "I don't even know where to start."

"But you must start."

"Why don't you?"

"Me? I find writing difficult now. I've started being scared of having a piece of blank paper in front of me."

"How can you say that? You used to write with all the élan of a poet. And what am I supposed to write? Don't you know the sociological point of view rots the imagination at the root? For ten years they train you to view man as a societal phenomenon, and then there you are at the end of it all, totally incapable of looking at him as a different, unique person, whose authenticity lies inside his mind, in the cells of his brain."

"If that's not the way you can see Walid," said Ibrahim, handing me his lighter, "you'd do better not to write."

I lit my pipe, then handed him back the lighter. He lit a cigarette for himself.

"The greatest wars have lasted just a few years—the last world war, for example, and the one before it—and then people go back to some sort of situation that's normal, logical, and humanitarian. But what about Walid and his colleagues? Fifty years, fifty years of struggle, of hate, the conflux of bombardment and hatred, stubborn resistance. What other nation in history has ever known such a long and terrifying period of enmity and fighting? How could any Palestinian manage, in this bitter, arid, painful atmosphere, to think, work, build, or write when he's had to spend all his time resisting tyrants, tin-pot dictators, and oppressors every way he turns? But in spite of it all, just look! Walid's life has been unlike any other person's among us, unlike yours or mine. He resisted, produced, made himself wealthy, and gave birth to some ideas; he left a heritage behind him whose dimensions will take us a great deal of time to define. What is this contradiction? Where does the explanation lie?"

"All I know," I replied, "is that Walid wanted to approach life from every angle. And then . . . he tossed it aside in one gesture."

"Are you aware, Jawad," he asked, looking straight at me as usual, "that twenty-five years ago he was advocating the formation of secret groups like the fedayeen today, but no one was prepared to listen to him?"

"The life he led seems to fit that. He wanted to take on everything. Do you remember how he used to say: 'This project you regard as feasible, how feasible really is it?' Life's potentialities are there, and you're always surrounded by a thousand circles; how many of them can you take on, penetrate, eventually fulfill?"

"Just look on life, Jawad, as a jewel in your hand, right there in your palm. How would you finger it, enjoy its colors and its luster and the way the glints keep changing on its different surfaces? Life is fruit on a tree, but there's no Eve there to be tempted by the serpent into tasting the fruit and then tempt you, too, Adam. No. The fruit itself is the ever present temptation that you accept as you move and respond to as a continuous way of reviving the cells in your body and soul, and as a means of reigniting the fires in your veins that are forever on the point of dying down. How old are you now, Jawad?"

"Do you have to remind me of my age?" I retorted with a laugh.

"It really doesn't matter," he said. "You've known Walid all these years, yet you've never even seen the fruit he's been dangling in front of your nose every single day! Kazim's brighter than you are. He saw what Walid saw, but jealousy destroyed him, because every time he stretched his hand out, the fruit cheated him, but it never cheated this stranger who came from the valleys of the unknown. Listen. What do you believe in? Society? Intellect? What do I believe in? The masses? What did Kazim finish up, committed to in his own way? Imposing the proletariat on the bourgeoisie? It's always a commitment to the general not the particular . . . Fine. They'll set up statues of us in the Baghdad squares, dozens of them! Walid reeled like a madman between the general and the particular, between commitment to self and commitment to others, and saw that any effort on behalf of others achieves fruition by virtue of an internal initiation aimed at everything that's profound, ebullient, convulsive, and crying out for freedom. He was the least egotistical of men; what he loved most was what could be achieved by way of the self in its spiral orbit around the cells of society, consuming and being consumed, and never finished."

"But he is finished, Ibrahim. Finished."

He got up, went over to a cupboard on one side of his office, opened it, and took out a bottle and two glasses. "No," he said, "he isn't finished. We're the ones who are finished, you and I and the others. We're beating our heads against cement walls and aren't prepared to admit these very same walls are the end."

He poured out two glasses and offered me one, then returned to his chair, satisfied with the conclusion he'd reached. "We're the ones who are finished," he repeated. "Walid's still carrying on."

I wasn't convinced. "No, no, Ibrahim," I replied. "Tomorrow you'll admit you're exaggerating all this. I'm going now, before you try and wheedle me into agreeing with you." I took a big gulp from my glass.

"Are you going back to your papers?"

"My papers? I'm going back to look for that fruit you were talking about."

Ibrahim gave a loud laugh. "Yeah! Look for it! And if you find it, save a bit for me!"

I drank what was left in my glass and felt the alcohol warming my stomach. Then I got up to go. As he was escorting me to the door, he grabbed hold of my arm suddenly and stopped me. "There's something I'd like to ask you about," he said, staring straight at me to show how serious the question was.

"Yes?"

"Kazim and Tariq both saw Walid at Rutba on his last night."

"Yes."

"Isn't that a strange coincidence?"

"Ibrahim, how many times do we need to go back to this same old question? As soon as summer's under way hundreds of people drive out of the city in their cars for a summer break. Why is it strange that three friends should happen to meet at a border station during the summer?"

"Was there anything else between Dr. Tariq and Walid?"

"A certain indifference, perhaps, toward the end."

"Anything more than that?"

I suddenly remembered how I'd suspected Wisal Raouf, Tariq's sister, might have been the Shahd mentioned on Walid's tape. On those evenings at Amer Abd al-Hamid's home I had the impression of stumbling on an important secret, but I hadn't pursued the matter any further as it concerned Tariq himself, if indeed it did concern him. Actually, the fact that I hadn't even let my thoughts venture in that direction was sufficient proof that I didn't think the matter involved Tariq at all. Needless to say, I didn't, for more than one reason, mention that to Ibrahim or anyone else. Wasn't it likely, after all, that I was wrong or simply indulging in fancies?

"Absolutely nothing," I replied.

I got the impression he didn't believe me. "Never mind," he said. "Do you know I was the intermediary between Tariq and Kazim's sister in days gone by?"

"Good God, I'd forgotten," I replied with a laugh. "I do remember you got Tariq to intercede with his father over a case concerning Kazim before the 14th of July Revolution."

"To get him a decent job before he lost the ministry. You know what happened then. Tariq fell in love with Samira, and a few months later after the revolution, I saw the whole thing arranged. In fact, I was a witness at the engagement ceremony."

"I got the news when I was in Austin, Texas."

"The important thing is . . ."

"What?"

"The important thing, Jawad," he replied, as though revealing a piece of wisdom attainable only by the greatest minds, "is not to expect the best from anyone. They're all traitors."

I laughed. "You'll never change, Ibrahim," I said. "Good-bye!" And I left.

Behind my laughter there was a new concern. What precise link did Ibrahim see between Walid's disappearance and his meeting Kazim and Tariq on the very night of his disappearance? What feverish process was at work in Ibrahim's imagination?

Two or three weeks later, Ibrahim telephoned to invite my wife and me to dinner at his house. "Forget about cement walls," he said jokingly, "and leave the fruit for me! Have I got a lot of it?" Then he changed his tone. "Sawsan Abd al-Hadi's invited, too," he added. "Does that interest you?"

This time I laughed, too. "Are you dangling fruit in front of my nose, too?" I asked.

His laughter over the telephone was enough to split my eardrum. "You crafty old devil," he said. "You crafty old devil!"

3

Issa Nasser Witnesses the Death of Masoud Farhan, Having Known Him for Part of His Life

It was pouring, and we were hastily heaping muddy earth on top of Masoud Farhan's corpse. We sloshed it over his chest without a pause, as though we were afraid he might awaken from his final sleep. I managed to laugh despite the grief-laden situation I was taking part in. "If this poor wretch were to rise now," I whispered to the man beside me, "I swear he'd grab hold of us and demand we lay him to rest again!" This was why we did our job so quickly, setting a row of stones on the grave to be safe; the whole thing looked like a gigantic rosary that someone had carelessly thrown down on the mound of earth. The priest intoned the final phrase: "Deliver us from the eternal Abyss, as we cry to You and say: 'Glory be to You, O God, Glory be to You.'" He turned over the censer, tipped the embers and incense onto the center of this "rosary," then turned away. This was the cue for the world to leave the man for the last time—though in truth the world had left him long before his death. But when it left him now, he'd found refuge in a lovely place, beneath green pines decked with droplets of rain that dangled like pearls—or like tears, perhaps. Four or five of his relatives were standing to one side, accepting condolences, and we all shook hands with them. "May God have mercy upon his soul," we said one by one. "May your life be a long one." Our feet sank slowly into the mud, and heavy clumps of it stuck to our shoes as we walked.

The moment Masoud died, we all felt a heavy burden added to our shoulders, which were already too weak to take on another ceaseless heavy load. The night before his burial we all spent many hours thinking about his life and death, even though most of his friends were getting older now, their backs ready to sag under any load. For all the long illness that had slowly eaten away at his body, Abu Walid was a stocky man. His wife, Najma, had come knocking at the iron door of our house, while I was eating dinner with Um Yusuf. We let her in. "Abu Walid is dead! Abu Walid is dead!" she yelled. "He's left me all alone, he's gone ... He's left me, he's gone." Her eyes were wide open and bloodshot, and her cheekbones jutted through the wrinkled skin of her face. She beat her chest with a blanched hand knotted with countless protruding veins.

My wife and I went back with her to her house, on the other side of the alley in the Anatira quarter. There we pushed open the wooden door to find Abu Walid lying in a mattress on the floor in the dim light of an oil lamp, his eyes staring at us like two glass balls. I bent over him and gently closed his eyelids; his face was as cold and hard as ice. A little later some women came, whispering to each other and screaming. I left them there weeping and went to Antoun Salem's house to tell him what had happened. We agreed to hold a vigil in the dead man's house, and brought a huge candle from the church, which we set by his head and lit.

It was a long night. The others had already gone home. The rain started pattering against the door; then we heard it pouring down. In the flickering light of the candle Walid's mother and my wife were sitting on the floor near the dead man, looking like two propped-up corpses, each wrapped in a gray refugee's blanket; their hands lay in their laps, and their heads sagged in exhaustion. I was unsure whether the widow's eyes were closed because she was asleep or because of her crushing sorrow, which she'd stifled all through her husband's long illness. My wife was asleep. The candle flickered, and the immense black shadows wavered in response.

"They leave one by one," Antoun said, puffing out the cigarette smoke from his mouth and nostrils, "and they never come back. The moment we leave the cemetery tomorrow," he added, "we have to hurry off to another funeral. One by one, Issa, our men leave and never come back. All our young people are dispersed, in different countries, seeking out a piece of bread, in the cities and deserts of this world, while their parents die of need and grief right here, all alone, just like our friend Masoud. He left three young men behind, but none of them came to see him buried."

Bethlehem had always seemed to me like a piece of heaven on earth, but in those days, the only news we heard was of saints, holidays, and dead people, and when Christmas came with its merry bells and joyful carols, it was only like a brief life-giving rain in a long, dreary winter, filled with dirges in numerous languages and with different rites.

This happened, as I remember, in 1950 or a year later. Bethlehem was crammed with the thousands of people who'd taken refuge in it. The young men had left, though, the only ones who'd stayed being the old men and women and a few young women—many of the latter dreaming of leaving for faraway places where they could study or work. As for the refugees, they swarmed in the houses of the old city and in the shacks built on the surrounding hills, in the Dahisha quarters, among the rocks, on the outskirts or in orchards, on barren soil, under torn tents, yearning for a tempting hope, their minds shuttling back and forth between memories of gold-laden fields and their current futile reality. Life still went on, haphazardly, amid the stir and the clamor that was all for the sake of a few handfuls of flour and lentils from the UN relief agency; the insults kept coming, and the curses; officials issued cards; and there were policemen, and political leaders whose voices were heard from afar, promising and threatening—and life still went on, haphazardly. And those camps, that new, horrible social order, were becoming an integrated society that none could even imagine.

One flat mountain foot, rocky, full of thorns, heaving with thousands of animals! I've always said I'm not a philosopher, but you don't need philosophy to realize that rocks and thorns don't spawn life naturally, that if life's forced into the crevices of a rocky, thorny surface, it can only revert to rocks and thorns. But life can never put up with this, despite humanity's harshness and wickedness, because life always explodes forth in every direction. And if they force it to petrify, it'll explode in their faces like bombs one day, no matter how peaceful it seems now. A flat mountain foot, rocky, full of thorns, just one, heaving with thousands of animals. Isn't this a contradiction in terms? And does it take philosophy to see that? "Is there anything we haven't seen yet?" Masoud Farhan would say. "You're still young, Issa, you read books, like Walid. Our time's past. What will you do, young man?" Then he'd fall silent and shake his large head; and in the sway of that head, with its short white hair, and its grooves and its scars, I could see a summary of Masoud Farhan's life—a life like the rocky, thorny surface, and the contradiction in terms. I knew him for years, yet I only remember him as a huge man with a loud voice, whose laugh would shake the window panes. I was about six, I think, when he was a young man, and it seemed he was born a giant, with his huge feet that pounded heavily to the ground like a rock when he stood up, and flapped beneath him when he walked. I was a little boy when people talked about "beating the drum," and "*Safarbarlek*,"* when we ate bread that tasted of dirt, when people talked about bread made of acorns, when men told in the evenings how, in the Turkish Army, they carried water containers for miles like donkeys, and how they'd desert the army and return to their villages and relatives singing songs about their experiences. They talked about an English general who, when entering Jerusalem, got off his horse and went on foot out of respect for the Holy Land; little did they realize then what disasters his entrance into Jerusalem would bring to their Holy Land. People talked about Masoud Farhan and his wide travels—from Madaba to Salt, from Salt to Jerusalem, to Ghaza, and perhaps even to Aqaba and Cairo. They talked about his flight from the Turkish Army, how he was caught and sentenced to death, and how he then broke out of jail and returned to Bethlehem to witness the Turks themselves fleeing, to see his father's two horses, their ribs showing through their haggard frames, being used by this town dignitary and that.

Masoud's father had become old and feeble, and while awaiting his son's return, he no longer drove out in his carriage, keeping it idle throughout the days of war. But the moment Masoud returned, the carriage appeared in the streets once again, polished, freshly painted,

---

*Safarbarlek *was a term used during Ottoman rule signifying exile. When a person was exiled, he was sent to* Safarbarlek.

its bright black exterior highlighting an impeccable white interior, eminently worthy of its new driver. I'd hear a clatter on the road (which was still unpaved in those days), and I'd say, "There goes Masoud's carriage, heading toward Jerusalem." I used to listen to the rattle of the steel wheels and delight in the rhythmic fall of the horses' hooves on the pebbles and the jingling of their bells. I'd rush to the window overlooking the road to see Masoud sitting there in front of his passengers, his head craned upward, his back erect, like a prince, wearing a robe and a red fez. He held the reins with the gracefulness of a male dancer holding a ballerina's hand, and the horses were well bred, adorned with multicolored feathers, their muscles shimmering like silk as they reflected the morning sun. "Hey, Masoud!" I'd shout. "Let me come with you!" But the black carriage would sway past our house, swaying with its passengers, with Masoud raising the whip and shaking the reins, joyfully muttering, "Yah, yah, yah!"; and then the two red-brown horses would respond with a measured gait, and the carriage would undulate like a huge, strange animal, stirring the rocks and leaving a thin veil of dust behind it.

Masoud's carriage wasn't the only one in the town, but it represented all the carriages of the world. And the whole world was that town with its rising houses, one archway after another around Wadi "al-Jamal"; and the "city," Jerusalem, which Masoud ferried passengers to and from, just like a magician making one miracle after another. Every time he returned from the "city," the passengers would get down, carrying with them bags, baskets, packages, cans, new clothes, and shiny shoes, all of which Masoud would take from his carriage and hand to the passengers, as though they were gifts from him to them. Three or four times, he did take me with him to Jerusalem, seating me next to him in the driver's seat; and at the carriage station by Damascus Gate, he'd say to me, "Look after the carriage while I'm away." Then he'd go off and fetch a watermelon, which we'd eat together.

"Don't you want to get married, Masoud?"

"Haven't you found a decent woman yet, Masoud?"

"Isn't it sad, Masoud? You're twenty-five and still unmarried."

The old women never stopped teasing him; but he'd just laugh, holding the whip with one hand and the reins with the other.

"Leave me alone, you women," he'd say. "May God protect you. I must make some money first."

"But a woman is a treasure," an old woman would say. "She'd bring her own means of life with her."

And Masoud would laugh uproariously.

One day he visited us, opened his cigarette box, and handed one to my father.

"You're invited to the wedding at our house," he said.

"Congratulations, congratulations!"

Then he left, went to the neighbor's house, and offered them cigarettes.

"You're invited to the wedding."

"Congratulations!"

He went from house to house distributing cigarettes and inviting everyone. That night the whole town descended on the house of Masoud Farhan.

The women congregated in the only big room in the house, singing and clapping around the shy bride, Najma Humsiyya, who was modestly shrinking from all the attention directed at her. The children, sitting in the laps of some of the women, shouted and cried, before eventually drifting off to sleep. The drum moved from hand to hand, while singing and clapping shook the stuffy room. Sweat glimmered on the women's faces and necks, but the singing, an outlet for all their suppressed worries and emotions, went on unabated. Do women these days still sing with such tremendous joy? One woman recited a wedding song, while the others joined in with the chorus:

> Kookiyya stands tall and proud
> She wouldn't kiss white-haired men
> Her desire in life
> Is to marry a young knight
> Kookiyya O Kookiyya
> She's worth a million others
> Worthy of a Judge or Sheikh
> Or the mayor himself

The high-pitched singing billowed out into the sky, and spread through every house in the town.

As for the men, they sat in the large courtyard on low wicker chairs rented from the neighboring cafés, and in the center, under a strong oil lamp, sat the oud, violin, and tambourine players, singing and strumming on their instruments. Masoud, his brother, and some of their relatives went around offering small glasses of arrack to the guests, one by one.

With his great height, Masoud could be seen from every direction, and his voice, amid the singing, could be heard welcoming the newcomers, seating them and offering them drinks.

"Come on, Abu Farhan, dance!" one young man shouted, then went up to him, embraced him, and asked him again, clearing a space for him in the middle by pushing the chairs to the back. Abu Farhan obliged, went to the center of the space, raised his hands, holding a bottle in one hand and a glass in the other, and started to dance. The men clapped, getting more and more excited, while Masoud's beige-colored robe glistened on his body.

In a corner of the courtyard, a number of young men stood shoulder to shoulder, joined hands, and danced the Dabke around the lame Awda, who'd started playing his mandolin and singing.

All of a sudden there was a hostile cry. "Masoud, son of Farhan! Listen to me, son of Farhan!"

Everybody looked and saw Khamis Humsiyya standing at the edge of the courtyard, menacingly holding a stick high in the air and shouting, "Go ahead, Masoud, dance! But you'll settle with me first!"

The music stopped immediately, and the dancers froze in their spots.

"I swear I'll never let her get to the church tomorrow!" Khamis shouted.

"By God, people," Masoud pleaded, "you're my witnesses. I didn't start this!"

"Shame on you, Khamis," one of the older men said. "You should be celebrating your sister's wedding."

"I swear, I'll never let her get to the church tomorrow! You'll see!" Khamis repeated his threat. Then he lowered his stick and left.

"Go on, play," Masoud said to the musicians, filling their glasses. "Don't worry about it."

In a flash, the celebration resumed. A few men went after Khamis Humsiyya while he was still on the road, argued with him, rebuked him, and finally brought him round after promising him they'd persuade Masoud to pay three gold pounds more as part of his sister's dowry. It appeared that Najma had consented to the marriage with her mother's blessing, but in the face of her brother's objections.

The next morning, Khamis was at the front of the wedding procession, in which most of the people in the village took part, and which stretched from the Arch of Zarara all the way to Masoud's house. Well known for his love of singing and excitement, Khamis led the jubilant crowd on its way to the church, waving his stick in the air and singing:

> "Hear me well, my lawful bride!
> Hear me well, my lawful bride!"

Everyone intoned:

> "Hear me well, my lawful bride!
> Hear me well, my lawful bride!"

Khamis continued:

> "Dearest folk, say after me . . .
> Hear me well, my dearest bride . . .
> O Sister, give me a drink, I said,
> I'm going south a long, long way.
> Here, drink, she said, and may it bring
> you cheer forever and a day . . ."

After the wedding ceremony, the procession returned to Masoud's house. There in the courtyard, in the shade of the tall pine tree, a man was doing a sword dance, slicing the air with powerful blows. Everyone remained at a safe distance to avoid injury, except for Masoud himself, who, while moving among the singing and clapping guests, was accidentally hit on the cheek by the tip of the sword. The sword barely touched his face, but it was enough to leave a streak of blood. Masoud fell to the ground, and the dancer dropped his sword and bent over the bridegroom, crying and kissing his forehead. The men and women rushed toward him and cleaned the wound with arrack.

"Thank God you're all right!" they cried. "Thank God you're all right!"

Masoud pushed the concerned guests aside and stood up. "I swear," he shouted, "if you don't start singing and clapping again, I'll hit you with this sword!" The celebration resumed.

For months on end the scar on Masoud's face remained a favorite topic among the riders in his carriage as they traveled back and forth between Bethlehem and Jerusalem. Every time I looked at him my eyes were drawn to the scar, and I remembered the wedding and the singers. He himself loved singing. Whenever there was a wedding, he was sure to be invited, and he'd sit by the oud player, sipping arrack and singing. I'll never forget the day my mother praised his voice to my father. "Why hasn't God given you a lovely voice like Masoud's?" she said.

"Have you fallen in love with him, too?" my father said angrily. "Isn't the business of Regina and this carriage driver enough for us?"

"Shame on you, Nasser," my mother scolded. "What nonsense is this?"

My father shouted at her menacingly and put an end to the subject. But I never did find out what the business of Masoud and Regina was all about.

Even so, my father didn't object, soon afterward, to becoming a godfather to Masoud's son, who was named Khamis to appease his mother and her brother. I watched him grow like a desert flower. Even when he was an infant, I could tell he was different from the others, more tender, more agile, stronger. I was eight or nine years older than he was, and when he reached six or seven I'd already left school and started learning carpentry. I'd constantly see him leading a group of dust-covered children, playing barefoot in the streets, yet at other times I'd see him crouched beneath the branches of a mulberry tree or an almond tree, singing or reading. He used to do his homework clinging to the branches like a piece of fruit, overlooking Wadi al-Jamal. Then he'd slink down from the tree like a cat, lower a bucket into the well, and draw out water for himself and his friends to drink, or to water the onion or cauliflower patch. Sometimes, too, I'd see him sitting in the carriage next to his father, holding the horses' reins and driving the carriage part of the way—he reminded me of myself, ten years before. Every time he passed by the carpenter's shop, he'd make a point of looking in on me, picking his way through the piles of lumber and yelling to me so I could hear him amid the roar of the power saw. "Hello, Issa," he'd say. "Do you need some help?" or, "My mother needs a bag of wood shavings"; or he'd take a book out of his school bag and say, "Have you seen the new book our teacher gave us today?"

I don't precisely remember how his name changed to Walid. His peers started calling him Walid, then we followed suit, which made his uncle Khamis angry at first, but finally everyone got used to it. After two or three years, everyone—except for his mother—forgot that Walid Masoud was originally Khamis Masoud; and after a while, people started referring to his father as "Abu Walid" rather than "Abu Khamis."

"I wanted to call him Farhan, after my father," Abu Walid said once, "but his mother insisted on calling him Khamis. And then, when he got a bit older, he came home with his new name. 'Look,' I said, 'nobody in our family's called Walid!' I'm sure he got the name from one of those books he reads at night. He's always bickering with his mother over reading books at night, because he never turns off the lamp, and his mother can't sleep with the light on. And if you don't turn off the light, it burns a lot of kerosene, too, more than we can afford. May God help us with this child."

Within seven or eight years, Masoud had had five children, all of them boys. By that time cars had started competing with carriages, which made earning a living more difficult for him. He put his carriage up for sale, but no one offered to buy it; then one of the two horses died, and he couldn't afford another one. Finally, the day came when he gave up, sold the other horse, locked the carriage in the stables, and asked a friend to teach him how to drive a car.

Oh, for the good old days! Whenever I think back to the twenties and remember how the lover of horses was changed to a driver of cars, and how he gave up his robe and started wearing pants, I recognize the point where the times completely changed. I remember the day Farhan's expatriate brother said Farhan came to visit him and persuaded him to take him back with him to Colombia. We said then that he'd become wealthy in America, and that, later, he'd send for his family and the rest of us and make us all rich like him.

Walid's mother stayed alone in the town with her children, raising them with love and hard work. She bought an old Singer sewing machine and worked as a seamstress in her house. One of the children died, and Walid and his three other brothers, Farhan, Elias, and Bassam, remained with their mother who was still able to keep her brilliant smile, in spite of all the hardships she endured. She managed to send Walid to Father Antoun's Monastery to study Italian, learn to serve in the Church, and take up bookbinding. His family saw him only once a week, on Sunday evenings. I used to go sometimes with my father, as he was his godfather, to visit him in the big monastery, and he'd always be happy and smiling, wearing those huge sandals they made in the monastery, and eating big slices of bread from those wonderful loaves that had made the monastery bakery famous. I heard the monks raving to his mother about how smart he was, how he excelled in his studies. "Every time we give him a book to bind, he reads it, the little rascal," one of the monks boasted to Walid's mother. The monks asked his mother for permission to send Walid to Milan in the next two or three years to study theology.

"Theology?" Walid's mother asked. "What would he do with theology?"

"He'd become a learned monk," they told her.

"Dear me, my little devil becoming a monk?"

"No," they assured her, "not a devil, just a little rascal, perhaps. But he'll make an excellent monk. Then he'll come back to the monastery in Jerusalem, and you'll be very proud when you see him up in the pulpit, preaching to people with the tongue of angels."

"What do you say, Khamis?" Najma Humsiyya asked her son.

"I've told you a thousand times," he snapped. "My name is Walid!"

"Yes, all right. Do you want to go to Italy?"

"Yes," he said. "I want to go to Milan. I want to study and learn music. Please, Mother, give me your permission."

"It's better for him and all concerned that he goes," his mother said with apparent helplessness. "If he doesn't go, I'm sure he'll run away again and disappear into one of the caves in the valley. And we'll never find him this time."

She was referring, I realized, to that incident that had so terrified her and his brothers and had the solemn monastery in a state of unusual commotion. That day he'd run away with two of his friends from the monastery to a distant cave in Wadi al-Jamal, and two or three days later they were found there praying and chanting hymns—at least that's what they said they'd been doing, though no one believed them. Personally, I was sure he would come back because he couldn't stand being away from the organ that he played with unusual talent from the moment Father Giovanni began teaching him.

Walid was sent to Italy when he was thirteen or fourteen, one or two years, I think, before the General Strike—which was in 1937, the same year that Abu Walid returned from Bogotá, the capital city of Colombia. I remember this clearly because Masoud went with my father on his visits to seek the hands of young women in marriage for the young men in the town. As a rich returning emigrant, it was difficult for the young women's parents to rebuff him.

Masoud's "wealth" was actually a concoction of our imagination. He probably came back with some money, but he neither opened a store nor built a big house. He stayed unemployed for many months, working out how to "invest his money," as most of us thought. At last he bought an old car to take passengers from Bethlehem to Jerusalem and back, and once again the business with Regina was on everyone's tongue. In those days she was a widow pushing forty, her wide eyes made up to kill, her lips streaked red with lipstick, her breasts jutting out from the confines of her blouse, and her skirt almost splitting at the seams around her large hips. Najma ignored her crushingly, and went to great pains to try and convince her she knew nothing about her relationship with Masoud. Regina herself, though, never gave a second thought about being seen with Masoud in his car, which he soon had to sell, perhaps because he put it at Regina's disposal instead of using it for his passengers. Even today I still don't know what kind of relationship that handsome, illiterate man, who no longer had a job or trade to earn a living with, could have had with a woman like

Regina. At that time she lived with her old mother in a red stone house, which her late husband had left her along with a workshop for inlaid ornaments behind the Church of the Nativity. Later, she sold the workshop because she couldn't look after it properly.

Masoud's children started leaving school one by one to learn a trade. I used to see them on Sundays, each wearing his one elegant suit on the way to or from church, and woe betide anyone who dared say a bad word to them, or about them or their father or their relatives—they'd band together and "break his head." The people in the town referred to them as "Masoud's children," and stayed away from them. And when they accompanied either their father or their mother, they seemed, with their measured gaits and tall statures, like a royal guard accompanying the most exalted person in the town. My cousin Antoun Salem, or Abu Ibrahim, as he was known to the people in the town, was their neighbor and Masoud's childhood friend.

"The best one left," he'd say, "the intelligent one left and the rascals stayed behind . . ." We talked a lot about Walid, and every time his mother heard his name, tears swelled in her eyes.

"He'll come back, God willing," she'd say, proudly raising her head. "You'll all be proud of him, just as his father and I are."

"If you hadn't sent him abroad to become a monk," Abu Ibrahim would tease her, "I'd have given him the hand of my prettiest daughter."

"What makes you so sure he would have married any of them, even if he hadn't become a monk?" she'd ask.

"May God protect their honor!"

"Your daughter Rima is my favorite, Abu Ibrahim," she'd continue. "Rima belongs in our family, Abu Ibrahim."

"She's too young," he said. "She's not six yet."

"What can I do?" she asked. "She's always here entertaining me with her lovely stories and asking me to comb her hair and decorate it with ribbons. I have a surprise for you! I've made her a blue dress, and she'll wear it next Sunday. The prettiest dress for the prettiest girl."

If life in the thirties was difficult for the adults, it was even worse for the young, and Masoud's children started thinking of moving to Jerusalem where job opportunities were better. It seemed then that Regina had found work for Masoud in the city; it was said she knew

Father so and so and Bishop so and so, and had managed to get Masoud a job as a gatekeeper or messenger for the monastery in Jerusalem. But no sooner had the family moved to Jerusalem, while Walid was still in Italy, than Farhan left for Colombia to work for his uncle Said. And when the war started, the family, or what was left of it, had settled in a large room on the ground floor of a building in Jourat al-Nasna, among a large number of other poor families. Every time we passed by that room with its ever open door, we could hear, amid the lively sounds of the people in the quarter, the patter of the sewing machine, and we'd realize Najma was still hard at work. My wife and I would go there whenever we had the chance. Every time I looked at the scar on Masoud's face, it seemed more prominent, as though it had been carefully drawn on his face by some unseen, prophetic hand to separate the glorious days of his youth, when life was primitive and simple, from the complex days that followed. I saw him as a man who worked hard without achieving anything, who loved life and was rejected by it. A lot of people benefited from the war, in one way or another. I myself opened a large furniture factory, made a lot of money, drank more than I should have, and went from place to place looking for fun and pleasure. But all Masoud got out of the war was pain. His two children Walid and Farhan were away, and he was constantly worried about them, especially Walid, because Italy had turned into a fearful battleground after the Allied invasion. He dreamed in vain of receiving a letter, just a line or two.

"Why would anyone want to become a monk in this evil world?" he asked once. "Does he want to revive religion in Malta or what? That little rascal? One word from you, Walid, a mere word, would bring my spirits back!"

He placed all his hopes on Elias and Bassam, sending Bassam back to school and finding Elias a job in some government office. But just before the war ended, late in 1944 if memory serves, the office was blown up by Jewish terrorists, and Elias and several other people were killed. He was twenty years old. Masoud started suffering from nerve problems, most probably sciatica, some people thought, but others were convinced it was the start of a more serious disease that would ultimately lead to paralysis. He could hardly walk and had to leave his work. Suddenly, after the war ended in Italy, Walid came to Jerusalem to find his parents sunk in abject poverty and grief.

Masoud received a cable through the monastery, giving him the time of Walid's arrival from Cairo. I'll never forget Walid's face when we saw him get off the train at the station in Jerusalem. He'd left us a child, and now he came back a young man, with a striking resemblance to his father. This, indeed, was how I recognized him while his father, his brother, and I were looking at the faces of the passengers.

"You're joking," Masoud kept saying. "I swear Walid won't come. He won't come. Issa, can you see a monk among the passengers?"

My eyes fell on a tall, thin young man, with wide eyes and long hair, wearing a wool sweater that had seen better days. He was carrying a heavy suitcase.

"Walid!" I shouted.

Masoud was shaking. As the young man approached us, like a spirit from another world, he threw himself upon his father. Masoud started sobbing loudly, kissing his son over and over again, and his brother Bassam and I cried and kissed him on the cheeks.

"Where's Elias?" Walid asked, bewildered.

"We'll talk about that later," his father replied quickly. "Where are your things?"

Walid pointed at his one suitcase.

"How come you're not wearing your church clothes?" Masoud inquired.

"Oh, those!" he said. "I left the church a long time ago. Where's my mother?"

"At home, waiting for you," Masoud said.

We walked to the car, Masoud leaning on the shoulder of his prodigal son who'd finally come home.

His mother, dressed in black mourning clothes, was waiting outside the house with a group of women and neighbors. When Walid rushed toward her, she held her hand up to stop him, then lifted up a jar in her strong hands and smashed it on the ground by his feet. The jar broke into many pieces, pumpkin seeds and candy flew out of it in different directions, and all the kids rushed to pick them up. Only then did she embrace her son. The women ululated as if a bridegroom had descended on them from the skies.

I'll never, as I said, forget Walid's face that day; it's the face that's remained engraved in my memory from that moment on. People often talk about tragedies punctuated by happy occasions, about laughter overcome with tears, happiness dissipated by sorrow; they talk about resolve, despair, facing death while at the same time embracing beauty and splendor. Mix all these together, and you'll get a full, complete picture of Walid. It was as though I were back in my carpenter's shop of fifteen years ago; this person, I felt, had come to us by mistake, to a place he shouldn't have come. He came back a lover, a prodigal, a stranger, and he'd remain a lover, a prodigal, and a stranger, lonely, even though his parents, and the village people and the whole world, thronged around him day in and day out, as those children had fallen on the pumpkin seeds and the candy from the broken jar.

No, he hadn't become a monk. His mother had known him better than the monks who sent him to Italy. In that thin face of his—like his father's, yet firmer and more delicate, like a razor blade—I could see the fearful resolve of molten iron in a crucible. I wasn't surprised to find his suitcase full of books and papers, with just three or four pieces of clothing. And when his mother said, "They killed your brother—the Jewish terrorists killed your brother," he gave out a short cry and covered his face with his hands. The people in the room stopped talking, and we could hear his choked sobbing. That was the face I'd never, ever forget.

From that day on nothing I saw from him or heard about him surprised me. I'd come to realize years before that he was the exception every rule should have. In Italy he'd stopped studying theology, left the church, and worked, or perhaps studied, in many cities. In Jerusalem he wrote articles and worked in the Arab Bank, and his name was frequently mentioned in the Palestinian newspapers—a young man, twenty-four years old, who could hardly afford a new suit for himself or his father, yet his name was mentioned in places and situations where I'd be out of place. In the forties and fifties, the first years of Palestinian destitution, there were happenings and situations that fascinated me but that I couldn't understand. But they were the breath of life to Walid.

I rarely saw him after he came back, but I always felt I was in touch with him. I even gave the name Walid to my second son, who was born a few months after his return—Walid Issa Nasser, now a petroleum engineer in Abu Dhabi. My son knows I named him after Walid Masoud, and when he finds out about what happened, he'll be very upset. Walid had helped him a lot in Abu Dhabi, and had found him the job there.

In 1948 Walid's family returned to Bethlehem, like many of the old townspeople who had to leave the areas of Jerusalem occupied by the Zionists. But Walid didn't stay long with his family, joining the freedom fighters during the first few months of the year, then leaving for Damascus and enlisting in the Arab relief forces. One particular rainy night, when he was fighting the enemy in Jerusalem, it was rumored he'd played a part in blowing up a street in one of the city's new quarters where the enemy lived. Then his parents lost track of his whereabouts once again. At that time we were following the progress of the battles everywhere, especially in northern Palestine, where the Arab relief forces, despite the lack of arms and provisions, fought most of their battles. Masoud had become bedridden by then, hardly able to move, and Najma stayed by his side, catering to his needs.

"I swear, O Lord, if Walid dies in these battles I'll blaspheme Your name!" he'd say. "You've already taken one of my sons. Aren't You satisfied?"

"May God forgive us! May God forgive us!" Najma would say. "You have two other healthy children, besides Walid. Don't blaspheme!"

Then came the travesty of the armistice, and soon afterward Lod and Ramla fell to the enemy. We went out in a vast demonstration, shouting slogans, "Where's Lod? Where's Ramla? Give us weapons!" We moved toward the barracks of the Egyptian contingent on the outskirts of the town, shouting, "Give us weapons!" The commander, whom everyone loved and respected, told us weapons were scarce, and assured us the army would do its duty. A few weeks later, this same commander joined the ranks of the martyrs near Saint Elias Monastery, fighting the Jews with a few of his poorly armed soldiers. Soon afterward, I heard Walid had finally settled in Baghdad, and was once again working for the Arab Bank there.

After Masoud died, we cabled Walid in Baghdad and Bassam in Deir al-Zour, in Syria, but they managed to get to Bethlehem only three or four days later; in those days, Palestinians not only suffered the tragedy of exile from their birthplace, but had to put up, as well, with all kinds of restrictions placed on their movements from place to place. They were constantly under observation by this or that security office, as though they were common criminals. And all the Arab governments were calling for unity while at the same time setting up a thousand obstacles among themselves. But that's another story.

During those times Walid's mother was constantly worried Walid might marry a woman from outside the family, and be far away from her. Fortunately, it wasn't difficult to persuade him. Rima had studied at the nun's school and grown into a beautiful young woman, the envy of all eyes. During his quick visit after his father's funeral, Walid saw her helping his mother, and became engaged to her right away. The following summer they got married, and no one was happier than Walid, except Rima's father, Antoun Salem. On her wedding day she appeared in her bridal gown like one of those angels on Christmas Day, and her husband took her off to his new world, Baghdad.

Poor Rima!

Six or seven years after her marriage, God took pity on her father, who died before he saw what would happen to his daughter after she returned to Bethlehem. She wasn't alive, and she wasn't dead. We couldn't enjoy her company, and we couldn't disregard her. And how, how could we tell her about what happened? Is there no end to this bottomless sorrow?

Walid Masoud Remembers the Hermits in a Distant Cave

A little after sunset we slunk out through the gateway of the outer section of the building, one by one, just like escaping prisoners. It was a long way from the monastery to the "Gremlin's Path." First, we had to go down the wide steps of the little hill, with big houses on either side, then carry on along a road lit by oil lamps; Abu Nizar used to light them every evening, carrying his ladder from one lamp to the next, then at dawn he'd make the rounds again, blowing them all out. On this road was a café where many of the men of the town used to gather after a hard day's work to smoke a water pipe and play cards or dominoes, with a large lantern over the door that threw its glaring light across the roadway. As we went by, the regulars of the café were busy with their games and loud talk, so that none of them noticed us. It was only when we reached the approaches to the "New Road" that we felt we could relax, confident we wouldn't be discovered. We were constantly troubled, even so, by another kind of fear. "Gremlin's Path," which we'd chosen as the way we'd enter the valley, was so called because of the "gremlins" who, according to scores of stories we'd heard, stalked passers-by there every night, each one of them the ghost of a dead man whose body had been discarded in that particular place. The gremlin would appear with his face daubed in blood, catch up with the passer-by, and yell for revenge, finally seizing hold of him and . . . But these gremlins usually preferred dark nights, and it was almost as though they were startled by the sign of the cross and stayed away from anyone who made it. There was a moon on the night we'd chosen, and our hearts were overflowing with faith; each one of us was carrying a rosary in his pocket, and that was ample protection against gremlins—not just on "Gremlin's Path" but in every nook and cranny of the entire valley.

That night, the moon looked much larger to us than any moon had looked in Bethlehem for a long time, its greenish glow lighting up the uneven rocky slope of the path in a way we'd never seen before. The path ran alongside a quarry that the three of us knew well, as we did the terraces of olive groves that followed, and then the places where the old rock chains had been broken up so that the connecting fissures made small gateways leading us down toward the perpetual depths, down to the place where, Sulayman had said, he knew a big cave that God had provided for hermits in days gone by. It was ready and waiting for us now, and we felt sure we'd find it that very night, however long it took.

We started racing each other and jumping over things, pausing periodically to sit down on the rocks. We were singing, too, or rather chanting. Murad had a beautiful, sweet voice, and Sulayman's and mine were hardly less so. Every time we sat down, we faced north, or the direction we were pretty sure was north; we knew Jerusalem lay beyond the hills, which had a kind of twilight hovering over them throughout the night. It kept us moving toward the east, as we kept it on our left-hand side as we went on. In some parts of the valley, there were flashes of light, rather like stars coming down into the nighttime vines and wandering about among them. These we deliberately avoided. The vines were wonderful, but we were in search of the open spaces where there'd be neither grapes, nor figs, nor pomegranates, and no people either—nothing but the big cave from which we could address ourselves to God and receive his bounty every morning and evening. As the going became rockier and more difficult, our happiness increased still more.

Despite all the rocks, the ground felt soft under the pressure of our big shoes. We were hurt by the thorns we found everywhere (although this pleased us as well because, as Sulayman said, they were part of God's creation, too). The thorns kept scratching our shorts and bare legs, but we didn't care; in any case, their points were moistened by the night dew. The thing we were really afraid of was stinging nettles; they looked soft enough, but a single touch from them was enough to bring the skin out in a burning rash, and they were hard to see in the moonlight. Sometimes we'd come across strange flowers, swaying gently in the breeze of the moonlit night.

"Man's journey to God is long and thorny," said Sulayman, "but there are roses on the way, too."

"Are you two tired?" Murad asked.

"A bit," I replied.

"We're still only just starting," Sulayman told us. "I'm not tired. How about you, Murad?"

Suddenly, we heard a long, forlorn cry from far away. We stopped. From another direction came a cry of response. "Jackals," said Murad.

"We used to hear them all night," I said, "when we spent our summers in the vineyards."

The cries could be heard going back and forth across the valley. Some of them sounded quite close, and I wondered whether Sulayman and Murad could really be unafraid of these savage, mournful, frightening sounds. They were both a little older than me. For all my bravado, there was still a generous chunk of fear in a distant recess of my inner self.

"It's hyenas we should be afraid of," I said.

"They don't come into this valley," Sulayman replied. "You'll find them around the Saint Elias Monastery, and that's a long way off."

"If a hyena pisses on a person, it will follow him anywhere."

"I just told you, there are no hyenas in this valley," Sulayman replied testily. "So what are you afraid of?"

The full moon was moving rapidly into the center of the heavens. Delicate white clouds were scattered throughout the sky; they moved very slowly, their edges lit up by the moonlight, which made the moon itself seem to be on some continuous voyage across the heavens. There was total silence, apart from the sound of our shoes crunching against the rocks and an occasional hushed rustle of the breeze among the thorn branches or in the folds of the rock. And then the silence would be shattered by the howl of a jackal or a dog barking in one of the vineyards.

We took comfort from our own voices and the sounds we made. We kept kicking rocks, or else letting out yells and then waiting to hear the echo coming back a short while later. I was delighted when Sulayman admitted that he, too, was a little tired, and Murad and I felt no shame about admitting we were also tired. I told them my skin felt hot from nettle rash.

"Let's kneel down on this rock," Sulayman suggested, "and beseech God to grant us energy and strength to continue."

We chose a high rock and climbed up it with some difficulty. Then, facing Jerusalem, we knelt down somewhat precariously, raised our faces and hands to heaven, and prayed.

"Now let's chant the Ave Maris Stella," said Murad—it was one of the Latin hymns we loved to sing in the monastery chapel. We started singing it, even though the only thing we understood about it was that it was a greeting to the Virgin Mary and mentioned Archangel Gabriel. Murad loved to rhapsodize with his voice at the mention of Gabriel's name, as though he himself were the angel announcing the birth of Jesus. When we'd finished, we all felt wonderfully refreshed, and I had the impression that the entire valley—with all its interlocking expanses and incredible empty spaces—was smiling at us and would ward off any harm that might be lurking among its thickets, rocks, and caves. Such was the effect of Father Spiridon on us.

"Let your faith be like that of the Prophet Daniel. He was thrown into the lions' den, but managed to bridle the mouths of the beasts, made them submit to him and rub meekly against his feet...." This was how Father Spiridon used his eloquence to impress us children at each liturgy. "The prophets of God were not touched by the wild beasts in the wilderness nor by the predators in the mountains. It is the pious hermits who came closest to being prophets; God Almighty granted them strength from heaven so that they could praise and venerate his name in a life that was otherwise eaten up with filth and sin. Saint Jerome befriended a lion in a cave; Saint Anthony fed a panther and an eagle at the door of his cave; Simeon Stylites tolerated the lacerations of the sun's heat and the wind's blasts year after year, while spreading his learning among the people and feeding the birds of the air from his own hand, all this from the top of a pillar. God be praised! Every morning and evening, You (in Your Almighty power) send down from heaven food and drink to Your hermits, who pray to You and beg that man may be cleansed of his sins. They continually invoke the Trinity, Father, Son, and Holy Spirit, and contemplate the wonders of Your creation. (The Savior said: Consider the lilies, how they grow; they toil not, they spin not; yet I say unto you that Solomon in all his glory was not arrayed like one of these. If then God so clothes the grass, which is today in the field, and tomorrow is cast into the oven, how much more will he clothe you, O ye of little faith? And seek not what ye shall eat, or what ye shall drink, neither be ye of doubtful mind . . .) [Luke 12:27–29].

Whenever it was time for Father Spiridon's class, he used to tell us tales of saints and martyrs and make us repeat many of his words and expressions. Sulayman was, perhaps, the most eager of all of us to respond to this "holy" magic, and one evening he broached the subject with me after solemn benediction:

"Why don't we become hermits, Walid?"

"Would we become saints?" I asked.

"We'd spend all our lives in devotion and prayer in some cave in Wadi al-Jamal. Does that appeal to you?"

"Where would we find things to eat and drink?"

"Didn't you hear what Father Spiridon tells us every day? 'Seek not what ye shall eat, or what ye shall drink.'"

"Will God send down bread and water for us as he did for the saints?"

"Every day! All we have to do is pray and beseech God Almighty."

The thought occurred to me that the saints were always old men, whereas we were just children of no more than twelve or, at the most, thirteen years of age. But Sulayman had an answer for that.

"God welcomes young people before old. He loves children."

"Are you a true believer?" I asked.

"Oh, yes," he replied. "I have beautiful dreams. I can see us worshiping, and people will come, men and women, from every village and city, and ask us for help in their lives . . ."

"I have wonderful dreams, too—strange ones. I see myself flying in the sky like an eagle, soaring and swooping through the valleys. People will come to me and say in amazement: "Teach us to fly like you!" If we go and become hermits, can we change mankind, change the world?"

"The world is full of sin. It must be purged and changed."

These big words, which we'd heard morning and evening for several months from Father Spiridon, kept repeating themselves on our tongues. When we found out that Murad was also having dreams about being a hermit, the three of us decided to run away from the monastery and go down into the valley to look for the cave Sulayman told us he knew, far removed from people and the world, ready and waiting for us to devote ourselves to God.

"How much food shall we take with us?" Murad asked.

"Where's your faith?" Sulayman retorted with a touch of anger. "We won't take any food with us."

I supported him on this point, although I have to admit to a feeling of shame at the very small amount of doubt I felt but did not reveal. Even so, I suggested we take a few tomatoes with us, probably because I like them and used to eat them with a little salt. I defended my suggestion by pointing out that they weren't really serious food and contained fluid to moisten the mouth if we became thirsty while going down into the valley, before we begin our hermit rituals. At that Sulayman's resistance softened, and he even agreed we should take a loaf, just one loaf, of bread and some sweet-sour candy drops that my mother used to bring me when she came to visit the monastery on Sundays. "All this is provisions for the journey," Sulayman told us. "After that . . ."

I pictured in my mind a marvelous bird descending from the heavens every morning to the door of the cave and releasing from its talons a basket full of meat and fruit and then flying up into the heavens again on its mighty wings. But when I tried to describe this imaginary bird of mine, Sulayman stopped me. "Now don't be greedy, Walid," he said. "God won't send meat and fruit so easily to every sinner who sleeps in a cave. Perhaps he'll send dry bread, or barley bread maybe, to test our faith. As Jesus said, bread will be enough."

"But Jesus distributed fish with the bread," Murad pointed out.

"Well, we'll have fish to eat as well. God forgive me! Don't you see that, by saying these things, we are testing the Lord Almighty?"

On the evening we'd set to run away, we found we couldn't get the loaf we'd planned to take, so we made do with two pieces of bread each that we'd saved from our share from the feast day of Our Lady of the Spikenard. Sulayman managed to sneak some tomatoes out of the kitchen (asking the Virgin's forgiveness as he did so) on the day when he was supposed to help the cook get the food ready for the boys, cramming them all into his pocket and almost completely squashing them. For my part, I filled my pockets with all the sweet-sour candy drops I had.

We'd chosen the Feast of the Virgin to begin our hallowed journey, not only because it would be a propitious start, but also because on feast days the orphans used to mix in the afternoon with the boys in the outer playground if they wished to do so, and after benediction they could go with them to an evening film show. All this made it easy for us to leave by the huge iron gate reserved for their use, which was left open until the film show was over.

Sulayman had the faith to move mountains, and it was combined with an innate ability to lead and command. He had no doubts about what he wanted and always took the shortest route to achieve it without the slightest hesitation. This made things much easier for Murad and myself. Every time I felt the urge to object, I preferred to keep my feelings to myself and submit to his will. Even so, it occurred to me, as we proceeded on our way through the valley, stumbling, falling down, and picking ourselves up again, that perhaps Sulayman didn't, as he'd claimed, know of a cave where we could find refuge.

"Sulayman," I said, "how long has it been since we set off?"

He looked up at the moon that was now descending from its zenith. "It's about midnight," he replied, "so we've been gone about four hours."

"I'm tired and thirsty," said Murad.

"Are you sure you know the way to the cave?" I asked.

"Sure. We're heading toward it. All roads lead to the mill."

"Where is this mill?" Murad asked. "Are we going to keep walking till morning?"

"No. I'm sure we'll be there within an hour or two."

"Well, lads," I said, "we're right in the middle of the valley. As soon as we find the cave, we'll settle right down, and that'll be it!"

Suddenly, Sulayman stopped at the edge of a terrace, with a solitary olive tree on it. He looked down and then called out to us. We hurried over.

"Look at that rock over there," he said. "Let's get to it!"

We bounded over to the large rock, hearing a strange rustling sound and then the noise of something scurrying away between the brush and the rocks—some animal had been aroused by our voices and run away. The mouth of the cave was gaping wide, as though it had been waiting for our arrival since the very beginning of creation. Right at the entrance were wildflowers of all kinds, difficult to distinguish; it was very dark there because the moonlight shone on top of the rock and then projected its long shadow far from the entrance to the cave. Even so, I could make out a profusion of anemones scattered all around the rock, and inside the entrance, and pushing up between the nooks and crannies in the rock, swaying gently in the breeze.

"Consider the lilies . . ." I said.

Murad and I both shouted in amazement as Sulayman silently took a candle out of his pocket, struck a match, and lit it. He raised the candle with its tiny flame into the air, made the sign of the cross, and went into the cave. We followed behind, full of anticipation and awe.

"This morning at Mass," he said, "I asked Our Lady of Sorrows: 'What will we be needing, O Sacred Mother of God?' 'Candles, my son,' she replied, a tear glistening in her eye. The candle tray under her statue was full. 'Would you be angry,' I asked her, 'if I took these three candles?' 'No, my son,' she replied, shaking her head. 'Someday,' I said, 'I will come back to you with many, many candles and a bouquet of flowers.'"

The cave was damp and not very deep; it faced the heights that formed the beginnings of the Jerusalem hills, exactly as we wanted. We sat down on the ground, which was well endowed with vegetation and rocks. My legs and feet felt very tired, and my throat was parched. We put the candle in the middle between two pieces of rock; the flame kept rising and falling and moving to one side with every little waft of breeze, projecting our magnified shadows onto the ancient rock ceiling.

Sulayman took the few tomatoes he had from his pocket, and we each took one. How luscious they felt, how juicy and fresh, so soothing for the lips and throat!

"And now," said Sulayman, "let's give thanks to God for guiding us to this hallowed cave."

We knelt down on our bruised, battered, and exhausted knees, as the moonlight began to disappear from the bottom of the valley so that forms became magnified and everything around us looked weird. In the distance a jackal howled. The apprehension I'd been fighting came back, but praying made things easier for me. Then we took off the shoes that had been torturing our feet and bedded down on the rock as best we could.

"Tomorrow," I said, "we'll level off the ground. Tomorrow we'll start the life of righteousness and good deeds."

We all started moving the stones from where we were lying down to sleep, so that they wouldn't keep digging into us throughout the night. I was just on the point of falling asleep next to Sulayman, with Murad on his other side, when I heard Murad's tuneful voice intoning "*Miserere mei, Deus, secundum magnam misericordiam tuam. Et secundum multitudinem miserationum tuarum, dele iniquitatem meam. . . .*" I don't know how much of this psalm he managed to finish, because I fell sound asleep with the Latin words washing against me like a wave.

I woke up with a start, feeling cold and damp, my face cushioned by a stone covered in moss. My two colleagues were sprawled out among the rocks in a manner that suggested they were far from comfortable. Where was I, I asked myself in amazement for a couple of moments. Then I remembered. From my place in the cave I could see that the valley was filling up with a cold, gray-blue light. I put my arm under my head and lifted my weary knees up to my stomach in search of warmth. A sparrow alighted deftly on a distant olive tree and launched into song, but flew off again almost immediately. There was no foliage to speak of except for a few wilted and scattered olive trees. Yellow and violet flowers and anemones stretched as far as the eye could see, though they, too, were fairly sparse. Wherever you looked there were white and bluish rocks.

Before Sulayman and Murad woke up, I got up in my bare feet to take a look at our place of worship. Beyond the blue mountains in the distance the eastern horizon was splashed with the reddish yellow rays of the early morning sun. I was overwhelmed by the sight of the sun breaking through the wisps of light white cloud; it was as though I were seeing it for the first time. All the while the stones were hurting my feet, and the flowers spattered them with morning dew. I felt a touch of thirst, but paid no attention. I didn't go too far from the cave; in fact, I hurried back and, with a delicious sense of trepidation, started looking around by the entrance. Had God sent us bread and water while we were asleep? I didn't find any. I looked between the rocks and in the grass. I scrambled up one side of the rock and noticed some birds hovering above me, then flying away. But there was no bread or water.

Holding on to the edge of the rock, I leaned over toward my sleeping companions. "Sulayman! Murad!" I yelled. "The sun's up. Let's pray!"

Disappointment was written all over their faces when I told them I'd found no sign of any bread or water. But we knelt down and said the matins prayers facing toward Jerusalem. When we'd finished, I took one of the two slices of bread out of my pocket; I was feeling terribly hungry. Sulayman made no objection, and in fact he and Murad did exactly the same. We all ate enough to quell our hunger and then got out the prayer book. Sulayman read the first chapter, after which we chanted the Ave Maria and Pater Noster along with a number of beads from the rosary, following that with pleas to the Almighty Creator that he'd have mercy on naked, suffering man and give him clothing to ward off the cold and food to keep hunger at bay. I looked toward the heavens in search of a bird descending toward us, but all I could see were small sparrows frolicking in the valley in search of their own food and water.

Sulayman closed the book and cleared his throat. Then he started reciting in Syriac, something he was very proud of, because he believed the Messiah spoke in that language and the angels used it, too, to sing the praises of God. Murad and I listened humbly as he elaborated on the chant. But it seemed the bird of heaven was paying no attention to our prayers, even in Syriac.

Refusing to despair, we set about our daily chores. We began to make the ground of the cave more comfortable and remove the larger rocks, and whenever we found worms and various insects underneath them, we squashed them with our shoes; we believed, resolutely, that we were turning this place into a decent room for three hermits who wanted to be in touch with God night and day for the rest of their lives.

The sun became much hotter, and we set about our work with a will. I took out some sweet-sour candy drops, and we shared them. How marvelous they tasted! Before long, though, they made us feel very thirsty, the kind of thirst that would not go away. Suddenly, Murad had had enough. "I'm going to look for some water!" he said.

Sulayman stopped him for a moment. "Do you see those dry-looking trees over there in the distance, on that hill with a rock formation around it?"

We realized immediately what he was driving at: wherever trees were grouped together along a rock line, there had to be vines or some vestige of them. We agreed to make our way over there.

"It's inconceivable that God should desert His servants," said Sulayman.

As we walked, the sun beat down on us with its noonday heat, but it was still pleasant because there was a springtime breeze with it. Grasshoppers kept leaping from thorns to plants, and I caught a gleaming green beetle that had settled in the cup of a violet flower and carried it in the palm of my hand to the hill. Sulayman and Murad were chasing butterflies, catching them, and then letting them go.

The rise with the trees on it was farther than we'd imagined, and we still had to scramble and climb our way up to the rock formation. Once there we scaled it and found, to our surprise, a derelict hut with its walls in ruins and close by an old rotten wooden door. Around the hut were some vegetable patches with dried-out bushes, which must once have been almonds, apples, and apricots.

"The well. There has to be a well, but where is it?"

We bounded toward one of the patches, and there we found a holed well top like a millstone gleaming in the sunlight. Still to be seen in it were the grooves and notches caused by the dangling buckets over scores of years past. We ran over to it and lifted a rusty iron door from the middle. Water, water! I was so thirsty I felt like jumping right into the well and drowning myself in the water.

The well wasn't deep, but even so the water was beyond our reach. Sulayman started telling us that God provides man with the things he needs, but doesn't make it too easy, otherwise he'd get lazy.

"Cut out the philosophy!" I told him. "Where's the bucket? That's what counts. Every well has a bucket."

We spread out in search of the bucket. Then suddenly, Murad let out a joyful shout, and we went back to the well with Murad carrying a dented tin pail reddened by a thick encrustation of rust. There was no rope or chain, but we didn't hesitate. I took off the thin leather belt that was holding my trousers up and tied it to the handle, although I was worried in case the rusty handle might fall off. Sulayman gave me his belt, too, and I tied it on to the end of mine. I lowered the bucket from the middle of the well top. Murad was muttering prayers to himself, while I cried, "O Lord, O Lord!" The bucket reached the water. No one, it seemed, had drawn any water from this well since the winter before, because the water level was very high. I struck the water with the bucket, then lowered it as far as I could so as to dissolve any brackish layer on the surface. When I pulled, it came up swaying, full of water through God's grace. We drank and drank till we almost burst, and filled the ancient vineyard with our shouts.

There wasn't much shade in the vineyard, so we filled the bucket again and took the water back to the cave. I began to feel even hungrier, but I was ashamed to mention it. Without a word, each one of us took out the last piece of bread from his pocket and ate it. It was dry and hard by now, but the water made it easier to swallow. When exhaustion had finally taken its toll on us, we took off our shoes and lay down on the ground we'd cleared for ourselves. In fact, it was only slightly more gracious to us than it had been on the previous night.

"When we wake up again," said Sulayman, half asleep, "we'll say evening prayers, and God will provide us according to His will at sunset."

With this attractive prospect I closed my eyes. Yet, a nagging doubt was still plaguing me. "Get thee behind me, Satan!" I muttered to myself, then fell asleep.

But at sunset, the anticipated bird didn't appear with bread and water when we'd finished evening prayers and supplications; it didn't even bring the bread.

Darkness fell and the moon rose. We lit a candle and read another section of the prayer book. Night sounds made themselves heard again, along with the barking of dogs in the distance. A strange, unidentifiable rustling kept startling us. Once again we fell asleep, but this time our sleep was fitful. Then I heard the sound of sobbing. At first I thought I was dreaming, but when I opened my eyes, I could just see the figure of Sulayman through the darkness (the moon had gone down by now); he was on his knees praying and striving vainly to stifle his sobs. At that moment I felt afraid, with a fear that sent a shiver through my entire body. I bundled myself up, still feeling the night chill, blaming the cold for my shivering. Sulayman came over to me. "Walid!" he said, his whispers moistened by tears. "Can't you sleep either?"

"Why didn't we bring a cover or blanket with us?"

"How could we have done that without being discovered?"

Only Murad remained serenely asleep, his hands between his legs.

"Why were you crying?" I asked Sulayman.

"I felt my faith was wavering. Satan took advantage of me and made me regret coming here. So I got up and prayed, and then my faith came back as solid as a rock."

We started talking, and I told him about my father with his carriage and horses. He'd never known his own father; he knew only what his mother had told him. All he could remember was seeing his father laid out on the ground with groups of women sitting with his mother and wailing.

"My father was terrific!" I said. "He used to tell us stories every night and sing us songs. In the morning I used to help him feed the horses, and then we'd take them out of the stable and tether them to the carriage."

"How lucky you were!"

"But he left us to go to Colombia and make money."

Suddenly, Sulayman grabbed me around the neck, shuddering all over—a strange-looking animal was standing at the mouth of the cave, panting and baring its teeth! We couldn't make out what kind of animal it was; it looked huge, almost completely filling up the mouth of the cave, and there was a frightening growl coming from its throat. I clung on to Sulayman for dear life, my eyes riveted on the animal. We were both quivering with terror. "The candle!" I whispered in a dry, cracked voice.

The animal stood there, looking at us with eyes that flashed in the darkness. An age went by as Sulayman searched for a match in his pocket; he'd already handed me the candle, which I was clasping in my trembling hand. "It's the devil!" I shouted. I dearly hoped the candle would light spontaneously, but finally Sulayman managed to strike the match and lit the candle. The black creature immediately turned on its heels and vanished.

"My God!" Sulayman cried. "A miracle, a miracle. O Queen of heaven! Satan has fled the light of your unblemished candle! Peace be with you, Mary!"

Little by little we stopped shaking, and I began to feel a pleasant relaxation seep its way into my chest, thighs, knees, and legs. I stretched out on the ground, feeling myself enveloped in a friendly, tender darkness; Sulayman went on hugging me. When I opened my eyes again, the sun was high in the sky.

This time we weren't surprised when we didn't find any bread at the door of the cave. God was testing us, we told ourselves, but he'd provide us with the necessary strength.

"The valley's full of things to eat," I said, after we'd prayed. "This is the globe-thistle season. Why don't we look for some?"

We drank up the water left in the bucket and started searching inch by inch among the brush, thorns, and flowers for that wild plant that we could recognize by its yellow leaves. It wasn't there in abundance, but it was there. We started picking it, pulling off its thorny leaves and stuffing our pockets full; some of it we ate raw. There were some flowers we recognized, too, and we picked them, broke off the crowns, and sucked the scented sweet stuff inside them. In a few spots we came across crab apples gleaming like red glass balls amid the thick green foliage. We picked them to play with, wishing all the while we could eat them.

Then we went up to the vineyard to draw some more water, and started rubbing the bucket in an attempt to get off as much rust as we could. It was barely midday when we lit a fire and started boiling our supply of globe thistle in the bucket. This time we ate more than just enough. We no longer had any doubts and were determined to stay in the cave.

That afternoon we set about organizing our cave, moving extra rocks and setting them up as an altar on one side. In a small cleft immediately above it we placed a small cross and an icon that Murad used to wear around his neck. Sulayman put the remains of his candle and the two others between the rock and the altar.

At that time of day the birds began to increase in number. Swarms of swallows were soaring and swooping in the valley sky. We sat in a rock close by, feeling utterly worn out, and the old, accursed feeling of hunger came back. "If we had a slingshot," I said, "we could hunt some birds ... until God answers our prayers."

"If a bird doesn't come from heaven by tomorrow," Sulayman said with complete confidence, "we'll make a slingshot for each one of us."

"If necessary," Murad suggested, "one of us could go into the town and fetch slingshots ... and some food."

But Sulayman wouldn't agree, insisting we must content ourselves with the will of God and stay apart from the world, whatever the difficulties might be.

That night, though, was even worse than the one before. What was left of the globe thistle couldn't stave off our tremendous hunger. We turned our attention to devotions and looked upon our lack of food as a fast aimed at pleasing God, even though circumstances didn't require us to do so. When we lay down to sleep, the valley, illuminated by the greenish light of the moon, seemed to teem with different sounds. I had some peculiar dreams: I saw myself riding my father's horse, wandering through open deserts, penetrating rock and cave, and traversing waters where the waves tried to drown me, but I kept on swimming with my horse; and, no sooner had I reached the other side, than I turned around and started traversing the waters all over again. All of a sudden I woke up, completely oblivious of my two friends, with the feeling that God was angry with me for some reason. It was very cold. I turned over onto my stomach and put my head in my hands. I found myself sobbing! "Why, Lord, why, why?" There was that sound of panting and growling again. I turned around, and there was the black creature we'd seen the previous night, standing in the cave entrance, except that this time it looked much smaller. Though panic stricken, I grabbed as many stones as I could find in each hand, charged at the animal and threw a rock at it. I hit it between the eyes and followed my first throw with a second. Without any candle being lit, it turned around and fled with high-pitched cries of pain. I got up, picked up two more rocks, went outside the cave, and threw them both at the animal, which was disappearing, still making its cries, into the predawn darkness. I went back to my corner of the cave and was soon asleep again.

Next morning, before we began our hermit rituals, Sulayman went out to check the area all around us, hoping against hope, but he came back disappointed and frustrated, angry in fact. However, he asked for God's forgiveness. Then we turned to our primitive temple and started chanting, but Murad's voice seemed to have lost its purity of tone. "Come on," he said after a while, "let's look for some more globe thistle."

We went back to the vineyard, cooked the fruits of the earth we'd collected, and ate them. While we were scrambling over the rock formation on our way back to the cave, we were thunderstruck to see a man on a donkey in the distance swaying his way down between the rocks. He was singing a Taamari song; we couldn't follow the words exactly, but we recognized the rhythmic, sad, doleful tunes. Murad couldn't resist launching into the same tune; Sulayman, on the other hand, wasn't pleased by what he saw, and I had a premonition of evil consequences that I couldn't define.

As we reached our cave, the donkey rider was approaching slowly. He saw us, and he started moving deliberately in our direction and stopped singing. He was beating his donkey ceaselessly on the neck and spurring it on with his heels. The donkey started to go faster, stumbling its way through the scrub and the rocks.

"Greetings, boys!" he said, and at that moment my eyes fell on the huge club hanging from his arm and the curved dagger in his belt.

"Greetings! Where are you going?"

"Is one of you called Sulayman?"

He looked at each one of us in turn. Stunned, we said nothing.

"And is one of you the son of Masoud Farhan? I've forgotten the third name . . ."

In the distance we could see another man on a donkey, coming toward us from a different direction.

"What's your name, Sir?" I asked.

"Me? I'm Abu Deeb Hamdan," he replied. "Don't you know Abu Deeb?" Suddenly, the tone of his voice changed. "What are you doing here? Do you think there's no government in the world, or something?"

"Government? What's the government got to do with us?"

"You run away from the monastery school, and then ask what the government has got to do with you! Bethlehem's been turned upside down because of you. They've been looking for you everywhere; you should be ashamed of yourselves. Why did you run away from the monastery? What did they do to you? Did they hurt you? Did they starve you? Did they throw you out? Come on! Pack up your things and come with me!"

"Listen, good sir," Sulayman replied, ignoring his instructions. "Go your way and leave us alone to look for God's way. If you want our things, here they are: a prayer book and a few bits of globe thistle we cooked today."

"Globe thistle?" he replied. "Let me see that!"

I handed him some fresh cooked globe thistle from my pocket. He took it and tasted some. "It needs some salt," he said.

In the meantime, the other man had come closer. Abu Deeb shouted out to him, "These are the ones, Ulayyan. Okay, you boys, come with us!"

"I'm not going!" said Sulayman.

"Nor am I!" said I.

"Nor am I!" said Murad.

"Just stop fooling around," Abu Deeb said gruffly. "Trying to stick together, eh, you little bastards! Are you trying to cause trouble?"

"Listen, Abu Deeb, we came here to worship God."

"You can forget about worshiping. Come off it. Let's go; get your things together. Ulayyan, take this one on your donkey, and I'll take the other two. And listen, anyone who starts any funny business, God curse his father . . . Come on, before I beat you on the head with this club."

Ulayyan caught Sulayman unawares, picked him up, and put him forcibly on his donkey. Abu Deeb put me on his and then put Murad behind me.

"You're lucky we learned about you from your friend in the monastery. We thought at first you'd gone to Bayt Sahur. But then we decided that couldn't be; maybe you got as far as the monastery of Saint Saba, we thought, but no, that's too far. What brought you down here? We've been looking high and low for you yesterday and today, you shameless ingrates."

Sulayman turned in my direction. "Our friend, eh!" he said. "Some friend! It must have been Abdallah, who was going to come but changed his mind."

There were anemones all over the terraces we now began to climb so unwillingly. I took a long, hard look at Abu Deeb to try and guess how cruel he really was, then took a chance, and threw myself on the ground. I started picking the fresh red anemones, telling myself that in two days' time I'd come back to the valley.

"What do you want with that stuff, Ibn Masoud?" he asked with a laugh. "You and your friends are crazy, Ibn Masoud, do you know that?" With that he picked me up roughly and put me back on his donkey.

Sulayman surprised me by jumping off his donkey, rushing at me, snatching the anemones, and throwing them to the ground. "Are you going to take them for the Virgin," he yelled, "when she completely ignored us and refused to intercede with God so as to send us even a single loaf of bread? Never! I won't have it."

And so we were dragged back to the monastery, where I found my mother waiting along with some relatives of Sulayman and Murad. As soon as she saw me, she deluged me with curses. "I was worried to death," she went on. "May God be angry with you!" She threatened not to visit me again at the orphanage if I didn't repent and promise not to go on such a lunatic adventure again. Then it was Father Tartini's turn: he threatened us with expulsion if we didn't improve our behavior. As punishment we each got four strokes of the cane on the hand, and for three days we weren't allowed to enter the church to pray with the other boys.

Father Spiridon listened to us, believing and not believing what he heard. He kept shaking his gray head in disbelief. "Then what?" he kept saying, looking us closely in the face. Our greatest disappointment came when we'd finished our tale. "No, no!" he said, standing up. "It's impossible, absolutely impossible!"

5

Dr. Tariq Raouf Contemplates Capricorn

Walid Masoud was born under the sign of Capricorn, on the fifteenth of January, with Capricorn in the ascendant, as they say. Had I not been aware of his keen interest in the stars and their effect on people's lives, something bordering on a belief in the unknown, I wouldn't have bothered to point out his zodiac sign—Capricorn, Cancer, Virgo, or whatever. In Walid's case it was just a craving for knowledge, including the old and the useless. He was plagued with this kind of appetite; he devoured details and paid attention to little things, his mind taking nourishment from everything he saw. And as time passed his birth under the sign of Capricorn started having a special significance for him.

"You see, Tariq," he said, looking at me suddenly, "I'm a Capricorn, and there's nothing I can do about it." It was as though he saw in that reality a clear justification for something he'd done, or was going to do.

As I had no idea about fortune-telling or zodiacs, I didn't understand what he meant. "Surely," I said, laughing, "you, with your logic and clarity of mind, can't be interested in these trivialities magazines print on their last pages—'The Stars and You'?"

"Of course I'm not interested in nonsense of that sort," he said seriously. "What I am interested in is the mysterious forces that control man, and you won't find anything about those on the last pages of magazines."

"Can you find these forces, or something to lead you to them?" I said.

"Yes, in the stars; and in the books of people who read into them."

"In the occult, you mean? You surprise me."

"Don't be surprised. The ancient Babylonians and the Egyptians and the Greeks all knew that a man born under the zodiac of Capricorn—to take an example—would be controlled by inner inclinations conferring some of the characteristics of a kid."

"What does that mean?"

"I mean the ram; the goat, if you like."

"Do you mean agility or sexual desire?"

"Both, and everything connected with them, especially the violent inclination to everything sensual, to tyrannical appetite and voluptuous lust. Listen!" He pulled out a book, flipped through it, and stopped on a particular page. "Here's what the ancient scientist Pharmacus said. It's in Latin, but I'll translate." He started reading and translating. " 'Those born with Capricorn in the ascendant will have a deceptive look that hides their real personality. Their faces are calm, their beards are long, and their foreheads are wide and stubborn. Yet, all this is false and deceptive, for their real nature lies in lewdness. The fires of lust devour them. Often they fall prey to their own evil desires and are forced to commit suicide.' "

No matter what others said about him, this was a true picture, almost a caricature, of Walid Masoud. A calm voice and long beard (figuratively) and a broad, stubborn forehead; intelligence, acute discernment, and balance: that was Walid. But it was also deceptive, as Pharmacus had so bluntly said, a false appearance. A reversible mask hid Walid's real face, the lewd Walid, the voluptuary devoured by lust that led him, ultimately, to suicide. The way his deserted car stood in the middle of the highway, a little way from Rutba, hardly accorded with what people said about him.

I believe Walid committed suicide, even though there's evidence to the contrary. He was strong and muscular; even at fifty his muscles hadn't started to sag. We used to swim at the club together, and I was always impressed by his compact body, although a small paunch had begun to ruin his figure. He often told me that he took after his father, who used to put a hundred-kilogram bag of flour on his back and climb two flights of stairs without complaining. Walid came from the mountains in Palestine, where the people were all strong farmers engaged in a constant battle with the harsh, rocky land. He used to brag about this. Yet, his physical strength was only a cover for a different kind of strength that grew inside him. At the beginning of our friendship I didn't know precisely what that strength was; I thought it was mental, or perhaps a stubbornness typical of the mountain people, attractive and repulsive at the same time. It was always as though he was right and everyone else was wrong. I discovered later it was a strength of a different sort, and it was he himself who alerted me to it. It was a strength I wish I'd never discovered—his sexual strength. He was happy to have the determination of a ram. For him it was like a gift from God that he wouldn't refuse.

How many women had Walid known? I wish he'd told me. I gathered from some of the things he said (although, in fact, he said very little about his love affairs and rarely mentioned specific names), and also from what Jawad and Ibrahim told me, that he had relationships with more than one woman at the same time. I personally know at least three of them who were extremely frank with me about their "fondness" for him, and there were others whose names I didn't know, or I wasn't sure whether the rumors about them were true. But, where there's smoke, there's fire.

If God wants to curse a woman He visits the madness of lust on her. If, on the other hand, He wants to curse a man, He makes him prey to a woman smitten with this madness. For all his alertness and clarity of mind, Walid allowed the ram to control his instincts and so became involved with women of this kind, making the original madness a hundred times worse. I suspected this only after years of friendship and intimacy, and I became really sure of it only after his death or disappearance. One letter in particular opened my eyes and made me see everything I knew about him in a new light.

At first, Jinan al-Thamer denied that the letter was from him at all because the signature wasn't very clear, but I had no difficulty whatsoever recognizing his handwriting, because I'd had several letters from him myself. As with my letters, the crucial hidden meaning of this one could be appreciated only if the context and the time frame were also understood. It was the kind of letter that had to be placed at a point where many facts converged before it could emerge in its proper light.

Jinan was a close friend of another beautiful woman that Walid was involved with at the same time, or most probably later. Maybe there was a third woman, too, whom I knew nothing about. It became clear to me that his relationships contradicted one another, and that he could have lived through these contradictions only by pursuing them toward an inevitable end. It was clear, too, that his supernatural belief in what Capricorn had destined for him had allowed him to belittle the role of doubt and conscience in his relationships with women. Who knows—maybe the women, too, took to him because they themselves had belittled the role of doubt and conscience in what they did. I'm not saying Walid was a wolf among sheep, I'm sure he wasn't; he was a wolf among wolves, rather, an equal among equals. The important thing was that he knew who those equals (male or female) were. I can't imagine Walid ever seduced a woman without her full approval. That kind of seduction held little interest for him, and I imagine he was the prey in most cases. He enjoyed, perhaps, languishing in the fires that burned inside him, which no woman had ever succeeded in extinguishing totally.

I ventured once to call this the Oedipus complex, which, according to Carl Jung, appears in its negative mode as macho behavior. It's a strange psychological complex, because it contains serious contradictions; the great movers in history were in most cases lovers of numerous women. It appears, sometimes, that this persistent passion reflects the positive side of the Oedipus complex. It begins with different forms of manliness, resolution, ambition, fighting oppression, and the desire to sacrifice oneself heroically for the sake of truth. Its negative side manifests itself as love for one woman after another. Its positive side is manifested in this lust to explore the secrets of the universe coupled with the revolutionary spirit that strives to give the world a new face.

Dangerous words, which I utter with great caution because I don't know how many of them really apply to Walid. Perhaps I don't care to know—after all, grasping even one side of this complex is a difficult task in itself, and how much more difficult it is to grasp both sides! And who's to say, in any case, that the psychiatrist's always right? His art isn't, finally, totally removed from fortune-telling and magic. So let me go back to what I'm sure of, insofar as anyone can be sure of anything.

The letter I'm going to cite is a revealing psychological document, but it's also the sort of letter only someone with a long experience of literary writing could have produced. In other words, it's that kind of writing that its author uses as a screen between his inner self and other people, despite the claim that writers write to allow people to see their innermost feelings. It is, at best, a colored, transparent veil. The lights behind it make what the eyes see extremely revealing, make us imagine we see much more than what's really there.

There's one point, though, that I don't think I've entirely resolved: who was Walid writing his letter to? Was it Jinan, who denied he'd given her the letter and denied that the letter was written to her, then claimed later that the letter was "of course" written to her? How else would a letter like this fall into her hands? But I must make a number of points. First, the envelope's missing, so we don't now know the name of the addressee. Second, the letter didn't start in the usual manner; there's no "Dear so and so" or "My love so and so." It starts right away, without mentioning anyone's name. Third, was Jinan the kind of mistress the letter clearly indicates? It seems the letter predated her relationship with Walid, though it doesn't have a date that might help us. Most probably, Jinan somehow got the letter from the woman it was written to in the first place. In other words, I think—even though I'm not absolutely certain—that the woman in question gave her the letter for some reason after Walid had left her, and after she'd discovered his relationship with Jinan. And because the letter refers to "another" woman, I believe Jinan is, at most, the third woman, the one that Walid got involved with after the first two (although I'm not even sure of this chain of events!). But why would Jinan show me only one letter and refuse to show me others? And why did she claim the letter was written to her, even though this definitely wasn't so? And why did Walid stop writing to her? And why didn't he leave her a written confession of his love? These are questions that came to me afterward, when I wanted to uncover the sexual drives clamoring in Walid's soul. It's likely that my conclusions moved me away from the truth rather than closer to it. So let it be! Let me present the letter, which is the subject of the allegation:

"I just received your letter, which almost brought me to tears. It's been a long time since I read such words. You're a jewel. I can't believe that a woman like you actually exists. Your words stir my emotions, and strange feelings afflict me, while I feel my own words are, in the final analysis, simple and stupid. I think I know how you've been able to understand my mental state, how you understood what I wanted to confess to you and was afraid to confess. Have you really been able to understand the complexity of all this, from my incoherent words, my words that lacked the skill informing yours? How can anyone understand what love has done to us? For me to love you, to continue loving you in this impossible, contradictory way—and then suddenly another love, another madness, and no matter what I do I can't make one take the place of the other... Please, my love, don't accuse me of hypocrisy. Don't accuse me of lying. You're the only one, the only one who could ever understand all of this in me. I embrace your spirit, I make love to your picture. Your thoughts excite me, entice me, make me envious of your intelligence. I imagine your voice, the way you stand, even your clothes and your nakedness. You are very real, and love in such a situation is a logical matter for both of us. Only, through all this, another picture appears, a visual picture this time, tangible, yet there's no contradiction between the two pictures. This is what worries me. Which of the two is closer to the here and now? I don't know. I told you once that imagination and reality were, for me, interchangeable most of the time. You're no longer a fantasy of mine (as I thought once). Rather, you're as real as the bread I eat. I have felt you from the inside. You have engulfed me within you. (Do I flatter myself with these words?) And I have engulfed you within me. And now, this new thing happens, this marvelous, confusing, persistent thing. Yes. Just as you said, you and I should someday write a book together about love, about how we seek out torment by way of happiness and how, by way of torment, we cry out jubilantly to the God of Heaven and Earth. If you don't understand this, no one else will. But I know you do. It's a difficult, complex thing. Heaven and hell, impossible, startling, maddening, at times filled with nothing except pain. Here I am writing again, even though I know that writing stimulated by such a direct, moving action won't necessarily turn out the best kind. (Oh, I'm thinking of the poems my pen might produce now if I were writing poetry.) If I haven't gotten lost yet, I'm about to. I feel that I'm living on various levels at the same time and that all these may fall apart at any moment. Please, answer this letter. I enjoy every word you utter. I enjoy the many ways of your sensitive love. You say you won't be too upset about our separation because it's given love a new dimension, which has a new magic about it. As for me, I'm very upset, but what's the use? Write to me. Advise me. Chide me. Say you're upset, that you hate me, that you love me, that you're sick of me. Let next year (the rains haven't stopped since I started writing) be fuller of love, surprise, emotional strife, and chants to the God of Heaven, for your eyes' sake, your lips, your arms, your voice, your hands. The contradictory, intersecting ways of our love, who could understand them? And how can I justify, today, my love, my other love, so you would forgive me?

Walid

I don't know if any woman can resist this dangerous style, which is like a military plan, dealing in trickery and mental exhaustion, before delivering the final blow.

I pretended to believe Jinan when she claimed the letter was written to her.

"And have you forgiven him?" I asked.
"I didn't answer his letter," she said.
"And that was the end of it?"
"Sort of."
"What do you mean, 'Sort of'?"
"I saw him two or three times after that."
"And you found out who the other woman was?"
"More or less."
"Who was it?"
"I won't say."
"Where were you when he wrote you this letter?"
"In London, where I was with my mother during her treatment. I stayed there quite a few months."

"And what happened when you came back?"
"There was nothing left."
"Were you hurt?"
"What do you think?"

It wasn't that simple, no matter what Jinan claimed, because I knew Walid had gone to London, that he'd agreed to meet her and that they both lived there for a little while in a country house outside London, in Surrey, while her mother was bedridden in a London hospital. I don't think Walid wrote her any letters worth mentioning, whether at the beginning of their relationship in Baghdad or when she left London, because they were together all that time. Nor do I think Walid loved her with the kind of violent passion Jinan would like us to believe in.

The person the letter was really written to was, I believe, one of Jinan's closest friends, Maryam al-Saffar. She was several years older than Jinan, a woman with shapely legs, white, transparent skin, green eyes, long hair, and a strange voice that attracted a great deal of attention. She had a literary bent that her conversations reflected, even though she hadn't, as far as I knew, published any book up to then. It seemed that Walid was impressed with the style of her letters. She was a divorced woman, or rather about to be divorced, and Walid's interest in her was quite apparent every time we met at one of our friends' houses. I don't know if Walid originally had anything to do with her divorce, but I do know that after her divorce she enrolled at Sussex University in England to study for her master's.

All this happened in the mid-sixties. I have a record in my files of her first visit to my clinic, and I looked at her file a short while ago to refresh my memory over some of the details. She was thirty-two years old then. She complained of insomnia and a headache that often led to a kind of nausea, and it was clear enough to me that this sprang from her miserable relationship with her husband, together with what she called her "attraction" to Walid. I felt, though, after the visits that followed her divorce, that she wasn't merely attracted to a man she liked or loved. Rather, she was totally infatuated with him, especially with his incredible capacity for love—for sex. I don't know if Walid knew she'd been involved with more than one man before the time she met him and tried to possess him so totally and with such unyielding ferocity. She had every weapon a woman could possibly desire: beauty of face and body, eloquence, intelligent conversation, and that lust every man loves to imagine in his lover—until he realizes he's incapable of dealing with this sexual ardor that grows more violent by the day. But, if one believes what's often said about Capricorns, Walid was equal to the task, though he wasn't able to put an end to her insomnia and headaches. Perhaps I'm being hard on Maryam. I reread what I've written about her here, and it's clear she isn't the tender, exquisite woman I know, a woman who doesn't pay much attention to her appearance, yet looks beautiful and elegant. When she sits it's as though she doesn't want to attract attention to her body, but rather to her voice and words. It wasn't hard for her to reject her husband (who came with her during her first visits, before the divorce), even after he became president of some institution that was nationalized in those days, because he was tied up in his job, extremely disciplined, and extremely paltry. I don't think he had any goal in life more important or attractive than sitting in his black leather chair behind a wooden desk with two telephones, one white and one black, covered with incoming and outgoing papers written in a dead bureaucratic style, with even deader comments in the margins. All this while Maryam sat at home like an ember burning with emotion, imagination, and an intense desire to live; and on the other side was a man whose only claim to fame was a bottom worn out from straddling the seat of an illusory position of authority, in charge of clerks, inspectors, and directors who placated him with praise when he was there, only to turn around and stab him in the back afterward. The moment the husband left—what was his name? Hisham? Hashem?—Maryam would pick up the phone, not only to get in touch with her women friends, but with her lovers, too, or at least, for a significant period of time, with Walid Masoud. Nine or ten o'clock in the morning was the hour of telephone love, or for actual love, if Walid was able to leave his work. He'd hurry to her house in a taxi, and she'd meet him in her nightgown with all the fervor of an eager, hungry woman; and if he had to go back to work, leaving her worn out with the pleasure of making love, she'd immediately call him, or he'd call her, in order to renew their commitment to that pleasure. How else should love be? Fervent, risky, totally oblivious to convention. Why does society frown on love? Isn't it because love induces in lovers impulses that society fears, because all those restrictions become useless, and restrictions are so important if society's to preserve a structure of healthy relationships between people? Love, on the other hand, ignores all this, and it is as though lovers are in constant confrontation with the possibility of either killing or dying. Of course, this confrontation heightens both pleasure and pain, and increases the resolve to pursue it, and so lovers revolve in an endless empty circle.

It may seem here that I'm claiming to know the secrets of other people's lives; in fact, long years of observation and listening to the confessions of patients and seeing all those people who came to me for help or treatment have led me to discover and learn a lot. I've become familiar with many facts about other people's lives, facts intuited or deduced in the course of time. Maryam had a special place in my heart because I found myself getting involved little by little in complicated relationships I didn't think at first I was prepared for. I never expected as I tried to minister to Maryam's sickness—some kind of hysteria, no doubt—that I'd find myself attracted to her lips, her voice, her fear. I don't know why, after she got divorced, went abroad, and then came back to work in the university, she disclosed her relationship with Walid to me. One day she came to my clinic, took out a school notebook from her purse and waved it in front of my eyes. Her memoirs, her misery, and her agony.

"That's what was there," she said, her lips diffusing a heavenly scent. It was a hot evening, in spite of the cool air issuing from the rumbling air conditioner. I led her to the examination room, where I made sure to close the door firmly, then kissed her, with her long hair billowing over her face and mine. She didn't resist. I reached into her blouse, lifted her breasts and kissed the nipples, first one, then the other. She lay flat on the examination table. There she was, like a delectable fire in which people love to burn. She kept saying, "No, yes, no," almost fainting in my arms. And before she went she left the notebook on my desk.

The notebook sat there, daring me to touch it, but more than two hours passed before I did dare. I saw a number of patients that evening, and I took my time examining them because I knew the moment I'd finished with them I'd be left alone with the notebook and wouldn't be able to resist reading it. So I put it off. I was afraid her words in the notebook would ruin the sweetness I'd tasted, the sweetness of their author's body. Finally, with a courage born of recklessness, I picked it up and flipped through its pages. Why, I wondered, had she left me her confessions? Why should I care whom she loved, who loved her, or which nights she spent sleepless? Had Walid left her after her husband had, so that she found refuge in me, a doctor to minister to her sickness, a lover to satisfy her body, and a priest to celebrate the rites of her regular nightmares?

When a man lives among patients for eight or ten hours a day, listening to stories of pain, misery, and disappointment for hours on end, he becomes callous, his feelings grow numb. After twenty years of practice it's become difficult for me to be surprised or excited or shaken by anything. Yet, that evening, with my body still hot with what I'd experienced from Maryam's body, I found that my feelings weren't totally paralyzed as I'd feared, and that the secrets of that miserable, splendid woman unfolding before me were going to, unjustifiably, disturb me. I wonder if she surrendered to me that evening on purpose. Women like Maryam don't talk a great deal about love when they risk their bodies. They have a dreadful need that can't be fulfilled by love—a gaping chasm that even a flood can't fill.

"I read a book by Miguel Unamuno," she wrote in one of the pages. "I agree with every word he says." I must confess I hadn't heard of this Spanish writer, but I looked for his books later to find out the subject on which Maryam agreed with him. I must confess, too, that, without telling her, I gave the notebook to a typist the following morning and asked him to make me two copies for my "medical records."

"Someday," I thought, justifying my action to myself, "I'll write an article for the British Psychological Association showing how I used it in my treatment of Maryam." I must also confess that, when I returned the notebook to Maryam, I didn't tell her I'd made a typewritten copy of it.

The pages contained an incoherent mixture of incomplete sentences, symbols, and long passages that at times led to no particular conclusion. The single letters symbolized, most probably, the names of men, though some might have referred to women, too. It wasn't difficult for me to conclude that "M" referred to Masoud—Walid Masoud.

"Nine o'clock in the morning. Telephone M. Soul to soul."

"M. The deadly, splendid ordeal. Three hours. No way out."

"Every day. In the morning, in the afternoon, even at night if it was possible at night."

"Nothing has value anymore. Nor any person. Nothing. Nothing, and yet M?"

"Loneliness is the great horror, as it was with Unamuno, when I lose contact with the thou, as in the case of primitive man who had to talk to the thou. Dialogue with God, with the beloved, with illusion—this is air and water. What am I? Broken, incomplete, searching for my complement in the thou. Only your voice makes me forget my headache. How can voice be music, thunder, wind, the hissing of snakes, a paradise, forests, and jungles? I see you with my ears, my lips, my insides, and I float on deep, calm, vast seas; the sun shines red and yellow, bleeding red over the hill, gold over the rivers and my body, water and flame, in your voice, in your pleasure and your lust. How horrible loneliness is, when dialogue ceases—with you, with God, with illusion. I don't want this, but I can't breathe without it. A cage, a prison cell, and a little bird that doesn't sing except when surrounded by your high deaf walls, and my body is clamor like singing, like death, like horror, like sweeping currents. I hear laughter inside me, but I can't laugh. I shall open the window and cry out for the racing clouds."

"We're sleeping on the floor in your office. J and S and a third woman I don't know are there. We're all under blankets. I roll over you and J wakes up. You take her in your arms, and I fall off the other side. Water, it's as though I'd fallen from a boat. I pull you by the hand and so you fall in the water with me. You flirt with me while this water covers us, and we drift away while J and S and the other woman watch us and laugh. I leave the room and you run after me, I naked and you in an expensive suit. We go down the stairs; we go down, and the stairs never end, "I" meets us, messes up my hair, and I say, 'You're a snake,' and so we sit on the floor and—I forget, I forget the rest. A lot of people around us, and your hand squeezing me..."

"Nine in the morning. Talking until ten. I fell down on my face and cried. Salt and bitterness were still in my eyes."

"A rainy day. I went out and walked in the heavy rain. I couldn't go far away from the house. I came back and called. No answer. I took a shower. I slept on the couch and dreamt of H. I combed my hair again. Let me read the papers—news of misery and hatred except for one short poem (how did it sneak into the paper?). I'll lose everything, I'll have nothing left except—no, there'll be nothing left for me. Tomorrow I'll walk in the rain—if it rains."

"Yesterday afternoon I slept, and I had a dream. At night I had the same dream. And today after lunch I dozed off and the same dream came back to me. Each time it was fighting and making love. I'm ashamed of the details. I don't dare write them. I don't want to see this dream again tonight, please God. My body's afflicted with wounds, afflicted with wounds."

Those were just random paragraphs, whose disarray and confusion actually come clear only when one reads page after page of the incoherent words, seventy or eighty pages in all. I wasn't completely certain that the man denoted was always Walid Masoud. On the contrary, I didn't think it out of the question that Maryam was moving between two or three men always represented as Walid. But the atmosphere was always the same, and so was the tune: a furious lust that couldn't be extinguished. I never understood how Maryam could describe it, dared describe it with such strange honesty. It's possible, of course, that some of it is illusory or exaggerated. Daydreams, for some people, are several times more powerful than night dreams. It's difficult to define a morbid tendency of this kind and sort out the true in it from the imaginary. A long time had passed since Maryam's first visit; but that evening I felt I'd seen her as she really was, or at least as she largely was. Her surrendering her body to me was just another paragraph in her secret notebook.

The next evening she called me, then came to the clinic at the appointed time.

She was beautiful and exciting, wearing a navy-blue blouse, a short navy-blue skirt that uncovered half of her thighs, and navy-blue stockings that emphasized the freshness of her skin and the length of her legs. No sooner had she sat down in front of me than I found myself unable to stay in my seat behind my desk. I walked toward her, lifted her up, took her in my arms, and kissed her. But as I was about to lead her into the examination room, she refused to go. "No," she said. "Please, Dr. Tariq, I have a headache." I gave her a second long kiss. A powerful desire surged within me, but I didn't try to force her. She fell back into her chair and took out a cigarette from her purse. I lit it for her and went back behind my desk.

"I read the notebook," I said with the authority of a doctor.

"Do you want the rest?" she asked. I was surprised.

"Is there more?"

"Three other notebooks."

"The same kind?"

"Maybe more horrible."

"Why do you write such things? Aren't you afraid they might do you harm?"

"I had to write. Writing helps me to put up with it all."

"Have these notebooks ever fallen into your husband's hands?"

"I don't think so. I kept them carefully hidden."

"What if he were to see them?"

"If he saw them he'd kill me. He was insanely jealous. Every time we went to visit friends he'd interrogate me in the car about what I said to this person or did with that."

"Did he ever beat you?"

"Several times. When he became jealous he'd search every corner of the house, hoping to find a letter or a paper to prove he was right, and he'd hit me."

"You purposely aroused his jealousy, no doubt."

"You're the psychiatrist," she said with a laugh, as she put out her cigarette in the ashtray. "You could say that."

"You enjoyed that, didn't you?"

"And the next morning I'd betray him to prove to myself that he couldn't control me."

"With Walid?"

She shook her head in a way that was neither yes nor no.

"With Walid?" I repeated the question. "He's here in your notebook, as clear as day."

"I wish I could show you the other notebooks."

"And with other people, besides Walid?"

"Walid was enough. He was splendid. I felt I could spend all my life with him, every hour, every day and night, lying on his chest and never satisfied."

"And he? Wasn't he satisfied?"

"Never."

"Did he have other relationships in those days?"

"That's not important. I'm the one confessing to you, Doctor. I'm the only one involved in this diagnosis."

"Please answer my question. Was he involved with at least one other woman at the same time?"

"I didn't care about that. He was superb; he never got tired out. I used to rid him of the pains of the world, if only for an hour. He was everything to me."

"And the others?"

"Only occasionally."

"Why didn't you mention these matters during your first visits?"

"Was it possible then?"

"And now?"

"Everything's over. Everything's changed. Now I'm a free woman."

"What about him?"

"I wish I could say I hate him now, but he's in a different world."

"So he finally got tired?"

"No, but another woman came between us."

"Are you sure?"

"Yes. He wrote and told me about it."

"That's odd! Do you know her?"

"I'm not sure. I think I do. But it's all over anyway, because still another one came, and perhaps a third after her."

"Aren't you exaggerating?"

"Not at all."

The way she was sitting with her legs crossed made her look especially sexy. The long blue stockings through which her thighs shimmered attracted my gaze in spite of myself, filling me with a desire that I tried to control in order to continue the interview.

"Are you a Capricorn?" I asked her suddenly.

"Capricorn? What do you mean?"

I picked up a Lebanese weekly magazine from my desk and leafed through it until I located the horoscope page. I took it over to her, pointing to the picture of the goat, followed by the date: from December 21 to January 19.

"Were you born in this period?" I asked.

"What do you mean? Suppose I was a Capricorn, what of it?"

"Hasn't Walid talked to you about that?"

"No! In any case, my birthday's on August 28. Which sign is that?"

We examined the page together and found out she was a Virgo.

"You see," Maryam laughed sarcastically. "I'm a Virgo. I never knew that. Does it mean anything in particular? What does my horoscope say?" She read: "Be careful, or you'll be sorry. A new opportunity awaits you. Don't be conceited. You will receive happy news but you should. . . ." "Stupid," she said, handing the magazine back to me.

I pressed on.

"Capricorn and Virgo!" I said.

"A Greek myth?" she asked.

"Perhaps . . . It's not important."

There was noise in the waiting room. The bell rang, and Ali the concierge came in, whispering to me that there was a man outside who insisted on coming in because he said he'd been waiting a long time. Maryam extinguished her cigarette.

"As usual, I've taken more of your time than I should. Your waiting room's full of patients." She stood up and said, "It's funny, Dr. Tariq, but I feel much better now."

"The headache's gone?"

"Totally."

When she stretched out her hand to say good-bye, I didn't know exactly how to look at her.

"When will you come again?" I said in spite of myself.

"I'll call you," she said as she walked out.

Two or three hours later, as I was driving home, it occurred to me to pass by Walid's house. Seeing the lights were on and his car was in the garage, I stopped at the gate and rang the bell.

Walid opened the door himself, and when he saw from the streetlight who it was, he rushed out to welcome me. We went straight into his beautiful, sparsely furnished living room.

"Haven't seen you in ages," he said as we walked through it. I was apologizing for coming without prior warning. He suggested that we have dinner together, as his servant, Furat, was just preparing his.

A few moments later beer arrived, and Walid filled me a tall glass. He didn't have any himself because he rarely drank.

I didn't give any hint of what I'd come to see him about. I was waiting for the right moment. After dinner we went back to the living room, and his servant brought us coffee.

"You know," I said, bringing the subject up with a show of casualness, "Maryam still comes to see me."

"Maryam?" he asked, casually, too. "You've been treating her for some time, haven't you?"

"Her divorce didn't make things any better for her. Nor did her studies abroad."

"There's always the possibility of a relapse, with every patient."

"I think Maryam was never really cured to begin with."

"A splendid lady. But she's unlucky."

At that moment I decided to broach the subject, or at least part of it.

"Walid, you're an old friend of hers," I said, lighting a cigarette.

"Yes."

"You can help her."

"Help her?"

"Or rather, help me to find a cure for her."

"Do you want me to interfere in a medical matter I know nothing about?" he laughed, diplomatically shunning my suggestion.

"Were you in love with her?"

He wasn't taken aback by my question. He looked at me, still laughing, and didn't answer. "Did she tell you that?" he asked.

"The truth is she said she was in love with you, that she loved you a lot, in an unreasonable way."

"I don't know what to say. But if she said that and you're her doctor, you can believe her or not, depending on how you read her words."

"I know your relationship ended a long time ago, but it seems to me she never got over it completely."

He didn't say anything at first. He went to the bar, and picked up a bottle of brandy and two glasses. He poured the brandy and offered me a glass.

"The smell of good brandy's enough to make you drunk sometimes," he said, turning the glass in his hand and sniffing it. He took a sip and went on, "The most difficult thing in life is to define your relationship with any woman, between the two of you, or between you and yourself. It's even more difficult to discuss it with others."

"I'm sorry if I gave the impression of interfering in your private affairs."

"Not at all, not at all, Tariq. I know you're interested in Maryam—interested in helping her. She's a superb woman, and she should be rescued from her pain. I wish I could do that. What did she confess to you about? Excuse me, I'm sorry. Doctors are like priests. We shouldn't ask them about other people's secrets."

"Let me be frank with you about Maryam. I don't feel I'd be divulging any secrets if I talked to you about her. On the contrary, I want you to tell me her secret, so I could perhaps help her. Don't you see?"

"Let's assume I do know certain things you don't know, or things she refuses to disclose. How would knowing them help you?"

"Only one thing interests me. The truth. Is she really what she says she is? Or is she simply drowned in her illusions?"

"Who isn't drowned in his illusions?" He finished his drink, then gave me a brief look in which, I felt, sarcasm and sorrow were mixed. Then, suddenly, he stood up and said, "You want to hear the latest record I've bought?" He headed toward the pile of records. "Purcell's *Harpsichord Suite*," he said.

I laughed, apologized for having stayed so long, and said music required peace of mind. I stood up.

"Peace of mind?" he said. "You don't need music when you have peace of mind."

He lifted an album from the pile and took out a record.

"All right, Walid," I said. "So you don't want to talk about Maryam. Maybe some other time?"

He didn't answer me, and it was as though he hadn't even heard me. He put the record on the turntable and lowered the needle. The music blared out, but I didn't wait; I saw myself out to the sound of the music. I hadn't learned anything new that evening, at least, anything new about Maryam. I felt, though, that Walid had unintentionally revealed a facet of his soul I hadn't been aware of. His evasiveness wasn't new to me. He had every right to refuse to talk about a woman he loved, who loved him and other men, even if they were his friends. We're all drowned in our illusions he'd said. That wasn't anything new either, but I was beginning to see that Walid himself was drowned in his illusions, illusions he'd erected as a wall between himself and others. What illusions, precisely? I don't know. I don't even know what made me suspect he had a relationship with a new woman who preoccupied his mind and made him anxious, perhaps against his will. All this happened a year or so before his son, Marwan, was killed.

As I got into my car, something like anger stirred inside me. Why should I care about his illusions or his preoccupations, or the reasons for his anxiety? He could, if he'd wished, at least have helped me move one or two steps further in my quest. But no. The Walid of today was different from the Walid of yesterday. I wished I had the courage, when I got home, to call Maryam and tell her what had happened, without letting Samira know.

"You seem nervous," Samira said, the moment I arrived.

"I'm just tired," I said.

"Where've you been? You're very late and you didn't call me."

"I went to see Walid Masoud and had dinner with him."

"Why didn't you call? I haven't eaten. I've been waiting for you."

"I'm sorry, darling. What about the kids?"

"They ate and went to bed."

"Fine."

"Tariq, please call me when you're going to be late. When will you learn to do that?"

"I'll never learn. Or maybe in another ten years . . ."

I couldn't sleep. Walid was an insufferable burden, and now Maryam had become a second insufferable burden. I tossed and turned as if between two rocks. Around two o'clock I got out of bed. Samira was half awake.

"What's wrong with you?" she said drowsily. "Are you sick?"

"No, no," I said. "I just want a glass of water." I did actually go to the kitchen, and it crossed my mind that I might sneak into the library to call Maryam. God, I thought, what's happening to me? I went back to bed. Samira was asleep.

At precisely three o'clock I tiptoed barefoot to the library, without turning the light on; the night-light in the hall was enough for my purpose. As an extra precaution I closed the door of the library and opened the curtains in order to see the telephone dial in the dim light coming from the street. I dialed the number, surprised I remembered it so easily.

I heard the intermittent ringing at the other end. Twice, three times, four times. Then Maryam answered cautiously.

"Hello?"

"Maryam?"

"Who's speaking?"

"You seem to be awake. I didn't expect you to answer so quickly."

"Who is it? Dr. Tariq?"

"Yes."

"You know what time it is?"

"Yes. Only an idiot like me would call so late."

She was silent for a couple of seconds.

"Are you upset?" I asked.

"No," she said in a clear voice, almost breaking into laughter. "I'm surprised, that's all. Why are you whispering? Is your wife asleep next to you?"

"No. My voice is just choked. That's the way I feel. I went to see Walid after your visit, but he refused to talk to me about you."

"And why should you talk to him about me?"

I sensed some anger in her voice.

"Because I'm stupid."

"Listen."

"Yes."

"Never talk to him about me. Never ask him about me."

"OK. Fine."

"Go to sleep... Why don't you go back to bed?"
"Because you made it impossible for me to sleep a wink."
"Take some Valium."
"I did."
"Take some more."
"I did."
"All right," she sighed, with alluring sweetness. "Come over, then."
"Now?" I asked, clearly shaken up. "At 3:15 in the morning?"
"Yes."
"Is it all right with you?"
"If you have the courage."
"You know what?"
"What?"
"I love you."
"Tell me. Are you a Capricorn, too?" I could hear her laugh.
"I was born under the sign of bad luck. Saturn, Mercury."
"You're talking nonsense, Doctor. Everyone knows what the signs are. There's no Saturn or Mercury."
"Shall I come over?"
"Yes, come quickly. You know where my house is?"
"In al-Mansour. But where exactly?"
"It'll be dawn in an hour or two. Listen. I'll wait for you in my car at the street corner by the school. Do you know it?"
"I think I do."
"Don't be late." She hung up.

Was she serious? Or was she playing games with me? Did she want me to behave like a stupid idiot, make me come after her behind my wife's back in the dead of night, only to find no one there waiting for me?

And suppose she was going to wait for me. Was she alone at home? I didn't know whether she had children, or servants living with her. Was she feigning this wicked courage just to satisfy her lust? These thoughts didn't stop me from quickly putting on my pants and shoes. I grabbed the first shirt I could find in the dark and left.

In less than ten minutes I was at the gate of the Shumoua School. The street was deserted. There were no people, no cars, only trees. The moment I stopped the car I heard the distant whistle of one of the night guards, which was answered by another whistle. I drove to the end of the street, turned onto another, then back to the school. A car was heading toward me. The two cars met, light against light, then the other car turned around, and I followed.

A few minutes later the other car parked in a garage, and I parked behind it. Maryam got out of her car without a word, headed toward the door, opened it with her key, and entered.

"Come in, please," she said. I entered the house. All of a sudden, a dreadful thought came to me. What if there was a man in the house? What if it were Walid himself? No. Impossible.

Impossible?

From inside one of the rooms I heard a man yelling. There was no emotion, no surprise in his voice.

"Has Tariq arrived?" It was Walid's voice. Walid himself. No doubt of it.

Like someone who's bumped into a wall in the dark, or like a ball bouncing back from a wall, I turned back, opened the door, ran to my car, and started the engine. I don't remember how I managed to pull out without hitting the garage door, or the trees nearby. I drove like a maniac in the empty street, at 120 kilometers an hour, not knowing where I was headed. I found myself turning onto streets I was unsure of. The lights at night made all the streets look the same to me. I kept driving until dawn.

Had that really been Walid's voice, or was it my imagination? I was terrified.

No. The person in the bedroom—it was the bedroom obviously—had been none other than Walid himself. What had this wicked whore done to me? Why? Why?

The moment I walked into the house my wife met me. She seemed nervous and upset. "Another patient?"

"He died, " I said. "It's beyond me why they have to call the doctor when a man's fighting for his last breath."

"You look exhausted. Go to bed, darling, and get an hour or two's sleep."

Before Samira could ask me who it had been that died, I took off my clothes and threw myself onto the bed. She came back to bed, too.

"I hope the fee was worth all this trouble at least."

"The fee? Oh, yes, of course."

At around eight o'clock that evening Maryam called me at the clinic. I don't remember precisely what we talked about, and to this day I don't know how I managed to hold the receiver to my ear, listening to her through all those long minutes.

"What happened?"

"You're asking me that?"

"Why did you run off terrified like that?"

"So I didn't have to answer the man in your bedroom."

"What man?"

"What man? Maryam, why all this lying? You can lie to yourself all you want. You can lie to others, but why do you do this to me?"

"Dr. Tariq, you hurt me. I came to you, of my own free will, in the middle of the night. I opened my house to you, then you ran away."

"Did Walid stay till noon?"

"Walid?"

"You made me a laughing stock for Walid. You dragged me out of my house at three in the morning to prove to Walid you could still attract men, that men come running to you after midnight, that you could attract his friends, too, if you wanted to. Isn't that so?"

"You're imagining things. I swear to you, you're imagining things. There was no one at home when you came in."

"So how did you come to answer the phone that quickly? I suppose you were already awake—with Walid himself."

"I was awake, yes, because I suffer from insomnia, as I've told you a thousand times. Sometimes I don't sleep until dawn."

"Then who was that man who shouted out: 'Has Tariq arrived?'?"

"You're imagining things. No one shouted your name."

"Is this another one of your games?"

"I'm sorry. I'll never call you again." She hung up the telephone abruptly.

Our conversation was actually much longer than this, but what I remember most was an immense feeling of humiliation, a fear of becoming a party to one of that strange woman's games, a game I didn't like, or couldn't handle. Later, though, I couldn't be certain that I hadn't been imagining things, that I hadn't been afraid or nervous, and so perhaps I had heard a voice that wasn't there. She could have said something, and I imagined it was some man's voice. Despite my doubts, though, I decided I shouldn't let myself fall into Maryam's trap. I felt that no matter how much he might try to dodge the issue, I had to find out from Walid himself whether he had indeed been there at that hour. How could he lower himself to conspiring against me with Maryam, in such an insulting, disgusting manner?

I dialed Walid's number. His servant answered the phone and told me his master wasn't at home.

"Furat," I said, "this is Dr. Tariq. I had dinner at the house yesterday."

"Yes, Doctor."

"Where did Walid go after I left him yesterday?"

"I don't know, Sir. I went to bed."

"Was he at home this morning?"

"Of course. Can I give him a message when he comes?"

"Is he going to be late?"

"I don't know, Sir."

"Tell him I called."

"Very well, Sir. Good-bye."

Walid didn't call me that evening, which was a good thing perhaps. Many days passed, and neither of us contacted the other. At first I was torn between feelings of humiliation and anger, so much so that I dreaded meeting Walid even by chance. But, as the weeks passed, I convinced myself I'd been imagining things, that perhaps the person I'd heard wasn't Walid. And so it was that when Walid invited me and Samira to a dinner party at his house several months later, we reprimanded each other for not having kept in touch. It was the night after this party that Samira let me in on one of her friend Jinan's many secrets.

Samira served dinner. I was back late, as usual. She sat at the table facing me, then said, in the tone of someone who cherishes every detail, "Every day brings something new."

"What's up?" I asked.

"Today Jinan told me things I could never have imagined."

"What?" I asked.

"Do you know she was in love with your friend Walid?"

"No, I didn't."

"She was. They'd been having a relationship for a year or more. The poor woman suffered a lot on account of your friend, and all of a sudden he dropped her."

"You talk as though I'm responsible for it."

Samira laughed. "People are riddles," she said. "It's difficult to figure them out. It seems Walid's the kind of man who never spares any woman who happens to be there."

"Don't exaggerate. Relationships like that have two sides to them."

"Come on, don't deny women are more prone to be seduced than men."

"But women are better able to resist than men."

"Who said that, then? That's how you men want them! And when a woman yields to temptation, you devour her." Samira kept rattling off bits of traditional wisdom. She accused me of being no different from the others, and God knows she might have been right.

"And how could I be different when you come up with generalizations like that?" I asked.

"I swear I'll kill you," she said, half laughing, "if I ever find out you're involved with another woman. Shall we have coffee outside? It's a beautiful night."

"Good idea," I said. I got up, put my arms around her, and walked outside. I was thinking I should get in touch with Jinan to learn more. As for Samira, she was in a flirtatious mood. She gave me the coffee to drink, but I could tell she was wishing she could slake my thirst with her lips.

And that, in fact, is how I first saw the letter Jinan claimed had been written to her. The thirty-year-old friendship between my mother and Jinan's had fostered strong ties between our families, which none of us tried to undermine. For the past few years I'd been looking after Jinan's mother, and had helped her to go to London for treatment. Samira considered Jinan one of her dearest friends and always seemed to be looking for a husband for her. She was, I realized, upset with Jinan, first of all because Jinan hadn't told her about her love for Walid and only came to share her sorrow with her after the relationship had become old news, and second because Samira felt Jinan's little relationships could ruin her chances for marriage.

When I called Jinan from the clinic the next day she agreed without hesitation to come and see me—rather enthusiastically even, as though she wanted to share her pain with someone who knew Walid. We didn't say much during her first visit; she just mentioned that she and Walid had met by chance in London, where she was taking care of her hospitalized mother, and he was taking care of business—or at least that's what she claimed. Two or three days later, though, she brought me the letter I mentioned. I analyzed the details in my own way, and suddenly realized why she had the letter and why she'd shown it to me.

In the letter Walid confessed to Maryam that he had a new love, none other than Jinan herself. I don't know how Jinan managed to see a letter addressed to Maryam, but Maryam wasn't the cautious type, as I had good reason to know—my experience with her was still fresh in my memory, and still causing me a great deal of suffering. When Jinan realized she was the person referred to, she felt justified in taking the letter by any means she could. Did she actually tell Maryam she was the woman referred to in the letter? Quite possibly. Anyhow, I wasn't interested in Maryam's and Jinan's secrets, or in the confidences they shared. My sole preoccupation was with Walid himself. Every time I think about Walid now, I realize that he'd occupied a part of my very being, even though he himself had been totally bound up in his continuous love affairs. What Jinan wanted to emphasize to me was that Walid had a new relationship, as though she knew how much Walid's life concerned me. How strange it was! On the one hand she was secretly thrilled when Walid confessed to Maryam that he was in love with her. And on the other hand, she exploited the letter, "the document itself," by accusing Walid of loving another woman, other than herself. She claimed, further, that she knew who this woman was, yet refused to tell me her name.

I almost laughed at myself. Here I was, beating around the bush, using my preoccupation with Walid as an excuse to talk to Jinan. Why? Because she talked about Maryam now and then. And every time the conversation strayed away from Maryam I'd throw in a question to bring it back to her. I was still burning with desire for Maryam, hoping, constantly, that I'd go back to her, or she to me. Maybe I'd forgiven her that cruel night that, as the days passed, seemed more and more like a dream. Had I really been so crazy as to go out at three o'clock in the morning, and get in the car with a woman who was waiting to take me to her house? (Jinan! Talk to me about Maryam!) Was there a desire in my subconscious to follow Walid's steps by leaving Maryam for Jinan, and then leave Jinan for another woman? I just have to laugh at myself for getting into such emotional pitfalls, I, the psychiatrist, who's supposed to save his patients from falling into them! No, nothing about Jinan excited me. For me the long-standing friendship between our families ruled out any sexual interest in her. Let me get back to Maryam, then. Yet, Jinan—with all those fires burning inside her—damn! Walid was the one born under Capricorn, so why was I behaving as though I had been? (Yes. Nothing destroyed Walid except that lust that overwhelmed his mind, that dark satanic power that clouded his thinking, and brought him so low his mind became finally blinded to everything, and death became the sole inescapable end.)

What if I'd tried to come closer to Jinan, emotionally, than I should have? I would certainly have lost her friendship, and the possibility, too, of regaining Maryam's interest in me. It was Jinan who, without realizing it, brought me back to Maryam, making it possible for me to meet her a few days after she'd come back from Lebanon. I didn't think Maryam had told her about what had occurred between us. (But how could I be sure?) Anyhow, Maryam wasn't any less diplomatic or tactful than me. She didn't say a word about that crazy night—Dear God! So many months had passed, and that night was still fresh in my memory, as though it were yesterday. Maryam's absence made it only more vivid. She was a woman in her mid-thirties, beset by dreams, unable to distinguish between them and reality. After she got her M.A. she was appointed a lecturer in the university, and she'd talk about publishing her first book, with her long hair cascading over her shoulders and falling now and then to cover her face. She'd push it back, and I'd feel as though all the birds in this world were fluttering over my eyes. The sense of guilt, too, which I'd never paid any attention to in the past, would increase. Perhaps Samira was the reason for that, for she, too, showered Maryam with affection. Why didn't I keep quiet when Maryam came to visit us with some friends? I remember taking her aside and asking her, "How's Walid doing?"

"Ask another woman about that," she whispered.

"You mean Jinan?"

"No."

"Who, then?"

She whispered more softly, so that I could hardly hear her: "Wisal."

Then, when she realized I didn't understand, she repeated, "Wisal, your younger sister," and hurried off to join the others.

How could I ask Wisal? I'd never discussed subjects like that with her. Perhaps she, too... Or was this just Maryam's way (Maryam, who'd always confused reality and illusion) of antagonizing me and leading me off in a different direction? I dismissed the matter altogether and decided, then and there, never to bring up Walid's name again, especially if I wanted Maryam to be interested in me. Let Walid go to hell!

Of course, the matter remains open, with its many allusions, and still more ambiguities. When I heard about Walid's disappearance I felt as though a heavy burden had been removed from my shoulders. I felt a sense of relief, relief at last, and let Maryam say whatever she wants. Let all the others say whatever they want. But why was I, except for Kazim, the last one to see Walid and talk to him? It was as though it was left to me, among all his friends, to say good-bye to him. Even when I saw him at Rutba I wanted to ask him about Maryam, but I controlled myself. Kazim didn't know that when I asked Walid where his car was on that dark night, I actually went to the car to see if there was a woman waiting. Was it Maryam? But there was no one in the car, and I felt a sense of relief.

The tape Amer played for all of us a few weeks ago convinced me that my old enemy had, for whatever reason, finally withdrawn from the battlefield. Now, finally, I was laughing inside.

I couldn't forgive myself for this malicious joy, which I've always thought unworthy of me. Yet, I couldn't help but feel a kind of strange comfort because Walid had somehow "disappeared." In other words, he'd been defeated; he was the one who'd finally fallen in my illusionary battle with him. Maryam was the woman I wasn't to forgive, because she was the one who'd trapped me and pushed me to such a level of decadence, wallowing, it almost seems to me, in the dirt. Man hates himself sometimes, despises himself when he's beset by feelings unworthy of him, yet can't help but succumb to them. That's how I am sometimes; whenever I think of Walid. A friend, yes, but let me say it plainly, let me get it out of my system, an incorrigible lover, always devouring what others desire, leaving them only the crumbs. Yet, in spite of all this, I had to turn and turn around him in order to know a precious scrap of his reality.

Maybe Walid's Don Juan complex was in fact a manifestation of a deep-rooted fear of losing his masculinity, and that's why he'd flaunt it in bed, left and right. A lost man, actually, forsaken, one of many dispossessed people like him, forsaken to an illusion of power, and to an illusion of homeland, of belonging, which he strove toward with untiring resolve, yet never reached except in moments of despair, when he'd make up for it with his peculiar ability to get into relationships with women. Those people, women in most cases, who dwell in a state of bodily estrangement are enchanted by the passing stranger when the threads of life become worn out. They see in him the migrating bird, the legendary roc who lifts them, even if only for a day, from the valleys of sadness and from the desolation of mountain peaks that overlook the expanses of this world, its cities, and its mazes—and then flies away. It's this despair, this destitution, this hidden lust that forges a bond between people who are alike, and exploits the sojourns of strangers who remain outside social rules and restraints because they never stay long enough to be held accountable. That's how Walid passed, much like a migrating bird, and was shot down by some unknown hunter. Yet, perhaps the hunter never realized what bird he'd shot. Walid carried his own hunter with him, waiting for the right moment. So, if I'm right, if Walid killed himself in order to be rid of all those complications that wrapped around him like ropes, then he had no alternative. He'd already prepared the way for the hunter within him and offered him the opportunity again and again. Did Maryam know any of this? Did Jinan? Or my stupid sister, Wisal? My poor sister, Wisal!

Walid Masoud Writes the First Pages of His Autobiography

Ever since I can recall, the conflict has been one and the same: between me and myself, me and the others, me and the world. The conflict of a love that I wanted for every single thing, for every human being. And, if I wanted to convert the world to love (what a delusion!), then I had to change other people; and, if I wanted to change others, I had to change myself.

I wanted to change the world according to my own perception. There I was, looking down from a tree onto the road as people went to and fro, and beyond it to the valley. As I sat perched among the tree branches eating the green almonds, I wanted the world to change. And I wanted to change myself, when I was a mere ten years old and so had no idea of what I had to do in order to change.

The poor people were filling the roads and markets with movement and noise, and sleeping on the ground in their old ramshackle houses. Like demons, they'd laugh, cry, and argue with each other. They used to pray dutifully, and on feast days they'd come out into the streets and markets with cheerful faces, forgetting their poverty, and the tattered clothes they wore, and the mothers who struggled, laughed, and cried. It was because of them that I wanted to change something that lay deep in the very core of life itself. Whenever I conceived of the earth changing, in motion and assuming new hues, I'd feel a pleasant shudder deep down inside me. It wasn't the way politicians bring about change (as I was to realize when I grew older), but that of rebels not yet familiar with theories and revolutionary planning;

and the kind of change such rebels aspire to has no connection at all with mere change in governmental systems and class conflict.

It was notions of rebellion like this that prompted me to live in the way I must if I was to achieve the thing I was envisioning, however unclearly—which meant rejecting laws and customs that were found to be incompatible with this absolute love and freedom. Life itself was the means, the vision, the way. It was as though I had to be rid of everything, of every relationship, and float like an unknown bird in unknown heavens; and, within the setting of my isolation from everything, I would actually, paradoxically, be in touch with my love of everything.

I soon realized all this would involve suffering; I'd have to walk naked through desert wastes swarming with wolves and vultures. Was that the reason prophets used to go out into the wilderness, to forests, to far-off caves, where they could achieve their own brand of rebellion? And what did they do once they were there? Did they concoct words and dreams? What use are such things when you're cut off from people? The words may resound like the tolling of a church bell, but what's the point if people can't hear them and then go forth intoxicated into the earth's defiles? Christ spent many years in the wilderness, and then came back to talk to man about love; and when he came back, they crucified him. The rebel, then, has to be crucified as well, and his victory will be in his crucifixion. But there are still those thirty years in which man has to prepare himself for the last three that really matter. What do we know about those thirty years? All I had to help me toward my goal was intuition, dreams, and a yearning for which I could find no logical justification. Every time I gazed into the distance at the hills and valleys and the violet-hued mountains that surged behind them, I got the feeling they were alive; deep down inside them were volcanoes that, from time to time, might spew forth lava and alter everything. But they weren't erupting. It all sent my mind flashing back to the 1927 earthquake.

I was six years old when it happened. It seemed as though the earth was being jolted by some fierce wind. I was sitting on the floor in a small school with several other children, and I thought for a moment that the raging gale was rocking the old building to and fro. But when all the children rushed outside in panic, I went out with them and was in time to see rocks falling in chunks from the top of the old building across the street, piling up before my very eyes in a terrifying white heap. From the rubble in which we found ourselves we looked toward the Church of the Nativity and prayed to God to save it from destruction. "If this is the Day of Resurrection," I heard some of the older children say, "then is God going to bury us under piles of rubble only to raise us up again?"

I ran home, where I found my mother with my infant brother, Bassam, on her arm. She was there with the other women of the quarter, outside in the courtyard. My other brothers, Farhan and Elias, were playing hopscotch with the rest of the children. There was old Sheikh Salem, with his ancient fez pushed over to one side, revealing his thick white hair, fiddling with a crooked stick he was holding. And close by Abu Samih and Abu Saliba were sitting on a wooden box. They were all chattering at the top of their voices about the earthquake, and Sheikh Salem was haranguing the gathering. "I tell you," he was saying. "This is the end of the world! I advise you not to go back into your homes. This is a sign from on high, a beginning of God's final judgment. There'll be another earthquake. This one's just broken up some houses and destroyed a few old buildings. The next one will destroy everything. No stone will be left standing on top of any other; all this to make way for the angels who'll descend to earth with swords of fire in their hands. They'll descend first on the hills of Jerusalem, then on Bayt Sahur at the Shepherd's Wood. And then they'll spread out across the length and breadth of the world to change the earth into a heavenly abode. Tonight the miracles will begin. Look to the mountains of Jerusalem, you people; go out into the orchards and groves, take to the open spaces, go down to the valleys, and look for the great coming!"

"What makes you say such dreadful things, Sheikh Salem?" asked Umm Samih. "What do angels want with us?"

Holding the crooked end, Sheikh Salem raised his stick and pointed to various imaginary spots in the firmament. "There are the signs. I see them there and there and there! Yesterday I had a dream such as I never dreamed before; and when I woke up, I said 'God help me!' I saw all the townsfolk gathering in Nativity Square, rich and poor alike. And which among us isn't poor, O Lord!? I saw them gathered there, all dancing in circles; circles of them there were, and an incredible light was shining on them from the heavens, and fires were starting around them... I dreamed this in the early morning. What can such a dream mean, when a few hours later an earthquake hits the entire town? Well, woman, what do you think it means, eh!?"

At that moment, my mother spotted me, rushed over, and hugged me to her warm body with her free arm. Then she took me off toward our home. "Where are you going, Najma?" Sheikh Salem yelled from his position in the middle of the assembled group. "You mark my words: don't go inside your house!"

My mother turned in his direction. "Don't play the prophet with me!" she yelled back. "Fear God, Abu Antoun!"

Surely, God should have given the earth a touch of heavenly paradise on that day—for our women, dressed in blue and red; for those farmers, cobblers, and carpenters; for those who sold grapes and tomatoes with all the pride and grace of princes and kings! Instead, terror was rampant, and what I'd always supposed to be the love of nature had turned into an inexplicable anger. Even so I retained my obscure sense that those mountains of ours contained forces that could change the world. Maybe I only wanted to change it so as to make it conform with the needs of my people and my small town.

I saw my hometown as it began to stir, yawning, stretching, gradually waking amid its own basic realities; there it was, a meeting point of ancient forces, historical, religious, and social, yet proceeding, too, along various untried paths. Much of the land was owned by the churches and monasteries, but there were also families who owned the olive groves in the surrounding valleys, and vineyards, too, here and there, yielding just enough to provide for the members of the family during the summer months. Families like these had owned their stone houses for a very long time, going all the way back to the beginnings of the four long, oppressive centuries of Ottoman rule; perhaps, indeed, they were even older than that.

The petty landowners were themselves so poor they were often forced to emigrate to South America, where they'd work as cloth salesmen. They used to carry their materials around on their shoulders, going from village to village in the unfamiliar cold of a country whose language they didn't know. This would continue until they settled down to a life of some prosperity, and then they'd send us the glad tidings.

The particular local trade was mother-of-pearl ware, and many families were involved in the process. You could hear the songs of the craftsmen everywhere as they sat on the floor of their workshops, which were open to the street, making mother-of-pearl handicrafts with their primitive instruments to the beat of the ancient songs: rosaries, crosses, figurines, and fine jewelry, all taken away as a blessing by pilgrims, as something made in the Holy Land. It was a good source of income, but the young folk were beginning to feel frustrated by the routine and self-effacement of it all.

Others were even poorer; they might own a dilapidated house and a vegetable patch or two with some olive, pomegranate, or almond trees in them. And below them, at the bottom of this downward slope of poverty, would be other groups who owned nothing at all. The Ottoman period, with its many injustices and a chaotic rule that had played fast and loose with the rights of individuals and communities alike, had deprived them of their lands and forced them to move from their own territory, to wander around the various parts of this sick "empire" in search of shelter and a bite to eat. Bethlehem had witnessed the arrival of many such vagrants since the middle of the nineteenth century; they came from the wastes of Mardin, Diyarbakr, and Tur Abdin; from the villages of northern Iraq and northern Syria; from east of the River Jordan, from the towns of Kerak, Ma'daba, and Salt. In Bethlehem, and sometimes in Jerusalem, too, the bonds of poverty and high aspiration would link them to a particular religious and social cadre, and they'd find work at jobs that the emigrants needed someone to do in their absence: in stone quarries, rock smashing, building, paving roads, wall plastering, driving carriages (and later, cars); as smiths, carpenters, cobblers, and gardeners in the large monasteries. They were generally illiterate when they came, and always destitute, but they were determined there'd be schools for their children and that every single child should go to a school of some kind. They thronged around their churches and used to contribute, from the fruits of their toil, sums that helped provide for their basic needs (though the priest in each church could hardly understand what it was he was reading, apart from the fact that it was "sacred scripture") and also for the basic requirements of the needy, widows, and the aged. It was a closed social system that met the needs of its members, if only on the most rudimentary level; at least it meant they didn't have to beg from others.

The houses they lived in (with each family having as many as ten people living in a room) were the ones the emigrants had left behind, or else others that time and neglect had allowed to fall into disrepair, or even huts that had been built in the yards for animals in times past and were now used by nesting rats. They had wooden ceilings, and the roof was covered with mud and shingle pressed down with heavy pieces of smooth rock. Their food consisted of thyme, oil, olives, lentils, and bread baked in earth ovens, which they made sometimes from wheat and other times from maize or barley that they used to buy in season by the sack. They'd grind it at Abu Iskandar's famous mill, where the staccato noise of the engine used to punctuate the surrounding silence with its beat, and the clanking turned all conversation inside into shouts. All the women and workers inside would have their faces turned white with the flour dust.

Tomatoes were plentiful and cheap, and during the summer grapes and melons were within the reach of almost anyone's pocket, as were oranges in winter. As for meat, many people used to buy beef and mutton bones from the butcher when they'd been cut away but still had some meat left on them. Sometimes, if they had a few piastres, they might move up to cow or sheep's heads, trotters, or tripes, while at times of celebration and joy they might buy a pound of mutton. Then the owner of the house would pour a glass of arrack for his wife and himself, and maybe for his elder children, too, saying all the while: "For once we don't need to save money!" And while the women cooked the food on a wood fire in the yard, he'd place his palms over his temples and cheeks and start singing softly to himself, "O night, O night . . ." till his throat had warmed up, whereupon he'd launch into a ballad, swaying from side to side to the pulse of its beat, and let come what may! All his cares melted away into melodies, if only for an hour.

To me they seemed beautiful people, and I was conscious of how harsh the world was to them; but they fought back in their own way and never gave up. I used to walk barefoot and would wander around with my friends in this world that must have been very much as at the beginning of creation, one that seemed to me full of sounds and melodies. We'd walk around, like a wandering herd of gazelles, starting at Ra's Fatis and moving on to Nativity Square, then down to "the Canal" that was always full and echoed to the shouts of girls who used to gather there to fill up their tins and pitchers with water; and they'd lift the hems of their billowing embroidered dresses to reveal legs with the sheen of ivory. From there we used to descend to al-Hindaza, then climb up the narrow road where the stone houses exuded a sense of times past and the smells of donkeys and camels, and then we'd move on again to al-Madbasa nestling in the shadow of the tall, conical bell tower of the Germans, and head toward al-Dahisa with its many houses dotted among the hills of olive and pine trees. Here we'd be met by a strong wind and would begin to head back to our homes, which were all close to each other, feeling deliciously tired. Once home we used to eat tasty bread rubbed in garlic and salt, and each one of us would wait for his father's return from work.

One afternoon, after we'd crossed the town from one end to the other, we were sitting under the tree at our house, overlooking the road, when some trucks loaded with men came past; the men were firing into the air and shouting: "We're the fighters, drawing near."

We all started waving to them. "We're the fighters, drawing near," we chanted to them, "we're the fighters, with no fear!"

We kept repeating the slogan till we felt hoarse. That night my father told me about al-Buraq and the al-Aqsa Mosque, al-Khalil and the fighters. I imagined the world being rocked by another earthquake; there it was, breaking open first and then collapsing, and from the rubble there emerged a new, changed world that began at the far eastern horizon and extended to the hills of Jerusalem opposite our house. This image stayed with me day after day, along with those ringing shouts from the men in the trucks; it became bigger and bigger, till it enveloped the universe, or at least that small part with which I was familiar. Next morning I was helping my father take the two horses out of the stable. "Father," I asked, "are you a fighter?" He laughed at me. "God willing," he said, "you'll be a fighter yourself one day." Then he went on brushing the blaze of one of the horses, which, out of love for me, he called "Walid's colt." "My son," he continued,

"I've always been a fighter, since the days of Safarbarlek. But my time's past; now it's your time, yours and your friends'. It's God's will. Hand me the water bucket..."

At that moment I wished I could get on the horse and speed off to wonderful worlds that no one knew about, not even my own father. I'd take with me all the boys of the town, who'd turned instantly into men with masked faces, headbands around their temples, and swords brandished in the face of the world. But actually I had to collect my book, notebook, and pencil case, thrust them into my school bag, and rush off to school, where I might learn something new about God's will.

Occasionally, I found myself clashing with the cruelty of others. I couldn't understand such people, or they me. One Easter Day, I went out into the street wearing my new shoes and carrying three colored boiled eggs. There were droves of children in the streets, all wearing their best clothes, or the ones with the fewest patches. They were all swapping candy, pumpkin seeds, and pistachios, and betting cheerfully on the eggs. A boy who was slightly older than me came up to me; his name was Nasri, and his father was a car driver while my father still drove my grandfather's carriage. He had a bundle of eggs in his hand, too. "Do you want to play?" he asked, and I said I did. I took a red egg out of his hand and tapped the top of it lightly with my front teeth to test its strength and then the bottom as well. He took a blue egg out of my hand and tested it in the same way. We began to play. I hit the top of his egg with the top of mine and it broke. He turned it over, and I hit the bottom with the bottom of mine. It broke again, and so I won it. We played again, and I won another egg, and then another, till I'd won all five of his red eggs. I couldn't believe my eyes as I filled my pockets and one of my hands with eggs. Then suddenly, he grabbed me by the throat. "Walid!" he said. "Give me back my eggs!"

If he'd said it politely, I might well have given them back, or at least some of them. But, even though I was obviously very skinny to look at, I had all the stubbornness of the mountain folk if anyone tried to threaten me. "I won them!" I replied. "You were quite happy enough to play. I won't give them back!"

"If you don't," he said, "I'm going to strangle you!"

I mustered all my strength to get his grip off my throat. It occurred to me that, if we had a fight, all the eggs would break; and I decided that, if the fight went on for a while, I'd put the eggs in my hand and pockets on the pavement, so as to leave myself free, and then I'd get him on the ground. But he didn't give me the chance to do any of that. He quickly moved about two meters away from me, bent down to pick up a huge stone the size of his head and came back aiming the stone straight at me. "Give them back!" he yelled.

"Put that stone down!" I yelled back. I'd long ago resolved never to swear at anyone, even when I was being attacked. It never occurred to me for a single second that he'd really use the stone.

But that's what he did. He came right up and dealt me a crushing blow on the face with it, which knocked me down screaming. My vision was blurred by a thick screen, and I thought I'd gone blind. The next thing I knew was a crowd of boys, men, and women all lifting me up, saying, "I hope he's not badly hurt." I put my hand to my eye and felt blood all around it. The cheek bone was fractured at the base of my left eye socket, but I was still able to see, thank God. Nasri, meanwhile, had vanished. I took the eggs out of my pocket and started smashing them to the ground one by one; what was the point of all this cruelty, I asked myself, and was God's will somehow involved in it?

Then there was the day, too, some years later, when I ran away from the monastery with Sulayman and Murad to live as hermits in a cave in a remote valley, wasn't I spurred on once more by the same defiant, obscure desire to be in touch with the will of God, and so gain some understanding of it? How could we make other people comprehend our own internal elation and our attempts to change ourselves as a prelude to changing them too?

When I grew older, I discovered that many people have wanted to change the world and to change history. I came to realize that my own childish vision had been given a logic by others and had been provided with theories and revolutions. I was still taken by the words of the Messiah to the effect that the poor should inherit the earth, and supposed, accordingly, that the fighters in the villages of Palestine were the ones who'd eventually change everything. When I was sent to Italy to study theology at the Santa Maria Dolorosa Monastery in

Milan, I expected to find there the logic that would justify my dream, the dream I hadn't been able to understand in the cave in Wadi al-Jamal. As it was, I discovered the thing they'd sent me to study had been turned into a means of maintaining the world as it is, not changing it. What I had in mind was to change the profundities, those things whereby mankind would be created anew. But all I found was intense activity devoted to changing the mere surface and covering over the deeper things that really mattered.

That's the way I viewed the barking armies crowded into the squares, goose-stepping in their heavy boots and then moving off to a fate that both bewildered me and made me angry. None of my companions realized what it was this Arab boy from Palestine had in mind. He believed in the fighters of the mountains he came from, but not in the armies of the new Rome. One of them (I can still remember his name: Pietro Brachi) launched into me one day as we were strolling along a low-arched colonnade: "What's all this nonsense of yours about?" he said. There I was, clutching my Latin book as he turned toward me, stopping me in my tracks. "If you want the world to change," he went on, "as you claim, then go and join those people yelling and screaming in the Cathedral Square, because that's what they're going to do, too. Either that, or else stay as you are, reading books in this old courtyard and walking to and fro inside these ancient, crumbling walls. That way, you can wait for the Day of Judgment itself. So you can either go to war now, or else sit on your bottom in the monastery and keep your mouth shut!"

"But the Messiah didn't use weapons," I replied. "Look what he managed to do with just twelve poverty-stricken disciples, the most prominent one a mere fisherman from Tiberias. In two or three centuries he'd changed the world. But then the aging Roman Empire came along, and took over Christianity and absorbed it. So change came to a halt."

My companion shook his head at my logic.

"The Roman Empire set up Christ in place of Caesar," I continued, "and made him a Caesar for all time, with them ruling in his name. And so people became slaves again for another thousand years."

"What sort of interpretation of history do you call that?" he shouted, in a tone that had turned from contempt to anger. "Do you really think that was the Church's role in it all? What books are you reading these days? Is that the way for a postulant to a brotherhood of monks to talk, in a Catholic monastery? You need a great deal of fasting and prayer, and penitence, too." He grabbed hold of the lapels of my cassock, his eyes bulging: "Do you realize, my dear *penseur*, that you're abusing the generosity of those who've taken you into an Italian monastery, when all you were doing was roaming around starving in a Palestinian village!"

"You'll never understand what I mean," I replied calmly.

"I understand," he yelled back, "only too well!" Then he went off to tell Father Bramanti, the head of the monastery, all about me.

This was one of the critical moments of my entire life: I decided once and for all to leave the monastery, whatever trials and tribulations I might have to face in a strange country that was moving toward a war it wasn't fitted for. So I decided to run away into the world.

This decision of mine sprang from something more than a sense of frustration at what I'd been studying; after months of confusion and anxiety, it had become something absolutely essential if I wished to preserve my integrity toward myself, my homeland, and the world, to be loyal to my own freedom and that of other people, and if I wanted to continue in my quest for that profound change that still excited and tortured my spirit because I couldn't yet grasp its real dimensions. Here I was in a strange country, where I couldn't respond to the people and their problems, only to the pictures, statues, and music, because I felt that they all pointed to my country, to Bethlehem, Jerusalem, and Tiberias, to Palestine with its plains and mountains and springs.

I was reading books of all kinds, openly and in secret, in Arabic, Italian, Latin, and English. In the margins I kept making comments that, one day, I was resolved I'd use as the basis of studies to help me explain so many mysteries, apart from the seven sacraments of the Church that clerical college books kept urging us to contemplate. Much as I enjoyed meditating on theological abstractions, my desire for action also started to take hold, and I felt the need to move, to go out and meet people, and confront things that went beyond the confrontation with ancient words.

Whenever I was frank with myself, as I intoned the "Act of Contrition" each day, I found I couldn't deny my body entirely. My eyes ate up the faces of the girls in church, with a voracious greed; it was as though they were trying to enfold beauty inside them, which could serve as food for my imprisoned pleasure on those many days and nights when I never set eyes on a woman's face inside the monastery wall. The act of admitting this wasn't enough to purge me of this greed; I was, after all, approaching twenty years of age. So I had to acknowledge the truth once again: I wasn't cut out to be a monk . . .

I ran away, and this time for good.

A few weeks later I was working at the Banco di Roma, in Rome itself. One of my friends, who was also a theology student, had given me a letter to an uncle of his in the capital, which was where I was aiming to go. "So you know Arabic, do you?" said Salvatore Bruno, one of the bank directors, surveying me from head to foot, while I was quaking all the while in my tawdry clothes. He went over to a file cabinet and took out some papers with Arabic script on them and marginal comments in Italian. "We used to have dealings with Arab countries before the war, as you know," he said, pushing them in my direction. "Most of them are closed to us now, but we still have some papers that need to be cleared, and many of them are in Arabic. All our young men have been conscripted, unfortunately." It was this, I believe, that had me appointed a clerk in the bank, though at a meager salary.

A lame man used to work in the bank alongside me; his name was Carlo, and he was full of jokes and loved to talk. "So you wanted to be a monk, and you failed! Ha, ha! Did they throw you out of the monastery? Tell me the truth. Did you put your hand on a nun's behind and like what you felt? Would anyone but a stupid Arab like you leave a life of ease, eating, drinking, and sitting around in Santa Maria Dolorosa? In two days you changed from worshiping God to worshiping Mammon."

A hideous devil, that's what Carlo was. "Walido," he kept saying to me, "I'm an angel divided by fate into two parts: inside, choirs are chanting the motets of Palestrina, while outside all I enjoy is imagining my tongue wandering crazily over the lips of women." But what woman would look at this bald, ugly man?

When I'd been working alongside him for just two weeks, he took me out with him. It was a dark night, and the blackout that war was to impose on all the European cities had begun. We went to a house in an old, decrepit alley close to the place where I was staying near the station, and there he pulled me into a gloomy passageway that led to a brilliantly lit room. There were five or six women sitting there in poses so brazen I didn't know where to look; I almost died of sheer shame and cowardice. Their thighs and breasts were completely exposed. I'd never set eyes on a naked woman before.

"Choose the one you like best," he said. I shook my head, feeling utterly confused, while the girls laughed and carried on with their conversation. Carlo, where was that beauty I'd longed for in the women who passed by me each day?

He knew one of the girls and went over to her, and she got up and took him off to her room. Another girl came up to me in an attempt to calm my nerves. She was wearing a thick coating of lipstick, and bits of it were smeared on her big teeth. "Cigarette?" she said.

"What?" I asked.

"Cigarette. Give me a cigarette."

"I'm sorry, Signorina, I don't smoke."

She shrugged her shoulders and turned around, expressing with a sideways gesture of one of her buttocks her indifference to this young man who didn't even know how to talk to a prostitute.

At that moment a girl with black hair came in, wearing a nontransparent dress that covered her entire body. I liked the look of her and walked over. This is really a different type of girl, I thought to myself. She took my hand immediately, as though I were her child, and led me out into the passageway, up some stairs, and into her room. Without either of us saying a word, she took off her dress in a single movement, threw herself onto the bed, opened her legs, and raised her arms in my direction. "Come on!" she said.

In front of me I saw a huge body, with white thighs parted to reveal a hairless fissure like a cow's. "Come on!" No, no, impossible . . . "I'll show you how," she said, laughing at me. "Take your coat off first . . ."

"No, no, thank you, Signorina."

She pointed to the alarm clock on a bedside table close by her. "You can stay with me for ten minutes," she said, "just ten minutes. Get moving, for God's sake!"

No, this bleak, bisected lump of flesh wasn't what I'd been dreaming of. I turned around and saw my stark, gaunt face in a mirror. "Have you . . . a comb?" I asked.

"A comb?" she shouted in amazement. "What for?"

"To comb my hair," I replied.

She opened a drawer in the bedside table and took out a blue comb with a set of large teeth. I took it and started combing my hair. Behind me the woman was putting her hands on her large thighs. I gave her back the comb, uttered a word of thanks between my dry lips, and headed for the door.

If this is what women were, then I would have nothing to do with them! I went out, feeling my way down the stairs to the passageway and out into the street. At the doorway, I had to lean on the wall, struck by an attack of nausea; I wanted to vomit, but, for all the nausea in my stomach, I couldn't. It was a long time before I got rid of this feeling.

What sort of love could this be that I felt toward people, women, things, and the world in general? Was it through horrible, repeated rituals like this one that I was to leave behind childhood and adolescence, as I'd left the monastery, full of grief, disgust, and bewilderment at the vast chasm I knew nothing about, that ever gaping chasm between my own childish impulses and the horrors of reality? What ugliness was this that I had to tackle every single day, in order to prove there was still some point to the vision of that poor boy perching amid the branches of a tree overlooking the valley, eating green almonds, to prove that changing the world to love was still worth the trouble and efforts of man?

"I know what your problem is, Walido," said Carlo. His dreadful bald head was bent over the antique wooden table, and he was holding a lead pencil. "It's the Virgin Mary you want, but she flew up to heaven ages ago. Ask the pope . . . ha, ha, ha!"

By getting away from the life of contemplation that, so I'd been taught, was the only valid life of the spirit, I had, at last, fallen into the world of the flesh, the world of the senses, the world of time. Did I have any choice but to carry in my heart many of the sayings of Saint Augustine (who'd spent three important years of his life in Milan many centuries before I did) and see, sometimes, that some of my sufferings were in a language I'd learned from his books? I came to realize that I'd now started the "Great March" he spoke of somewhere; the Great March into time through time: my soul fell from "Eternity" into the abyss of "Time" when I allowed that deep concern about it to control me, so that I wanted to abandon the contemplation of what is continuous and makes me a part of God's eternity, in favor of a desire for my soul's experience in the world of time and sensual realities.

Let pain be my fortune from now on, I felt. This is the fate of man when he falls. Falling into time is simply entry into the world of action.

But as I walked along the streets of Rome, or sat on the stones by the Fontana Isidra, which was ten minutes' walk from my cheap room, I used to wish that when the world of action came within my grasp (in my country, I used to say, in my country!) I might establish some mutual intellectual bonds between this world and the world of contemplation, for in these, I knew, Saint Augustine himself would have seen my salvation.

7

Maryam al-Saffar Hangs On to a Rock Deep Inside Her

Where would a person like Naji Abd al-Hamid fit in the social fabric of a city like Baghdad? You can always find three or four men of his kind in any large city in the West, competing among themselves to attract people endowed with fame, beauty and attractive personalities. They may or may not have aristocratic names, but they usually have big aristocratic houses, and are immune to all the supposed theories and practices of social equality. They all have fortunes that they spend freely, throwing flashy parties in their homes and organizing gatherings that remain off-limits to those newspapers and magazines that spin off the myths and rumors of society—the latest fads, the love affairs, the scandals, and the ideas that crystallize into schools of thought, trends, or gimmicks, sparing neither art nor literature nor politics. Men such as these, with their wives, mistresses, friends, and foes, may last for a decade or two, then disappear before the rampaging advance of others and become mere names, references, and anecdotes. Indeed, they might end up as memories of a minor group that rose and fell and was gobbled up by time.

Amer Naji Abd al-Hamid was one of these—perhaps the only one in Baghdad, whose society was so totally unlike the societies around it. He was less a social phenomenon than someone from a different world and a different time. In its long history Baghdad had known everything known to the civilizations of today; and perhaps Amer wasn't just a borrowing from Paris or London, but rather a borrowing from his own city's past, the city that, more than a thousand years ago, was the world's center for everything man did or thought about. Amid the intrigues of the various regimes, the insurrections of armies, and the clashes between the men of religion, one could still hear the most beautiful poetry, the most lovely music, and the most brilliant discussions between the angels and the devils, the heretics and the faithful, the conservatives and the liberals—as long as they outdid the others in charm, brilliance, or eloquence.

You could say this about Amer, if you were to look at him from the outside, and it could be expressed in a way that wouldn't, most probably, appeal to him; for today Amer's almost afraid of looking back. He thinks of his childhood, his youth, his school days only when hounded by painful memories, memories in which he can find not the least beauty. And that's why he refuses to look back at the past, to his country's history. To him all history started with his grandfather, when he was fighting the Ottomans during the last years of the nineteenth century, then continued with the British occupation of Iraq, when his father distinguished himself as a nationalist fighter, sustained by the dream that every time he was jailed or placed under house arrest, his country came closer to the day of liberation. But liberation remained a dream. From the time Amer crossed over into his forties, he felt his immediate history had been severed from him, with a suddenness he never cared to justify. He kept close to the old events that he thought of as large rooms filled with accumulated objects he didn't dare look at; so he closed those rooms and buried the keys deep in his consciousness, which in its turn was filled with other keys of various shapes and sizes.

Amer lived for the present, and for the present alone, for the particular fleeting moment that passed like a summer cloud in the skies of Baghdad. For him Baghdad was his house (which he inherited from his father and remodeled), its big garden and his library filled with Western books. Unlike his father, he hardly read anything in Arabic, except perhaps some writings by his friends, such as Walid Masoud. In the last years, he'd ask his wife, Ann, to read a particular English book that interested him, and she'd then summarize it and urge him to read particular paragraphs. For him, Baghdad was the banquets he gave, his modern kitchen filled with provisions that could feed a whole city quarter, his French and German wines, his Scotch and Japanese whiskey, and his numerous kinds of French, English, Swiss, and Danish cheeses.

His perspective was a futuristic one, not only with regard to art, science, and architecture, but also toward life as he imagined it should be lived. And this futuristic perspective had, according to him, been responsible for those ambiguous bonds that tied him to Walid for so many years and so bewildered their friends. On the surface, they were opposites in a lot of ways, but over the years they managed to show that they complemented each other. Even in their personalities they were like two opposite poles. Walid tended to be eloquent, and clearly savored words, both Arabic and English. In happy times, his meetings with his friends were occasions for a staccato burst of ideas and images that exploded like fireworks. Amer, on the other hand, was given more to silence, searching for his words carefully, if he spoke at all. There was always a feeling that his words were inadequate to express his ideas; yet, when he spoke, his words were shocking, surprising, annoying, or very funny. As far as Amer was concerned, Walid was the one who unraveled his tongue for him, unleashing it like an unruly horse within the thickets of his ideas. Walid enjoyed all this. He found in Amer a justification for his own whimsical and unruly thoughts, and the other's adventurous way of speaking was a great help to him.

He wasn't surprised when Amer told him he was the first person who'd opened his eyes to communist literature. Amer's father, who'd had friends with socialist leanings, had constantly supplied Amer with Marxist books and pamphlets, and when he went to London to study at the London School of Economics, he was happy to be able to read Marxist literature with total freedom and attend the lectures of excellent professors whose high intellect fascinated him. He was still full of all this when he returned to Baghdad in the fifties, but it took only a few years to shake his old ideologies, and little by little he began to realize he didn't actually believe in anything. His excessive intelligence made him see contradictions, not only in his own ideas, but also in the ideas of those he met. Ultimately, this made him try to reconcile his many internal contradictions, only to conclude that those issues in which contradictions remained ought to be discarded, and that though the immense knowledge he'd attained in his life might not be able to solve the problems of society, it nevertheless gave him a vibrant pleasure. Like many members of the rich classes who opened their eyes to the poverty around them and were shocked, he started out espousing the cause of the proletariat. He ended up believing in one thing only: technology.

The belief in Man that Amer discerned in Walid Masoud's opinions and statements made him laugh at times. "Belief in Man," Amer once said, "becomes belief in people, in general, if you give this belief concrete form and multiply it, say, a thousand times. And people are those individuals who race against each other, shout at each other, make decisions one day and forget them the next. They refuse to change—except by force, and plenty of force, too, because otherwise they'd go back to racing, shouting, deciding, and forgetting, and searching for someone to bow their necks to, someone to put a new yoke on them."

"So you think change stems from some power from above?" Walid asked. "That kind of change," he continued, "is a mere transition from one kind of slavery to another. I, on the other hand, think of effecting change through a power that issues from within. From slavery to freedom, from the inside of man, Amer! This is the power you yourself feel in your blood, in your guts, the power that makes you stronger than the people who'd like to put the yoke on your neck."

"This inner power isn't something I can give to anyone," Amer responded. "It's futile even to try. I once memorized whole passages from *Das Kapital* in search of change, change from any source. But now I no longer care to change the world, the world of man. The computer will do that for me."

"But by attaching yourself to the computer, you're effectively changing the world, by the exercise of your own will—whether for worse or for better is a different matter altogether."

"The end result is determined by the matter under scrutiny, yet I don't think I want to change the world. What do you say, Maryam? Do you or Hisham want to change the world?" Amer asked, offering me a piece of chocolate from the box.

"I don't pay any attention to the clichés of the great writers," I said, as I unwrapped the piece of chocolate. "Changing the world or changing history, those are grand-sounding clichés I hear every day, and I don't know what they mean exactly."

"You hear them every day," Ibrahim Nawfal said, "and you don't know what they mean. I don't know anyone who believes in them totally, who devotes all his thinking and all his daily activities to them. A frog's croaking is bigger than its body. And the story stays just a story, no matter how big it gets."

"Don't let Amer deceive you, Ibrahim," Walid said suddenly, to Ibrahim's surprise. "However much he may deny it, he tries night and day to make the cliché a reality. Amer," Walid continued, as he picked up a few peanuts from the engraved wooden platter, shelled them, and started eating them one by one, "in one of those dark corners in your soul, you guard, I'm sure, a hope dear to your heart, like some jewel you deposited for safekeeping in a bank, confident it will always be there for you no matter how much you ignore it or undermine it—the hope that your theories about architectural planning have brought about some change in society, in people. Your own office that, with the help of the computer, draws plans for the highways and the buildings, and the growing cities on the Gulf Coast, is simply a formidable machine for designs and forms; you know that quite well. So, you're not interested in changing the world? Fine, but you know quite well that when forms change, their meanings change, too. And so, while you work on changing the forms and the physical relationships among them in your own milieu, you cherish the secret hope that ultimately something else beyond these forms and their relationships will change. Only so could you justify, to yourself at least, your avoidance of people and the philosophy of your vision. Then suddenly you'd go to the safe in the bank and open your little steel box to make sure your jewel was still there."

"Then, I'm not the egotistical monster I sometimes imagine myself to be," Amer said, clearly pleased by Walid's words. He let out a loud laugh, casting a quick look at the faces of the people sitting around him.

"With that tongue of his," he said, "Walid controls all those who deal with him, from Dubai to London. He produces diamonds from the heaps of coal in their chests." Then he assumed a more serious tone, although even when he's serious he can never totally suppress the tone of sarcasm in his voice. "In reality, I'm more interested in the operation that goes into creating the thing than in the final result. I'm fascinated by brilliant improvisations that lead to still more brilliant ones. Creating something, like a drawing or a poem, starts with some inspiration, some madness, and ends where others look and are fascinated."

"For you, then," I said, "change is an aesthetic experience."

"What has aesthetics got to do with it?" my husband said. "I don't understand."

"You don't always understand, Hisham," I was forced to tell him.

"If you ask primitive people," Walid said, " 'Why do you work?' they'll answer, 'In order to dance, in order to get agitated physically, aesthetically, and collectively.' It is a change of a sort, after all, even if only for an hour."

"But this change," Ibrahim said, having taken a sip from his drink, "would it, I wonder, lead to revolution? Lenin says," he continued unexpectedly, "that when the lower classes realize they don't want the old ways, and when the upper classes realize they can no longer continue with their ways, only then does revolution succeed."

"And alas! The world will change in the batting of an eye," Jinan said, bringing her hands together and throwing them up in the air as though she was setting two birds free.

And so the conversation continued until a late hour, on one of those hot summer nights. We were all in the big garden, the breeze wafting around us, the water murmuring softly from several fountains; there was cognac, pretty women (wives and others), baroque music issuing from the Japanese stereos, all somehow erasing the demarcating lines of form and time between Baghdad and the rest of the capitals of the world, old and new. Someone mentioned one of Walid's books on civilization. Jawad Husni spoke about how backwardness was in reality "cultural absence," how difficult it is to ascend to the "theater of presence" when "deeds are framed by moral values and are judged by them." And what are moral values? Are they all truly rational? A long silence ensued. Amer, who was barely listening to the conversation, pounded the table several times with his fist and said, "All civilizations are right here on this table, embodied in our women, in you, in your words, in the sounds of the flutes and the harpsichords, in the Iraqi musical mode, and the paintings of Jawad Salem and Faiq Hassan. Isn't it wonderful that we can appreciate all this at one time, bringing it together from Sumer, from the Florence of the Medicis, from the Baghdad of the Caliph al-Ma'mun, from the space age, the satellites landing on the moon and Mars. Leave everything else behind. Forget it. Values should be cultural, or they shouldn't exist at all. And if someone were to disagree and say that there's backwardness all around us, then let him disagree. Backwardness can't be cured. Either you transcend it or you don't. So let me be with those who've transcended backwardness before I become another one of its victims. There's nothing of Christ in me, Walid. I refuse to be a victim."

Of course, it wasn't difficult for Amer to "transcend" backwardness, or imagine he transcended it, because money wasn't a problem for him anymore. It appeared that every time he spent money, his income increased. And if Walid had come back from Abu Dhabi and Dubai with some money, then Amer's construction contracts—as they were throughout the Gulf, including Kuwait and Bahrain, and covering close to half the world, with partners pitching in with their money and expertise in architecture—had made him wealthy beyond all his dreams. He could therefore claim he was building the world of the future right in the middle of backwardness itself. His one problem was: how could he most efficiently use his money to achieve an intellectual or physical joy on a level consistent with his intelligence?

"After a certain age," he said once, "my passport will be ready for the last trip . . ." He imagined he wouldn't be afraid to die after fifty. Yet, when he came close to fifty, his wealth had doubled and his capacity for joy had increased. So he postponed it to sixty, and might even postpone it to seventy . . .

Why is it that whenever I want to talk about Walid, I end up talking about Amer instead? Are they, despite their contradictory characters, the two sides of the same coin? Whenever I talk about one of them, I find myself forced to talk about the other, and it doesn't matter who I start with first. I met them together, and I was impressed by them together. I feel I must mention this here, at the very start, in order to thrust aside any evasion or fear of being equivocal. Yet, Walid's trapped me (or did I trap him?) in some sort of a whirlpool that I can't talk about in any manner I find satisfying. Maybe, when I'm done with these careful, balanced words, I'll go back to that whirlpool that swept me round and round like an idiot for months on end, without actually drowning me. Or could it be that I drowned, and now I'm a voice from the beyond? In the past few months I've taught myself silence. I've imposed silence upon myself. And it doesn't take much intelligence to realize that's meant being torn from the inside. How can the wheel be stopped while the axle's still madly turning? Be that as it may, I am what I am. For a while, I devoted my time to my memoirs, to Walid, and it would have been better to go back to them. Yet, now I'm afraid of reading them, afraid of hearing something new about Walid, which might open a window, no matter how small, for hope. If Walid was killed, it doesn't matter how he was killed. If he disappeared on his way to fight for Palestine, as he'd always wished to do, then let him stay where he is, giving rise to guessing and conjecture. (Every time I go to give a lecture at the university, I fear there'll be a letter waiting for me to tell me Walid's somewhere, waiting.) As for me, I won't guess.

I'd no sooner graduated from Beirut College for Women (which was called, unjustifiably, I think, Junior College, even after it started offering graduate degrees) than I found Hisham in Baghdad, coming to our house with his family, for a very clear purpose. Maryam graduated! All she needs now is to get married! And although Hisham was ten years older, he was handsome in his mid-thirties; as his mother used to say, half the young women in Baghdad wished he'd get engaged to them. He was sent to Manchester on a grant in the late forties, came back to occupy a government position, and was promoted to the rank of executive director. He loved cameras and taking pictures, and he traveled a lot. His family, who were well-to-do, wanted him to marry a wealthy relative. And so we got married (the bridal dowry contract stipulated one thousand dinars in advance and ten thousand dinars suspended), spent our honeymoon in Rome, London, and the Lebanese resort of Bhamdun, and a year later Cyrene was born. The 1958 revolution made Hisham nervous at first, but less than a year later his position improved and he was appointed director general. At the same time he knew very well how to invest our money during those years immediately before nationalization, and within two or three years we'd built a big house in al-Mansour quarter on an area of sixteen hundred square meters. (I paid half the expenses, and the house is now all I own.)

On the surface, then, there was an improvement in our financial status—judging, that is, by the new house we owned, in addition to the house Hisham owned in the Aazamiyya quarter, overlooking the Tigris, and the house in Catifiyya (a wedding present from my father) where we lived during the first few years of our marriage and where my mother and younger sister now live. Then there were all those other signs: a car for Hisham, a car for me, a servant, a nanny, a cook, a gardener, vacations in Lebanon or, sometimes, in England. I don't deny things changed later, when our income couldn't keep up with our expenditures. We felt the financial crunch, but one way or another, we were able to preserve appearances.

In reality, though, things were different. There was a quiet tension between us that eventually erupted. The more I got to know the people in Amer Abd al-Hamid's group, the more I felt I'd married an uninteresting man. He didn't like what I liked, and I didn't care about his interests in life. His reactions were always nervous, changing suddenly to violence and threats to kill me or commit suicide. More than once he got physically violent with me, hitting me and taking me by force. (How could I ever forget those long, infernal nights?) Six or seven years of life with him passed in a kind of painful affluence. I hated it when he touched me; I hated his voice and his sexual advances. For his part his jealousy made him say and do stupid things, which I encouraged on purpose. It's no fault of mine if I'm beautiful, if I attract men without any conscious effort on my part. Did this make him jealous? Very well then, let me display my beauty even more, let me attract still more men to me! I wanted to go back to school to get a master's degree, but only as a way of getting away from him for a year or two. I wanted to write a novel, to invite artists, sculptors, poets to my house. I didn't want to hear a word about jobs, employees, and employers. I wanted to see famous people in my house: Arabs, foreigners, professors, journalists, diplomats, politicians. And the more sensitive, unpredictable, and marvelous Amer or Walid appeared to me, the more dull, repetitious, and uninteresting Hisham seemed. Then there were all those other friends: Ihsan, Ibrahim, Ala',

Jawad, and others, each one interesting, in his own way, they and their women, whether they were friends of mine or not.

Perhaps it was all an illusion, but I developed a chronic headache and started wishing the lives of others for myself, while rejecting my own life. I found some solace in my darling Cyrene, and spent a lot of time with her, teaching her drawing and ballet and reading her stories from A Thousand and One Nights. But after that I'd withdraw into myself, into my private darkness, waiting for a friend to show up or call. Then there was Amer, and, after him, Walid. Time passed and one day I was twenty, then thirty. As I approached forty, terror took hold of me. Then, at last, I became, once again, a free woman—a traveler, a student, writing a thesis on history! A woman reborn? I don't know. A day came that erupted like a volcano, and I erupted along with it. Then the chronic headaches returned, so that I cried with pain, and the insomnia returned, too. I reverted to the old Maryam, the Maryam with whom students and friends alike flirted, but who was too proud to respond to their advances. Finally, they gave up on me, and my defenses collapsed. I knew that as soon as I had time from my lectures, I'd sit down and write—everything.

Hisham had been Amer's friend ever since they met in England during their student days. They came back to Baghdad the same year, and, for some time, worked together in the same department. Hisham remained an employee, satisfied with his salary, but Amer left his job and sought new opportunities, which no one thought were there before the revolution. Then he came back from one of his trips abroad with a blond British wife. Ultimately, each of them achieved exactly what he deserved.

When I met Amer and Ann, after my marriage, I found it difficult to get along with them at first. Soon, though, I got to like Ann for her simplicity, her quiet, "classical" beauty, and her interest in her husband's friends, especially us. Two or three years later, my opinion of Amer changed, too, and I started liking him. I saw him change and mature; the number of his friends increased, and he became more attractive. Ann was his greatest support. She took care of their two children and kept herself in the background of her husband's busy life, seemingly satisfied to be close to him, take care of him, and pamper him, while at the same time, with her dreamy eyes, smiling lips, and long neck, looking as though she'd just stepped out of a Gainsborough painting. I was quite the opposite, for it was clear that Hisham was the one standing in the background of our own canvases. Perhaps the mutual attraction between Ann and me was the attraction of opposites, just as Amer's attraction to me was due to the stark difference between me and his own wife. And no doubt, I in turn was attracted to Amer because of his difference from Hisham.

These words smack of special pleading and self-justification, and they don't even convince me as I say them. There came a time when my relationship with Hisham was at its worst, and I left him and went back home to my mother and sister. During that period, I was like chaff that would ignite at the slightest spark. In those days, and for some time afterward, my attachment to Walid was simpler, more logical. Everyone knew that his wife had, for years, been committed to the mental hospital in Bethlehem, that he was for all practical purposes a bachelor. With Amer, on the other hand, I had to forget (impossible though that was) that his wife was a friend, someone I really cared for; I had to convince myself that he deserved the kind of love he wanted from me. Amer was an extraordinary man, certainly not lacking in genius. Even his nihilism was part of that genius, and so was our relationship. I don't deny I found a wicked sort of pleasure in using my feminine charms to seduce a man like him, so haughty, proud, and well known, a man who mingled with scores of men and women, only to wind up in my arms like a naïve, helpless child, asking me to protect him from the world. How stupid! There I was between two millstones: my foolish impetuosity and my marital turmoil. I'd look at my face in the mirror and take a narcissistic delight in its beauty, but at the same time there was a feeling of damnation I didn't know how to protect myself from.

That night I was paying a visit to Sawsan Abd al-Hadi, an innocent visit to a friend who was closer to me than my own sister, a friend willing to listen with concern and sympathy to the details of my problems with Hisham, and with his family and mine, especially after the upsetting separation that left me neither married nor divorced. That night Amer also came to visit Sawsan and Ala', but Ala' wasn't in fact at home; he'd gone to Basra or Musil on some job, which made me think the visit had been deliberately arranged. Sawsan was well aware I'd be spending the evening at her house; in fact, she came herself to pick me up in her car. Amer too knew that Ala' was out, and he came without Ann on the pretext that he wanted to have his portrait painted...

The visit had, then, obviously been arranged. So, let me confess exactly what happened without beating around the bush as Amer did when he made the meeting look like a mere coincidence. One day I went to visit Sawsan and found her, as usual, painting. The canvas she'd been working on before I came in was propped up on the easel; it was in its first stages, an incomplete "portrait" of a face that seemed familiar to me.

"Don't I know this face, Sawsan?" I asked. "Or is it my imagination?"

"Of course you know it, for God's sake!" she cried out, throwing her paintbrush into a vase full of brushes of various sizes. "Isn't the resemblance obvious?"

"I've a vague idea. The portrait's still in its early stages... Shall I say who I think it is?"

"Save yourself the trouble. It's Amer Abd al-Hamid."

"Oh! Of course! The resemblance is obvious," I said, to put her mind at ease.

She wiped her hands on a soiled cloth, then walked with me to the bathroom to wash her hands.

"It was Ann, his wife, who wanted the portrait," she said. "As you know, I dread painting portraits. I can paint myself, but other people, ha! Who can satisfy their vanity? But Amer has an impressive face, doesn't he? Faces like his I do like to paint. Ann wants the portrait for the bedroom."

We went back to the living room where Sawsan does her painting. She gave me a cigarette and lit it, taking one herself.

"The important thing is to bring out this power you mentioned," I said, looking at the portrait on the easel. "Resemblance isn't important."

"I'll try. You know the story about Picasso, don't you, when he painted Gertrude Stein? When he'd finished the portrait, someone said to him, 'That doesn't look like Gertrude Stein.' 'It will,' he said, 'and Gertrude Stein herself will think she's changed to look like my painting.'"

"Please, Sawsan," I said, laughing, "make the picture look like him . . . at least a little bit. Leave him as he is."

"I know you're secretly interested in him. Be sensible, Maryam," she said, shaking her head and blowing her cigarette smoke in my face.

At that moment it occurred to me to ask for her help.

"Are you worried about me?" I said. "Then help me."

"How? Does he know you're interested in him?"

"Is there a man in this world who can't tell right away when a woman's giving him special attention? Listen, does he come here often for his portrait?"

"He came last night and the night before. Ala' was at home, of course."

"Did he come alone? Without Ann?"

"Yes. Why should he crucify his wife while I paint him?"

"Next time, Sawsan, let me know."

"But Ala' will be here."

"Fix it for when he's away. His work often takes him to Musil and Basra, doesn't it?"

"For a day or two, yes."

"Isn't that enough?"

"Damn you! Do you really love him?"

"A lot. And he knows it."

"I agreed with him not to come tomorrow or the day after because Ala' will be away."

"Then call him. Ask him to come tomorrow evening. Please! Then come to my house and pick me up. I don't want my car to be seen outside the house with his car, OK?"

"All right, fine. And Hisham, how's he?"

"I haven't seen him for a couple of weeks. Sometimes he blockades the house and asks me to come out to him. He goes to our friends' houses, too, hoping to find me there. What a disaster, Sawsan."

Sawsan wanted to test me out, as though she was wondering how far this headstrong woman was willing to go in her relationship with Amer. She may have wanted to test Amer, too. Was there a human being of flesh and blood behind the conservative, haughty mask? And how far was she herself, in agreeing to set up the meeting, innocent of other motives I couldn't pinpoint?

My happiness knew no limit that evening. For the first time, years after first meeting him, I was almost alone with Amer in that little library Sawsan prefers to her living room. We started speaking plainly and frankly, and when Sawsan left us alone to prepare some food in the kitchen, I fell into Amer's arms, like a woman who'd been starved of love for years. We kissed, and the walls between us came tumbling down. I wished he'd ask me for everything I had so I could give it to him from my heart. (It occurred to me during those moments that Walid, too, would come to me with that kind of intensity if I wanted him to.)

Suddenly, the doorbell rang. Damn you, whoever you are, I thought, coming out of the blue like this to destroy our pleasure! What brought you here in this magnificent stolen moment? Sawsan came in, confused and perplexed. She turned on the big light in the library, as the room was only dimly lit.

"It's your husband!" she said. Her face was pale. "Hisham! He's standing by the door. I saw him from the kitchen window."

"Damn him! He goes from house to house looking for me!"

"What shall we do?"

"Let's go out together. Keep calm. Don't ask him to come in."

Only Amer was unmoved.

"Should I go out to him?" he said.

"No! Stay where you are," Sawsan ordered.

Sawsan and I went to the door. Hisham was ten meters away, standing by the iron gate.

"Hisham! . . . Welcome."

"Ah. Here's Maryam with you," he shouted.

"Yes," I said. "What do you want? You've humiliated me among my friends and relatives, going from house to house asking for me. What do you want?"

Sawsan and I walked toward him, and he stepped forward.

"Maryam, please," he said pleadingly, his voice progressively rising. "Be sensible. I'm tired. I want you to come back to me. I'm tired, Maryam. I'm finished."

"Hush! Don't raise your voice. Do you know who's inside? Ala', Amer, and Ann. We came out to you so they wouldn't hear us, so they wouldn't hear your shouting."

"Would you care to come in?" Sawsan said, trying to help me. "Although, perhaps, if you came in in this state, there'd . . ."

"Of course not, Sawsan, no. It's out of the question. I can't face my friends like this. But I wish you'd persuade Maryam to come back to me, to come home with me. Now, if possible."

"All right, Hisham," I said, indulgently. "Let's not go on like this. Sawsan, you go back inside, so they won't wonder what's going on and come out. I'll go with Hisham. I'll go with you, Hisham, but to my mother's house. Do you understand?"

"All right, fine," he said, as though he hadn't expected such a quick response. "Let's go."

"Just a moment. You go on to the car. I'll go get my purse and follow you."

Hisham went to his car, and I quickly went back into the house with Sawsan.

"We convinced him!" we cried out together. "We did it! We've really spared ourselves some embarrassment!"

"I'll go and come back later," I said to Amer, who was coolly leafing through a book he'd pulled out from one of the shelves in the library. "Wait here for me. Sawsan, I'll be back."

In the car Hisham started pleading again, and threatening, too. He stretched out his right arm to me while he was driving, put his arm around my shoulder, then forcibly pulled me to him and kissed me. His hands and lips disgusted me, but I didn't make an issue of it. Going home with him was the price I had to pay to get rid of him for the night. When we reached my mother's house in Catifiyya we both got out of the car. He wanted to come inside with me, but I refused.

"If you don't go home this very moment, I'll scream, I swear it, and the whole neighborhood will come out after you," I said.

He went back to his car, satisfied or angry, I don't know which, started it up, and roared off at top speed. I waited a few minutes, then went to my car, backed out into the street, and started off, also at high speed, for Sawsan's house. I took a different road, longer and safer.

When a dam collapses, the water carries you with it wherever it flows. It wasn't just that my will was paralyzed; I was driven by some obscure power to a point where both thought and logic ceased to be. Deep inside me there was a magnificent glow, a horrifying glow I'd never experienced before. When a woman crosses the first barrier all the other barriers collapse without much effort. And so when Sawsan opened the door for me a second time I said, "I'm sorry I caused you so much trouble tonight. Hello, Amer."

I walked toward him as though he was the only love I'd ever known, and embraced him like a madwoman, right in front of Sawsan. I didn't care. Let Sawsan enjoy her discovery of the truth, all of it. I couldn't hide it from her any longer. When a secret goes beyond the confines of two people, it becomes public. So be it.

Yet, the secret never did become public, at least as far as I knew. I went back to Hisham, and to our house, as though I was punishing myself for my sin, trying to resume our life together and at the same time keep up my secret relationship with Amer. It didn't really work, though, not because my attachment to Amer kept interfering and spoiling the attempt (Amer, in fact, insisted I keep up my marriage and also keep my relationship with him secret) but rather because Amer's other side, Walid, entered and caught me unawares. It happened at a time when all the barriers in front of me had come tumbling down, and he forced me into temptations I'd always feared facing right up to that very moment. All of a sudden I wanted to pursue those temptations and record them on paper. At first Hisham was all tenderness and sweetness, and I went back home with the vigor of someone who'd just been given new blood; I'd experienced love, forbidden or not, for the first time. I no longer took time to reflect. The most important thing was that I went back to Hisham with a new kind of satisfaction, as though I wanted to reward him for making possible for me, without knowing it, something I'd never dreamed would be possible. At the same time I started balancing, within myself, a number of conflicting situations and emotions. And when I asked him to let me go to Lebanon for two or three weeks in the stifling heat of July, he made no objection.

"It's a present for you, my love," he said. Unfortunately, he added, his work wouldn't permit him to come with me, though he'd probably follow later and spend a few days with me. I'd already realized all this.

Did I want to go to Beirut because I hoped distancing myself from Baghdad would also help distance me from my own distraught self? So I could see my steps more clearly along this dark, rugged road I'd chosen, in full knowledge of all the danger and excitement involved? Or was it quite simply because I knew Amer was there?

Amer had bought a house in Shemlan, one of those old mountain houses that stud the mountainside as you look at it from a distance, lodged between the pine trees and the rocks. He'd often described his house to his friends, like a horseman describing a cherished horse, and he'd invite them there if they came to Lebanon in the summer and he was there with his family. He'd talk about the pine trees, the walnut trees, the fig trees, the vineyards, and the birds that filled your ears with their songs in the morning, followed at noontime by the buzzing of the millions of cicadas. I'd already heard about all of this during my school days in Beirut—and how I yearned for the sensations of those innocent days, which now began to appear before me amid the clamor of my soul, like distant islands of concord and clarity surrounded by an angry, tumultuous sea.

When the plane landed at the Beirut airport I went along with the other passengers to the immigration hall and baggage claim area, feeling as though I'd been set free from one of King Solomon's bottles, into the vast realm of sky. But if anyone wanted to find me, he didn't have to cross the City of Brass, the city of death and sorrow. Here I was, Maryam al-Saffar, a genie who'd rebelled against Solomon's oppression and broken the lead seal he'd set on his bottle; here I was, filling the skies of the world and its vast expanse. All the cities of brass sank beneath my feet, disappeared forever—or at least for three weeks. The first thing I did, when I arrived in my air-conditioned hotel room close to Hamra Street, was to make a telephone call to Shemlan, dialing the number Amer had given me. It took a long time to get through, and I felt as though someone was clipping my wings. Then I heard a voice at the other end of the line.

"Amer Abd al-Hamid? He's not here, sorry."

"Will he be coming back?"
"Yes, in three weeks."
"He's left Lebanon, then?"
"Yes, he's gone to London, with the family. Who's calling, please?"
"It's not important." As I uttered the words, I felt wretched (had Amer run away from me on purpose?), and I was about to hang up when, at the last moment, it occurred to me to ask who was speaking. "Walid Masoud," the voice replied.
"Walid? Really?"
"You must be Iraqi. I think I know you."
"Of course you know me. The strange thing is, I didn't recognize your voice."
"You sound a long way away . . . It's a bad connection."
"This is Maryam."
"al-Saffar?"
"Yes."
"Welcome to Lebanon. When did you get here?"
"Today. A few minutes ago."
"And Hisham?"
"I came alone. Hisham may come in a few days."
"Is there anything I can do for you?"
"No, thank you."
"Can I see you?"
"Why not?" ("Play hard to get, Maryam," I said to myself.)
"Would you like to see Amer's house here?"
"Why not? Who's living in it at the moment?"
"I am. You know I always have keys to the house."
"How do I get to Shemlan? Via Aley and Souk al-Gharb, if I remember correctly?"
"Yes, that's right."
"OK."
"What hotel are you staying in?"
"The Mayflower."
"What's your phone number?"
"I don't know."
"It's printed on the phone right in front of you."

I gave him the number. I was afraid he'd hang up then because there was nothing else to say.

"Do you see a lot of friends here?" I asked.

"I've a lot of friends here. Would you like to meet some of them?"

"Yes. I know a lot of people here, too. Don't forget I spent four years studying in Beirut."

"Good. You won't feel lonely then."

"No, no, I won't."

"Listen."

"Yes?"

"I'm giving a dinner party tomorrow."

"Where?"

"Here in Shemlan. It's going to be a big party. Would you like to come? You can bring anyone you want."

("Play it cool, Maryam," I said to myself.) "Who's invited?"

"Oh, a bunch of writers, poets, journalists, bankers."

"I trust your taste. I'll be there."

"Make it 8:00. Ask for Abu Razzouk's store and then go there and ask for the Iraqi's house. Have you got that?"

"Yes, I have."

"I'll see you tomorrow then."

"Yes, good-bye."

The next day for all my eagerness to get there, I arrived at the "Iraqi's house" late. It didn't make any difference, though. I never in my whole life saw such an array of people, some very famous and some not so famous. There were at least seventy or eighty men and women spread through the little house, out on the balcony, and in the garden among the trees and the rocks. Walid started introducing me to his guests. I was quite impressed to meet writers whose books I'd read and luminaries who'd often been at the hub of social controversy. The men wore casual clothes, but the women were elegantly dressed, their faces elaborately made up and their hair styled in the latest fashions. A large number of the guests were sitting on the floor, or on cushions in the candlelit living room. For the first few minutes I felt uneasy, out of things. I didn't know anyone, except Walid, so I stuck by him at first.

"Take care of me," I whispered to him. "Don't leave me alone."

"Don't worry," he said, laughing. "They'll be after you, head over heels, in a few minutes." He was right, for no sooner had I sat down on a chair someone offered me than I saw a man walking toward me with a glass in his hand.

"This lady's Iraqi, isn't she?" I heard him say to Walid. Then he whispered to him in English, still loud enough for me to hear. "She's absolutely ravishing." Of course, I was very flattered. Walid introduced him to me, then another man came, and another. Two young women followed; one said her mother was Iraqi. A young man wearing a pair of jeans and an open shirt that bared his hairy chest offered me a glass of wine.

"Wine?" he asked. "Or whiskey?"

"Wine, red, that would be perfect," I said. We talked about everything and nothing. The wine really was perfect. Walid was mingling with the guests, but he made a point of checking on me. "Can you hear what they're saying?" he whispered once. "They're talking about your hair and your eyes. They're saying that when Iraqi women are beautiful, their beauty's absolutely stunning. Where have you been all this time, Maryam?"

"Where have you been all this evening, my dear lady?" a well-known poet asked, echoing Walid. "That alabaster face of yours, that hair tinged with gold."

"I've been waiting for a word from you. I've been watching for a pearl, my dear sir," I answered—both to him and to Walid.

There was general agreement that Iraqis were all poets, that they were fighters and lovers at the same time.

"The women of Baghdad have always been beautiful," one of the guests said, "and aloof too . . ."

"Of course," I said. "Otherwise, where would the inspiration come from?"

"My dear madam," the poet answered, "inspiration is danger, horror." Everyone laughed.

"Inspiration means losing oneself in what one sees," Walid said. "I don't mean with the eyes; I mean a visionary, dreamlike perception in addition to what you see with your eyes, like the experience of the Sumerian artists five thousand years ago. Do you remember," he asked me, "those strange Sumerian sculptures of men and women with eyes blackened with tar to heighten their size, because the men and women who possessed them were in contact with some deep, unearthly vision? But then you find their hands are so small, almost insignificant. And why? Because it's the hands that emphasize the presence of the body, which vanishes in the particular perspective the artist has, whereas the perceiving eyes, which are the windows of the soul, become everything. The body reverts to nothing. That's inspiration, almost like a crossing from the human to the divine." He stopped talking. The others looked at him, and I regarded him with wide eyes.

"We're all eyes," the young man in jeans said. "Let the body disappear, but not tonight. The body's important, Walid, important." More wine was served.

I could hardly help noticing that, among the many women there, two in particular were hovering around Walid, in a way no woman could miss. Everyone was interested in those two: Rabah Kamal and Hanan Awad, and I felt, somehow, that they belonged to me, or that I belonged to them. Rabah was beautiful, more like a wild, unfettered animal, close to forty, but with the body of a twenty year old. I found out later that she was the widow of a wealthy Lebanese, high-spirited perhaps, but with an aristocratic pride. She wasn't afraid of anyone, and her personality, if ostentatious, was by no means cheap, no matter how tackily she behaved. Hanan, on the other hand, was a gorgeous woman (why on earth were they saying I was the beautiful one?), clearly under thirty, with short black hair against a fresh white complexion, rosy cheeks, and blue eyes whose beauty was sharpened by kohl and eye shadow. She spoke and laughed continuously, and her beauty flooded the whole place. (She seemed to have the same problems I had, poor woman!) It was obvious they'd been brought together partly by a special interest in Walid (or in love, perhaps?).

"Walid, Walid, Walid!" They bounced his name back and forth as though they were sharing their flirtations in a spirit of arch innocence. After a while they joined me, and my name rolled off their tongues with a strange sweetness. "Maryam, Margarita, Marushka . . ." I didn't understand. They added me jubilantly to their club: the Walid Club.

How could all this possibly have happened so fast? Wine shortens time. And after all those days of disappointment, pain, and dissembling, after the days of patience, endurance, and internal strife, after dryness, drought, and thirst, ecstasy was realized in a matter of seconds, like a hallucination that launches the mind and the senses, with lightning speed, to a clean, delicious, laughing concourse of stars. The circling started, but without dizziness. I was in constant motion, among serious, lecherous people who pretended to be naïve and cunning. I believed everything and nothing. My eyes were fixed on Walid, following him wherever he turned, however much they tried to divert my attention with their maneuvers. Walid had a distinctive voice and a distinctive laugh. White hair merged with black on his temples and sideburns, his eyes burned like the eyes of an eagle, and his wide mouth spoke of stubbornness, power, and temptation.

"How long have you known Walid?" Rabah asked me. "In Baghdad, of course, I mean."

"Oh . . . four or five years," I answered. "How about you? How long have you known him?"

"Ever since I opened my eyes! Twenty years! Ever since he was in Jerusalem. When he didn't know anyone, and no one knew him. Don't tell anybody, Marushka," she whispered in my ear, "but Walid was the first man who ever kissed me. But he's naughty, too. He never finishes what he starts. Of course, I was just about to get married then. And I did get married. And . . . Let's not talk about my life, darling. Do you like Um Kulthum? I saw her in Cairo recently, singing 'Anta Umri.' Do you like that song? You should see her sing it. It's incredible. How can I get in touch with you tomorrow?"

I didn't know exactly what that song had to do with the subject of our conversation. But that isn't important; the conversation itself was the important thing—I'd taken off, flown away from Amer's snares, and his technological ideologies. After tonight the genie would never return to the bottle. I wanted Rabah and Hanan to know my special interest in Walid was no less than theirs, and that he was paying me more attention than he was paying any of the others. He might fly away from me like a bird, but a bird whose leg was tied to a string I held in my hand. I'd pull the string, and he'd come fluttering back to me!

After dinner the guests started leaving, some of them suggesting making parties to go to the nightclubs in the mountains. I left Walid in no doubt about what I intended to do.

"I'm staying," I told him. "I'll be the last one to go."

"Let's have coffee alone on the balcony when everyone's left," he said, squeezing my arm.

Rabah and Hanan were among the last to go down to the street where cars were waiting. It was then about two in the morning. Even then Hanan hung back a little.

"Do you need a ride to Beirut?" she asked me.

"No thanks," I answered. She gave me a knowing look out of her blue eyes.

"Watch out for him," she said. "Bye-bye."

At last we were alone, the clamor still echoing in my head. Alone at last.

Walid left me on the balcony and went to prepare coffee in the kitchen. Then he came back carrying a coffeepot and two cups. The coffee was better than any wine. The dizziness grew stronger. We entered the house, walking between the mess of chairs, cushions, cups, and saucers, and headed straight to the bedroom, which was in no better state. There we threw ourselves on the bed, and we didn't leave it until the next evening . . . We heard the morning birds chirping as we lay there, then the buzz of the cicadas at noon. The telephone rang several times, and the evening calm fell on the trees and the house, and on the whole world. We stayed in bed all this time.

We saw Beirut from the window, glimmering anew in the dead of night.

"Maryam," Walid suddenly said, "I'm hungry. Aren't you?"

"I'm starving," I said.

"Shall we go to Cliff House?"

"No! Let's eat here."

"Yesterday's leftovers?"

He jumped into a pair of pants and a shirt. I could hear him making noise in the kitchen.

"Cold chicken with tomatoes, Madam," he said, bringing two plates with him. He handed me one while I was still sitting in bed.

"Honestly now," he said. "Have you ever had dinner naked like this?"

Suddenly, I was aware of my nakedness. I ran my fingers through my disheveled hair and lifted it away from my face. Then I peered at him through the darkness relieved only by the faraway lights of the mountains and the city.

There he was with a plate in his hand, standing there and contemplating me. He seemed tall, a giant, his eyes filling not only his face, but the whole room, the whole world.

"Walid," I said, "is this how a person moves from—what were your words?—from the human to the divine?"

"Don't you mean the return from the divine to the human?" he asked, shaking his head.

He put the plate aside, took out a tape from a red case, and put it in the cassette player. I felt the choral music blaring out of the tape deck was like nothing I'd ever heard before. It was, I knew, the kind of religious music Walid loved, but I had little knowledge of it. He turned toward me and started swaying with the music, singing along with it, his eyes fixed on me.

"Walid," I said, laughing, "are you dancing to religious music?"

"Can't you hear the choirs singing—in Latin, of course: 'My soul praises the Lord because He chose me from among all women' . . . and how else could praise be rendered except with song and dance?"

He kept turning and swaying in the little space between the wall and the bed. He'd take a piece of chicken, then start swaying again around me. He'd bend over me while I was eating, steal a quick kiss, and wave his arms in nervous, rhythmic movements.

Then he turned the volume on full blast, so loud the room almost shook with the splendid, competing voices.

"Monteverdi, Magnificat for six voices, 1610," he shouted, "or do you already know it?"

All of a sudden I felt the room explode. I tossed the plate aside, threw off the covers, and jumped out of bed. I had to scream to hear my own voice through the thunder of the music.

"Walid! You're horrible, you're wicked, wicked. You've destroyed me. You've ruined me. I want you. I desire you. I'll kill you, tear you apart, into small pieces and eat every bit of you." I charged at him, pounding his chest with my fists, and broke out into such a fit of tears as I've never experienced in my whole life. My body convulsed like the body of an animal offered for sacrifice. He held me tight between his arms while I shook and screamed in fearful ecstasy.

Scream out, trumpets of heaven, you angels of fear, scream out, scream out. But I was the one screaming, while Walid held my head tight to his bare chest to muffle my voice. I could feel my tears wetting his body, rolling over his chest. He started patting my hair, kissing it, and whispering in my ear, "Shush, shush, please, Maryam. Calm down. Control yourself."

"How?" I asked as he held me in his arms. "How?" But little by little my screams changed to sobs and gasps, and my convulsions became less frequent and finally stopped. Finally, I stopped crying. I felt a great desire to sleep, with my face glued to his chest. I felt my knees giving way under me, and I was on the verge of collapsing when he guided me toward the bed and lifted me onto it. The moment I lay down I fell into a deep sleep. When I woke up I found myself under a blanket that covered me up to my neck, while Walid was sitting in a big chair watching me. All I could see in the darkness were his eyes and hands. Silence engulfed everything.

"Walid, have you stopped dancing?"

"A long time ago."

"Did you dance for me?"

"Maybe."

"You danced for me and you know it."

"Fine, I danced for you . . . And for you, you cried . . . Was it for me or over me?"

"Over me, over my self, the self I've burdened with more than it can take."

"Then you'll cry again and again, Maryam."

"Why are you so cruel to me?"

"I only live when I burden my self with more than it can take. It's only then that the world becomes a toy in my hands. This damned, cruel world becomes a game, a toy. Imagine, I stand it on its feet and it opens its wide eyes and winks at me with one of them. Then I lay it on its back, and its eyelids, with their long lashes, close. I poke it in the belly, and it says 'ouch.'"

"And now I'm the one saying it: ouch . . . You've made me a toy. I wanted you to make me a toy, so you could poke me in the belly and I'd sigh for you, feel sorry for you. When that happens to me I scream like some electric appliance that can take only so much voltage. That's how it seems. If the voltage goes beyond the limit I catch fire, and . . . I go crazy. If you see me go out to the garden right now and run naked among the trees, don't be surprised—will you?"

"That's just precisely what we'll do together."

"No. No. You stay where you are and wait for me to come back to you. You think I'm making it up? Watch." I threw off the covers and jumped naked to the floor, feeling an incredible resolve in my body. I took his hand and led him to the door.

"You stand there. Don't move. You understand, darling?"

I left him and ran barefoot to the trees that were new to me. In the mellow, cold, tender darkness I ran around the tree trunks and circled each and every rock. I felt the sharp broken stones stabbing into my feet, but that made them only lighter. My pagan body, sprawled out before the wildness of the star-studded night, pierced all things, and all things in turn pierced it. What was this passion? Annihilation? Or being, an utterly violent being? I reached down to a path overgrown with trees, where some people were walking.

"Walid!" I screamed from where I was standing. "Shall I go down this path, to the bottom of the world?"

"Come back!" he said, waving for me to return. "Come back!"

I ran back, hurtling through a bed of rosebushes surrounded by rocks, pricking my thighs left and right. Then I stopped suddenly. I bent down and picked up a rock, and carried it despite its weight. Then I went back to Walid who hadn't moved from where I left him. He was watching my mad antics and laughing.

"Take this," I said, panting, and gave him the rock. He took it from me.

"It's magnificent," he said, "like you." He pushed me gently inside with the rock, and I could feel its cool hardness against my waist. We went back to the bedroom, and I threw myself onto his big chair, still panting. He threw the rock onto the bed, without saying a word, then turned toward me and knelt between my knees.

"You'll be the death of me, I'm sure," he said. He fell over my breasts and lips and took me for the tenth time, yet as though it were the first time. I grabbed his hair and lifted his head to devour his mouth. From time to time I could see the rock behind him, sinking into the bed under its weight.

What did that rock mean in those moments? And what did Walid think I meant by it? Why does it remain, always, in front of me, like a lovely, tempting riddle, a symbol fraught with what all my words fail to express, no matter how hard I try, year after year? I've seen the rock grow bigger and bigger, become a mountain, with me on top of it, holding on to it as the hurricanes of desire tear me apart. I've seen it grow smaller and smaller and sink into the bed, with me sinking with it, looking for it. I've wanted to catch hold of it, but it's always slipped from my fingers.

The next morning we saw bloodstains on the floor, stretching in a crooked line from the entrance of the house to the bedroom. Both my feet were cut, with blood dripping from them. I hadn't been aware of it; but, when I put my shoes on, the pain was piercing (a pain I'd never, ever forget). It was Monday morning, and I had to leave before the maid, Um Riyad, arrived. Walid and I went to the main highway leading to Souk al-Gharb and Aley, and there I took the taxi alone, looking behind me as the car sped on, seeing Walid recede farther and farther. I felt there was a huge chasm separating me from one o'clock in the afternoon when Walid would come to me in Beirut, an immense gulf I thought neither of us would be able to cross. Five hours? More like five eons that no man's life could span. I found pleasure in feeling the pain of the wounds, the scratches and the bruises on my thighs and feet. Pain proved to me that everything I'd done, and was doing, was real, not a dream, that truth follows from the logic of reality, and that time in this reality is what the small watch on my wrist measures. So let me believe.

At the hotel the receptionist gave me the key to my room and a telephone message from Hisham in Baghdad. I read it. It was a missive from a different world. Baghdad? Where was Baghdad? Who was Hisham? Maryam al-Saffar's husband? And who was Maryam? I was a different person, in a new world whose land was made of stones that love, and cut the feet that love, whose air is a fantastic wine. I told the receptionist I'd spent the two previous nights in the Cedars.

"You look as though you have. Your face is tanned from the glare of the snow," he answered, with sly politeness. I threw Hisham's letter in the wastebasket and took the elevator to my room. Then, for two weeks, I lived in a dizzying whirl, a whirl of people, places, restaurants, the sea, the mountains, and the nightclubs. Walid, Walid, Walid. And then there was Hanan. (She reminded me, as I told her, of my friend Jinan al-Thamer, not just because their names were similar, but because they had the same kind of personality and lightness of spirit. Jinan, though, was tied to her house and family; the confining walls of her house sapped her of her vigor.)

"All this frantic to-and-fro-ing between Beirut and the mountains has drained me dry," Hanan said. "I'm going to finish with it. Once I get my life together again, I'll go back to painting. I'll do nothing but paint." Then there was Rabah, Aref, Unsi, Riyad, Nizar, and . . . I forget all their names. We visited Marwan at his summer school in Brummana and spent the whole day with him; he was following the political scene avidly, although he still wasn't fourteen yet. He was Palestinian to the roots of his hair, tall for his age, with a thin face like any intelligent teenager, and there was always a sparkle in his eyes. He didn't pay much attention to me. Did he, I wonder, know where his mother was? I didn't ask Walid any embarrassing questions. He used to leave me to go and visit his Palestinian friends, and I used to wait for him in the cafés on Hamra Street. Then, in the evening, I'd get to the "Iraqi's house" in Shemlan before him, in a constant state of expectation, and a constant state of fulfillment. Dinner with our friends at Cliff House, with the fifty meze hors d'oeuvres dishes, the tabbouleh, raw kibbe, shish kebobs, barbecued chicken, bottles of arrack, all this kept me always wanting more, wanting more of everything, more words, laughter, food, crying, love, and sleep on Walid's chest. If I ever wondered whether our relationship had reached the point of scandal, I'd shrug my shoulders. I didn't want to hear the answer, even from myself. Unbridled genie, the world's full of sobbing, and your turn will come, so why hurry?

Then without any previous warning, Walid said he had to fly to Jerusalem the next day. I begged him to postpone his trip, but he said he had appointments he couldn't break. What appointments? He wouldn't be specific. He was to fly the next Saturday on Middle East Airlines. The plane was scheduled to leave at 2:30, and he had to be at the airport an hour before; he'd go there straight from Shemlan. We'd meet in Baghdad in another two or three weeks. Was that all right?

Yes, yes, that was quite all right. Maryam was to become a widow for two or three weeks, and whoever said it was easy to meet in Baghdad? Who was to say Baghdad wouldn't make me more of a widow even, more of an orphan, wouldn't deepen my anguish?

The next day, Saturday, at 1:30 in the afternoon, Maryam stood at the Middle East Airlines counter at the airport. Passport. A ticket to Qalandya Airport, Jerusalem. Two suitcases, slightly overweight. Walid came a little late and saw me standing there, waiting.

"Maryam! You came to say good-bye to me. I love you!"

"You love me, yet you want to run away from me?"

"No. It's so your love will grow while I'm away."

"That's an old formula. It doesn't work with me."

He finished with his papers, picked up his briefcase, and walked toward the passport checkpoint. I walked along with him. At the gate, he stopped and looked at me.

"Take care of yourself," he said. "Go to Baghdad soon." He handed over his passport, and I took out my own passport from my handbag and gave it to the officer. Walid was shocked.

"What's this?" he said.

I laughed as I walked with him to the gate.

"Where you go, I go," I said. "I can't think of visiting Jerusalem with anyone better than you."

He looked flustered (had I angered him with this surprise of mine?), but his face was full of love.

"I adore you," he whispered, leaning over me. "You'll be the death of me yet. I know you will." He planted a quick kiss on my cheek, sending shivers down my spine. I looked around me to make sure there was no one I knew.

This all happened in the summer preceding the summer of the June defeat (of the Six Day War), and if I had nothing left of Walid but the memory of Jerusalem and its walls, its valleys, and its hills, that would have been enough. I went there full of ecstasy, fear, excitement, sorrow, and bewilderment. I went there having possessed Walid, having possessed the whole world, though I knew, too, I was on the brink of disaster. In just a few months, I'd lost everything. Openly and secretly, everything remained submerged in the depths of my soul, just like that rock. The enchanting city. Those few magical nights whose depths span all the centuries of civilization and all of history. I lost myself in it, and it lost itself in me. As soon as the plane landed at Qalandya I felt an urge to weep. That nature, that air, those colors, were all new to me. I felt I didn't deserve them. That wide road between the green and violet hills studded with white houses built of stone—God, how easy it was to reach paradise, as easy as the piercing of a sharp knife through the heart. I knew Walid had painted a rosy picture for me, made it more complex, more interesting. He'd doubled my feeling of pleasure and disaster alike, playing the role of guide for a tourist hopelessly in love. There was Ramallah and here was Beyt Hanina, to the right stood Jerusalem, Jerusalem raped by the enemy and beyond the help of all. There was Jerusalem, which we'd defend with our blood even if we couldn't count on anybody's help. At Damascus Gate we got into the car a second time and drove along a narrow, winding road, adjacent to the city walls and surrounded by olive trees. Mount Toor and the Mount of Olives were behind us. As the car wound its way up and down, I held on to Walid's arm, and he spoke of this land he knew, inch by inch, as he'd never known any other land, or any woman's body. A half hour later we were on the outskirts of Bethlehem, and from there we went up and up, between the olive trees and the pine trees and the vineyards. Where were we climbing to? To Beyt Jala, a small town where the road winds between old, large houses and people standing by their doors laughing, to other heights, to more olive trees, more pine trees and vineyards. At the summit was a hotel, which we reached as the setting sun glowed from the distance, like a huge, golden disc, its intensity having diminished, and the wind wafting its cool breeze across blue transparent horizons that never end.

We checked into two adjacent rooms. Everyone in the area knew him, Walid said, but we'd deal with the situation as best we could, to avoid any gossip. But of course, people would gossip.

"The fact is," he added, "I have a small house in Bethlehem. My aunt lives in it and prepares it for me when I visit once or twice a year." During the next three days I was constantly moving among the churches, the monasteries, the narrow, winding streets filled with people, merchants, donkeys, cars, children, school girls in their pretty dresses, and women wearing long blue or red skirts and pure white scarves on their heads. The women villagers there didn't have to wear black, as the women in Iraq customarily did from the moment they opened their eyes. How wide the gap is between that symbol of mourning, darkness, and denial of life, and those positive colors drawn from pleasure and the dawning of day!

"It's an attitude to life that nothing can overcome," I said to Walid. He took me to the Dahisha refugee camp on the outskirts of Bethlehem, a crowded city full of stone houses with different-size rocks protruding from the walls, a city teeming with movement, faces, and voices. For all its repressed nervousness it had a semblance of organization, a strange organization, with children roaming everywhere.

"Here are the cells of the revolution," Walid said. "There are problems, insurmountable obstacles of every shape and color. But the cells of the revolution are spawning in every inch of these rocks." Men came over and shook our hands warmly. We drank coffee and tea with them. They knew Walid as one of their own, and they whispered to him and treated me like one of them, too. The most beautiful thing I heard was the comment of a woman Walid greeted.

"How pretty she is, Walid," she said. "Is she your wife?" I immediately embraced her and kissed her on both cheeks.

Every time I entered a church and saw an icon or a statue of the Virgin, my namesake, I lit a candle, put some money in the tray or box, uttered a few words to myself, and refused to tell Walid about the vows I was making. Time and again, in the dark cave of the Church of the Nativity, which was lit with old oil lanterns, I felt, unexpectedly, that I was part of its holiness, that my love was as holy as it was, that I should persevere in that love, no matter what.

That's what I did, too, in Jerusalem, where we moved later, staying in a hotel outside the city walls. I shall always hear those strange sounds and remember those dark, covered alleyways leading, all of a sudden, to the wide open space in whose center the

Dome of the Rock sparkled. I spent a lot of time walking there, along with countless other people, circling around it, overwhelmed by it all, while Walid supplied me with dates, events, and numbers. When I wanted to enter al-Aqsa Mosque, an old man stopped me at the door.

"Madam," he said politely, "you can't enter like this, with bare arms." And before I realized what he meant, another distinguished-looking old man came to my rescue.

"Here," he said, "take my headdress." He removed his *kufiyya* and spread it over my shoulders, covering my arms, and I went in along with the other visitors. How little I knew about our culture, I realized, and me, a student of history! When I came out the distinguished old man was standing there near the door, waiting for his *kufiyya*. I gave it back and thanked him for his kindness.

Walid wasn't always with me. The many appointments he'd come for in the first place kept him busy for many hours. I knew nothing about them, and I didn't insist on questioning him about them because I realized he was unwilling to go into details. All I cared about was that he shouldn't stay away too long, that he shouldn't leave me at night. (He did in fact leave me alone for two nights, and I didn't sleep a wink.) I found out, as I'd already suspected, that he was a member of a guerrilla unit. He spoke of it with great enthusiasm, but never let on that he was actively involved. (I only realized this after he was captured and tortured by the Zionists in the fall of the following year, after they occupied the West Bank. I heard the details from Jinan when I was studying for my master's degree in England.) I've never doubted he remained an active member in the organization until the very end.

Ah! That rock! Six years or more had passed, yet there it was still right in front of me, like a symbol tempting me to slip into the folds of my memory and my wandering illusions. All this while I could not clarify precisely my rebellion and recklessness, nor did I know just how much Walid loved me. All I knew was how much I loved him, with a burning kind of love; despite all those vows and all those candles I'd lit in the churches, or perhaps because of them, it was a love that fanned the embers of pleasure and longing inside me, for months on end, utterly changing my life. Then he left me to wander about aimlessly.

I reached Baghdad before Walid. My whirling life now touched new levels of madness and delusion, and I got into one problem after another with Hisham as I tried to hide all this from him at least. A few weeks later we separated for the last time, after a dreadful succession of painful family quarrels. Then we got divorced, I giving up my right to the suspended bridal dowry and he relinquishing his share of the house, where I've lived ever since. Hisham, as it happened, got married soon after to a woman he'd picked up on some street corner.

Then there were those months with Walid that seemed too few when measured in terms of days and weeks, yet, measured by the depth of every hour of every day, appeared as though they'd devoured half the years of my life—or rather as though they'd doubled the number of years. Every hour brought forward a dilemma and a salvation. Every day led to a new, unfettered plunge toward further, more distant shores. And so I became as vast as the universe itself. I felt the tiniest particle assumed the splendor of many suns and the horror of many hurricanes, till, in the end, I could no longer sense any difference between dreaming and being awake, between the feelings of the body and the illusions of the mind, between ecstasy and torture.

But the torment increased, and the clamor of the city grew more intense in my mind. I told Walid about my strange dreams (I still, now, write them down in my notebook), then about the nightmares as they kept recurring. With the coming of the rains, my ecstasy shook me hard. Every time I told Sawsan about what was happening to me she said, "Aren't you worried about your mind, Maryam? Do something drastic. Change your way of life."

Amer and I had lost touch, and he couldn't understand what had happened to me; or rather, I was sure he pretended not to understand so as to save me the embarrassment and make things easier for me, so as not to put me under any kind of pressure. When Walid went off on one of his long business trips I realized I had, once and for all, to act on the decision I'd actually made more than a year before, when I received my acceptance from Sussex University to continue my studies. And so, one cloudy, cold day Sawsan drove me to the airport.

During the short trip from my house to the airport, I felt the irony of the situation with especially painful intensity.

"Do you remember that evening," I said to Sawsan, "when you drove me to your house in this same car to wait for Amer?"

She kept her eyes on the road. "Ha!" she said. "It was an unexpected beginning to an unexpected ending. Let this be yet another beginning."

"Yes," I said, "to an unexpected ending."

My mother and my sister were there at the airport to see me off. I kissed them both.

"Take care of Cyrene," I said, "and write to me every week."

"Say hello to you know who, and write me about them," I said as I kissed Sawsan good-bye.

"What? Every week?" she asked, laughing.

Walid wrote to me and I responded. I was sick for a while, and then there was the disaster of the June Six Day War. We lost touch.

I still dread those sudden migraine headaches that render me useless. I could never love anyone else after Walid. (Sex? No. Sex was something else. It has nothing to do with love.) Walid, so I heard, kept getting involved in new relationships, but I never knew how much truth there was in this. That was something I left for others to figure out. I saw him a lot at parties. He was like a dear friend, always ready to enter into a discussion, but I always dreaded long conversations with him alone. Amer and Ann found, every day, some new, surprising way of entertaining their friends, and dispelling some of their own anxiety. Amer was too proud to utter so much as a word about what had happened between us. For a time, his social evenings reverted to dancing parties; for a year or two after the grief and degradation of the 1967 defeat, frivolity and the lust to forget prevailed. Miniskirts were in fashion, and the clamor of rock and roll was everywhere.

As for me, I was suffering from a different kind of clamor, a destructive one that forced me into confession. How could I have rid myself of that cursed, delightful rock weighing so heavily within me, how could I have destroyed it, crushed it to pieces, except by making it the center of conversation, by bringing it out into the light over and over again? Yet, when I entrusted it to the care of the psychiatrist Dr. Tariq Raouf, it didn't crumble, or melt away. It transformed itself into two rocks, rather, just like a dragon that sprouts two heads when one's cut off. Every time the dragon's head was cut off, I realized, many heads sprouted in its place. I was horrified, and stopped seeing Dr. Raouf. Though I didn't feel sorry for Tariq, I certainly did for Samira, his wife. He could take care of his own rock, however he wished. But what sin had Samira committed that I should cause her misery like mine?

When, when will I write everything in the clear, detailed, precise way I should be writing it? I'll never forget, though, that pleasant French writer I met once at one of Amer and Ann's parties, who said to me in English, colored by his French accent, "Do you want to write, Madame? Why would a beautiful woman like you burden herself with the labors of writing?" Then he kissed my hand and left.

Why, just why do I want to write? The rock will always be there in its place, a reality, a hallucination, an anxiety about what can never be. And then, if the writing itself had any real value at all, it would only serve to kindle the fires of scandal, which I could easily do without. Maybe I should finish writing my lectures on Dawoud Basha, the famous Ottoman provincial governor; writing about him is much easier, and more useful, too. After all, he's not part of me, and his memory doesn't bother me on summer nights. I never dug out a rock from his garden, nor could he interfere in any aspect of my life. What I write about him, the university will help me publish, but I don't think it would help me publish anything I might write about my own life, or about Walid.

8

Walid Masoud Passes Through Rain that Keeps Recurring

Rain. How sweet it is, and how bitter. Love, fear, anticipation; all these things I feel for it. I watch for it, want it to continue, want it to stop. The sound of it, drumming, pounding, wheezing, excites me. It makes me want to love and sing, to fade away and die. The rain filled the valleys and roads and just scoffed at our houses, coming in through the sad roofs and searching out their innermost secrets. Do the poor have secrets, I wonder? Children and mothers, can they have any secrets with the rain pouring down on them in the night? It looks so wonderful as it comes down in torrents, pounding the leaves on the trees and the window panes, and covering the world with a mantilla of beads. For a while a rainbow bursts out over the hillocks and ravines, and then the rain starts falling again, murmuring, knocking and pounding as it dispatches the flood's crows into the regions of the earth.

How pleasant it always is to walk along the city pavements in the rain at nightfall. The water's streaming into gutters and people are hurrying on their way, trying to keep themselves dry with newspapers and raincoats. How pleasant it is to stumble one's way through the puddles that reflect the gleam of the city lights. The hair gets more and more tangled on top of your head and around your face, and tiny rivulets of water cascade down your cheeks and nose and chin. Rain, rain. Showers pounding the stonework of the big black walls that for countless centuries have lurked there in the broad expanse of darkness, pierced by tiny distant lights, cracked by thunder and lightning, and punctured by wind, whistles, and howls.

By the entrance to the al-Khalil Gate, around a fire made from old wooden boxes; dampness, exhaustion, and cold. A woolen scarf around the neck, a heavy black raincoat, and wet feet that refuse to get warm. The flames leap up, twist, and smoke, and in the dancing light our faces are transformed from one mask to another. Deep down inside questions can be heard that seem to emerge from the depths of a bottomless well: Who am I? Who are you? What am I doing here? And who are these people around you laughing, laughing in the face of death while hour after hour the savage beast is devouring the city limb by limb? And all the while the rain comes pouring down in torrents, roaring along with the storm. All this sadness, what dire catastrophe can it be foretelling? Everything is black, ancient, antique; and still the rain comes down. Rain, rain, rain, rain, rain . . . A wonderful life poised in the depths bursts forth, black changes into green, the antique begins to dance, and the ancient blooms into full flower . . . Rain, rain, rain . . . So let me die!

That night I wanted to die. Bashir, Tahbub, and I took the British soldier to a room near the neighboring police station and stripped him of his khaki uniform so I could use it as a disguise. He didn't resist at all. A few hours later the whole operation was completed, and I could hear the shattering, screaming, reverberating sound of gunfire. I could picture the whole thing. So let me die then, if my death will allow you to live on, my city. Saint Augustine of Carthage, what would you have to say if you knew about it? Here's my defenseless people; they're killing them, uprooting them, pulverizing them, and scattering their limbs across the valleys and mountains of the earth. Rain, rain, rain, rain. Very well, let me kill and afterward let me die. The walls collapsed, and the cry went up. The rain kept falling; the water skins of the heavens were spewing their entire contents over the poor wounded city, the beloved city, which is being violated in the rain, at night, in the morning, and at high noon; in fair weather and cloud, in storm and silence. I wept in silence, as my face was buffeted by the wind and rain. I mourned my dead brother, my dead family, my friends, and my nation; I even mourned those who'd been killed at that precise moment and those who would be killed, too. The rain kept pounding on the doors and windows, trying to penetrate houses and locked and impenetrable recesses, to flow in streams into nooks and crannies, presaging death, saving from death those I love and those to whom I'll give birth, proclaiming a life that will ignite, rage on its way, and reproduce openly and in secret... O rain, O black dawn that never brightens, O hours laden down with debris and destruction, with refuse and ruin, O morning spluttering with streams of blood that pour forth today, tomorrow, the day after, next year, on and on without ceasing through fifty years of struggle and wounds, in every one of those oppressive, tear-laden hours.

• • •

After something less than twenty years, they came to my house in Bethlehem and beat on the door. The rain was beating down its accompaniment as they pounded on the door. Three of them came in, shaking the rain off their coats. Walid Masoud Farhan? they asked. Yes, I replied. Come with us. In this rain? We're sorry to bother you. Have you always lived here? So what's that supposed to mean? This is my country, isn't it, my city, my land? OK, OK, OK. Come along with us. Will you allow me to put my coat on? Yes. Who lives here with you? No one. We'll search the house. So they searched all the rooms, turned the chairs over, opened all the cupboards. They put handcuffs on me and pushed me toward the door. We went down the steps. The military vehicle was standing some twenty meters away from the front door of the house, and we had to cover the distance in the pouring rain. We all got soaking wet. They put me in the back of the vehicle, between two of them, while the third sat in front with the driver. The roads were deserted. The whole town was wearing rain, much as a bereaved woman wears mourning. I saw this town, as in times past, gleaming like a jewel, its skies full of swallows. I saw it with almond and apricot blossoms clinging to its houses and cries of joy issuing from its windows. I saw it when the roads and roofs were covered with snow like a bridal gown. I saw it on the seventh of June when Israeli guns were pounding its houses and killing its people; and later in the afternoon they came in as conquerors and occupiers. During the first rains of autumn and after the olive harvest, the whole atmosphere of the town was saturated with tears. I saw the city wounded as I sat in the back of the jeep with handcuffs on my wrists. In silence I gazed at the valley and the distant hills beyond those sad, beautiful veils of rain. My city, if you can still live through my torture and my death, then let them torture me and let me die. Who are these faceless invaders? I know them and I don't. I've seen them in the histories that weigh down my mind. They come, they destroy, they kill, and then they fall down and collapse.

The jeep rattled and groaned its way downhill toward al-Mourida and then started uphill on the twisting road that goes past the monastery of Saint Elias. Every rock and every tree I knew was still in its place. But where were the swings, the earthen jar vendors, the people squabbling and laughing around the water well, the sellers of kebab, livers, and spleens, the smell of grilling as it wafted among the olive trees? Where were the bottles of arrack, the beautiful girls and the singers of the traditional folk ballads? My poor hills, are you weeping? Should I jump out of the jeep into your orchards, bury myself in your mud, and become part of your soil, your thorns, and your anemones? We kept climbing, up to the al-Khalil Gate. The huge stone walls lay there like wild beasts, waiting, beneath the onslaught of the rain and the pounding of the invaders' army boots, waiting. Not smiling and not weeping. Waiting. We climbed up parallel to this wall and went into the *Maskobiyya*, the old Russian church that still stood there. But they took me in another direction and put me in a cell; then, later, they took me into a room with men in it whom I knew instantly without having seen them before, tired, pale, stubborn, beautiful. I heard coarse voices, cries, bodies being dragged along the floor. I came face to face with my interrogators in that vile but commonplace interrogation, known around the globe, interrogation that never ends. Your name, age, address; your father's name, your mother's. A slap across the face that blinds you for a couple of moments. Nasri had hit me on the face with a rock because I'd won five colored eggs from him on Easter Day, but he'd hit me and then run away. In this place they don't run away. They hit you and stand right over you because your hands are tied behind your back and your whole people is tied, too. What's your connection with Fatah? they ask. You went to Baghdad. You stayed in the Gulf. In Beirut. What are you doing in Bethlehem? Who did you see in Hebron? In Bayt Sahur? In Nablus? In Ramallah? In al-Bira? The only person I saw was my wife. Your wife's a pretty feeble excuse. Never.

The cell was damp, and I was too tall to stand up in it. They locked the door. It was completely dark: there were no cracks in the walls, and not even a keyhole. Just a latrine can. Oh, if only I could sleep, and lose consciousness. Hours later I could hear screams and moans from my cell. Walid, remember your childhood. Think of your days at the monastery, the war days in Milan and Rome, days in Jerusalem. Remember the shattered remains of Elias buried under the debris, and that wonderful, terrifying night with the rain pouring down when you drove that "sequestered" jeep loaded with dynamite across area J, then area A, then area B. You were wearing the British soldier's uniform and alongside you was the other English soldier who also wanted his revenge on behalf of his squad. Winter 1948, and it seems just like yesterday! Twenty years, do you realize that? And here they are asking you whom you've seen, and what you're doing here. The crucial thing is not to break down. It's enough that Rima's had a breakdown, that she's living the life of the dead in a clinic. They pulled me by my arms and my hair, they kicked me in the buttocks, pushed me into the other room full of my colleagues whom I don't know, yet I know them all. "Beware of Shimon," they say. We whisper our names to each other: Tahir, Umar, Yasir, Zuhdi . . . and the interrogation starts again.

A stick came crashing down on my shoulders and sent an electric charge right through my body. Then they threw me to the ground on my back, viciously grabbed hold of my mouth, and used their nails to thrust a hose into my mouth. They filled me up with water like some water skin. I'm going to die, I told myself, but I must not break down. Then they turned me over on my face on the filthy floor, and the water came pouring out mixed with vomit. The interrogation started once again. They gave me a cigarette and offered me hot tea. This time, they were joking with me. We know all about your books, they said, and your movements, too, and your membership in Fatah. We want to help you relax. Who are you, exactly? Whom have you seen? Who, who, who . . . and then back to the cell and the black darkness, and then back once more to the fearful, intensely lit room for more questions. Then came that foul attack that caught me by surprise, when they tied my arms behind my back and pulled my trousers down. Suddenly, Shimon grabbed hold of my testicles and started burning the skin of my scrotum with his thick cigar, now here, now there, then stubbed it out slowly on my penis. I screamed. It was the scream of a forty-six-year-old man who feels in his heart he's a proud young man of twenty-six. My crying helped ease the pain. Where's Tahbub, they asked me suddenly; who is Tahbub? Weren't you with him on that demolition operation in Ben Somekh Street in 1948? I don't know what you're talking about. So they know about that wonderful, terrifying night twenty years ago; they're mentioning Tahbub's name. It's as though they could read my mind. Even so, I realized from their questions they weren't sure of anything. If they were, then why all this torture and madness? The crucial thing was not to break down. Endure and remain silent till death. But where was death? Death would seem so easy if it came. Pain is far more frightening than death.

Has the rain stopped? I wonder. Has the sun come out again and begun to warm the city once more? They dragged me off to the cell again. I no longer have any idea of time. They pull me from one room to another. My companions keep changing, and so do my torturers; or perhaps it's just that I can't distinguish between their faces anymore. The dampness, the walls, and the cold floor all remind me of things hidden in the recesses of the past. I'll tell all this to Marwan when I see him; if I don't die, that is. I wonder what he's doing now in Brummana. Is he studying his lessons, or playing basketball? You're very good at basketball, so good they made you captain of the school team. Marwan, my darling, remember your father; keep his name pure and unsullied, even if they kill him here like a dog. The important thing is not to break down. People do break down; I'm not made of steel, but I won't break down.

Suddenly a scream fills the whole world, a hoarse scream followed by women shrieking. Major Shapir. How can one man harbor such a horrific load of hatred in his heart? Hatred? he said. There's no hatred here; we just want to help you relax, and put an end to your torture. Don't imagine you're Tarzan. You'll confess, sooner or later. Here's a piece of paper. Write on it ten lines of the things we've asked you about, and it'll all be over. Have a cigarette. Oh, so you don't want to smoke? You refuse to write anything? Take him away. Always the same, forever, time after time. Take him away, make him understand, fix him, get him to talk. And then, at last, through a tiny window at the top of the wall some wonderful light from a blue sky pours into the cell; the thick bars convert it into squares. Ten, twenty, how many men are we? I wonder. We go to sleep on the same floor clasping one another. Time's divided into segments by the times a tepid broth's thrown at us in tin cans, a dry substance they call bread, and a cold liquid they term tea. For several days they left me alone. They kept shouting out names continually through loudspeakers; they'd open the door suddenly, and then we all had to stand up. They forced us to our feet with sticks. By now I could get to my feet only with an enormous effort. Every joint in my body groaned. Every bone felt as though it was separated from the rest. They'd take one or two of us away at a time, and the one they took might never come back or else would be utterly shattered; his clothes would be torn, he'd be splattered with blood and would lie there spread-eagle on the floor, groaning and groaning. One day they called my name and number, and took me away. The interrogation room was full of them: Shimon, Shapir, and many others. Some of them were seated; others were standing. They brought Mahmud Kamila in for me to see. He looked like someone who'd just come out of a grave. He started walking around in a daze with his hands tied behind him. Do you know this man? No. Do you know him? No. Do you know him? No. They made us face each other. Mahmud was magnificent. He didn't bat an eyelid when he saw me. His mouth was bloody from the beating he'd taken. Good God! I mustn't break down! Mahmud was my key contact in the region, as firm as a knife's edge, and not yet thirty years old. Shimon gave a nod to one of his assistants who caught me unawares with two vicious punches to the stomach. Do you know him? No. At this point, reality becomes confused with dreams and nightmares. Consciousness, unconsciousness, and the sounds of groans and screams become mixed up. I'm shuffled back and forth. Time goes by, as heavy as lead, as black as the night of the dead.

I longed for Baghdad. I longed for my home, for music, for the valley of Bethlehem, for Abu Dhabi, Beirut, Shemlan, for Marwan! My mouth was full of blood. Mother, O Mother, are you crying? Is my father weeping, too? And the angels, are they weeping? And what of God Himself, is He weeping? Saint Augustine, is he beating his breast and weeping? Monica and the Virgin Mary, how about them? Days went by until the nightmares became commonplace, mere points of reference in man's barbaric history.

They gave me papers in Hebrew and told me it was an expulsion order. Then they pushed me toward a jeep. The three soldiers and driver were all silent. The rain was pouring from a sky that looked as gray as lead. Their boots, belts, and rifles filled up the small space in the jeep, and I sat there in silence squeezed between two of them, watching the rain. They were grumbling to each other about the rain and how long the trip was. There won't be rain like this, they kept saying, in the Jordan Valley. In two hours, one of them said in an Iraqi accent, we're going to leave you. Will you go to Baghdad? I looked at his face, his eyes; they looked sad, very sad. I nodded my head. At the destroyed bridge there were other formalities. My strength was so depleted and feeble I could hardly stand on my own two feet. There I was in my dusty raincoat that now billowed around me, as I'd lost half my total weight in two months. There were Arab soldiers, too, who looked at me as though I was returning from the world of the dead, just like Mahmud. But the sight of people returning from that world wasn't a shock to anyone anymore. It's repeated a thousand times every single day. The important thing is I must stay on my feet; I mustn't break down; I have to get to Marwan.

I'd been lucky; others had suffered agony and still are suffering. The enemy wanted my head because I'd struck it more than once, and because I'd taken part in attacks on it more than once. I was lucky because I'd managed to outfox it once again, because, though my body had been torn limb from limb, my mind had held together under the dictates of my iron will. Yet, if my body were to be exposed to the same dismemberment again today, I wonder if my will could still stand the horrors of it all, could bring about such a miracle a second time.

I emerged from all this with the feeling I'd won life all over again, in its entirety. I was breathing in the cool air; how good it was, how delicious! I emerged with a child's view on life, even though my body was crippled and I had to pull myself together. Intellectually, psychologically, I was running over the expanses of the earth, cavorting like panthers and gazelles. Yet, I was faced with problems, too, and in order to confront them I had to learn various things again, from the alphabet onward. And what an alphabet it was, more taxing than any cuneiform and hieroglyphics! As, for example, when I saw countries I consider my own, for which I'd been prepared to go through the tortures of hell, themselves applying these selfsame tortures to anyone who fell into the hands of those with influence. From the Arab Gulf to the Atlantic Ocean I heard cries, I heard weeping and the sound of sticks and plastic hoses. Capitals and Casbahs, the secret police were everywhere, and on mountain peaks and in the valleys below. Men in neat civilian suits walking to and fro like a thousand shuttles in a thousand looms, taking away to the centers of darkness people by the tens and hundreds, losing them in labyrinths of cellars and dungeons, and night and day the sound of questions, denial, and confession could be heard, the noise of rubber coming down on naked flesh; accusations and calumnies pile up in dossiers, and people's mouths fill with blood. How can I ever learn all that and come to accept it as a part of life? Marwan, whenever rain falls, I think of you, I remember all those I love; I remember Tahbub, Bashir, and Mahmud. Then my heart swells with pride and well-being. Whenever rain falls, I recall the concerns of my nation, its confusion, and its pains, and then I'm filled with a sense of sadness and calamity.

Wisal Raouf Reveals Her Secrets

1

Miracles! From the heavens above they descend on you, like a purse stuffed full of pearls that some bird, huge, gorgeous, and mysterious, drops into your lap one crazy morning.

Such gifts from above truly are miracles. All of a sudden you see the glory of existence embodied right in front of you: the wonders of the universe, trees, fruits, forests, mountains, seas, all the cascading rapids of the world. In a fleeting moment of vast duration you know everything and forget everything. All forms of delight are focused on your eyes, your hands, and your lips.

I've known Walid for many years, ever since I was a student at college, and I used to imagine to myself that he found me beautiful and desirable, but kept up a pretense. I did the same myself. I had nothing to do with his particular world. When I met him, I'd usually be with my brother or father or sister. There'd be greetings, chat, some laughter, and then farewells; after which all would be forgotten. Years passed, and during that time my feelings for him, and his for me, hovered between reality and unreality. Whenever he'd had an affair with a woman, and she no longer cared for him or he for her, I fancied I'd occur to him as a prospect, like some flash of the unattainable. For my part, I felt bound by some obscure feeling I was afraid to reveal even to myself.

One October morning, when the summer heat was beginning to slacken off somewhat and the poinsettias were a blaze of color outside the window, I was eating breakfast, quite late. I took out the telephone directory and looked up Walid Masoud's number. Then, taking a large swallow of tea, I rushed over to the phone.

"Hello?"

"Hello!"

"Does the world look as good to you as it does to me?"

"Even better!"

"Impossible!"

"Who's speaking?"

"Is it Walid I'm talking to?"

"Yes. Who is it?"

"I thought you'd be quicker than that! Have you forgotten our chat last night already?"

"Wisal?"

"Thank God! The thing is, we didn't get anywhere with our conversation last night."

"With all that noise and loud music, how could we have? Would you like me to listen to your poem?"

"Over the phone? Have you had breakfast yet? As you said yourself, great poetry's a prophetic intuition. Let the prophets beware!"

"No, I've finished breakfast, and I'm quite ready to deal with intuition, prophetic or otherwise."

"Your intuition didn't tell you who it was on the telephone so early, did it? Are you very busy?"

"Was it last night you made up your mind to call me today?"

"I've been thinking about it all night. I didn't sleep. Maybe it was the glass of whiskey I drank just to please you. You know I never drink. I had another glass, too. That you didn't know about."

"Just two glasses, and you were deprived of the sleep of poets?"

"No! More likely, it was what you had to say. Do you remember what you said?"

"Did I say something to stop someone else getting to sleep?"

"Stop avoiding the subject!"

"I'm afraid I had a lot to drink. Maybe I said some inappropriate things."

"Oh no, not at all! I'll remind you later. Are you busy this morning? Can I come and see you?"

"My dear lady, for your sake all the cares of the world can wait!"
"Walid, I'm being serious!"
"So am I."
"Can you drive to my house in a little while then?"
"To your house? Now?"
"Don't worry about your reputation!"
"Oh, is that so! We'll see who's worried. Are you ready now?"
"Give me fifteen minutes."
"Fifteen minutes! This gorgeous morning won't go on forever, as you well know."
"But I need to comb my hair and . . ."
"Okay then, ten minutes."
"I'll be waiting by the door."

That's the way it was. No preliminaries—or perhaps after preliminaries that lasted a few years and an evening at Amer's house. It was one of those occasions that only Amer and his wife can do well. Their home's filled with objets d'art and books, and they have a huge garden, big enough to hold a thousand people, filled with palm trees, pyracanthas, and rose beds. It was divided up into sections, separated by walls of varying heights set up here and there. Some of them were blank with lights reflecting off them; others had delicate archways that led out onto a number of paths through the gardens. Frogs could be heard on either side of these walkways, which led to other walls shrouded in darkness. The modernized minotaur's labyrinth in miniature, an accurate reflection of the mind of Amer Abd al-Hamid, himself a man of many twists and turns who thoroughly enjoyed leading both himself and others astray; deep within some dark recess of his personality there lurked a minotaur that devoured people, ideas, and things without ever seeming to be sated. Walid seemed to attract such complex and highly wrought characters; or perhaps they attracted him. I got the impression many of the guests who'd come to the party on the previous evening, both men and women, were eager to hunt such an easy and choice prey. For my part, I was determined not to let the opportunity slip this time. It was a gorgeous night, and the labyrinth extended far and wide. Walid wouldn't escape my clutches unless he decided I was a fool with no charm whatsoever. I had no idea how I was going to turn the conversation the way I wanted it to go; but when I saw him there standing underneath one of the arches with a glass in his hand, I suddenly felt a wave lift me up to an enormous, dizzying height. For a moment he was alone, before the crows descended to perch by him. Wisal, I told myself, this is your big chance. At last! I made a beeline for him.

"Alone?" I asked. "Are you lost, or has everyone deserted you?"

"What?" he asked with a start.

I kept up my attack. "You really are lost, aren't you?!"

"No, I'm not," he replied simply. "I went to get a refill. Can I get you anything?"

"Yes, please," I replied, even though I don't drink.

I went over with him to a candlelit table close by.

"Whiskey? On the rocks? Water?"

He handed me the glass, and I decided to drink it down even if it was poison. Almost immediately we were surrounded by other people who'd come over to refill their glasses. I deliberately made off with my victim to a distant corner, where we found a large palm tree with low leaves.

"How very odd," I said, taking no care even to make sure that what I was saying made any sense. "We always imagine it's the other people who are all lost, but then we find out that it's really us. Isn't that so, Mr. Walid? Sometimes I can walk four meters and feel I've crossed the widest desert in the world. Aren't these dates wonderful? What type are they? Maktoum? You don't know much about dates. How do you know they're Maktoum? I suppose Amer told you so. There's only one chair here. Just a minute, I'll get another one. You'll get it? Thank you very much. Let me help you. I mean, I'll come with you while you bring it. I've a lot to talk to you about. Here beneath the dangling branches, as they say."

At that moment I thought of the Virgin Mary and the birth of Christ. Should I shake the trunk of the palm tree? Here I was, the Virgin called Wisal, "love bond," by her father, his own "Wisal" or love bond with the one he loved, his second wife. I was just going to tell Walid no human being has ever touched me when I spotted Maryam al-Saffar hurrying in our direction. She had a gorgeous figure, and her hair cascaded over her shoulders like a golden curtain. At that particular moment, I felt afraid of her; I loathed her. I was stabbed with jealousy when she exclaimed, "Walid, where have you been hiding? We're all waiting for you!"

"I'll join you in a while," he said—really meaning, "Go away! I've found something more interesting here! This virgin who's drinking whiskey just for me." My jealousy subsided.

"Hello, Wisal," she said, "and how are you keeping Walid occupied?" Before I could even reply, she'd turned on her heels and gone back the way she came.

"What a stunning woman," I said. "Why don't you go back to your group? Oh, I haven't even tasted the drink you got for me yet. I don't need it. Yet, I get the feeling it will give me some kind of strength to add to my own. You're very diplomatic, I know. Where do I get strength from? I'm forever being exposed to winds that blast me from unknown directions and tear me apart. Do you know the story of the man who stood before the judge with the phrase "Out of luck" written on his forehead? Well, the judge delivered a verdict that proved him right. I feel I've written something like that on my forehead, too. So, please don't laugh. Or rather, yes, do laugh! Go on, please! Laugh! What do we have to do with luck? You can talk to the happiest of people, and they'll tell you they're out of luck. No one's ever satisfied with their own lot or what they've achieved. Take you, for example. Are you happy?"

"To a certain extent," he replied.

"What do you mean, 'to a certain extent'? Yes or no? Why don't you give me a straight answer?"

"Very well then. Yes and no."

"I can figure out why you're happy, but I'll never understand why you're not."

"That's a long story."

"Tell me some of it, please."

He shook the ice in his glass. "Problems, sorrows, crises . . ."

"Anyone who sees you anywhere, reads the things you write, or listens to you talking to people would imagine you're always radiant and optimistic; in other words, happy."

"In spite of all the problems, sorrows, and crises? Perhaps I'm one of those people who insists on being optimistic, even though I firmly believe that in most cases optimism really signifies stupidity and lack of insight. My own resolve has weakened recently. I can feel the onset of darkness, growing more intense day by day, both around me and on me. Life's full of evil, poverty, and injustice."

"Please tell me something a little bit original!"

"There are some abrupt pleasures to be had, too, wonderful things that manage to transport us, if only for a few fleeting moments, to those few places where the fires of pleasure and joy burn so brightly."

"But they soon go out, don't they!"

"Such moments come seldom, but we still cling to them. We savor the sheer pleasure drop by drop. They seem like a rare wine that we drink only in small amounts because there's so little of it to be had. Winds keep blowing and knocking you down, you say? Never mind! Maybe you need knocking down. Winds have to blow. Some storms bring the sweet balm of rain with them. They can be moments of sheer joy . . ."

"What's the point?" I asked. "The rain barely starts coming down before it stops again!"

"So that you won't get inundated, Wisal!"

"Walid! May I call you that? I've known you for more than seven years now. Haven't I earned the right to call you by your first name? Walid, you're still treating me and talking to me like a child. Don't you think I deserve better? I'm twenty-six now. Don't you realize it?"

"I still think of you as being twenty. Ever since that time I saw you in the Red Crescent Building selling those Palestinian clothes with the Bethlehem and Ramallah designs. Do you know, my mother used to wear dresses like the ones you were selling that day?"

"You forgot all about me as soon as you'd bought the dress. Every time we met, I had to remind you I was the one who sold you the dress you didn't need."

"Not true! I've never forgotten for a single instant."

"You're flattering me as usual."

"Certainly not."

"That's a risky sort of admission to make. Why didn't you forget me?"

"Oh, things like that are extremely complicated and difficult to pin down."

"Oh, come one, give me one or two reasons."

"What do you want me to say? Because you're beautiful? Fine. Because you're beautiful. Because you've got unforgettable, honey-colored eyes. Because your hands are so small and pretty. Because your laugh . . ."

"Why didn't you say things like this before? Why haven't you written me a poem?"

"Do I have to write a poem to every pretty woman I meet? I've no idea how to write a love poem."

"This whiskey's gone straight to my head."

"So quickly?"

"Yes. This is the first time in my life I've drunk any liquor. Do you think I'll get dizzy from the very first glass? I wanted to read you a poem I've written, but now my tongue won't be able to keep it straight."

He laughed. "Don't you think," I seem to remember him saying, "I'll get giddy from a very first poem?"

"I don't want to make you giddy," I said.

"Please do," he replied, "but no . . . I don't get giddy. I'll either get totally drunk or not at all."

"In that case you won't be getting drunk," I said. "Whiskey's better for you!"

"Better than the voice of prophecy? Of course it's not!" He leaned over toward me and whispered: "Are you a prophet . . . a minor prophet perhaps?"

At that moment I wished he would take me in his arms and kiss me, but he pulled back and gulped down the rest of the whiskey in his glass.

"I'm no prophet," I replied, "not even a pseudoprophet. Just an interloper, butting in on poetry, on the world, even on you."

"Then why haven't you butted in on me before?"

"I will."

"Is it a deal?"

"Too bad for you! Are you joking? Aren't you afraid of my threats? Actually, I'm the one who's afraid. Do you realize that? Up to this evening I was scared to get too close to you. Are you really that frightening?"

He kept laughing without making any reply.

"What I mean," I went on, "is that you seem so daunting. When I'm close to you, it's like being near a fire; if I'm not too careful, my clothes will get caught in it. Will you listen to my poem? I'm no prophet, and I've no desire to be one. I'm a sentimentalist. I've no idea how to use my mind for more than three minutes at a time."

"Intuition," he said, interrupting me in a serious tone. "That's what's important: intuition, prophetic intuition."

At this point the music was extremely loud, painfully so. My head was spinning, and my arms felt delightfully relaxed.

"I'm full of intuition," I said, raising my voice. "At this very moment, I'm having intuitive feelings, things I haven't even spoken to you about . . ."

"Please don't scare me."

"Why not?"

"Because I take a transcendental view of such things, especially about the intuition of a gorgeous girl drinking whiskey for the first time."

"Mr. Walid, you've said it again!"

"What?"

"That I'm beautiful."

"You're very beautiful."

"Oh dear, here they come to gobble you up."

Maryam was approaching once again, bringing Jinan with her, and another man I didn't recognize. I stood up and made my way toward the other guests, so as not to say or do anything I might regret later. The music was as loud as ever. I went over to the other table and got myself another whiskey. I noticed my brother.

"Tariq," I said, "isn't this a marvelous party—or am I just imagining things?"

"What's going on?" he asked. "Are you drinking?"

"Don't you have any poetry or prophetic vision in you?"

"You're drunk, my dear! You've had more than enough to drink!"

"Oh no, my dear brother. You get back to your wife. You can stop her from doing what she wants to, but not me!"

I looked around again, but Walid wasn't there anymore; the labyrinth had swallowed him up in a matter of seconds. I felt like sitting there on the grass and crying, something I hadn't done for years and years. I made up my mind to call him the very next morning, come what may.

It was a gorgeous morning. I leaped out of bed feeling once again as though a wave had picked me up and now here I was gazing down from its dazzling crest. I never believed my brief telephone call could achieve everything I wanted with such speed. In less than a quarter of an hour I was standing by the door. Walid drove up, and I got in the car beside him. The wave started to get higher and higher, and we set off to finish the previous night's conversation, as though the whole thing had never been interrupted.

"Now read me your poem," he demanded.

"After all this chatter it's going to sound stupid."

"Read it!"

I took the piece of paper out of my handbag. "Do you realize," I asked him, "that you're the man I've always dreamed of above all?"

He looked at me in bewilderment, but didn't say a word.

"As a child," I went on, "as a teenager, and now as a woman. Do you realize that?"

"Read the poem!"

I turned toward him, aware somehow of the hand with which I was holding the piece of paper undoing the zip on my blouse. I felt my right breast pop halfway out of my brassiere in a movement all its own. When he looked at me again, he was stunned to see my half-naked bosom bulging out of the open blouse. He didn't say a word, but took a good long look before turning his eyes to the front again to concentrate on his driving.

Then I started reading the poem.

He didn't look toward me again until I'd finished reading it. I waited for him to say something. He'd been listening to me in silence, without interrupting me, focusing his mind on my words or maybe on the road, I don't know which. He looked at me, then lowered his gaze to my breasts.

"Your breast is superb," he said, "full of youth, a golden dome in miniature."

I adjusted my position in the seat and pulled the zipper up. "My poem's no good. Is that what you mean?"

"Your poem? I didn't hear your poem. I just heard your voice."

"My poem! Walid, you didn't even listen to it! My recitation, my skill, my prophetic vision, were they all in vain?!"

"Read it again."

"Certainly not!"

"With your breasts uncovered."

"Never!"

"Please!"

"OK, provided you concentrate on the words this time!"

"Of course."

How could I do anything but say yes? It was a glorious day, crazily wonderful. The wave was carrying me up and up; I never imagined I could be so bold and devilish. Walid wasn't driving in any particular direction, just away from the city, toward the desert. "Faluja's ahead," he said, "and then Ramadi; after that, it's the desert, but let's come back to the poinsettias now; they're at their most spectacular. The desert can come later. There's always time for the desert, but poinsettias..."

"On fire today, snuffed out tomorrow? Never! We'll never let them be snuffed out. We'll set them alight, rekindle them, always, always, from now on, forever!"

Walid laughed, chuckled in fact, as though he'd heard the funniest joke in the world. "Forever?" he said. "My dear lady, isn't today enough for you? What are you talking about 'forever' for? What concern is the everlasting for us?"

"I don't know. It's just the way I feel."

"You don't know! That's what you tell me after every single thing you say. You're good at knowing really, Wisal; in fact, you're a veritable fortune-teller, a sibyl. The veils shrouding the future have been lifted, so that you can see what's to come."

"Now you're making fun of me!"

"No, I'm convinced of it. Your eyes are so penetrating."

"All right, I know: two balconies from which..."

"No, no, I don't mean that. I mean they can penetrate into the unknown. What can you see, my fortune-teller?"

My blouse was open right down to the waist as I turned toward him. I put out my hand and squeezed his face. "I see love," I intoned in a deep, solemn voice. "I see burning passion; I see your face bloodied by kisses. I see people jealous of you sharpening their skewers while Wisal's there to protect you from their talons, with her teeth and her talons..."

"I'm desperately in love with your teeth and your talons," he said.

He took me home with him. I was afraid of nothing and nobody. As I entered his house, it felt as though this were a meeting destined since the day of my birth. In full sight of the poinsettias by the window, he took me into his arms on the couch. He was talking and so was I. What did we say? I can't remember. What we said afterward I can remember vividly. I scratched his chest with my nails. "That's so you won't forget," I told him. He replied that surface scratches heal in a week or two, to which my response was to threaten him with even deeper scratches that wouldn't heal so quickly.

Little did I realize then that later he'd give me wounds that wouldn't heal, like the five wounds of his Jesus.

All of a sudden I found myself searching for words, words different from the ones I already knew, words that could talk of new, fresh things, that would both deepen and pour balm on the wounds. I felt I wanted to define my ideas in forms that had never occurred to me before.

When compared with my other experiences, the time I spent with him shook the very ground beneath my feet. The things I experience—and I may well be like other people in this—usually set me at a distance from others sharing the same experience. I used to be aware of myself as a separate entity, as something affected by forces external to it with which it wasn't merged in any way. Yet, with Walid, came the peculiar discovery that I was totally merged, transforming, meshing, and emerging as a completely different person from before. As he talked to me, argued, discussed, and flirted with me, I felt I'd penetrated into the inner sanctum of another human being; as though someone had allowed me to enter a huge, dark house with wonderful rooms in it, carrying a candle and wandering around among all the furniture and objets d'art. I got to know Walid from the inside; I traveled along his mental orbits and his psychological and emotional ones as well. I started to know and to love him; I began to feel jealous. Time and again, the illusion came to me that Walid was actually me. I began knowing and loving him as I did my own self. If I didn't see him, I was still always talking to him—to my own self. Our conversation always had its own unique savor to it; as he flirted with me, words would come pouring out of his mouth all over my body, so much so that every pore used to listen to him in a frenzy of excitement. As a result I had no choice but to find new words to define what it was I wanted to say. In fact, the things I wished to say were sometimes in conflict with what he wanted to say, while at other times they were either a completion or a substitute. The fact that I was he or vice versa should not be taken to mean there was some tacit agreement between us. There were conflicts; nothing was expressed simply in terms of black and white. I found myself becoming his facsimile; love made me like him, tolerating all the contradictions and refusing to settle merely for an ultimate abstract idea.

Is it that, I wonder, which made us so necessary for each other? For a long time, I freely admit, I felt the thing binding us together wasn't mere bodily lust; even though he desired me with a violent passion, I'm still amazed he was able to keep it going. The feeling between us was the fervent longing to be together again after being apart, or perhaps the secret fear our two halves might indeed come apart after coming together and forming a perfect, heavenly unity (*heavenly* is the word he used; for my part, I only fully understood what he meant by it on occasions like this). He told me our relationship was a confirmation of some paragraphs in one of Plato's dialogues. I'd read them in the *Symposium* and laughed, and he'd laughed at my laughter.

"I'm not convinced," I said, whereupon he carried me naked around the room with me resisting all the way and then put me down on the floor. He proceeded to put Plato's theory into practice, or at least to confirm its veracity, all this entirely in accordance with his own passionate desires.

"Words, words, words . . ." He whispered into my ear between the strands of my hair. He'd been hugging me from behind, but now turned me around to face him.

"What a crafty devil Shakespeare is!" he said, looking straight into my eyes. "He makes Hamlet say that, and many people imagine that what he's saying is 'Void, void, void!' For some people that may well be true: people deficient in language, people with speech impediments, parrots. But Shakespeare's al-Mutanabbi's brother; they're both masters of words. What Shakespeare wants to do is make Hamlet scream in the face of all the parrots of this world: 'Words, words, words!' The most wonderful thing God's given to man! Just imagine if someone like al-Mutanabbi was in love with you. What would he be saying? The words would come pouring out of his mouth and hands; he'd clean them and polish them, and then apply them to everything to be found in life in return for some pearls just like these dinars, 'shadows scurrying away from the fingertips' as he himself puts it. Words are everything. In the long run, words are all that's left of anything; if there are no words left, there's nothing. Intrigue, folly, murder, they're all in words; hatred, tedium, suicide, moonlit nights, sleepless nights, nights that refuse to come to an end, nights that melt into a sweet, passionate embrace. Words. They may be: 'No, no,' or 'Yes, yes,' or even mewing and purring. If a woman has al-Mutanabbi's gifts, then she can rob him of his sleep, not just through pain and torment, but, more, through sheer elation as his body's ripped apart with wicked delights. There are silent heroes, Wisal, and others who talk; I'm aware of that. There are silent and articulate scoundrels, too. Some are dead through silence, others through speaking; some can signify by talking, others can't even utter a coherent phrase. I realize all that, too. But words ... those who control words flagellate themselves with the bewitching sounds of letters; they adore the vibrations in the throat. When words of love are no longer to be heard on lovers' lips, doesn't the love itself disappear as well? Words are everything. We'll make the first such word this very day, and it'll be the one I'll call you by from now on: Shahd."

For a while, we played the game of words with each other. He wanted to outwit the intolerable cruelty of not being able to meet every day. I'd write something to him every night, and he'd do the same. I'd pass by his house in my car (outwitting the entire world in order to pass by his house at the same hour every day). I'd find him standing there by his iron gate, then like conspirators we'd exchange letters, and I'd rush away with my treasure.

Once I wrote to him "Now we see through a glass" (he knew what the source was, of course):

> Now we see through a glass
> Darkly,
> but then we shall see
> face to face,
> As clear as the day.
> Is love to be
> my glass, my darkness,
> in which to see your face in mine,
> that it may one day become
> as clear as the day to me?
>
> But why do I question?
> It is enough that I
> can see your face,
> even though it be
> a cloud in the murky gloom,
> a specter in the depths of my glass
> a mirage in the clear of the day.
>
> Your love is my glass, I know
> full well; the dark in my night,
> the sun in my day.
> So I cease my questions.

Next day I sent him this:

> Neither day nor night
> can veil your face from me.
> Every hour of loneliness
> is a battlefield with
> my own frustration.
> Is it only your eyes
> that hover so close to mine;
> no other lips but yours.
> Such is my waiting that
> I am a prey to dreams
> repeated night after night

from a place that is
forever different from yours.
Whenever I meet you, will I have
to don my veil hurriedly,
when all the while you
behind your own veil realize
that all I desire is to implant
myself on your lips
and to hug you in my arms,
like a rose, a handful of perfume,
a jewel that I keep hidden
inside my blouse between my breasts.

A passion that can only end with death.

For his part, he wrote this to me (and I was well aware of his source, too):

Never has a woman the likes of you
emerged from her clothes,
with a beauty like yours.
My lady, I am the morning,
I am the dew, and you
are the tree.

My lady, no tree has ever grown
in our land with branches
like your arms
or fruit to rival your breasts.
You, you are the tree,
and I am the daylight.
Illumine me with the
gleam of your eyes.
I am the breeze blowing
hither and yon, filling
the world with the fragrance
of your arms and breasts.

> Never has a pair of knees
> appeared from beneath
> a dress to equal yours.
> Nor a pair of legs
> as wonderful as yours, my lady.
> You, you are the tree,
> and I am the sun pouring
> my fire down onto you;
> I am also the night,
> concealing you finally
> like a secret
> in my chest,
> so jealous am I.

Walid! How well I knew you and loved you! I used to be furious with you, jealous about you, crazy about you. I've spent thousands of hours raving at you; and even as I did it, I knew well enough you were doing exactly the same thing, losing your mind and feeling jealous, deserted by sleep and tossed to and fro by seas of words until eventually dawn came. Then sheer lack of sleep would coat your eyes just as it did mine. "Your mascaraed eyes greet me," you'd say... Walid, we have to talk now; that mascaraed eye is looking for you. In your interconnecting rooms, amid your scattered furniture and files of paperwork. Why don't I admit it: I'm searching for you here, in my very blood, within my innermost self, in those very fires that you could make to flare up or die away at will. Very well then, so let me speak. That will bring you to life again, and it will do the same thing, too, for me.

With me, Walid, your sins are numerous. Not the least of them is that you taught me the meaning of the word *body*. Of all the people I've met in my life, you're the one most intensely devoted to spiritual and cerebral matters that have nothing whatsoever to do with the world. That's how you managed to embroil me in your sin, by setting fire to the body and then looking for the embers in the spirit. The trouble is the body often catches fire, then all that's left of the spirit is ashes. How I wish you were here with me now, so I could hear what you had to say in your own defense. You involved me in your sin, but forgot to leave me any of the benefits that accompany it, any of the embers of the spirit. Ashes, that's all that's left in my veins now. Can you see from over there? Where are you? Tell me, where? Why didn't you take me with you, you cruel, evil man, to finish me off as well? How am I supposed to blow on the ashes, to find, perhaps, some last piece of live ember amid all the desolation? I'm dying, I'm telling myself lies. I'm lying because, every time I talk to you, my body starts shuddering, going rigid again. Very well then, I'll talk to you, flirt with you, accuse you, argue with you. I love you like a maniac, like a prostitute, and I won't marry you. You convince me I'm you, then send me home feeling utterly destroyed like one of your shattered cast-offs; all this so I can tell the world I'm waiting here in my father's, mother's, and brother's house, for some young man to come along, ask for my hand in marriage, and become a new part of my life. As though such a thing were possible for anyone who's become part of you, a part that can fit only into the mold of your lips, your hands, and your chest! Who made the impossible remain impossible? Am I the one, with my perpetual rejection, or is it you, up to your very neck in impossibilities? For your sake I'm deceiving people: I travel, I come home, back and forth, I stay close to my father; I get engaged and then break it off. And then there's Marwan. I almost fell in love with him because of you. He has your eyes and hands, I used to tell myself. I'd say he was more handsome than you, and you'd laugh. Were you as good-looking as him when you were young? I don't think so. But who's ever suggested that I loved you for your good or bad looks, or because you were tall or short? But I don't want to talk about such silly things, or about the ways you were able to seduce me; you'd done that many years before, when I was still an adolescent, without even realizing it. What I want to talk about is the way you uproot me and then try to plant me in your own soil. There I stay, planted but unpicked, to face the sun's heat and the waters of the earth. Even so, I'm still uprooted, entwined around your trunk and branches; neither sun nor waters can provide my life with the sustenance it needs; that can come only from the sap I suck out from your tree.

But, you'll reject the charge, I know. You'll insist that what attracted you to me was the fact that I am what I am; you didn't uproot me, but rather embraced me, only to let me go for a while, then come back and hug me again, leave again, hug me again, and so on. Now you've left me for the last time—if I'm to believe what you're saying—and you didn't expect me to be coming back to get a last hug from you. But I'm lying now, too, or at least I think I am; I was the one who didn't come back, who in my ignorance and sheer impetuosity was afraid to come back. And when I did come back, you weren't there. I gave my word and then broke it. Then, when I changed my mind and came back, you'd gone. How then can I claim I'm actually you, when I had no idea of what was going on in your mind in those final moments? After today, I'll never believe in the thought of love again (as though there is any room for love after today!). All I can see, in this city of mine, is eyes gleaming with death, betrayal, death, betrayal, death. Is it possible to see the gleam of death and betrayal in people's eyes?

My darling, I no longer remember the words you taught me. I've forgotten everything in two short days. When I heard about your death—have they really killed you, or is it just jealous nonentities showing their malice? How can I say the unsayable? Here I am saying it: they've killed you, they've felled you. At that moment, I would have loved to wrap my arms around your waist and chest to protect you from the bullets and bruises, when you started crashing from one rock to another, to save your face from being marred; I would have kept my mouth on yours to stave off all the bullets the world could aim at you. In just two days I've forgotten all speech, all intelligence and logic. When I put on mourning clothes, my mother was thunderstruck.

"Who are you wearing that for?" she asked.

"For the whole of humanity," I replied.

"Then you'd better start wearing it all the time," she said. "People's woes are never-ending."

"Actually," I went on, "I'm wearing it for one particular man."

"A man?" she said in amazement.

"Yes, Mother, a man I've loved for some time now. I've just heard he's been killed."

She looked around to make sure no one had heard what I'd been saying. "Don't say that again," she said. "We're in enough trouble already. Go upstairs and change your clothes."

"I mean to wear black," I went on, "for all those young Palestinian men who are fighting as fedayeen. Don't I have the right to do that, just for two or three days?"

She became flustered, stood up, and left me on my own. She never mentioned the subject again.

Such things as wearing mourning, going without food and sleep, and having nightmares if dozing off for a moment if possible, aren't important for a woman. What really matters is that she should retain her sense and resolution, her ability to make decisions. Decisions about what? I feel as though I'm on a steep downhill slope, skiing down the Alps toward a horrendous abyss with no way of saving myself. I feel dizzy, furious, resentful. I know what you'll say, as you always do: "Rise above it all! Don't feel resentful! Don't stoop to other people's levels." How very hard that is. My natural impulse is to raise my hand to strike someone, to launch into a series of curses, but you'll never accept that. You'll take me home and show me the latest Iraqi painting you've bought, and I'll put my favorite cassette in the recorder, and then you'll enclose us both in the shell you have against the whole world. Then, piece by piece, you'll take my clothes off and let me share your delirium as you consume my body, make me die of sheer passion, in order to live anew.

That poem I read to you on that wonderful October morning—what was it, I wonder, that made me read it to you?! You started asking me for a new poem every day. "Where are the metaphors?" you'd ask. "Where are the allusions, the wonders of creation, the wounds, the disasters, the joy, the self-sacrifice? Where, where, where?" You had the force of the sea striking a pebble on the beach. "Where are the rocks, the forests, and the angels?" you'd ask next. I did paint rocks, forests, and angels for you. I painted women, cities, and storms. That's the way I regarded my poems. But you weren't satisfied.

Then came the day when I discovered I wasn't the only woman in your life—or at least after that magical morning in October. I went mad. Was that why you wanted the whole universe: rocks, forests, angels, women, cities, and storms? When, oh when would you ever have enough? Was death the only thing that could give you what you wanted—that thing that made me continually afraid for your sake? I was distraught then, but I was satisfied with your confession, too. The papers you gave me every time we met were checks guaranteeing forgiveness in advance. The things you wrote in prose were much more beautiful than all my poems put together, perhaps because, in your letters, I was the center, the pivot, the compass, distance and space, length, breadth, and height, all rolled into one; or else because you were all those things as far as I was concerned... anything you wrote became, for me, a matter of conviction and faith; until, that is, the day you put your confession in my hand admitting that there was another woman you'd been fooling around with. Then I stopped seeing you because I really thought I was going to be married at last. Here I was playing the role of a reflective woman who knows that, sooner or later, she's going to have to get married, in spite of all her love and passion.

When I took your confession home and read it, I went completely to pieces. I hear your words my slain beloved. Let Jinan die once and Shahd a thousand times:

> I couldn't see you. I wrote to you every day; sometimes it was a few lines, other times several pages. I felt I was talking to you. The world changed before my very eyes. It became majestic in an unbearable way, and frightening, too, in a way that was equally unbearable, because you weren't there. Everything cries out your name, suggests your presence. Shahd, you were the one who put an end to my indifference, my personal limitations, my stupor. Maybe you shouldn't have done it. Now that I don't have it, the pain I feel stuns me, tears me apart; it's been doing it for days now. When we meet, I feel torn apart with sheer joy and pleasure. How luscious your kisses are, your mouth, your tongue. Then I go back to the world, which is wonderful because of you, and frightening because you aren't there with me. The solitude I used to crave is a prison for me now. In the world outside I seem like an imbecile. I go to see Jinan, and with her I betray our love; I do it deliberately, trying not to remember you. The vision of you fills my head. Shahd, you came as a punishment for me. Jinan believes she has me to herself, not realizing she possesses me for only those few moments when my despair over you

drives me insane. She used to have her doubts about our relationship, but she's afraid of finding out the real truth and doesn't pursue the matter to a final confession. But your love was my punishment, the thing I relished, which aggravated me, and eventually made me want still more. One day I was talking to Jawad. "Every morning," he said, "when I get up, I do some exercises to keep my body in good shape. How about you?" "When I wake up," I replied, "I think of the woman I love; that's my only physical exercise!"

It was that which gave me such a cursed relish for life and made it seem so precious and dear, something worth all the exhaustion, sacrifice, and tenacity. But you know all that, Shahd. I'm only repeating it here to bring back those wonderful times when you gave yourself to me, to recall the touch of your skin to my hand, of your thigh and stomach to my face, your frenzied, incredible whispers, like some sword coming down on our necks whenever we finished making love. The vast expanses contracted and closed in on us; there was no longer any sun, or trees, or birds, or pictures or people worth looking at—just your face, still more beautiful than the sun, your body more beautiful than any bird or painting. Whenever I had to leave you— against my will as always—I'd stumble back into a world without you, only to discover that all those vast expanses had contracted, were closed up and dark. This was the punishment: to be deprived of all other pleasures at one go. If I hadn't felt (and I'm not always sure of it myself) that the self same thing was happening to you, too, that you were involved in the very same situation, I would have declared my revolt and demanded an end to my love, even if it meant death. But contradictions continue to dominate my life. Everything's wonderful; everything cries out your name, everything I long for because of you. But it's all gloomy, too, unappetizing, because you're not part of it.

Jinan used to get very excited as I pushed her—in spite of myself—toward the climax of her passion. I'd watch her writhing and groaning, and I'd be hugging my own misery to myself, hating myself, feeling so utterly stupid because I couldn't find contentment in that great love, because in all the wonder of life

I could find happiness only with you, you, you, Shahd, my Shahd. Everything I said was directed at you. I kept looking for the other half of me till I found you, and then I came to realize the utter horror of your separation from me: I was, in truth, cut into two segments wanting to come together again. I was waiting for my reunification with you, the woman with whom, so the fates decreed, I could be united in only a few moments of a rapture as profound as the oceans themselves and as swift as the sweep of a hurricane.

Walid, how could you bring yourself even to mention Jinan, even though you were trying to use her to prove you loved me? That day you managed once more to tear me apart; but whereas before it had been love, this time it was jealousy. You forced me to come running back to you, out of jealousy, nothing else. I wanted you to enter a monastery, to suffer, to be deprived of all women after me. Off you went with your half of our relationship and tried to get my half back through Jinan! I made a firm resolution on the spot, that very day, that I'd never get married, just to keep you for myself even if I didn't come back to you. I did come back. Did I ever ask you about Jinan? Did I argue with you about her? Any other woman but me would have left you as soon as she found out another woman was involved, whatever excuses were made. With me it was just the opposite. I came back to you, but this time with feelings of doubt I hadn't known before. Were you still seeing Jinan every time I had to go away? I kept all this to myself, pretending your letter hadn't revealed anything new.

Did you run away from everything at the last moment, just to rid yourself of your wavering over Jinan and myself? Is that possible, even conceivable? Am I supposed to believe you were able to put me in a balance with another woman, Jinan or whoever? I went back to my delirium. Why should I make myself a focus for your tragedy, knowing full well it did indeed have a focus that I dearly wanted not to have to believe in. Flawed angels botched the job of forming the universe, so the universe was full of flaws, too. That's what one of your Greek authors said. Now here I am confirming the truth of what he said. You arrived as a stranger, at war; and that's the way you stayed, a stranger fighting on various fronts in a world molded with flaws. Oh God! "Wasted is the time that we do not spend in love . . ." But the losses were great indeed, my beloved, and time wasn't the only thing wasted. When you lost Marwan, I, too, realized I'd lost everything. Yet, the world stayed the way it was with all its flaws; nothing changed. You came as a stranger and left the same way. You turned me into a stranger in the midst of my own family and friends. Only I have changed. The bougainvillea at our house is in full bloom, and I don't understand why. It's almost as though it wants to spur me on to lift the receiver and call you again to arrange to read my poetry, with my body firing all your senses. Miracles! A purse filled with pearls, dropped from the heavens into my lap. Yes indeed! Now here's another purse dropped from heaven, but this one's full of scorpions.

2

It was no easy task finding Marwan in Beirut, even though Walid's friend Khalid Abu Matar had given me directions. In the end Khalid went with me himself to the Sabra refugee camp, and after a lot of questions we found Marwan there. "What do you want?" he asked, looking curiously at me. I didn't know what to say. His eyes, gorgeous eyes, were exactly like his father's, but they had a brighter gleam to them and a cruelty totally missing from Walid's. I wanted to imagine it was Walid I was seeing in khaki camouflage uniform and fedayeen headdress, carrying a *Kalashnikov*. But all I saw was Marwan, tall, unsmiling, rejecting everything except his new comrades in this tented city, which I could feel taking me back to the forgotten essence of life.

"I'm Wisal Raouf," I said, "and I've come from Baghdad. I've got a letter for you from your father."

He took the letter and read it. We were standing in the middle of a roadway crowded with people. I kept looking at his youthful face and the slight moustache barely visible over his lip. He took Khalid and me to a small office, where we sat down on wooden chairs. He's asked me about his father, and introduced us to two of his colleagues who were wearing the same uniform; they brought us some tea. The whole encounter was awkward, but the conversation kept going and gradually became more heated. We toured the camp, and Marwan introduced me to a number of people. "Welcome to the lady from Baghdad!" I could imagine any one of them as a mother for Walid. We met some young people, too, who knew Baghdad; some of them had studied there. I wanted them to let me stay with them.

"Teach me how to fire a gun," I said to Marwan.

He looked at me in my tight-fitting pants. "Whenever you want to try it!" he replied.

Next day at lunchtime he came to the hotel and we went out to a seaside restaurant. The waiter filled the table with hors d'oeuvres. "Marwan," I said, when the waiter had left, "you've no idea how much your father loves you; you're all he has in the world. Why don't you come to Baghdad?"

He glanced at me for a brief moment, then looked out to sea. He was shy, and hardly said or ate anything. "I've no need to go to Baghdad," he said. "My life's here in the camp. We have lots to do."

"Well, take care of yourself, anyway," I said.

"Why on earth did I join the front then?" he asked in astonishment. "To take care of myself?"

I wanted to tell him to finish his university studies first and then come back to the front, but realized that would just annoy him. I took a packet of banknotes out of my handbag and handed them to him. "These are for you," I whispered. "Your father sent them with me."

He stared at them, there in my hand, as though they were some strange creatures he was afraid to touch. "What's that?" he said.

"Two hundred dinars. You may need them."

"No thanks," he replied, shaking his head. "I don't want them."

"Please!"

"I don't want them."

"I beg you! Please, take them before the customers notice."

"No! I've got quite enough. Really!"

"How strange you are!"

"No, I'm not! I don't need any money. What am I supposed to do with it anyway?"

"Come on, Marwan! Just take it and stop arguing!"

"Forget it! I'll throw it all in the sea if you like!"

"For heaven's sake! If you don't take it, now, I'll throw it in the sea for you."

"Go ahead. I hope the fish enjoy it!"

"You're just like your father. Stubborn as hell! You Palestinians, you're all stubborn!"

I put the money back in my handbag. "Do you know anything about my relationship with your father?" I asked him abruptly.

"Are you in love with him?" he asked coldly.

I felt a pain piercing to my very core. "I adore him," I replied. "I'd die for him."

He looked at me silently, then raised his hand from the table and put it on top of mine; I could feel it trembling. "I love him, too," he said, "and my mother used to worship him. But . . ."

Tears welled in my eyes, and my voice broke. "But what . . . what?" I asked.

He withdrew his hand. "He's been fighting the whole of his life," he said with a sigh, "and he's tired. He refuses to give up. Do you think you can help him . . . ease up, at least a little bit?"

I wasn't certain what he meant exactly.

"Oh Marwan!" I answered, my voice breaking again. "If only I could! Life's so complicated and always asks so much of us. If only you knew what a man he is!"

He took out a handkerchief and handed it to me. "Well, then, help him, will you?!"

I dried my eyes with the handkerchief, then paused. "Help him? Me?"

"He insists on going on with the fight himself. He keeps demanding they include him in operations. Don't you realize that?"

"I'm not the slightest bit surprised. But he doesn't talk to me about things like that. He's so secretive."

"When he was here last winter, he brought the matter up with his group, and then with me, too; it really annoyed me. Operations involve a lot of hard training beforehand; they need young men who can run hard, jump, go hungry, and put up with hardship. My father thinks he's still the young man he was twenty-five years ago. I told him if he wanted to commit suicide, to find some other way of doing it. He got very angry and we had a big fight; he swore at me and then went back to Baghdad. He hasn't written a word to me all these past months, and the letter you brought with you is the first one I've had from him since that day. I hear he's renewed his request to be involved with the fighting . . ."

I kept looking at Marwan and imagining to myself that it was Walid talking. The son had the same forceful tone in his voice as the father.

"But how can you deny your father the very things you've chosen for yourself?" I asked.

His face flushed in anger. "Because my role's completely different from his," he replied. "We're in a different phase of operations now. A fifty-year-old carrying an RPG is of no use to us. He's needed for organizing, financing, and making the necessary connections as a background to the fighting. Isn't all that enough for him? He's spent a lot of time fighting in any case . . ."

I didn't answer. As we sat there, silent, I saw the sea pounding the shore beside us, gleaming and restless. That sea belonged to Marwan, and to Walid. I felt at that particular moment it belonged to me, too, because I longed to plunge into the depths of both of them. What kind of fighting had my own father had to do to be appointed minister in the 1950s? What ideas had he put forward, what struggle had he articulated, except, that is, for his struggle against disease ever since he married my mother? What yearning, what passion, what agony had there been?

I put these thoughts out of my mind, so as to concentrate on the roaring mass of blue that seemed to encircle Marwan's face.

"What about now?" I asked. "Are you happy with your father?"

He looked astonished, as though the question had come straight at him from nowhere. "Am I happy with him? The main thing is: is he happy with me? That's what I'd like you to help me with. Can't you see?"

With a laugh I handed him back his handkerchief. "But you're not being any help to me."

"How can I be?"

"Don't you realize that by refusing to take this money you'll annoy him all over again? Marwan, please take it."

I opened my handbag again and was on the point of taking the package out when he pushed my hand back and closed the bag. "No, no," he said. "I told you, I don't want money."

I looked at him in silent despair. He was smiling; yes, for the first time I actually saw him smile! "Marwan!" I exclaimed, giving full vent to my shout. "You actually smiled!"

"What of it?" he asked with a chuckle. "Is that such a miracle?"

"It certainly is! My life's full of miracles these days. Do you know what I mean?"

"You should say thank God for that, then."

"Oh, I do, a thousand times a day! Now what are you going to get me to eat in this glorious spot?"

"Anything your heart desires."

"How about some fish? What's it called here: Sultan Ibrahim?"

The waiter came over and took our order.

"Wisal," he said, calling me by my name for the first time.

"Yes?"

"You have beautiful hair. Do you always keep it short like that?"

"But Marwan, you amaze me! You've actually started noticing me."

"So? Another miracle!"

"True enough! I cut it two days ago. Do you like it?"

"Very much. It reminds me of . . ."

"Of what? Who? One of your girlfriends?"

"Of another Iraqi woman who came to visit me with my father when I was a schoolboy at Brummana; that was about four years ago."

"What was her name?" I asked without the least attempt at subterfuge.

"I can't remember," he replied, "but she had really long, beautiful hair. I was twenty-four then."

"Was she Iraqi?"

"Yes. She had green eyes, too. Do you know who she is?"

My heart sank. "Maryam, was that her name? Maryam al-Saffar?"

"Maryam! Yes, that's it!"

"She came to visit you with your father?"

"Yes. I think they'd met accidentally in Beirut."

"Could be," I commented. In fact, I was thinking the very reverse; it certainly hadn't been an accident. Marwan, I thought to myself, are you really trying to remind me I'm just another woman in Walid's life? But why should I be bothered about what woman he loved, or what woman was in love with him, four long years ago?

"Oh, she's one of our many acquaintances," I told Marwan. "She's a professor at Baghdad University now. Do you have any special message for her?"

"Oh no! I don't think she'd even remember me."

I laughed. "I don't think she'd forget anything to do with your father," I said as though to poke fun at myself.

The waiter took the hors d'oeuvres away and brought the fish. "Do you have any girlfriends here?" I asked.

At first he frowned, then his expression relaxed. "The . . . er . . . there are plenty of women around here, even in the camp, but I'm too busy with other things that are more important." For a moment he was silent, then he went on: "My platoon and I go through really tough drills. I can't wait to cross the border. The situation in Amman's extremely tense." There was an abrupt flare of anger in his eyes, then he looked out to sea again with his jaw set in a strange way.

"Marwan," I said, trying to put him in a happier mood again, "this fish is superb."

He turned and looked at me again, determination still written all across his face. "I'll make you a promise," he said.

"A promise?"

"One day I'll make fish for you from Lake Tiberias, with myself, you, and my father sitting by the shore. It may take five or ten years. Do you accept?"

"With all my heart. I'll be waiting . . ."

At this point he took up his knife and fork, and so did I. My heart was pounding with all kinds of emotion, and I didn't know whether to admire or be afraid of this young man who'd made me feel the sea was roaring and pounding all around my head.

The waves kept crashing down on the rocks nearby, turning the headlong rush of blue into a laughing cascade of white that dwindled away into foam, only to confront yet another onslaught of waves.

3

I sent Walid many cards and letters. Then, when I got back to Baghdad at the beginning of September, I found he'd already left. His "disappearance," without any notice given to his friends, was nothing unusual in itself. He could have been pursuing his interests in Abu Dhabi, London, or even Beirut itself; that, at least, was what people were assuming. But this time he was actually in Jordan, and about two months later he came back, exhausted and broken. Eventually, he revealed some of his secrets to me. I spent another October morning with him, but this time it was agonizing. He started to tell me about the insane, disgusting massacre he'd been involved in, carrying a *Kalashnikov* he'd never even dreamed of knowing how to fire.

"Don't you ever think of me?" I asked furiously. "Don't you realize how selfish I am about you? Here you are close to fifty..."

He let out such a scream as I'd never heard from a human being before. "Shut up," he yelled, "shut up!" and put both his hands over his face, then he turned to the closest wall and leaned on it, sobbing and moaning horribly. I was riveted to the spot in terror, as I watched him banging his head against the wall. His body was shaking and trembling. The room felt too small for the two of us, as though the walls were collapsing in on us. I felt my head spinning; I wanted to stop but couldn't. I fell to the ground, grabbing at it to keep myself steady, then crawled over toward him, till my face sank down at his feet and I found myself retching and sobbing, with no idea of what was happening. Much later—I have no idea whether I fainted or what—I found him collapsed over me, piled in a heap on top of me. I took his wan face in my hands. "Walid," I whispered, "oh Walid." I found it difficult even to utter his name, my throat felt so exhausted.

He fell into my arms and put his lips to my ear. "If I have the right to make love to you and fight the whole world for your sake, and all this when I'm pushing fifty, don't I have the right to love my country, too, and fight the rest of the world for its sake, too, even if I were ninety?"

"Of course you do," I said, laying him down beside me on the floor and resting his head on my chest. Was it one hour, two hours? The whole day went by, with us like a pair of corpses, wrapped one around the other. The world doesn't understand and never will; and accordingly, I reject a world that doesn't understand me. I must keep my wounds to myself, not tell anyone else about them; I must continue my rejection and join the other rejectionists.

4

My brother, Tariq, would occasionally visit us on Fridays, bringing Samira with him and sometimes the three children as well. He'd bring my father some free drug samples that companies present to doctors, and then they'd play a couple of games of backgammon and discuss the only three things in the world that occupied my father. The first was the garden, to which he'd devoted most of his energy after the 1958 revolution. As he himself put it, it was the only thing he'd ever learned from Voltaire, and he used to acquire all sorts of bulbs and flowers for it from all corners of the globe. Then there was his health. He imagined his very life was continually under threat from all sorts of dire diseases, and it was Tariq's job to assure him otherwise. Last, there was his own political career, from the 1920 revolution when he was a young man of eighteen until the last time he held a ministerial post in 1957; he was forever hoping to be able to write his memoirs of that era. In summer he went to London; in winter he could never keep his knees warm no matter what he did, and so he found it impossible to concentrate on anything; spring was the season for enjoying the garden to the fullest; and autumn hardly gave enough time to prune the bougainvillea and get the winter plants ready. In any case he didn't really like writing; he much preferred talking because it afforded him the opportunity to elaborate on his tales and heroic acts with no one ever asking him for the precision and clarification he'd have to provide whenever he put pen to paper. Once in a while Tariq would accuse him, jokingly, of not having stayed as devoted to his first wife, Tariq's own mother (who'd died in 1939), as he was to his second wife, whom he'd married when his first wife's body had hardly had the chance to get cold in its final resting place in the Imam al-Aazam cemetery. That, my father said, wasn't true, but he'd admit he'd been somewhat hasty in marrying my mother. "She was a stunningly beautiful girl," he said. "I was afraid of losing her if I waited too long . . . and then, my dear sir, who was supposed to look after you, Faysal, and Lamaan when you were still children?"

Tariq and I never had the feeling we weren't full brother and sister. He was my favorite among all the members of the family, save for my mother and father, the only one I always found leaving a bridge open between myself and him. He was a full sixteen years older than me, which meant he always kept a sympathetic, protective eye on me, not to mention the love he showed me. My father used to spoil me, but would admit, at the same time, that I wasn't always too responsive to all the people who spoke loving words to me. I'd graduated when I was twenty and got a job at the Arab Bank a year or two before it was nationalized (it was there I saw Walid for the first time, before he started his major financial adventures in the Gulf). From that moment on, I found I got a great deal of pleasure out of the intellectual challenge of arguing with Tariq; he'd insist on the need for me to study more economics, and all the time I'd be talking about my interest in poetry. I used to read some poems to him, but he'd just raise his hands in despair. "Riddles," he'd say. "Riddles, that's all they are! As if the ones my patients tell me aren't enough!"

That's the way those Friday visits would end up, too, whenever he came, that is. He hardly ever visited us on any other day. But there was one particular evening when he paid us a visit after nine at night, on his way home from the clinic. My father wasn't at home, and my mother and I were anxious to get him some dinner, but he was in a hurry. He took me to one side for a moment. "Listen, Wisal," he said. "Let's go out for a ride in my car. I've got something I want to talk to you about. Something I don't want your mother to hear."

I felt the blood draining from my face. "But why?" I asked.

"Hurry up!" he muttered. "It's urgent." Then he raised his voice. "Mother, I want to take Wisal to my club. Samira's waiting for us."

He took me by the hand, and we went out together. I had a definite feeling that, at long last, he was going to talk to me about my relationship with Walid.

He didn't waste any time; we'd barely settled into our seats and moved out of the drive before he broached the subject. I was sitting there quietly, trying to decide whether or not my hunch was correct, while he, for his part, was looking straight in front of him with his hands on the steering wheel.

"Listen, Wisal," he said. "Do you know what you're doing?"

"About what exactly?" I asked, feigning ignorance.

"You know very well what I mean. I've been meaning to talk to you about it for some time."

"Tariq, what are you talking about?"

"Walid. Who else? Are you seeing a lot of him?"

"A lot? No . . . I see him as often as I can."

"Why?"

"Why? Why does any woman see a man?!"

"That's wonderful, Wisal!"

"Is that the urgent problem you were going on about? When did you find out I was meeting Walid?"

"I've known for ages."

"So why are you bringing it up only now?"

"Because I can't bear to stay silent any longer. Lots of our friends have found out about it."

"Who, for example?"

"Are you trying to cross-examine me, or what? The point is, I can't stand the thought of it any longer."

I had to marshal all my courage and obstinacy. "Tariq," I said, "you know no one's closer to me than you are; perhaps even more than my own mother and father..."

"That's why I'm bringing the subject up in the first place," he interrupted. "I don't want you to get hurt. Do you understand?"

I carried on with what I wanted to say. "Is it such a big thing," I said, "for me to have a relationship with a man who's been one of your closest friends for so many years? Don't you love him as a friend?"

"But... there's such a big difference in age... and in background... a... a thousand differences. Walid's a famous man; any relationship you have with him will be public knowledge in no time."

"The relationship's been going on for more than two years, in case you didn't know."

"Are you planning to get married to him?"

"Probably not."

"Then what's the point of..."

"I love him. Isn't that enough?"

"Of course it's not enough. You speak as though you were born yesterday. Listen. You've got to stop seeing him. I don't see him much myself these days, as you know."

"That doesn't matter as far as I'm concerned."

Tariq didn't answer. He drove the car in the direction of the suspension bridge, which we crossed before heading toward al-Jadiriyya and the university buildings. It was a splendid night, beautiful and sad, as April nights often are. I dearly wished my companion could be Walid himself, with all his sorrows.

"Don't you find Walid strange, cryptic, incomprehensible even?" Tariq suddenly asked me, as though his prolonged silence had been an extension of his own thoughts.

"What do you mean?"

"Every woman he's had an affair with . . ." He looked in my direction in the darkness, then stopped.

"Yes?"

"Every woman he's had an affair with has been driven to madness or hysteria. You may not be aware of it, but I treated his wife some years back, in 1957, if I remember. You know she went mad, don't you . . . ?"

"Rima? Tell me about her."

"Then there's Maryam al-Saffar. Has he told you about her?"

"No, but I know enough."

"No, you don't. You don't know a thing. I treated her, too; she was right on the brink of madness, and I managed to save her. What do you know of things like that? Do you want me to see the day I have to treat you, too?"

"My darling Tariq, the day I go mad, just leave me alone, I beg you. If you really love me, don't interfere in my relationship with that man. What does he have left? His books?"

"He has a lot left, so don't get sad. He has money and friends, and you know who they are."

"Yes, and he has enemies, too!"

"And he has Wisal Raouf as well. How lucky he is to have her!"

"Tariq!" I said slowly, almost as though I were showing him a part of himself he'd unsuccessfully been trying to keep hidden. "Tariq, you're jealous, jealous of Walid! It's incredible! Why are you jealous when he's never been your rival in anything?"

He gave me a furious look, and seemed about to make some terse response. Then he calmed down and looked straight ahead at the road again. "You're free to do as you please," he said. "Shall we go to the club?"

He didn't say anything more about it after that, or threaten me with violence. For my part, I didn't burst out into anger or weeping. That was a phase I'd already passed through and left behind me.

Or perhaps, rather, it was a phase reserved for the unseen future, and the not-too-distant future at that.

5

Two or three weeks later Tariq came to visit, bringing Samira and the children, and Kazim Ismail came as well. I hadn't seen him in a while, ever since that day he'd come to see us carrying the burden of all mankind's miseries on his shoulders, because Sawsan Abd al-Hadi had turned him down as a husband even though his family and ours had interceded on his behalf. She was sorry, she'd said, but although she had a great deal of respect for him, he was much older than she was! What she really meant, I had no doubt whatsoever, was that, though Kazim might be an author of a certain significance, he'd never achieved anything in his life to make a woman want to throw herself at him, even if she was a widow—in this case a widow with a superb figure who spent her life living out her dreams in paintings that she filled with her real lovers. Who is there, Walid, apart from you and me, who understands all this?

I wasn't all that keen on greeting our guests, but they were all involved in family merriment and insisted on dragging me into it. My father took them out to the garden to show them his latest rare roses, especially a violet-colored one he'd at last managed to grow, and three others. "As splendid as dawn itself," my father said, remembering all the right clichés by heart in true politician's fashion. "I'm going to call it 'Wisal,'" he told them all, "and I'll write to the Rose Society in London to tell them about it. I'll spell it W-i-s-a-l, the French way. What do you think, Doctor?"

"The doctor shares his father's opinion," Tariq replied with a laugh. "How could he even dare to say anything else?"

"Abu Tariq," Kazim said, "I'd like three clippings from your wonderful bush, bird's beak."

"You're too late," my father replied. "You should have told me last February. I'll save some for you next autumn, though." And then he added archly, "By that time we hope you'll have found some nice girl who suits you. What on earth are you doing, fooling around with artists, you devil?!"

Kazim gave me a really miserable look, and my heart sank. I felt like shouting right into his face: "Don't I have enough misery of my own, you wretch?!" I went back inside the house, and after dinner I retired to my room. I was surprised to see Tariq come in and close the door behind him.

"Are you cross with me?" he asked. "Come on, give me a kiss!"

He kissed me on the cheek, just as he did when I was a little girl. Then he stood there in front of me and looked straight into my eyes. "What news do you have of him?"

I shook my head and said nothing.

"Kazim and I visited him a few days ago. Did he tell you?"

Once again I shook my head.

"When's he going away?" he continued.

"In two or three days," I replied.

"When exactly?"

"Wednesday, by car."

"Really? That's the same day Kazim and I are leaving."

"How odd!" I said.

"It certainly is odd!" he replied. "We're going to Lebanon and Greece in my car. Do you want to come with us?"

"Oh yes, I'll get ready right away!" I said sarcastically. "If you happen to meet Walid," I went on, "look after him, won't you?"

"As you command, Madam," Tariq responded with a laugh. "But do give just a little smile! Don't you realize: the world's still going around as usual?"

With that he opened the door and left.

10

Marwan Walid Attacks Umm al-Ayn with His Colleagues

Ramat Yusif is almost on the border. It was originally an Arab village called Umm al-Ayn, and was occupied by the Israelis in 1948, after which they expelled the Arab inhabitants and changed its name. Then they fortified it and, in recent years, bolstered its defenses with artillery, machine guns, and some armored cars. It's a mountain village of medium size, surrounded by orchards, and all around them are olive trees and oak groves climbing up to the very topmost point of the rise, in the middle of which the village was built. Day after day we studied the layout of the village on the maps we had with us, and its topographical features were explained to us by Uncle Uziyy, who knew all about it, because he'd been one of the inhabitants forced to leave twenty-three years before. He'd been a young man in his twenties then.

The Front decided we should attack Umm al-Ayn in an operation involving three groups; the first would attack it from the northeast side of the hill; the second from the east, which was where the oaks began; the third from the south. It was to this third group that I belonged. To avoid detection, we had to descend a rocky valley full of boulders and thorns, and then move upward toward the village.

Our group moved toward the target area at ten o'clock on a moonlit night, and we walked in single file as far as the area close by it. There were about forty of us in this particular group, moving in small subgroups of ten men with weapons and ammunition. One of us, Abd al-Rahman, carried a medium machine gun to give us greater firepower, while another, Jamal, carried a first-aid pouch in addition to his machine gun. Everyone was carrying extra ammunition along with their weapons. I myself was carrying a mortar and four shells, and in my belt was a small revolver Usama had given me at the base, to protect myself if my shells gave out and I found myself facing the enemy directly.

At eleven, we received the order to start the operation, and we moved forward, group by group, in total silence broken only by the sound of gun belts and pouches banging against our bodies. It was a long walk to the point from which the village was to be attacked and penetrated. The side of the valley was extremely steep, and, as we moved down, the downward pull of our heavy weapons dragged us forward, and the legs of our trousers were full of thorns. After a while we changed direction and started climbing among the rocks and trees until we reached our positions. Then we spread out, each group moving to its particular point of alignment with the hill, according to our prearranged plan, so that it would be directly in line with its primary targets. We began to creep forward carefully, getting as close as possible to our targets without being spotted, while the other two groups moved into their own respective assault positions. We moved forward with our bodies bent, then on all fours, and finally crawling, until at last we were within sight of the first distant buildings marking the edge of the village. At this point, we paused, waiting for the signal to attack.

This was my third operation, but it was a much larger one than the previous two . . . I felt a sense of inner satisfaction I wasn't expecting. It was strange how I didn't feel afraid or tense, nor was there any of that debilitating nervous enthusiasm I imagined must precede combat, which I'd certainly felt the two previous times. I looked at myself deliberately, calmly—as if from a distance, as though I wasn't actually lying there with cautious resolution among the olive trees. I was filled with a sense of satisfaction at what I was doing; the Palestinian night was quiet, and there was a wonderful cold nip in the air. Beyond the olives I could see the cascades of apple blossoms gleaming a green-silver color in the moonlight, and I savored the smell of the dewy soil. The sky was clear, and the light of the waning moon still left several stars visible. Calmly, I rested my head on my weapon. "Are you happy,

Abu Awf?" I whispered to Abd al-Rahman. He clasped my hand without saying a word.

We received the signal to start the assault. We'd already decided not to move at once, but to wait for a little while. The sky lit up all at once, while Abd al-Rahman and I were still lying in a depression in the ground, waiting. I felt impatient, yet, at the same time, unruffled, a strange contrast of emotion. Explosions followed along with the sound of gunfire; the air became thick with the flashes from explosions and the tracery of bullets. Meanwhile, the groups to the left and right of us set off, letting loose a mixed barrage of gunfire and rockets on the fortified posts and the positions facing us. For a period all I saw was the flashes of exploding shells. Whenever a rocket was launched, there was a powerful flash that lit up the trees all the way to the horizon. It would head toward its target, and I'd watch it speeding on its way like some brilliant red star that quickly died away.

The enemy responded with the same intensity, bombarding us with heavy machine-gun fire. The bullets were flying over our heads; they came from a point high up on the escarpment overlooking us, and there was another machine gun firing at us from straight in front, while a third position was lobbing shells at us, not from the village itself, but across the dark, deep valley from the top of a mountain far to the south. The bullet trails crisscrossed in the sky, painting stunning designs across the different parts of it, to which was added the tracery of other bullets that ricocheted from rocks and flew in other directions. The view from the hillside seemed full of white stars scattered throughout the heavens, with other lights from bullets reaching the end of their journey, or else exploding in the sky, adding yet more flashing stars to the scene.

Then our group's turn came. Our first target was a position made up from piles of sand, which was just in front of us, on the ground-floor level of a three-story building. In a trice we were exchanging fire with guns in every window of the building. Then, suddenly, we found ourselves under attack from the rapid fire of a machine gun coming from the window of another house a short distance to our left, but at a level lower than ourselves. None of us was hit; an enemy soldier was probably firing it at random to scare us and give himself some courage. Abd al-Rahman put his medium machine gun between his legs and started firing in long bursts. Jamal and his group now started engaging the fire of the three-story building, while I joined the action by firing a rocket at the window in the other building. There was an incredible flash, and the enemy machine gun stopped firing immediately. Two soldiers emerged from the building and started running, but Abu Awf got them with his machine gun, and I saw them fall to the ground simultaneously.

Our reactions and responses in the attack were swift, and I was surprised how undisturbed I was by the enemy fire, as we lay there sprawled or sitting on the ground. I surveyed the spectacle with a cool, conscious eye, noting the way the flashes from the machine guns and rockets lit up the entire orchard; it was as though the mountain terraces were a theater illuminated by gunpowder, while we were the spectators, and the thunderous noises were playing their various parts.

We managed to finish off this nearby position fairly quickly. Even so, there was still a great deal of gunfire from various directions, and the roar of explosions became louder and more frequent, getting gradually closer to our position. We realized this was a counterbombardment. As the shells cascaded down all around us, Abd al-Rahman and Muhannad cursed them for all they were worth. I remained silent, watching and listening. Sometimes, I could hear the whistle of shells as they approached, above the din of the battle; at others, the first thing I was aware of was the explosion itself. The brilliant flash would catch my eye, and it would be followed by the shattering percussion of the explosion. I noticed a strange noise accompanying the explosion of the shells, like the beating of gigantic flying insects. This, I realized, was the sound of shrapnel, scattering and bringing death with it. It was falling all around me now after every explosion, like olives falling from the branches of the trees over my head.

The sounds of shells and bullets blended together, and the pounding of the machine gun across the valley continued, producing a continuous red tracery of gunfire, in a curved line like a stream of red urine. And then there came a new sound to permeate the atmosphere, the whining sound of the incendiary shells the enemy was firing to light up the battlefield and identify the position of each one of us. Whenever one of them burst, it made a whispering noise like the sound of a candle being lit. With these brilliant moons descending all around me, I lay spread-eagle on the ground, tailoring my body to the contours of the land, waiting all the while for a fresh order to move. I took the rocket pouch off my back and put it under my body together with my rifle to protect the heads of the rockets from the possibility of being hit and exploding. My left cheek was against the ground, my right touching the cold steel.

Meanwhile, the group to the left of us had been moving forward in accordance with our plan, led by our unit commander, Abu Raaid, a daring, stubborn, impetuous man with a tremendous love for the men under his command, and equally fanatical with them if the slightest mistake occurred. I aimed the launcher and fired a rocket a specific distance in front of him. The group waited for a short while, and I fired another rocket. "The village is finished now," said Abd al-Rahman. "We're going in . . ."

We started running between the trees one by one toward the darkened village, and our group, Abu Raaid's, started going through the houses, clearing them as we went. We were stopped by a sniper. Abu Raaid took cover for a moment, and we heard him open a savage burst of fire. Then he came back into view, waving us forward. In the center of the village we seized a heavy machine gun. Muhannad rushed over to it, turned it toward one of the houses, and unleashed a burst of fire at it, laughing and cursing the whole time as he did it.

By now it was almost four o'clock in the morning. Each commander did the rounds of his unit, checking both men and ammunition. We had some wounded, but they were able to walk, with whatever difficulty, except for two who needed to be carried by their colleagues. Then we started the return journey through all the rocks and thorns, moving in single file as we'd done coming in. Shells started falling all around us again from the distance, accompanied by the bullets of snipers searching us out in the darkness. The moon had set now, and it was pitch-dark.

The return journey's never like the one coming in; it's hard moving downhill, but going uphill's even harder. But my mind was clear. I'd entered Palestine as a fighter! I'd give my father all the details, sending him the news in Baghdad when I got back to the base. I'd ask him to tell Wisal, "This is the start of my fulfillment of the pledge." She'd understand. My mind was clear, and my pouch, with its last remaining rocket, was banging against my back. A shell exploded in the sky overhead, painting the entire hillside in a silvery light, and for a fleeting moment dozens of moving black shapes could be seen, black shadows caught in the light. Then the approaching shell warned us with its usual whining noise, and everyone threw themselves onto the ground behind rocks or in the grass.

For all the repeated glare and the dwindling gunfire, we'd gotten away from the points of real combat. My heavy load, though, made me feel tired; lying low one minute, leaping up the next, and walking bent over the next—all this had exhausted me. I decided to raise my head and take in a lungful of cool, moist Palestinian air. For a couple of moments I walked erect to my full height, ignoring the whistle of bullets and scoffing at the possibility I might be hit, as though after this experience I'd acquired some magic protection against all enemy bullets. "Get down, Marwan!" yelled Abu Raaid from I don't know where. "The whole world can see you."

I got down. Abd al-Rahman, who'd taken part in a number of operations before, was my guide. "Death's a tricky customer!" I remember him saying. "You've got to have even more tricks of your own up your sleeve, all the time." This time I got up extremely cautiously. I had to get back to the base. We covered a section of the rocky slope slowly and with great difficulty. As soon as we could turn north, the hill would provide protection.

Suddenly, my eyes were dazzled, and a noise that seemed to weigh many tons enveloped my head; I had no idea what it was. "Marwan!" I heard Abu Awf yell. "Marwan's been hit! Marwan!" The broad expanse of the sky was filled with one incredible face.

"Father, Father," I shouted, but no one heard me.

11

Ibrahim al-Hajj Nawfal Reveals Secrets Till Dawn

You trees of the Khabur River, of the Tigris and the Euphrates, of all the rivers of the whole world, how is it I see you in leaf? It's as though you feel no sorrow for . . . but no! You trees will never have any feelings of sorrow. If mankind feels no sorrow, why should you? Who is there today who can summon up any feelings of sorrow? I shall proclaim mourning by putting on brightly colored clothes, and by drinking arrack and whiskey, whichever's easier to get hold of. Show your leaves then, trees, and burst forth . . .

Every single night, I miss him; every day I think of him. I see him in every eye where a glance of love appears. We'd talk and argue without ceasing, he and I, and arguing with him was far more enjoyable than agreeing with others.

"This conversation of ours is very revealing," I used to tell him. "It tells us a lot, doesn't it, about the hidden recesses of our thoughts?"

"No," he'd reply, "it tells us very little; in fact, it covers up a great deal. Do we have the necessary courage to delve into all the corners of our inner feelings, our desires, our dreams, our fears, our joys, what we're afraid of and what we hope for, our experiences, both enjoyable and scandalous? Shouldn't we leave them completely or at least partially in the dark, in case something comes out? Suppose I were to try and say everything? How difficult that would be!"

That's the way he used to talk; and like me, he enjoyed talking far more than most other men like fondling a woman's breasts. Every time I start by saying I'll try to peel off just one of the many layers enclosing my own self or selves; but no sooner do I peel off that one layer than I find myself putting another in its place. Even so, I'll try.

In a way Walid reminds me of Alexander on the day he decided to acquire the secret of eternity. These conquering tyrants subdue the world (because they love it so much!), then go searching for eternity. Gilgamesh did exactly the same thing: the people of Uruk suffered at his hands, and then he grew up, came to his senses, and decided to acquire the secret of eternity. And when, after much struggle and hardship, he got hold of the plant that would give it to him, a serpent ate it and gained eternity in his place. Alexander went to Babylon (where they no doubt told him the tale of Gilgamesh), but he didn't learn his lesson.

Alexander mounted his horse and took a girl along with him to act as his servant. That at least is the way it was in the story my father told me, but we all know those world conquerors can't keep their hands off a woman for a single night, and in the end find themselves conquered, in their turn, by the fair sex. There came a Greek or Babylonian goddess, Juno, perhaps, or Inanna or Ishtar, to guide him (or was it to lead him astray!). Traversing the desert wastes, Alexander was amazed by the limitless plains of Iraq. Eventually, he came to a well guarded by serpents and knew at once he'd reached his goal. The water of eternity was gushing from the depths of the well, and all he had to do was kill the serpents and take a drink. "O Alexander!" said one of the serpents, reading his mind. "It's vain for you to try to kill us. Rather, fill up your water skin with the well water, but don't drink it here. If you try, one of us will bite you before the water even reaches your lips. Take the water with you and travel for twenty parasangs. There you'll find a beautiful orchard. Hang the water skin on the branch of a tree and sleep beneath it until you're fully rested. Then get up and take a drink, alone and slowly. Thereafter you'll be one of the immortal..."

Alexander filled his water skin, loaded it behind the girl, and urged his horse on toward the promised orchard. But, although the horse galloped at full speed, it still wasn't reaching it. This went on for several hours until at last Alexander saw some trees in the distance, which he took as a good sign. He had hardly gotten there, though, when he felt extremely tired, dismounted, and told the girl to hang the water skin on one of the branches and keep watch over it. He tied the horse to a tree, lay down on the green grass, in the luxuriant shade, and was soon sound asleep . . . Suddenly, along came a black raven, which landed on the water skin in full view of the girl, pecked at the water skin with its sharp beak, and pierced it. The precious water started leaking out, and the girl sipped a small amount of it as it was falling to the ground; the raven, meanwhile, drank its fill.

The girl woke Alexander, who was very angry at what he saw, after all the effort he'd gone to and all the exhaustion he'd suffered. Then, when the girl told him the raven had drunk from the water of eternity and she'd taken some, too, he lost his mind, struck her with his sword, and cut off her nose.

Soon, though, he took pity on her and made her a nose out of clay. The result of all Alexander's efforts was that it was the raven who became immortal! According to the tale, the girl's still alive today, and throws herself onto the chest of any man she sees sleeping and gives him such a terrible nightmare he can scarcely breathe. She imagines that he's Alexander and refuses to get off his chest until he threatens to cut off her nose . . . all because she's afraid someone will find out her nose is made of clay!

All this reminds me of Walid, although, of course, with one major difference. He aspired in his own way, and achieved various things so that a raven here and another raven there could enjoy the fruits of his achievements, but he never managed to acquire even a grave that anyone could say with certainty was his. I have no doubt, either, that he, too, left more than one woman searching for him among all the others, fearing all the while someone might find out her nose was made of clay, but still searching nevertheless.

But I mustn't get carried away by analogies and stray too far from the facts, or else I might say something I didn't mean to say—just like the prince who said: "O Judge in Qom,"—and then got so carried away by his love of rhyming phrases that he went on: "You're dismissed, so be gone!" He couldn't think of anything else to say that would rhyme. No! I won't dismiss anyone, either from a love of rhyme or through a desire for perfection, even though there are many people I'd like to dismiss, people I see every day, who are much less innocent, far more iniquitous and deceitful than that poor judge in Qom. But then, God didn't make me a prince nor did He grant me a ceremonial sword from Yemen. Instead He thrust a bottle into my hand, so I could relish the sound when the top of it clanged against my glass and poured that golden fire from within it. "Ibrahim," He said, "speak!" So I spoke. And if the golden bottle doesn't make me talk, then the wolves of humanity do—if not in words, then in shouts. I long to shout, the same longing a prisoner has for freedom. I've seen many prisoners in my time, in Abu Gharib and elsewhere, who've told me I have freedom within my grasp, to which I've replied that it was beyond my reach, behind walls that conceal it, yet don't conceal it, as though there's clouded glass between it and me, and all my attempts to smash this glass, so that I can reach out to it and see it as it really is, as its Lord created it, all fail—the glass is bulletproof, and not even a hammer can smash it.

When I was young, I used to raise hell and cry in the house, every summer, about how I needed to travel to Europe, and it was through those journeys that I found some of the clamor I longed for. I knew well enough that my father, al-Hajj Nawfal Ibrahim, had large amounts of money that he kept hidden even from his wife, let alone his children. Who was he keeping all this money for, I used to ask, when he gave every appearance himself of being the pious pilgrim, ascetic in this life and aspiring to the life to come? In all the forty years he spent in business in the banking district on Rashid Street, my father never lost his instinctive skill. He made me study economics, even though he'd mastered it all himself without recourse to books or teachers. He managed to marry off all of my four sisters, Najla, Nawal, Naaus, and Nadaar, to "suitable" husbands, when they'd graduated from college and obtained jobs. He found each one (if she didn't find him for herself) a spouse who was reasonably well off. I remained at home, reading books, flirting with the Left (or so they said), longing for the proletarian revolution, and—out of either laziness or defiance—not lifting a finger at any serious job. Even in my father's office I found the so-called economic operation mechanical and wearisome, and begged my father to release me from the tedium of it all. My only interest was in writing. I even wrote about economics, and also about oil in the days when Iraq's demand for a 20 percent share in the revenues from the British Petroleum Company was regarded as a difficult national goal, one that would require perseverance and determination. When I had to find a job, I worked as a teacher in a private secondary school. My subject was English language, but through it, whenever I could, I also spread heretical views on economic and political subjects as well, something that didn't escape the notice of those in charge of the school, or of the government authorities.

I had some friends who were artists and gravitated to their circles, where I found that I had what they called hidden artistic tendencies, and decided to unleash them. And so I began to write about art. In the fifties (and, let's be frank, it's been true ever since), you could always write about art if you couldn't find anything else to write about. It never occurred to anybody to ask you what qualifications you thought you had that allowed you to set yourself up as a judge of artists. My own qualifications were my love for what the eye can see, my friendships with artists, and my ability to use my pen in any direction I wished. Every time I came home with Jawad Husni or Kazim Ismail, carrying yet another oil painting to hang on the wall in my room, my father would grumble at the futility of the whole thing and take me aside. "If you carry on like this," he used to say, "you'll land in prison or in al-Shammaaiyya. When are you going to behave like a rational human being?"

"Never mind, Father," I'd answer with a laugh. "I need ten dinars."

"Ten dinars? What for?"

"It's what the painting cost."

"Ten dinars? Are you mad? I wouldn't pay ten fils for it."

"Ten dinars, Father. You'll see later that I'm right."

"Heaven help us . . ."

At the beginning of the summer, voices would be raised in argument; there was no avoiding it. I knew very well that even though my father refused to give me any money at first, he'd untie the purse strings eventually. He'd always throw one or two hundred dinars in cash on the table, and then I'd pick them up and rush to the bank to change them into traveler's checks (having already prepared my passport for the purpose).

Thus it was that I got to know Walid Masoud in the early fifties; at the Arab Bank to be precise, with which my father did business. Our introduction was easy and quick, as Walid knew my name and I knew his, which the newspapers kept mentioning. We're the generation of the great leap forward, I used to say—although, in fact, Walid didn't come to Baghdad in the first part of 1948, but a year later, so he didn't see us all in the days of the great leap that was the beginning of real life: politics (as we understood it then), writing, art, arrests, and incredible utopian vision. We used to write in the local press and send our articles in batches to Lebanon and Egypt; by "we," I mean myself, Kazim, Jawad, Walid, and some others. We were all arrested in the wake of the 1956 demonstrations, and at the detention station in the government house we kept repeating the verses we'd memorized from al-Jawahiri:

> Consciousness is a disgrace, liberation is an outrage,
> whispering is a crime, and talking is forbidden.
>
> Anyone who defends himself is a saboteur,
> anyone who seeks his rights a wrecker.

On this occasion Walid was taken from his office to a police car and driven off to the Jordanian border where, because he wasn't carrying his papers, the Jordanian authorities refused to allow him across. So he was taken back to Rutba, then back to the desert again, then back to Rutba. They were just playing a cat-and-mouse game with him. All the while decent people in Baghdad were working on his behalf; we were all involved. Rima, his wife, was so worried about him she almost had a nervous breakdown. Eventually, the authorities agreed to allow him back when a merchant registered at the chamber of commerce posted a bond. He was placed under surveillance for a year, and subjected to various other kinds of constraint that are well enough known.

His book, *Man and Civilization*, was at the printers in Beirut at the time, and when he returned, we all advised him to have the date of publication delayed, but he insisted on seeing it published. The book arrived at the end of the year and raised a storm. Kazim Ismail made an entirely illogical attack on it, which was really an ad hominem attack on the author, then, a few months later, wrote another piece in which, in contrast, he dealt with the things we'd all liked about the book. None of us knew whether this was because he'd reread the book and changed his mind, or because he was trying to repair a friendship that had begun to show cracks at the seams, between Walid and himself, and, indeed, between me and him during this difficult period in our lives. Was the work really so incredibly important?

Years before that, at the beginning of 1951, I believe, Walid had been sitting opposite me at a table preparing an exchange transaction at the bank where he worked. Something about his appearance caught my attention and has stayed with me ever since. Was it his lean face? His wide eyes? His long hair? It's difficult to be specific. He looked like a hermit; there was something monkish about him that made him seem distant from you and close to you at the same time. It came as no surprise to me when I learned later that he had in fact been a novice in his youth. He could exert himself, concentrate, show discretion, laugh, and love all at once. He worked for himself and for you at the same time, and gave the impression that there was, within him, a capacity for sadness that was inexhaustible. At times he could be irritating in his insistence on the need for fairness, for the use of reason, for basing decisions on love and not on hate, as he used to put it. These were ideals that I was prepared to appreciate in other people, but certainly not in myself. When I felt love, I wanted to devour my beloved, but when it was a question of hatred, I wanted to smash and destroy. No reason, no fairness. But Walid was Walid. Whenever you argued with him about himself, he used to laugh and change the subject.

The day I met him, as I described above, he was submitting an economics exam to London University as an external student, and his books were on the table, along with piles of money orders, letters, and checks. He'd begun his studies several years earlier in Jerusalem, but his departure from there and his arrival in Baghdad (bringing, he said, only the clothes he was wearing) had delayed his studies somewhat. For a short while in 1948 he'd apparently joined the Arab Salvation Army in Damascus, until it was disbanded. He decided Baghdad should be a fresh start for him and for every Palestinian—in fact, for every Arab. It was to be the beginning of the second half of the century, the first real Arab revolution; and for the revolution to begin, there had to be a fresh vision of everything, from economics to poetry, one based on genuine knowledge. You had to know what everything you intended to reject really was, so that you could have a full understanding of its alternative. The purpose of vision (in the final analysis, after each political, economic, and artistic theory, after every clash and struggle) is to achieve a man closer to the ideal, a free man, a man who can be convinced, who can disagree, and who can reject. Such a man is the one who will, finally, renew the nation, give it a second birth, so that it can share in the progress of mankind.

All this is, of course, a gross simplification of the never-ending series of conversations we had. But I noticed something about Walid. Theoretically, his mind was wide open, and he refused to adhere to any one intellectual school (such as Marxism) that would assist him by channeling his energies in increasingly integrative directions. Instead, he imposed on his thinking a circular motion, which may have taken him up in a spiral toward some noble goal, but which also failed to provide him with a complete springboard for all his powers. He seemed very much like a bird with huge wings, flying around in a big hall and eventually bumping against the ceiling, unable to break through to the sky beyond.

That, though, wasn't the way he saw things. He believed his intellectual commitment didn't imply confinement within objective boundaries, and that it was his previous adherence to schools of thought that was like being cooped up in that huge hall, rather than flying in the limitless skies. In the final analysis, this is what lies behind the tragedy in Walid Masoud's life. He wanted to be a saint in a world of sin and corruption, an independent theorist in a world of political parties, an undogmatic dogmatist in a world of rigid primness. He wanted to talk in symbols whose semantic force he thought people would understand, but he forgot they aren't the same symbols that people carry around their necks like charms. He was amazed that (when all was said and done) only a few people really understood him, and those few were the ones who loved his ideas because they loved him personally, a love based on something that sprang from his eyes, his hands, and his voice.

Rima was always worried about him (this was before that fateful year when she finally broke down totally). She used to cling to him, argue with him, worry every time he went out, in case he got lost on the way home. God help Walid if he was ever late! She used to go out of the house and pace up and down in the street waiting for him, then she'd get in touch with all his friends one by one and ask for him. More than once she contacted the local police station and told them he was lost; and they'd go out and look for him, just as though he were a five-year-old child! That's why those days of his arrest and banishment were so terrifying for her; they gave her a cruel jolt and disturbed her mind.

She was a wonderful woman, and we all adored her. I was fond of her in a particular way. I seem to be especially taken by women who have a touch of madness about them: the roaming eyes, the disheveled hair cascading down like splinters of wood, the impetuous laugh, and coupled to that the suggestion of an enormous capacity to enjoy love and sex. He brought her from Jerusalem in the autumn of 1951, a short while after I first met him, and she provided him with a nice house near Antara Square where he could entertain his friends. In the two or three years before that time he'd met them in cafés on Abu Nuwas Street, in seedy hotels on Rashid Street, and in even seedier rooms with some families in al-Batwiyyeen. Then, all of a sudden, Walid became something new, a social being; he had, in any case, a lot of acquaintances and friends. But, from the psychological and humanistic points of view, he never changed till his very last day. Rima was effusive and merry—quite the opposite of what we'd been led to expect from his description of her background. She loved discussions and arguments, and the things she said created an impression of emotional tension that made her seem continually on the move. She was so proud of Walid it occasionally embarrassed him, and she tackled life with élan and enthusiasm. In addition to all this, she possessed a terrifying pride that everyone was afraid of rubbing the wrong way, because if that did happen she'd fly into a rage she made no attempt to hide. If she hated someone, she'd treat that person with unconcealed distaste, leaving him or her in no doubts as to her feelings. I admired her and feared her at one and the same time. Then, suddenly, she withdrew into herself and closed up like a cocoon, shutting herself off from everyone, even Walid. She no longer even cared about her son, Marwan, whom she had adored. This was the sad way it all ended.

There's more than one reason I remember all this about Rima after so many years. Some of these reasons have to do with me, others with Walid. As I've already said, and will keep saying, I like this type of woman who grabs at everything only to see it all slip from her grasp. In recent years I've grown, too, to admire that other woman in whom I see a touch of madness, Maryam al-Saffar. This overpowering folly in a woman, which turns her life, her relationships, her driving of a car, and her writings into total chaos, brings out the chaotic from deep within me, arouses the impetuous ape, the mad dog that I can no longer keep quiet.

And so I drink to confirm that this mangy, deceitful world I live in really is crazy. The day I learned Rima had been taken to the mental asylum, I wept, with a weeping so abject it sounded like the bellowing of a bull. Here are all these utter imbeciles around me, who deserve nothing better than to be chained up in a mental hospital dungeon created in the dark ages, filling the earth with their noises and their obscenities and their ugliness, while this beautiful creature, whose laughter pealed out like one of the bells of paradise, and whose lips suggested the luscious taste of pistachio, was put in an asylum forever. How can it be? Nature's cruel, criminal; existence knows no logic. I shall continue to reject it and any accommodation with it. Maybe that's why I've never married. The wonderful possessed women don't fall into my hands; they're afraid of my tongue and temper. If only they realized that my tongue and temper have other people as their targets, not them! I'd marry Maryam even if I had only one day left to live. I'd abandon all these other women; I'm tired of their big backsides and their cheap perfume and their coarse laughter. My father—God have mercy on him!—would forgive me; in fact, he'd be happy to see his sole male offspring marrying a woman who's "educated, rich, and well connected" and a university professor at that. Maybe then we'd be able to reform the world, too—now that it's too late.

What one-eyed devil prompts me to say all this? Perhaps the same one that once told me things that didn't so much surprise me as provide me with extra proofs of my craziness. It happened the day I accepted employment for a short while in the civil service before leaving it for good. It was Hisham al-Saffar who urged me to do it, immediately before his divorce from the dear lady Maryam. He invited me to a directors' meeting in his department, where I'd been given a post as an expert in foreign trade matters, the purpose of the meeting being to discuss an urgent moral problem. It had come to light that one of the senior civil servants in the department was having an affair with a young girl working in his office—at least that was what was being said, after due investigation, etc.... Mr. Hisham was extremely hard, in this closed meeting, on anyone who let themselves be seduced into fooling around. "Those who abandon the traditions of our people," he said sharply, "who advocate libertinism and exploit the naïveté of young girls..."—and soon to the end of the performance—"should be treated with the utmost severity. Laws should be promulgated to fine, dismiss, and imprison them, so that this virus of corruption can be eradicated from our society." Tremendous, absolutely splendid. But I also, thanks to my one-eyed devil, happen to know what went on that very evening.

Mr. Hisham went home after having dinner with some of his colleagues at the club, then took a short nap. I can imagine him getting up, having a bath, and then going directly to the kitchen to make sure the fridge had enough food for the evening. Then he took some ice cubes out of the freezer and put them in a silver ice bucket. In the bedroom he put a bottle of whiskey and two glasses on his wife's dressing table. Actually, he'd sent poor Maryam, his wife, away to Lebanon because she needed a rest, and his little daughter had been sent to her grandmother's to be taken care of there while her mother was away. No doubt the little girl enjoyed staying with her grandmother.

He headed for the telephone and dialed a number. "It's fine weather," he whispered, and a woman's voice answered, "Yes, but it's a bit hot." Half an hour later, when it was beginning to get dark in the city, a Volkswagen car pulled into the garage and stopped behind his own. Our friend came out quickly, shut the garage door, and bolted it; then, as the woman got out of her car, he took her hand and led her into the house. "What is all this?" the beautiful woman asked, bending and swaying as she fell into his arms. "I've been waiting for ages. Don't your meetings ever end?"

In the bedroom he showed her the new camera he was going to give her as a present—a Polaroid that could take color pictures and produce them on the spot. "It's wonderful!" he said. "Just like a tape recorder that can record whatever you want and play it back for you immediately. Isn't science wonderful . . ." She started to undress, one piece of clothing at a time, and he kept taking pictures of her and showing them to her. Terrific! Just like that. Turn this way a little . . . lift your breasts . . . jiggle them . . . fantastic . . . snap. Look! Your thighs, your buttocks . . . snap. Lie out on the cushion and hold this mirror in your hand . . . look dreamy . . . Goddess of love, that's you . . . snap. Some whiskey? Let me pour it into your navel so it'll flow down into the thickets of those love forests . . . then I can drink some of it . . . the recorder's on, of course . . . listen, those are your hot, exciting sighs . . ."

"Just imagine if your wife saw those pictures and heard that recording," she said with her naked leg in the air and the glass touching her lips. "Ha, ha, wouldn't that be funny?"

"Don't spoil my fun, please," he replied.

Next morning the meeting reconvened in the office to make a final decision. Once again, Mr. Hisham was extremely severe and filled our ears with the wisdom of generations. "Corruption," he told us all, "spreads through the body of society. We need an explicit law to deal with it. The institution of the family is in danger because of these debauchers who set sin and corruption in the place of a regular, upright life." That very afternoon, the same goddess of love was in my house telling me what she'd been doing with Hisham the night before. I, in turn, told her what he'd said to us in the meeting about the norms of virtue. She asked me to take some pictures of her with the camera, but I photographed her with all her clothes on. I refused to be like Hisham.

Within three or four months, Hisham and Maryam were divorced in a gruesome atmosphere of mutual recriminations that reached the ears of their friends in spite of all attempts to keep it a secret. I don't deny I heard some people whispering the name of Walid Masoud. (If he was in love with Maryam, good luck to him! Like me, he loves women who are possessed.) I didn't stay in my job in Hisham's department either, although there were other reasons for my resignation. I'd discovered that being a civil servant was a waste of time as far as I was concerned, quite apart from the fact that it's an insult to humanity most of the time. It is, I came to realize, an alternative form of slavery, one that's been organized since the days of Babylon and the pharaohs, is continually expanding, and allows masters to hold sway while their very underlings enslave underlings of their own. In this type of servitude every slave has his own pitiful portion of livelihood; every day the whip's cracked over his head in the form of orders and penalties, until, twenty or thirty years later, they're finally released as the time comes to retire. This freedom comes at a time in their lives when they've lost everything that might enable them to enjoy it; they've wasted their lives sitting behind paltry tables, oblivious of what they were doing to their own freedom, so they feel a longing for their old slavery again, and the longing itself is a further kind of slavery. No! I preferred the office my father left me after his death, even though business has shrunk considerably. For a while I kept up my connection with Hisham by way of the love goddess, Saadiyya Ulwan, and I've no doubt whatsoever that she supplied my friend with accounts of her antics with me. They're all traitors, the whole lot of them.

Oh yea! Come to the lamentations, all the joys of the marketplace, the congress of buyers and sellers! Another glass and things will get much clearer. Night's for wine, day for business. Night's a wedding, day's a funeral; from one ritual to another, RIP, and so on... I was talking about Rima's breakdown, the tragedy of Walid, and my own love for any woman who veers away from the logic of mankind. I recall the stories about that famous politician who went to a very quiet reception and sat down on one of the chairs that had been arranged in rows. He raised his palms in the air and began reciting the opening chapter of the Quran, and was amazed to be reprimanded by the person sitting beside him. The politician turned to his neighbor, "Tell me, for God's sake," he said, "is this a wedding or a funeral? I've forgotten."

"It's a wedding, my dear sir," was the reply.

The aged politician wasn't in the least put out. "There's no difference," he muttered to himself, then proceeded to drink the sherbet that was offered to him. No, there's no difference! Come to the lamentations, all the joys of the marketplace, the congress of buyers and sellers. The main thing is to keep moving.

Rima's breakdown was an incredible rebirth for Walid. He took care to get her treated in a clinic in Bethlehem, but for his own part he began living recklessly. Despair and hope were the same thing to him, and there was no difference between weddings and funerals. It became obvious to him that Rima would never recover. She remained in a total mental torpor, and this condition of hers behind the walls of the hospital unleashed a surging demon inside Walid himself. In just a few years his work and his ideas had taken him wandering among Baghdad, the Gulf states, and every region of the world. An innate bedouin streak, lurking in his very blood, was suddenly bursting irresistibly out. How did he manage to keep writing in spite of all this business and travel? He maintained his base in Baghdad among his many friends. It amazed me he didn't go and set up base in Beirut like so many other brilliant Palestinians. "I've put down roots in this city," he used to say. "Only those who've become addicted to this city can possibly know how wonderful it is. Each time I'm impatient to leave it and equally impatient to return. Until we can go back to Palestine, I want my son, Marwan, to live here." Who was it, I wonder, who told him Baghdad would be more faithful to him than it had been to me? Walid used to say things like: "The important thing is to love other people, not that they should love you." Amazing! What age were you living in, Walid? If people don't like me, I bring the world crashing down on their heads and then turn my back on them. They're all traitors.

OK, another glass. "What's all this money you and your colleagues have amassed, Walid?!" other Palestinians used to ask. "Why don't you live in the refugee camps and get your hands dirty? People like you would rather set up shop in the Arab capitals and get on with big business. It all makes other people jealous and makes you forget your first duty, toward your own country that we've been robbed of. Why aren't you coming forward to fight, with your bare hands, the wars all the Arab states with their armies are shirking?" And, of course, every time you do make a move, they'll hit you over the head again and pulverize the ground under your feet. They know well enough you're that fearful explosive force that's just waiting for the right moment to come, that you alone are the people who don't forget, and that without you the Arab world won't move forward a single inch. Paralyzed and petrified, these people want you to be paralyzed and petrified, too. They expect the volcano to swallow its fires and bury its lava inside its guts . . .

In those days I used to say a lot of things like that to him. And my hunch wasn't wrong either; the end of the sixties and the beginning of the seventies brought tangible proof of that. Walid was the kind of Palestinian who rejected, pioneered, built, and united (if my people can ever be united); he was a scholar, architect, technocrat, rebuilder, and violent goader of the Arab conscience. As I knew him, Walid would refuse to undertake any role he hadn't mastered. His most important task was to foster the new spirit based on knowledge, freedom, love, and a revolt against looking back—all this as a means of achieving the complete Arab revolution. In his view revolution wasn't merely a class-based change in governmental system, or a matter of replacing the Right with the Left or vice versa. To him revolution involved placing the Arabs within the ambit of the big wide world, then fostering their ability to persevere on the one hand and make a contribution on the other. If I don't consider Walid's life in this light, I'll never be able to understand him. I'll keep arguing with him, disagreeing and debating every point, but I've come to realize he's one of those exiles who'll use that vantage point to shake the Arab world into reexamining everything it's ever thought or made, and to fill the whole world with the word *Arab*, whatever epithets may be attached to it by enemies with all their complexes.

Wherever you find outstanding achievement in science, finance, ideas, literature, or innovation, you'll come across that exiled Palestinian: he'll be doing things, urging, theorizing, and achieving everything that's different. Whenever there's anything worthwhile, involving self-sacrifice, you'll find the Palestinian.

With that in mind, it's not surprising someone like Kazim Ismail should lean over and whisper in my ear: "Palestinians are dangerous . . . really dangerous." They come at you from behind, Walid. And you're not worried, you don't turn around, and you don't forget.

Come to the lamentations, all the joys of the marketplace. I've no idea anymore whether I'm optimistic or pessimistic. Wine can sort some things out in your mind very clearly, but other things just get fused together. Someone, I can't remember who, said that progress, when it's optimistic, always promises to bring a kind of divergence from history as we know it, a type of impetus toward another plateau in life. And sometimes I get the feeling we've started that "divergence from history as we know it." Everything's in the process of changing, thanks to my own recalcitrant generation. What plateau are we heading toward? Maybe Walid had the answer one day when the Zionists put him in prison after the June defeat of 1967, tortured him, and then threw him across the river. What plateau did he think we were heading toward then?

Whenever catastrophe's struck a man like him, he's emerged from the experience a more powerful, obdurate person. The plateau he was working toward then was right at the top of the mountain, even though he was limping and coughing and his hand shook when he lit a cigarette. For my part I spat on the world, and ever since then I've kept having dreams in which I spit on the world. When I get up in the morning, I don't feel like speaking to anyone; I'm afraid of seeing someone and being forced to say something. So I take refuge in the garden and water the grass and the flowers. I find I can have the sweetest conversation with them, or rather they talk to me in the sweetest possible way. People say I've become a misanthropist. And why not? Is there anyone who deserves to be loved—apart, that is, from Maryam and two or three others? I'm diverging from history toward a plateau I don't understand.

I'll go back now to that ancient Florentine writer, whose writings are so remarkable for their optimism. Walid translated one of his sayings for me once, and I gave it to Khalid the calligrapher to be done in Kufic script, then hung it up in the library where I can contemplate it afresh.

> God said to man: "You alone are bound by no constraint unless you adopt it through the will that We have given you. In the middle of the world I have placed you to make it easy for you to look around and see everything in it. I have made you a created being, neither earthly nor heavenly, neither ephemeral nor eternal, so that you might be the creator or your own self and choose which form to adopt for yourself."
>
> Pico Della Mirandola

How many times I've wanted to believe that! How often I've wished to be the creator of myself, to look around me from the center of the world and see what's in it! Under such an impulse, I've often written, spoken, traveled, loved, hated, and drunk. Looking around me and seeing, I take in everything. I reject any restraint, direct my will against any curb, and find the justification for relieving myself of anything not in tune with my wishes. Walid's undoubtedly linked to this in some way because of his insistence on that inner liberation I always reckoned was the real source of his incredible abilities. After so many years, with such a variety of intellectual and political affiliations, I found myself following his lead, or at least what I imagined was his lead. I never openly admitted it to him, nor did I pay any attention to his allusions to Saint Augustine. I was never able to follow the logic in Saint Augustine's difficult writings, whereby submission of his own self to the will of God had given him a freedom the intellect was incapable of grasping. In any case, the result I achieved was exactly the opposite of Walid's. All I could see in human beings was evil, meanness, and ignominy, and I wasn't for a moment convinced by their excuses.

Yet, in spite of it all, I can't isolate myself from people altogether. The cock dies with his eye on the dung heap; and inside the human dung heap I find temptations that are irresistible. Walid, on the other hand, whatever he may have said and however he may have behaved, could cut himself off from people in the last period of his life, even before his son, Marwan, was killed in a fedayeen raid, in which Walid himself would have preferred to be the one to die. Man isn't made of steel. A few months earlier I'd noticed he was keeping to his own company as much as possible, but, when the dire news came, I saw him go to pieces. He couldn't bear to see anyone, except for a few close friends, and those he'd listen to without saying a word.

For my part, I've seen just about everything that needed to be seen to make me keep well away from the human dung heap. I've kept prying, kept exploring, but, every time I do, the stench gets worse and I begin to drink even more. People say I'm a misanthropist, but I'm not. I love people for their black eyes. I love tramps and monkeys and pygmies when they boastfully display their private parts—as though God created them and then smashed the mold to pieces! Walid's well aware of my feelings; he's my opposite, my counselor, the one who despairs over me. Maryam should hear this, too, Maryam with her ivory skin and intense eyes, and wonderful temples. Without knowing it she stole me from Sawsan Abd al-Hadi, who for several months had been my shady oasis in the deserts of tedium and anger.

• • •

"Do you know Sawsan Abd al-Hadi?" Nawal asked me once.

"The artist?" I replied. "I've met her once or twice at Amer Abd al-Hamid's house. Isn't she married to Ala' al-din Sabri, the architect?"

"That's right," she said. "He designed our new house for us. He died a while ago. Did you know?"

"Ala' is dead?" I said in amazement. "He was a young man, wasn't he, about my age?"

"He got out of bed one morning, went to the bathroom, and fell down on the floor. Two hours later he was dead."

I was very sorry to hear it, because he'd been a gifted architect. "His poor wife!" I said. "To be widowed so young..."

It emerged that she was a friend of Nawal, who was the sister I felt the closest to, she being a few years younger than me. In her younger days she used to look to me as the one who'd guide people from the ways of error, and she'd always come to me whenever she found her homework too difficult or needed some kind of help she was afraid to ask from her father or mother. She'd read what I wrote, question me about my friends, and, when I grew a bit older, warn me about getting involved in things (she meant politics, of course) that might get me into trouble. Later, whenever trouble did come my way, she was always the first one in the family to come to my aid and take care of me. I wanted her to be married to one of my friends, but my father had more authority than I did, and he arranged for her to be married to one of our relatives. She made no objection herself.

"If you do find life unbearable with Wahhab," I told her a day or two before the ceremony, "don't come running to me for help! Do you understand?"

She burst into tears and put her head on my shoulder.

"OK," I said, relenting. "OK. You can come running! Marry him, and I hope I'll see you running to me every single day."

She carried on crying, and eventually the whole thing began to get on my nerves.

"I accept the whole thing, my sweet," I said. "I hope you'll both be happy together."

And, strange to tell, she was happy in her marriage, quite contrary to my expectations. She was just right for him, it seems; Wahhab must have known more about her than I did.

"Sawsan has a rotten life," Nawal told me.

"You should give her as much time as you can," I replied, "and not just you, Nawal, but Wahhab as well."

Just then a thought occurred to me, which stunned me at first; then the whole thing made me laugh. "I hope," I said, "you're not expecting me to marry her?!"

"You never stop joking, do you? I've suggested fifty girls to you before now, and you've refused them all. I'm not going to suggest any more from now on."

"Then send her my greetings, please."

"Have you seen her paintings?"

"Once or twice. They're not bad, considering she's a rare female in an area crowded with men."

"You don't care about my friends, Ibrahim. My dear brother, could I ask you to do something for me?"

"For you, my sweet, anything. Provided, that is, that marriage isn't part of the deal."

"No, I'm being serious. I'll take you to her house to look at the paintings, and, if you like them . . ."

"I know what you're going to say, Nawal. You want me to write an article about her. That's it, isn't it? Did she ask you herself?"

"Yes, she did, actually."

"And what will people say about Ibrahim al-Hajj Nawfal if he writes an article about Sawsan Abd al-Hadi after her husband's death?"

"When did you ever care what people said? Please don't start making excuses."

Without any particular enthusiasm, I agreed to go with Nawal to Sawsan's house. We went on the late afternoon of a many-colored day, and found her waiting for us, wearing a black dress. She had another friend with her, Jinan al-Thamer, and, in accordance with the social code, her younger brother was there, too; I forget his name. As I looked at her oil paintings, I started to feel a mounting interest in them. They were large, or the size I'd been urging artists to paint for many years, and they had a femininity about them that I couldn't pinpoint at first; then I began to discern its principal features. I looked closely at Sawsan's eyes, as though I were trying to detect some secret link between them and her paintings. Nawal and Jinan were looking at the pictures with me, and kept listening to my cautious comments and encouraging me to say more.

"Madame Sawsan," I said finally, "all these people are you: the children, the adolescents, the naked women riding horses among the rocks on the shore, divided and superimposed faces, they're all you . . . in a continuous dreamworld."

"Well, Mr. Ibrahim," she said, handing me a cup of tea, "is that what you'll write about me if you decide to do it?"

I took the cup without replying, not wanting to be overhasty and commit myself. I looked into her eyes and laughed.

Being in mourning, she wasn't wearing full makeup, and it was that, perhaps, coupled with the fact that she was wearing a black dress, which accentuated the paleness of her waxen features, the fleshiness of her generous lips, and the blackness of her eyes (which she'd made wider with some lines of mascara). Her face was clear and radiant, more like the face of a child gleaming with good health than of a woman giving out sexual attractiveness. Her black hair was tied up in a bun behind her head, which again highlighted the simple openness of her appearance and the whiteness of her neck. But, she certainly wasn't as innocent as her face might suggest. When you took a look at her paintings, they seemed more like time bombs wrapped in gaily colored paper. I decided to write about her, without worrying whether my decision reflected weakness toward her at that particular moment or a genuine interest in her paintings.

We were both ready to play, and scared as well. I wanted to see her pictures a number of times, and she made me welcome. On the initial visits, there were other people there, too, but then we started to meet alone. Our relationship lasted for a year or less, during which time I carefully reconsidered the whole question of art and its role in life.

"Art alludes to the liberation of man at the time of his creative impulse," I used to tell Sawsan, "and as such it can give other people the taste of freedom forever. Your pictures are a proof of this, a reflection of your attempt to find liberty. When I talk about art, I'm not talking about just your pictures or even only about painting. By art I mean all creativity, whether in pictures or in words. My writings, like those of every poet or novelist, find their existence crushed by the fever of creation. We're all slaves; we all want to find liberty, to give other people what we artists gain in those moments of incredible, painful ecstasy."

She'd fix me with her anxious, penetrating gaze. "You're the only one who understands my secret, Ibrahim," she'd say. "You're the only one. Liberation. I'm afraid to pronounce the word, yet, every time I hold a paintbrush and stand in front of an empty canvas, I can bring its meaning to fruition. The picture's my promised paradise, and, every time I finish a picture, I enter that paradise afresh. I enter it on the run, seeking refuge, feeling the agony of creation, enjoying a pleasure like the pleasure of love and a fear like the fear of death. Do you understand me, Ibrahim? What comes out in the end may not suggest these things because perhaps I'll fail. But the important aspect of it is the dizzying labyrinth I walk through on the way, which makes me feel as though I'd drunk ten bottles of wine."

I wrote a long article about Sawsan Abd al-Hadi's paintings, full of circumlocutions, and of my own doubts and ponderings. Every time I wrote a new paragraph in the morning, I stopped to see whether my aesthetic judgment and critical acumen had been disturbed by the sweet lips I'd sucked the night before like a man possessed. There weren't many hours of love, but those that did come were intense. "Ibrahim," Sawsan would always ask me, "how can you keep such control over yourself?"

"Control?" I'd ask.

"Yes, control. Can't you tell I'm going crazy, crumbling in your very hands. But you, who are so violent in everything you write and say, suddenly turn into the rational, logical philosopher. You give just so much . . . Oh . . . Oh, Ibrahim . . ."

That luscious green oasis almost managed to bring me back to reason, and love, and working for a future everyone claimed they were dreaming about—poor deluded fools and phonies that they were! I almost forgot about the human dung heap, feeling I'd once more become part of that creative operation that Walid, I, and others always say is the operation to save mankind... Walid had stayed behind in the Occupied Territories after the June War of 1967, and, when I started to get interested in Sawsan, we didn't know what had happened to him. Art at that time provided a means of deepening the wounds and soothing them at one and the same time; so in fact did my writings, although I wasn't publishing very much.

"Man needs art," Sawsan used to say. "It makes him reconsider his existence and his universe, his passions and his own being. Please, Ibrahim, will you teach me how to talk about my paintings? Your study will be published in the exhibition guide, which will give the critics something to talk about and make it easier for them to write something. But I should have something to say that is different from what you've written. Don't you agree?"

Poor Sawsan! The exhibition she was planning only became a reality a long time later. Maybe she was using painting as a way of rescuing herself from the pains of widowhood and loneliness, but in the months I spent with her I wasn't entirely happy with the works she produced—which only drove her to work harder. She produced a large number of pictures, painting every single day, night and day, and eventually I began to feel her painting had matured. She started putting in a lot of hidden allusions to our relationship; in fact, she never finished a picture without including some symbol or other with a sexual connotation, one that we both understood and that was tied up with our private experiences together. In her paintings I was looking for the same thing as in my own writings—if only I'd written anything of value—the kind of thing I saw in Walid's writings in years gone by: man's confrontation with the world, in his own particular way. Confrontation. Victory. Confirmation of the unique vision. Metaphysical revelation through the matter of life...

"Your problem, Sawsan," I told her, "is that, though you're clever, skillful, and beautiful, too, experience hasn't taken a big enough bite out of your flesh yet. You dream of experience. You used to dream about it all the time when you were young, and during your marriage, too, and you still do. Perhaps it's all because you're a woman and a

Middle Eastern woman at that. Your vision's stayed far removed from the human dung heap. It's merely ornamental—brilliant but marginal. Am I asking you for something I have no right to ask from a woman? Maybe, but you manage to put up with me, along with my drinking and my moods. Before society pounces on you, ignoring your artistic talents, I'd like to review the entire past, the history of humanity, from the time man used to kill wild animals and then perform a gyrating dance for his tyrant deity, making the night and the stars spin till he collapsed on the ground in a faint . . . I want the past to exist in the present. No, Sawsan, I don't just mean our heritage, but something more profound, more remote and important than that: all times, as they force the human intellect between the unknown regions of consciousness and unconsciousness . . . The labyrinths of the past are expanding, continually, and we're the masters of them all . . . We carry them with us as we wander aimlessly through the inner spaces of time . . . No, I'm not gabbling meaninglessly. The spaces of time that are carried by every second passing over the cells of our bodies, Sawsan, like the moments of your nakedness over my body, open amazing doors of consciousness, and we pass through them each of us following the other. Then we look behind but see neither walls nor doors . . . Is it love I'm talking about or art? Or something else? The moment I go out and hear your door shut behind me, the world expands in a way my mind can't believe . . . and then suddenly, there in front of me, I see the human dung heap."

Why was I so fond, at that time, of imagining Sawsan as someone far removed from bitter, hurtful knowledge based on experience? Why did I want to imagine the woman I loved as having just emerged from a crystal bath, purged of all the filth and slime of the swamp and keeping her memory free of all encumbrances but beauty alone—and a false and ridiculous beauty at that—and so on and so on? Our meetings became more difficult, more cautious and tense. They no longer satisfied my ever growing need to touch that playful feminine essence that lay hidden behind Sawsan's lips and eyes and voice. Then came the day when she "broke out" of her mourning, putting on a yellow blouse that vividly showed the curvature of her breasts and red slacks that did the same for her buttocks. She let her hair down, and it cascaded to her shoulders, black, thick, and gleaming.

Her laughter pealed in my ears like a Chinese cymbal. That day I finally realized that Ibrahim al-Hajj Nawfal was a stupid idiot who understood nothing about the world; cheated, a victim, a poseur. If Sawsan had killed me that day, I would have told her to kill me again, then a third and a fourth time. I went into politics and emerged empty-handed. I went into economics and came out of that empty-handed, too. I tried art, and emerged empty-handed yet again. I went into love, and all I wanted from it was death, for me to die so it was all over. The world's full of treacherous people. How can I possibly live in it without another glass, and another, and another?

"Sawsan," I told her, "kill me! Kill me as you alone know how my killing should be."

She looked at me from behind some locks of hair that had fallen over her face, her black eyes gleaming like a leopard's. Slowly, she ran her hands down her red slacks, over the edge of her buttocks, and then toward her middle where they met, while I stood in front of her, relishing every move she made. She was silent and determined. She came toward me and undid her side leather belt. Then, pushing me toward the chair behind me, she made me sit down, then sat on my knees, looking straight at me, with her legs wide open.

"OK," I shouted, "I surrender! Marriage, marriage!" That's an easy way of solving problems, I thought to myself.

But Sawsan didn't say anything. As her perfume filled my head with the clanging of cymbals, she just laughed and laughed and laughed.

Meanwhile, Walid had returned, carrying the world's tragedies in his eyes and on his shoulders; he was in a pugnacious mood and wanted to stay and carry on the struggle. He kept coming and going, visiting the capitals of the world. I used to see him in his house, in our house, and in the homes of Amer Abd al-Hamid and Jawad Husni. With a certain hesitancy I talked to him about Sawsan and discovered he'd known her and her husband, Ala', for years. He'd always thought, he said, that she was gifted, but her husband had been jealous of her and played down her talents. "As soon as she manages to break loose," Walid told me, "assuming that by some miracle she can, she'll be able to bring out her artistic aspirations. I don't think even she realizes how intense they really are." Her friend Jinan used to defend her, and, in particular, her need for a degree of inner stability so she could devote all her talents to her work. When Jinan came back from her visit to England with her mother, she was amazed to see the number of pictures her friend had painted and looked them all over one by one, hardly believing her eyes. "At last you've broken the circle for her, Ibrahim," she kept telling me. "Now, where do things go from here?"

One evening, Sawsan brought five large pictures to a dinner party at Amer Abd al-Hamid's house, and his wife, Ann (after taking down the other pictures that Amer had collected with his usual discretion and taste), hung them side by side on a wall of their large living room. The pictures were the talk of the evening, and it seems to have been this that launched Sawsan into areas of life she'd never encountered before. Maryam al-Saffar was there again, too, that night, having returned from her studies at Sussex University in England, and I'd hardly had time to shake her hand to welcome her home than I had a powerful, disturbing intuition: that, if I didn't watch out, this woman would disturb the peace of my life, shake my very existence, Sawsan or no Sawsan. In recent months Sawsan had been talking to me about Maryam nonstop, reading me her letters and telling me what she was writing to Maryam in return. Every time I told her how much I admired revolutionary women like Maryam, she'd tell me I knew nothing about her; she knew all Maryam's secrets, she said, and Maryam was far more brilliant than I could ever imagine.

"I'm going to write to her about you," Sawsan said.

And so she did. Then Maryam wrote back asking about me: Had I come to my senses? Had I written anything new? Had I said anything spectacular that was worth recording?

When I shook her hand, the feel of her palm and the friendly way she grasped my hand with her fingers (like a telegram delivered to me in Morse code) suggested she knew everything about me, and that I'd be like putty in her hands whenever she decided. I had the sudden desire to turn my back on her, so as to avoid seeing her eyes or figure, and have the power to reject this idea that was yelling and screaming inside me. I immediately sought refuge with Walid, who was deep in conversation with Amer and Jawad Husni about events in the Gulf. Sawsan and Jinan came toward us, while Maryam turned her attention to the many other people who wanted to hug her and kiss her and welcome her home. Then they all started looking at the pictures again. "Sawsan," they kept saying, "come over here and tell me! When did you change your style like this? Poor Ala', if only he were alive to see . . ." And so on and so on.

The next day Nawal came to see me unexpectedly, on her own. I'd just woken up and asked her to wait in the library while I took a quick shower. When I finally came in and suggested we go into the sitting room, she refused.

"There's no need," she said. "This is the room for me. New books? New pictures? Piled up all over the place! Why don't you let someone put your affairs in order!"

"That may happen in spite of myself, eh, Nawal."

"You obviously don't listen to gossip!"

"Gossip?"

"About you and Sawsan."

"Nawal, the whole thing was your doing. Are you sorry now for what you started?"

"I value Sawsan more than you realize."

"I know you like her. She likes you a lot, too."

"And I've started to hear some disturbing gossip."

"Yes, Madam, we understand! We'll get married and put an end to all the problems."

"They say Sawsan had an affair—before Ala' died, I mean—with . . ."

"Nawal, how much longer are you going to carry on with this nonsense?"

"Listen to me first. She had an affair with Amer Abd al-Hamid."

"Lies! I don't believe it! Friendship between the two families—that's all it was."

"She also had a relationship with your friend Walid."

"With Walid? And who else?"

"She paved the way for him with Maryam al-Saffar, Hisham's wife, before her divorce."

"What is all this senseless talk? Please, Nawal, this is just women's gossip, that's all. How could she have had an affair with Walid, and then moved aside so he could have an affair with her friend as well?"

"How am I supposed to know?"

"Don't believe everything you hear in this city."

"What matters, Ibrahim, is that I'm beginning to get worried about your involvement with her."

"Are they gossiping about me, too?"

"What do you think? Are they supposed to save you for some special occasion?"

"It's a serious relationship I have with her, Nawal."

"Please think about it a bit."

"The one who's really to blame is the one who started it."

"I asked you to write an article about her pictures, not get involved with a young widow who's prepared to seduce any man, married or unmarried. The strange thing is I've never heard any of these stories before."

"She's your friend, Nawal, remember that. And I'm forty-two years old. I don't need advice from my younger sister, even if she is my favorite and my darling... Jasim, bring in the tea!"

"It's just that Wahhab filled my head with all this stuff."

"Aha! So it's Wahhab you've gotten all these stories from! And where has he gotten them from?"

"From Hisham."

"Your honorable friend! Listen, my darling, one of Sawsan's old shoes is worth more than the whole of Hisham's head, and one of Maryam's old shoes..."

"That's enough! I don't know why I interfered in your affairs."

"Because you love me."

"Because I only want the very best the world has to offer for my only brother, marriage included."

"In that case don't listen to your spiteful friend. In fact, cut him off."

"Ugh! Give me some tea."

"I've got some cake in the fridge."

"Made by Sawsan?"

"Nawal!"

"I'm only joking. I daren't eat any cake. Can't you see I've put on weight in the last few months?"

"You'll get fatter still yet. Jasim, bring the cake from the fridge!"

"A lot of help you are, you wretch! Look, you know how fond I am of Sawsan. But I'm worried, very worried. Do you realize she's never once mentioned there's anything between you? How's that possible? But now keep calm and listen to the rest of what I have to tell you."

"The final scandal? The scandal to end all scandals?"

"Listen. It doesn't matter to me. Sawsan must be a very deep well, and I never realized it."

"I'm all ears. Tell me all."

"They say Sawsan is having an affair with Kazim Ismail. Do you know about that?"

"Ha! He's the only one of my friends left."

"Don't believe it if you don't want to. That's what I've heard. Do you want the truth? I've never heard anything about you and Sawsan except from you yourself. Maybe it's because I'm your sister. Nobody ever says anything bad about you in front of me. But they say Kazim's going to marry her, and here you are thinking you're going to! Have you ever mentioned marriage to her?"

"Kazim? That's funny! The three of us have met together, it's true. But it never occurred to me . . ."

"My dear, another cup of tea, please."

"Everything you say is nonsense, Nawal. Do you realize that?"

"I hope it is."

"Tell me, do you know Maryam?"

"Hisham's ex-wife? Of course, you idiot. You keep forgetting Hisham's one of Wahhab's oldest friends. But we don't see much of Maryam these days."

"She's been abroad and now she's back."

"So? Don't you know her?"

"Yes, but I'd like to see more of her."

"From a widow to a divorcée! What comes after that, Ibrahim?!"

"She's a wonderful woman."

"Clever, very clever. But she's disorganized and confused. I'm surprised she managed to finish her studies. Sawsan's very fond of her. If you decide to marry Sawsan, you're bound to see a lot of her."

"God help me!"

"Look, my dear. Get these women out of your mind. Think of Jinan al-Thamer. At least she's not married."

"No, no, please, Nawal! Jinan isn't my type."

"So, are Sawsan and Maryam your type? OK, listen. Do you know Wisal Raouf, Dr. Tariq Raouf's sister?"

"Who? Oh, yes, I know her. I've met her a number of times. She's a beautiful girl, but she's young, very young."

"What do you mean, young? She's more than twenty-five, if not closer to thirty."

"No, no! Wisal reminds me of a tiny genie who's gotten lost. We've spent all this time together, Nawal, yet you've no idea of my taste in women."

"OK, fine! But please think things over a little. Friendship's one thing, but marriage is quite another."

"Any more advice for me? Each piece will cost you a piece of cake piled high with cream."

"If you'd only listen to me, I'd eat the whole cake and get as fat as a bear. Ah well, 'if she'd only seen my eyes . . .'"

"Ah, if she'd only seen my eyes." O generation of vipers! Another bottle, like a bride . . . I drink to your memory, Walid, father of Marwan, till my whole head turns gray, and all my friends and all the most gorgeous women follow suit. I'm still at the center of the world, looking around me, seeing ravens pecking away at the water skins, one after another, and letting all the water out in the hope of getting a couple of drops out of it. I've never seen an evil person who didn't want to live forever. So let's fill the water skins with urine, with filth, colocynth, foul poison. Then let the traitors drink just as much as they can. They're all traitors. And that was Kazim's portion of the fabled water skin. He didn't marry Sawsan. They were engaged and so on, but I don't know exactly what happened because I didn't want to know. I didn't ask him, Sawsan, or anyone else. The important thing was that this brought about another break between Kazim and the others, and once again a new streak of rancor came into his writings, which were bitter enough in the first place.

For my part, after that one occasion on the day Sawsan "broke out" of her mourning, I never raised the subject of marriage with her again. Maybe she realized, with that keen artist's sensitivity of hers, that when I felt my emotions getting the better of me and keeping me awake at night, I prepared my way to beat a dignified retreat. The gossip Nawal passed on to me (which was wrong for the most part) didn't serve to sharpen my resolve for the challenge; rather, it provided me with the turning point I'd been waiting for. I've no doubt I would have reached this same turning point, and followed it up, even if Sawsan hadn't had other lovers or suitors. Maryam was a wonderful turning point, too! It was just as though someone had been walking on rugged mountain terrain, then suddenly came across a side turning that brought him into a deep green valley with fruit glistening on the trees and water cascading from its rocks . . . Oh, I'm a traitor. I'm the one who said Sawsan was my oasis, then, a mere half hour later, I've made her a rocky path in the mountains. I've never preserved a mountain or valley in all my lifetime. Did I keep running away from women only to brush with them again, as Walid did (or, at least, seemed to me to do)? How many women had he known before Rima and then, more to the point, how many after her? I felt there was something deep down inside him that he refused to submit to any woman. As soon as his emotions reached the point of bursting, and he began to worry something deep inside him might take fire, he'd give his beloved the cold shoulder as a means of prevention, of protection; it was as though his decision were based on some inner experience, and he were unwilling to release his control over it. After such an experience, what did women have left? A suppressed love or a hatred that appeared as mere insouciance on the surface, but deep down was a self-consuming flame?

The night's long. I had no idea I'd be able to keep watching it as it moves along like a train, getting smaller and faster and never ending; or like one of Alexander's serpents, moving yet always in front of me. I stagger my way back through the rainy night on the earth pavements, going back where the police stations are and the prisons that look like colonies of ants. I break the traffic regulations and pay the fines. The old dark schools with their never-ending noise, their foul breath and squandered enthusiasms, they're still there filling up the scene that's forever expanding and contracting (but it's not the scene of the valley, of the dear enticing stealer and savior Maryam). I go back to where the bald and the bushy-haired are equal; to every party that looks like the feast of a jackal or a stork, to where the sparrow laughs at the stork; to where you've no sooner recovered from the hand of the robber than you fall into the hands of the fortune-teller. The people of the marketplace fall all over you, and the smile beneath the bushy moustache says to you: "You want a rabbit, take a rabbit; you want a gazelle, take a rabbit." But I came to my senses and repented. The night's long. I still have the wish not to disappoint my father in his grave. I'll add to the money I inherited from him, even if it's only two dinars. Or at least I won't lose more than half of it, or maybe three-quarters . . .

I don't know what my sisters and their husbands want from me. If I sell off land, its my property and I've the right to do it. If they feel like complaining, they should wait till I start cheating and swindling and selling off their land and houses, and then spending the proceeds in London and Berlin and Paris. Many's the time I've marched with demonstrators in London, without caring just what it was they were demonstrating about. They were against something established, and I'm against everything established, so why shouldn't my shouts be added to theirs? But they don't shout in London the way we did in the old days in Baghdad. If the guerrillas had agreed to take me, I would have been with them every time they decided to hijack a plane. But they say I'm too old! They don't believe me when I tell them how in May 1968, when I was in Paris trying to bring off a business deal, I joined the students in their wild, destructive demonstrations. I used to write to Sawsan every day, telling her about the poems written on walls, the attacks on smart storefronts, the overturning and burning of cars on the Boulevard Saint Michel . . . Ibrahim al-Hajj Nawfal, you tissue of problems, lover of crises, broken reed, leaning wall, exhausted searcher for freedom! But I didn't write to Sawsan about the young revolutionary Yolande, twenty years old, wearing a denim shirt that revealed two rebellious breasts. She spoke with all the eloquence of Robespierre, demanding that all traitors should be executed. I didn't tell Sawsan how this girl took me back in the evening to her small room on the eighth floor of a building in Montmartre; we had to climb the stairs to get there because there was no lift. All there was in the room was an unmade bed and a table loaded with books, magazines, and posters. All through the night, she had me between her thighs and then she rolled over on to my chest. The sun came up.

"Ah!" she said with her lips on my neck. "The sun has no shame. It's caressing my buttocks!"

"What do expect it to do," I asked, muttering into her hair, "when you flash your buttocks at it?"

"Ow! Don't bite me," she yelled. "It hurts!"

We went down to the old café in the building, where we drank some café au lait and ate croissants and sweetened bread. She kept talking about Baron Haussmann, who, when he made his designs for Paris a century earlier, hadn't left a single boulevard without other streets crossing it—with police stations dotted around among them, of course, to put an end to any rebellion.

"Authority knows how to perpetuate itself," she said, "or at least it deludes itself it does."

That was the last I saw of the beautiful revolutionary. I returned to Baghdad without bringing off my deal (in fact, I completed things later in Baghdad and made an unexpected profit—and all thanks to Yolande, although she doesn't know it!).

The night's merciless. It doesn't move, yet it flies, like a lover's night. I keep digressing because my life's one long digression; then suddenly, the sun's up, like a one-eyed ugly hag, staring at me with her single eye, saying with a horrid chuckle: "Another day, Mr. Ibrahim!" Never mind, who cares! There's still some drink in the bottle, and the night's not over yet. They're all traitors, timetable makers, almanac compilers, star readers, those fortune-tellers who claim to know the unknowable. One thing I do know, Walid—it's not Socrates who said it, but someone else—and that's that you came and went, and it seemed as if you'd never come or gone. Yet, the nights we spent with you in this very room are preserved in stone on the walls. I can see them and hear them, like tiny statues, each one shedding a tear; they're drowning me in a flood of tears, deafening me with the noise of their wailing.

But, as you know far better than I do, all these things are merely allusions poets might make, things that, at one and the same time, embody reality and wipe it out. You're not here, and the nights don't cling to my walls. You're a hurricane raging inside my mind, and I carry your voice in my own when I pose the kind of questions you know full well: Which man is there who, when his son asks him for some bread, will give him a stone? Or when he asks for a fish, will give him a viper? We asked for bread and fish, and they gave us stones and vipers; and in the end your anger burst out in spite of all your love and composure. Something happened, and that was the straw that broke the camel's back. From June 1967 to September 1970 and March 1971, when your son, Marwan, gave his young blood as a sacrifice for the cause you believed in—I don't remember all the previous dates; how many of them there are!—you were angry and sad, but you didn't despair. Or did you, too, feel despondent? I'll never believe it. I'll never believe you simply disappeared into the desert like some mirage, as a statement of your final attitude toward the world. I knew you too well for that. The hurricane that is you still roars on in many people's minds, not just in mine. Can I contradict myself? I've done it so often before, so why shouldn't I do it again? I feel you're sitting on this chair right in front of me, taking short sips from a glass—out of politeness to me, because you really don't want anything to drink. What you want to do is talk and listen to me as I do one of my disgusting readings, which are bound to start something moving somewhere, someday.

But I know, without your needing to tell me, that "it takes more than humus to have a party." I see myself sitting in my office in the morning; I welcome a man, pay my respects, and offer him a cup of tea.

"Look, Mr. Ibrahim," he says, "you know me. I'm a simple man and frank, too. I like those kinds of people."

I nod my head in agreement.

"I like you, respect you, and wish you well," he continues.

"Thank you, thank you," I reply.

"Whenever I don't pay you a visit for a long time, my conscience pricks me and says, 'When are you going to see Mr. Ibrahim again?' I ask myself why I haven't been to see you. The thing is, not only do I like what you have to say, but, to tell you the truth, and I wouldn't say it only to your face but in front of witnesses as well, it's because I get knowledge and culture through what you have to say."

"Thank you, thank you," I say again, feeling embarrassed.

"My friend," he carries on, "how few really well-educated people we come across these days, people whose words are a pleasure to hear. Actually, the problem . . ."

At this point I anticipate a significant revelation. My friend slows his voice down to measured tones to give emphasis to what he's about to say.

"The problem is hypocrisy. People praise you to your face, but turn your back and God help you! You know me well, Mr. Ibrahim..."

Actually, I hardly know him at all, but I'm probably going to get to know him well. I listen in silence as he continues.

"You know me. I don't like hypocrisy or hypocrites. I don't like gossiping about people and saying things about them behind their backs. It's wrong, very wrong. That man, so and so, you know him, he's a nice fellow, not bad at all. At least, he seems nice enough at first. But it's deceptive. He's got a tongue like a serpent's. In fact, when you take a close look at him, that's exactly what he's like, a serpent, a slimy yellow serpent. If he weren't my friend, things would be easy. But a man knows more about his friends than other people do, Mr. Ibrahim. I know all his comings and goings and how he fills his pockets. He can't fool me with his pretenses."

What can you say to a swine like that, who talks about his friends and acquaintances in such a way? My hand wanted to reach out to the teacup on the table and throw it in his face, but I restrained myself. "It seems, my friend," I said, "as though you've just come out of the human dung heap. Is that right?"

He didn't realize I was putting him down, although he did seem a little bit doubtful. He gave a hollow laugh, and the words "Yes, that's right," escaped from between his teeth.

It's like that every day, multiplied by ten. Come to the lamentations, all the joys of the marketplace, the congress of buyers and sellers! I meet these buyers and these sellers, so it can be said that I'm doing something profitable, to keep self-respect, and my servant, Jasim, and my old car, and this drink, too... I'm going to sell our house in al-Aazamiyya with its view of the river. House prices are going up, and my bank account's going down. So let the buyers and sellers come together. Maybe among them I'll meet my beloved who must still be chewing over the details of my affair with Sawsan. I'm pretty sure now that, whenever Sawsan finishes a picture, a lover appears in the guise of a buyer who's read the things I've written about her and whispers them in her ear.

A few months after Walid's disappearance, Sawsan came up with a strange surprise. After a long period when we hadn't seen each other, she telephoned to say she'd decided to present me with one of her pictures. Her exhibition the previous month had been a success, and she'd sold most of the pictures. A number of articles had appeared: some complimentary, others bickering, still others steeped in envy. Malice was the hallmark of some, while others were dotted with something resembling the language of criticism, a curious blend of politics and art that was supposed to be taken seriously. But it was just more of the same pretentious drivel that fills the markets these days because there are no really good horses to be found... My own article was published in the exhibition guide and served as a convenient handle for extollers and detractors alike to use. And why not?

When Sawsan told me she was going to give me one of her pictures, but refused to tell me which one she'd be bringing to my house, I naturally assumed it would be one of the pictures that had been exhibited but not sold. Two hours later Sawsan was outside the door, opening the trunk of her car to get the picture, and turning it away from me so that I wouldn't see it until she'd gotten into the house. As usual her hair was tied back from her temples and over her ears into two ponytails. "With my profound gratitude," she said, in an almost official tone of voice.

It was a portrait of Walid Masoud, which she'd started many years earlier but never finished. Then, when he disappeared, she'd gone back to it and with a few strokes of her skillful brush created one of her most forceful pictures. In accordance with her style, she made minimum use of color, so the picture emerged as a mixture of drawing and painting. It had something of the style of Andrea Mantinea, the Italian Renaissance painter, of whom Walid was very fond because of the rock-solid firmness and sensitivity of his work. Walid had given Sawsan a huge book filled with his paintings; God knows when and on what occasion. She'd devoted a lot of study to it and tried to use it as an inspiration for her own style—in her own particular way.

I was delighted with the painting. "Wonderful!" I yelled and gave her a big hug before she even realized what my reaction was. Then I gave her a big kiss on the cheek. It was cold and as smooth as marble. I was amazed to find myself feeling as though I was kissing my sister, not the woman I'd regarded as my lover at one time! I took another look at the painting. "Where shall I hang it?" I asked.

"In the library," she replied. "It's the nicest room in your house."

I immediately got a hammer and nail, and we decided on the one possible place where the picture could hang—books covered almost all the rest of the wall space. We hung it there, and I agreed to invite her along with some friends to a dinner party at my house two or three days later. Then I had an agreeable idea. "I'd like to invite your friend Maryam as well," I said. "She's never been here before."

"I know you've admired her for ages," she said. "I'll tell her. In fact, why don't you write down her telephone number and get in touch with her yourself?" She gave me the number.

So it was that Maryam came to my house for dinner a few days later with Sawsan. Amer Abd al-Hamid and his wife, Ann, and Jawad Husni and his wife, Hala, also came. We all talked again about Walid, whose place was so obviously empty, and each of us took a look at the picture after dinner when we moved to the library, feeling as though he was with us again. Jawad, in fact, stood in front of the picture, perusing it with all the scrutiny of an art critic (something I hadn't seen in him before). "Wonderful!" he kept saying. "Wonderful!" This forged a bond between the artist and her admirer.

"Did you see my recent exhibition, Dr. Jawad?" she asked.

I didn't catch his reply, because I was too busy paying attention to Maryam. He clasped his huge pipe between his teeth, lit it, and let out a cloud of smoke. I noticed the two of them talking together, for several minutes, while we each took a chair. Then they came back, and I imagined his wife, Hala, heaving a sigh of relief as she saw her husband return to the fold after a reckless adventure—if only for two or three minutes—into regions fraught with unknown risks; here he was now, restored to the august demeanor of the great professor who clung to reason and avoided all perils.

Jasim brought in the coffee and handed it around, along with large glasses into which he started pouring cognac one by one. At this point Maryam got up and, with a movement of her head, pushed her hair away from her face. The beautiful glass in her hand looked like a rose from paradise. She walked over to a shelf where a number of Walid Masoud's books were all arranged together, and started running her fingers over them and counting: "One, two, three, four . . . I had no idea he wrote all these books. Have you read them, Ibrahim?"

"All of them. And I discussed each one of them with him as he was writing it."

"What about you, Amer?"

"I've read most of them. They're very revealing of his personality as I knew it. I can almost guess what's in the book before reading it. In my opinion, *Single, Multiple, and Absolute* is his best. Have you read it?"

"Yes. It may be his most mature work. But I prefer *The Well*, where he talks about his youth. He does it in such a way that I don't really know whether it's autobiographical or an attempt at writing a novel."

"It's part of his autobiography," said Jawad. "I urged him to write it for ages, but for him it had become a matter of recording his childhood, something he kept circling around and stopping at, but hardly ever broaching."

"Have you read all his books?"

"Of course, Maryam. I'm taking a second look at them now. I want to come to some conclusion. If nothing else than to sort out all the problems with my wife who keeps telling me to write my book about him and set her free!"

Hala laughed and crossed her legs. "I want Jawad to finish his work on the subject," she said, "so he can start thinking about something else besides Walid—God have mercy on him."

"God have mercy on him?" Maryam asked in amazement. "Why do you say that? Do you think he's dead?"

It was Hala's turn to be amazed now. "Isn't he dead? Where's he gone then?"

That was enough to start the same old argument all over again: where had he gone? Maryam wasn't able to confirm he was alive, but her intuition, she told us, made her think he was, although she couldn't explain how. "He's alive, just as he is in this picture," she added.

"So the two of us agree then," Sawsan shouted gleefully. "I wanted my picture to be my personal affirmation that he's alive—for always."

Maryam looked at me with her wide green eyes. (Maryam, if I don't marry you this year, then let me be eaten by the highway dogs!)

"Ibrahim," she said, "you know a number of Palestinians through your work and various friendships. Do you think Walid was a typical Palestinian?"

I didn't have time to reply. "Excuse me!" she went on, shaking her head to get her hair away from her right cheek. "That's a silly question. No one's typical, all the more so when he's someone as unusual as Walid. My real question is this: did Walid arouse all the interest, love, and maybe hatred that he did because he was a Palestinian, and because Palestinians have a particular corner of the Arab conscience these days? As far as I'm concerned, the answer is a categorical no."

It occurred to me, as I'm sure it did to Jawad and Amer as well, that, though she'd been accused in the past of being in love with him, she undoubtedly considered him important for other reasons connected with her own character. But Jawad insisted that Walid's background, from the point of view of both birth and political cause, was an important component of the subject.

Maryam didn't pay much attention to what he said. "That's true," she said, "but only to a certain extent. The important thing is that Walid was something else, something unique, different from other people and a contrast to anyone else. There are ideologues and populists who want to start an uproar and have the ability to do it; they like the whole world to know about it because they feel that's their right. But Walid wasn't like that. Absolutely not. At least, not as far as I knew him. There's also the man who does things, the activist, prepared to throw bombs, write secret posters, set booby traps for the enemy, all this without worrying whether the world knows about it. Walid had a lot of that type of thing about him; he wouldn't say anything about it or make it a pretext for his existence on earth. It was just a spontaneous part of his being, or a single aspect of it; and that was because there was an additional pretext for his existence that nourished the other aspect, and it, too, was spontaneous and essential. And therein lies the merit of this man who left you all without saying the usual good-byes to any one of you. And, alongside this anxious, self-questioning doer, there's the contemplative ascetic who, deep down, wanted to keep away from crowds and was bound up in his thoughts and dreams. Were these two levels in his life in conflict with each other? Who can know? The tragedy for us is that we know so little about his life. What do you think, Dr. Jawad?"

"You're right," he replied. "I don't think we know much about his life, or at least much that isn't full of errors and illusions, although we'd be justified in inferring a great deal from his books."

Maryam was revealing her true colors in this discussion. She seemed determined to shed light on something that had apparently been occupying her thoughts a great deal, but that she hadn't been able to clarify completely.

"Facts themselves are mercurial most of the time," she said, still standing by the bookshelf and fingering them with her right hand. "And Walid found himself following mercurial paths, slippery paths, just like all of us, except that his paths were worse than ours. They took him toward complex, unclear goals that involved a remarkable mixture of politics and theology. He may have been surprised when they crumbled in his hands, one after the other..."

Amer got to his feet, took a puff of his cigarette, and walked toward the oil painting hanging on the wall. He stared at it for a while. "We can do the rounds in talking about Walid, if we want," he said, still facing the picture. "But, as I see him, he was really a poet who wanted to write that one marvelous poem that... that can't be written... His life, his views, his end are simply parts of that poem he couldn't write. Here we all are, Maryam, myself and all of you, trying to recite the few scattered verses of his that we can remember, the way the reciters used to do for poets in the period before Islam... If only we could collect them all, program them, and put them on a computer..." He turned to face us.

At last I had the chance to express the view that had been turning around in my mind. "The answer would be," I said, "that Walid Masoud was kidnapped against his will, and when he put up a fight, they killed him."

There was a short silence. "Who kidnapped him then?" asked Maryam in a shaky, barely audible voice.

"There are two possibilities," I replied. "First, the enemy or their agents; and second, personal enemies driven by particular motives."

"But how?" she asked, shaking her head. "How?" She came over from where she'd been standing and sat in a leather chair in front of me.

"Please," said Ann in English, "speak slowly so I can understand."

"This is what happened as I see it," I said. "When Walid left Rutba and headed west toward the Syria-Jordan border, another car followed him; it may have been tailing him ever since he left Baghdad. What's important is that the people in this other car succeeded somehow in making him move over and stop, and, on some pretext or other, asked him to get out. Maybe they said they needed some help with their own car. Walid, as you know, was never slow to help anyone, however difficult things might be. Then they pushed him inside their car, drugged him, and took off, leaving his car in the middle of the road with everything still in it. We know that's the way it was found, full of his belongings; even the tape recorder was still on. At Abu al-Shamat border post they took his passport out of his pocket and had it stamped together with their passports. Every time he woke up, they drugged him again, but with just half a dose, so he'd look as though he were awake. Even so, he couldn't think. The same operation was repeated at the Syria-Lebanon border. It seems as though they wanted to kidnap him to Beirut. They were after some secret or other and had decided to get it out of him, so they needed him alive. Or else other agents of the enemy needed him alive in Beirut . . ."

"But all the rumors said they'd found him murdered in Dahr al-Baydar," Maryam said. "Or at least they found somebody they thought was Walid Masoud. Is it reasonable to suppose they took him all that way across the desert and then murdered him on the outskirts of Beirut?"

"Of course not," I replied. "What happened, it seems to me, was that, as the car was climbing the mountain road a little way outside Shtoura, Walid woke up and made the kidnappers believe he'd cooperate if they didn't harm him. The higher the car climbed, the more Walid recovered consciousness in the mountain air. And then suddenly, as the car rounded a bend high in the mountains just before Sofar, the car door opened, or else he himself managed to open it. He either jumped out himself or else pushed the kidnapper who was sitting next to him out of the open door and onto the road . . ."

At this point Jawad put his hand on my arm to stop me for a moment. "Ibrahim," he said, puffing a fine smoke ring from his pipe, "are you repeating the same business he had with Kazim Ismail?"

"What do you mean?" I asked. "What business?"

"Something that happened about fifteen years ago. But never mind. Go on, go on. I'm sorry!"

"We all know," I went on, "that Walid had tremendous muscular strength. But one of the kidnappers, maybe the driver as there were only two of them, stopped the car when this happened, and I can see him leaping out of the car and grabbing hold of Walid. They struggled. Then, before they attracted the attention of drivers in other cars, or else because they were afraid they'd get the worst of things, they shot him, carried him off, and threw him down among the rocks. Or maybe he was the one who was running away, leaping his way down the slope, and they shot him. The corpse they found was said to be riddled with bullets, and the face was badly disfigured... I'm sure that if one of us checked the records of travelers on that day and the following night in Abu al-Shamat, in al-Jadida and al-Masna, he'd find Walid Masoud's name. And if he examined the names that appeared each time with his at the three border posts..."

"What a wonderful detective story," Hala interrupted with a laugh.

But Amer was serious. "It's a marvelous idea," he said. "The trouble is that hundreds of travelers cross at those three border posts, and the majority of them are repeated because most of them are traveling from Rutba to Beirut by those precise posts. But it's a great idea all the same and quite feasible. Just one question, Ibrahim. Why, in your opinion, did they kidnap Walid?"

"Because he certainly was an active member of a guerilla organization. I know he was. They put him in prison in Bethlehem many years ago, and then expelled him from the West Bank. He'd been involved ever since 1948."

"That's true," said Maryam, pushing her long hair back from her face. "We all knew that."

"This applies," I continued, "if the kidnappers were enemy agents. As for enemies or rivals of Walid's who were carrying out a plan for reasons of their own, we have to admit Walid wasn't short of enemies, whatever the reason may have been."

"Your story may sound convincing," said Maryam, "but I don't believe it. I'm sorry, Ibrahim. I don't believe a word of it."

"Of course you don't," I responded, looking at her gorgeous eyes. "Because you insist he's still alive."

"Certainly, I do!"

What a wonderful, difficult creature she is, I thought. Is she still in love with him in her own particular way? Well, at any rate, let's both of us come together in our love for him!

"You all know him very well," Maryam continued. "Yet, you come to a conclusion that doesn't fit with the things you know about him. Even that tape we heard a few days ago at your house, Amer—provided it wasn't a setup or fake by some fiendish devil—gave exactly the opposite impression of what you're all suggesting."

"The tape?" Amer commented. "If you want my frank opinion, I've come to the conclusion Walid was going crazy when he recorded it. I agree with Tariq Raouf on that point. I don't care if it's an Oedipus complex or, more obviously, straightforward madness."

"Is this what Tariq thinks now?" I asked. "Weren't he and Kazim the last people to see him? But neither Tariq nor Kazim said they noticed any sign of madness in Walid when they saw him at Rutba. He seemed lost; that's what they said. I still can't forget how they both bumped into him there, on that particular night . . ."

Amer gave a strange laugh. "The only thing left for you to say after that," he said, "is that they kidnapped him!"

"Impossible," Jawad said. "Impossible."

"Even though," I asked, unable to restrain myself, "there may have been motives we know nothing about?"

"Ibrahim, you're talking rubbish!" said Maryam, giving me a piercing green look of reprimand. "What motives could there have possibly been? They were all friends . . . Oh dear, if we aren't careful, we'll start imagining the most dreadful, convoluted things."

She got up, went over to the books again, and started reading out the titles in a loud voice. My books have never been arranged according to any particular system: Arabic and English books are mixed up, and I'm the only one who knows where to find a particular book in the library. Maryam read out a selection of titles, then turned her back on them. "Man is the product of his culture," she said, addressing her comments to me (give me more, sweetheart!), "don't you agree?"

Her question struck me as odd, but even so I said I agreed.

"In other words," she went on, "everyone's the product of what they read, what nourishes their knowledge and fills their moments of meditation."

"Correct."

"As far as these books of yours are concerned, then, your own cultural education of which you're the product has no connection with class or country . . . and so you yourself have no connection with . . ."

"All right, that's enough!" I said. "You're going to start me imagining the most dreadful, convoluted things if I'm not careful, just as you said. In two seconds you'll turn me into a Martian, and I've never managed to shake the mud of the Tigris off my feet . . ."

Everyone laughed, and the one who laughed loudest of all was Sawsan. "At last someone's come along that you can't push around!" she said.

Maryam waited for a few moments for the laughter to die down. "We were discussing this with some of our professors this morning," she said. "The idea's gaining currency every day because it appeals to the ignorant, and they're increasing in number every day, too, thank God. The notion's based on what seems, on the surface, to be a logical process, which goes like this: Man is a product of his culture. Now, the source of culture today may well be Western books or else the university with its academic programs that are really based on the West as well. So the cultured person is actually a Western product and as such, his ideas have, basically, no connection with his class or his country, and so on."

"And what if his cultural education's been a traditional Arab religious one?" interrupted Jawad.

"No doubt people will say," I answered, "that he, too, is a reactionary product, drawn from an idealized retrospective thought system that rejects both class and country . . ."

"So where does all this lead?" asked Hala.

"The conclusion from this kind of logic," Maryam responded cunningly, "is that culture implies the severance of man's ties to his class and his country. In other words, it's a kind of treason. All these books of yours, Ibrahim al-Hajj Nawfal, angry critic and thinker, are a treacherous plague!"

"Let's burn the lot of them then!" I yelled, raising my glass. "Let's drink a toast to the great blaze to come, when people with no culture will be the only patriots!"

Amer laughed, raised his glass, and took a big gulp of his drink. "You people who live by the pen and writing books," he said, licking his lips, "should really be worried about that."

"Nonsense, Amer, nonsense," said Jawad, blowing a cloud of smoke from his pipe.

"All I'm trying to do is warn you," Amer continued. "Walid and I would often discuss the subject, every time he wanted to publish a new book. You people who insist on earning a living by the word, I used to tell him, should be on your guard. I don't have to worry about things like that."

"Because you don't write?" asked Jawad.

"Exactly. I don't write; I don't express my views on paper. You keep battling against the lords of ignorance. One day you'll find they'll burn your books and they may burn you on top of the pile. For my part, I maneuver myself out of their reach. All I do is work, all the time. I arrange working relationships; I build government buildings, parliament buildings, phony or not, it doesn't bother me. I plan farms for raising chickens or producing cattle. I put up school buildings by the hundreds, which may be able to boast one day that they reject all civilization's books because they didn't write them. Meanwhile, money pours in from all sides, and I use it to have a good time as my cultural education leads me to see fit. It may be the product of the cultures of all the devils put together, but I don't care. I don't talk to anyone about it; it's all done in my own secretive fashion! No critic will ever attack me; they're all too busy writing about you people, you writers. In any case, they've no idea of the real meaning of the things I build and put up. But God help you people! You're going to be the new heathen, and like all heathen, you'll be pursued, banished, and burned. Your pockets will be as empty as your bellies. Martyrs of civilization, as Walid used to say? Certainly. We aren't in disagreement. But what's the point of being a martyr when you're deprived of what you've been extolling? Ha, ha, ha!"

I got up and poured him another glass of cognac. "I didn't realize you were quite so pessimistic!" I said.

"Pessimistic?" he said, taking the glass from my hand. "What, me? Heaven forbid!" He looked at Jawad. "Am I a pessimist, Jawad? I don't know the meaning of the word; only what people tell me, and I don't understand exactly what they're getting at."

I directed my question at his wife, in English. "Ann, don't you think Amer's a pessimist?"

"No, I don't," she replied. "Amer's a fatalist; he believes in everything."

Maryam couldn't restrain herself. "You mean, he doesn't believe in anything."

Ann laughed. "Is there any difference?" she asked.

"None at all," Maryam replied with a wonderful gurgle from her throat. "There's not a shred of difference, whatever Jawad or Ibrahim may say."

I got up to refill Maryam's glass, but she held it away. "I learned my lesson a long time ago," I said. "Our friend Kazim Ismail collected all his articles, at Walid's insistence, and published them as a book called *A Time for Challenge*. I believe he coined the title from a line of Eliot's. When Walid urged me to collect my articles into book form as well, I asked him whether society really needed yet another book that would never be read. His reply was that wolves need a prey. Were we to leave the poor things wincing with hunger? For God's sake, he wanted me to be a prey! I asked him whether that was why he kept urging Kazim to publish his book. 'Don't you see,' he replied with a laugh, 'events have become so momentous that all our faculties have shriveled up trying to cope with them. The disasters we've suffered can't be dealt with in verbal form; all the words have been pulverized.' That's why I'm going to follow your example, Amer."

"You, going to follow Amer's lead, Ibrahim?" asked Sawsan, letting fly at me. "You, who can't resist playing with words for a single moment? I don't believe you!"

My problem was that, even though I'd put a distance between Sawsan and myself, she continued to arouse something hidden deep inside some dark recess of my being. "Yes, Sawsan," I replied. "I'm not going to write anymore after today. I'll record anything I want to say on cassettes, and anyone with the necessary patience and tolerance is welcome to listen. But don't expect me to fill up pages so some debauchee can use them to cover up his doings at my expense. No..."

"Painting's safer," Sawsan replied.

Jawad took the cognac bottle and poured himself another glass. "Neither wolves nor anything else will stop me writing exactly what I please!" he said.

Amer emerged from his silence to play the spoiler, as usual. "My friends, I still reckon that if you learned how to sing and belly dance..."

"It's too late for that," I said. "Much too late."

We gave Amer's wife a translated summary of what we'd been saying. We all laughed. Sawsan got more fascinating as the evening progressed. Everyone became merrier. Each time we found ourselves perplexed, our certainty increased.

I was being very careful not to drink too much, so as to have all my faculties intact with regard to Maryam. I'd decided to broach with her the subject that was boiling inside me, which threatened to give me away when I didn't want that to happen. When they'd all gotten up to go to their cars and I'd escorted them all out to the street to say good-bye to them one by one, I took Maryam by the arm and led her gently to the other side of her car so that Sawsan wouldn't hear.

"Will you marry me, Maryam?" I whispered.

The cruel woman showed not the smallest sign of surprise. In fact, she let out a captivating laugh and stroked my cheek as though I were a cute little baby, then pursed her lips at me and gave me an imaginary kiss. "Some other time, Ibrahim," she said with a stinging sweetness. "Some other time. Goodnight!"

Goodnight, goodnight, all of you!

Here comes the dawn.

Dawn! Here's that one-eyed hag of yesterday, the sun! I've filled up three whole cassettes with my voice here, and anyone who has the necessary patience and tolerance can listen to them. I'm not going to put a single word of it down on paper.

Dr. Jawad Husni Promises More

After people have said what they've said, revealed, deliberately or not, what they've revealed, or else hidden, again deliberately or not, what they've kept hidden, we still have to ask the question: who was it they were actually talking about? Was it a man who occupied their minds and feelings at a certain point in time, or was it themselves and the fancies, frustrations, and uncertainties that beset them in their own lives? Were they in fact the mirror, with Walid serving as the face surveying them from its depths? Or was he the mirror, and their faces the ones rising up, while they, perhaps, weren't even aware of it?

Events have a habit of proliferating without end, just like young palms on dry ground nurtured by the sun and rain. They grow, they intertwine, they become ever thicker, and, before you know it, there's an impenetrable forest that can be breached in only a few places. The trees and thickets reach high into the sky, and some of them envelop others. Any investigation means a difficult walk right through the middle of them, and no sooner do we reach the other side of this congested microcosm than we realize all we've found enlightenment on, in the whole broad domain, is a little space here and another one over there; our only road, indeed, is the wilderness. We search for the horizon, we turn to left and to right, we withdraw and then turn around again, we peruse features and symbols, and we examine ancient monuments: they're a forest of innocence and recklessness, of faith and deception, of action and inaction, of murderer and victim— the enemy in front of you and the sea at your back. And whenever we manage to pierce this forest of events, we carry it with us, too, in the sounds of our throats, the dreams of our nights and days; we eat it in our bread and drink it in our water.

All this is by way of explaining why I didn't wade my way through the sea of papers that filled my desk with their particular brand of silent roar. From forest to sea! Traveling through either of them, like traveling inside mirrors, is both exciting and full of traps. If I've been carrying the forest around with me for more than a year, I'm now carrying the sea as well. I hardly ever sleep except very late, when I'm utterly exhausted. Hala keeps warning me not to get into the habit of taking sleeping pills. But she's no idea of how I'm trying to take all the elements back to square one, to compare part with part, to establish where the gaps are, to look for the lost pieces to fill them, to unravel the intermeshed folds with their obvious, yet scanty evidence, and finally to penetrate to that fastness deep within where motives are incessantly at work like bees in their hive. All these goals have remained my secret addiction and, at the same time, my true pleasure. The sad thing is that I haven't been able to tell anyone else about it; when I enter my office alone, I shut the door and exclude my family, my friends, and people in general. The universe is united in a small room, as crammed full as a forest, rolling like the waves of the sea. I'm at one here, too; I ignite, I'm fired, I circle in rotating heavens like a piece of the sun that's broken off. I feel my way through an unknown universe at once horrifying and wonderful. Yet, the only way I can express any of all this is through a feeble phrase here and an even more feeble phrase there.

In the end, though, I'm going to have to put some of all this down in words, however feeble it turns out to be. When were words bits of chaff, of flame, of rapture, like those that would come to me during the trances that thrust me around and dashed me in pieces just so as to reassemble me, then smashed me in pieces once more, so as to reassemble me once more, and so on ad infinitum? If I were a musician, the whole thing would be fairly easy, but the only commodity I have is words.

Was all this the result of my thinking about Walid Masoud's life? Wasn't I exaggerating things? From the strictly logical point of view, perhaps I was, but really, vitally, I don't think so. And when was my life, or the life of anyone else I know, governed by logic, except for the least significant parts of it?

In recent months certain specific things have happened. I won't venture an opinion as to whether they've reflected a degree of logic or lack of logic in the lives of those I knew; let's say, perhaps, they're a mixture of the two.

Ibrahim al-Hajj Nawfal let his beard grow and grow, till in the end it was so long he looked like a Hindu guru. His gleaming eyes were set in the middle of a face largely hidden behind a mixture of white and black hair, blended together in primordial chaos, and those same eyes gave you the impression of someone with extraordinary psychological powers. Then, suddenly, he shaved off the beard, and his face emerged as its normal circular self, shorn of all power. Thereafter he let his moustache grow for a while and kept trimming it, but when he discovered it lent his face a "melting loveliness," he shaved it off, then let it grow again, allowing it to dangle over his top lip and training it down to his chin on both sides of his mouth, so that he looked severe and morose even when he was laughing. And while he was sporting this new face, he married Sawsan Abd al-Hadi. After a noisy night at our house, he'd spoken to me about his distress over Maryam al-Saffar, and on the very next evening, I was one of the witnesses at his wedding to Sawsan, daughter of Abd al-Hadi Muhammad, widow, and so on and so on.

Two or three days later, we—Maryam and I, that is—were at the International Airport to say farewell to the newlyweds, who were on their way to Rome and London. I've no intention of trying to describe the feelings of Maryam, Ibrahim, or Sawsan during those moments. Everyone was kissing everyone else on the airport tarmac, and Sawsan was crying; I could see the tears in her eyes. Maryam was crying, too, her eyes flooded with tears. Ibrahim was laughing strangely. "Just imagine," he said, "if I were to run into Walid on a Rome street. What do you think, Jawad?"

"It's quite possible," I replied. "Take care of Sawsan, won't you," I went on, changing the subject. "Pamper her!"

"We're going to Florence just for her," he said, "to look for the paintings of Andrea Mantinea."

"And Venice, Padua, Mantua, and Milan as well," Sawsan added. She looked radiant and gorgeous, and her tears made her seem even more so—the tender fruit Ibrahim had wanted to wave in front of my nose, and then picked for himself!

Maryam soon stopped crying, and the newlyweds disappeared in the crowd of travelers. Maryam turned to me. "Marrying Sawsan's the best thing Ibrahim's ever done in his life," she said.

"I just hope," I responded, with a touch of cunning, "that marrying Ibrahim is the best thing Sawsan's ever done, too."

"Time will tell," she muttered, and began looking around.

"Where's your car?" I asked.

"It's at home; there's something wrong with it. I came by taxi."

"In that case, why not let me give you a lift?"

We walked toward my car in silence. For my part, I felt a little embarrassed, and Maryam seemed tense in the car, although she tried very hard to make me think she viewed Ibrahim's marriage as a relief from a burden that had been wearing her out.

"So now it's back to the same old vortex!" I said as the car sped along the long, empty road.

I sensed her giving me a long, silent look, even though I wasn't looking at her directly.

"Are you in it, too?" she asked me finally.

"To a certain extent," I replied frivolously, pushing the button on the cassette recorder to bring us Fayruz in a wonderful *muwashshah*. "Ibrahim," I just couldn't resist adding, "told me a great deal about you."

"Did he?"

"You know Ibrahim. He can't keep anything a secret."

"So what am I supposed to say?"

"About Ibrahim?"

"About . . . oh, anything. Life's so exhausting, Jawad. What does this lifetime want of me? Why don't we just stop at some marvelous point in the whole process, and then move no further for all time?"

Fayruz's voice on the cassette created a mood of sorrow, longing, and pleasure. "Do you know the story about al-Hallaj and the musician?" I asked.

"No."

"They say one of al-Hallaj's disciples heard the sound of the *nay* in the distance and asked his master what the noise was. Al-Hallaj replied that it was the sound of Satan lamenting the destruction of the world he'd wanted to save. Satan was weeping, al-Hallaj told his disciple, because everything goes to perdition, whereas Satan wants to bring everything back to life; but that quality belongs to God alone."

"Well, Jawad," she replied, "you should look on me as a daughter of Satan then. I also rue the destruction of a world I can't save. I'm trying, too, to give life back to everything. Just like this cassette player. You press a button and restore life to all these beautiful tunes."

I laughed. "Maryam," I said, "you can record a new tune every single day."

She put her hand over her eyes in surprise, then ran it through the hair that was billowing around her face. "You, too, Jawad!" she said. "Do you rue the destruction of the world, too? Here you are writing a book about a man who was, and then left!"

"It seems we're all from the same tribe," I said, letting out a deep sigh.

I saw her lean back in the seat, totally relaxed, and put her right elbow on the open window. "One profound experience annuls the entire future. One day I'll tell you everything."

During this period there was an almost total break between Ibrahim and Kazim Ismail. Their friendship had been a long one, but tumultuous as well; and but for the fact that the passage of time had blunted much of Kazim's old temper, Ibrahim might well have found himself faced with a friend confronting him not just with words, but with blows as well. Kazim had heard—probably via Amer Abd al-Hamid—the insulting insinuation Ibrahim had leveled at both him and Tariq on more than one occasion, to the effect that there was something suspicious about their chance meeting with Walid in Rutba on the very night he disappeared.

Kazim came to see me absolutely furious; in fact, I'd never seen him so annoyed. "Does that befuddled drunkard think I'm a kidnapper or something?" he stormed. "Does he think I've murdered a man I regarded as a brother for so many years?" I did my best to calm him down.

"I didn't sleep a wink last night," he said. "It's the truth, I swear to God. How can he accuse me of a despicable thing like that, if only by implication? Even if that sort of crazy idea did occur to him at some drunken moment, his own honor should have decreed he throttle it immediately... What is there between Walid and me to make him think such things? Even if you take the way Walid attacked me on that rainy night—do you remember, Jawad?—all those long years ago; I forgave him, didn't I? Didn't I even write an article about him, which is still one of the most favorable things written about him at the time? Or could it be, I wonder, that Ibrahim's attachment to Sawsan—who deserves someone a bit better than that bearded slanderer!—has shaken him out of his senses, and so he's come to regard me as a rival for her affections? My dear friend, when have I ever been anyone's rival over a woman? What is this vile slander? How can you explain such despicable behavior?" He went on like this for an hour or more.

His suffering was indescribable, and it was complex, too. At moments like these I looked on him as a fugitive creature pursued till his dying breath, then collapsing to the ground with a final cry of despair sticking in his throat. A few days earlier, his new book had come on the market: *A Time for Challenge,* a collection of the better articles he'd written in recent years. It was his second book, the first having appeared in the mid-fifties. A Lebanese journal proceeded to take this work, which he himself regarded as a distillation of the most important ideas in his life, and subject it to sarcastic and withering criticism, in an article by some unknown writer. Kazim swore the author was none other than Ibrahim al-Hajj Nawfal, who was keeping his true identity hidden under an assumed name. I didn't, needless to say, point out that this piece of defamation reminded me of his own attack on Walid Masoud's book fifteen years earlier. Instead, I told Kazim his book was an important one; in due course it would get the approbation it deserved; serious and fair studies would be written about it; its pioneering function concerning many problems connected with culture and literature would become obvious; and so on. At the same time I assured him Ibrahim didn't mean everything Kazim thought he did. The storm would soon blow over, I told him, and only the core would remain, namely, the warm friendship of old. I made use of these and all other available arguments to cope with his misery and anger.

"Kazim," I said, "you've sidetracked me with all this. I haven't had time to congratulate you."

"So you've heard the news," he replied with something more akin to a grin than a smile.

"I read it in the paper this morning. At long last, you've been made a director-general!"

"Yes, after the fall of Basra."

"So your efforts have been recognized at last."

"The publication of my book's more important."

"That's typical of you! Never satisfied about anything."

"I only hope my book won't cause me any trouble in my job now... but even so I mustn't hide the truth. If this new job has any value at all, it's that, for the first time in my life, the timing's exactly right."

"Exactly right with what?"

"My marriage."

The statement was made with the very least amount of excitement or joy a man could possibly muster. In fact, he seemed half sad and half joking.

"Your marriage?" I said in disbelief. "To whom? How could you keep something like that so secret from an old friend like me? Have you been doing things behind my back...?"

He said nothing but kept looking at me with the same expression, a peculiar blend of sorrow and humor, as though his misery wasn't to be shifted from his soul.

"Come on, man, tell me! Who is this fortunate, or, rather, this unlucky girl?"

The grin was suddenly transformed into a laugh. "The unlucky girl in question, Jawad, is Jinan, Jinan al-Thamer."

"That's wonderful! You're marvelous! Why didn't you do it sooner? Although, to be frank, I never realized the two of you had anything in common..."

"Does there have to be anything in common?"

"No," I replied, philosophizing. "Love's the important thing."

"Is love important?"

"Come now, Kazim, don't make fun of it! Of course love's important. Don't you love her, and doesn't she love you?"

"Yes, I love her now."

"Jinan's full of vitality, Kazim. She'll bring you back your youth. You've had enough suffering."

"It all depends on Jinan."

"And on you as well. Just take Ibrahim, your arch enemy, as an example!"

"Please don't mention his name in my presence."

"OK, fine. Aren't you going to ask me to be a witness at the marriage ceremony?"

"Of course, Jawad. How could I do without you?"

I got up and called Hala. He gave her the news, and she let out a marvelous trill of joy that she'd learned from her mother.

"Thank God!" she said. "Samira's convinced you at last!"

"This time," he replied, "I was the one who had to convince Samira! Please, Hala, could you give me one or two lessons about how to understand women's secrets?"

"What?" she said with a loud laugh. "Do you imagine I'd betray my own sex?"

"Let's drink to it!" I shouted. "Here's to your marriage and to women's secrets!"

Logical, illogical, or a blend of the two, here she was accepting him, willingly or reluctantly, when she knew all the facts, all the background, and all the man's strange characteristics. Every time I tried to get back to the real focal point of all these events (and I wonder what Walid would have said about this marriage?), I found my path blocked by ancillary issues. At this moment I recall the words of that author who died of love as a young man: "The greatest magician of all is the one who is prepared to use magic to elevate himself to a level where he comes to regard the creations of his own imagination as specters, each with its own will." Might that not be our situation, too? Did I project myself into the other dimension, till I began to envisage the real people I live with every day as being transformed into the specters of my own imagination, so that I could no longer distinguish their wills from my own? Might that possibly be my own situation?

A few days after Kazim's wedding I decided to have a big party in his honor at our house, and among the people I invited were Amer Abd al-Hamid and Ann, Tariq and Samira and Wisal. When I telephoned Wisal to invite her, she told me immediately she couldn't come, but gave no reason. Then, on the day of the party itself, an hour or two before it was due to start in fact, when we were all in the last-minute turmoil of preparations, she telephoned. My wife noticed, with some surprise, that she asked to speak to me.

"Can I come to your party this evening after all?" she asked.

"Of course you can," I replied. "We'll be delighted. You were one of the first people we thought of inviting!"

"And do you think, Dr. Jawad," she went on, "that I might have a few words with you alone sometime?"

"Yes, of course."

"Thank you!"

"Do you know how to get to our house? It's in the university district."

"I'll come with Tariq. That way I won't get lost."

So she came. She was, though, swallowed up among the large number of guests, and we couldn't spend any time alone because our house is so small. But I did manage to whisper in her ear, without anyone else noticing: "Why don't you come another day?"

She didn't waste any time. Just two days later, she asked if she could come and see me in the afternoon, and I told her she'd be welcome.

"Wisal Raouf's coming to consult me about something important," I told Hala. "We'll talk alone in the library."

My wife didn't take kindly to the idea, but she shrugged her shoulders. "These poor girls!" she said. "Their problems never end. Never mind! Just make sure I get a detailed report later!"

Wisal arrived in her small car, wearing blue jeans and a black shirt open at the neck to reveal a delicate gold pendant with a gold Quran in the middle.

"Walid's alive!" she said the moment I'd shut the library door, before I'd even had time to sit down opposite her on the other side of the couch. "He's alive and well!"

"Are you sure?"

"One hundred percent."

I paused for a moment. I really wanted to calm her down; her small hands were quivering. I lit her a cigarette and noticed how dry her lips were beneath the lipstick.

"Have you seen him?"

"Of course not," she replied. "He's in the Occupied Territories under some other name, and maybe with a new kind of life as well. I don't think anyone knows exactly where he is."

"How do you know all this? Why doesn't he find some way of sending news?"

"That's precisely what I'm upset about, Dr. Jawad. I want to join him."

"What?!" I asked, almost leaping out of my chair. "Join him?"

"Yes! Yes! If he's living in a cave, I'll live there with him!"

"Wisal, these are all wonderful fantasies, romantic dreams. Can't you see that, if Walid really is alive, the whole question's one of total rejection, of self-denial, of . . . ?"

"I know, I know," she interrupted, pounding her knees with her fists so that the blue started turning a whitish color. "He did it when he was a boy, but why do it now when he's older? When he was a boy, he had no one who really wanted him."

"He had his mother and brothers and his sisters, and his father in America."

"Don't you realize, Dr. Jawad, that a man finds his full self only when he detaches himself from his mother and father and brothers and sisters?"

She, it occurred to me, was still living with her mother and father and brothers and sisters. She may well have realized the thought had crossed my mind; in fact, I almost saw it written in the restless movement of her big eyes.

"Walid wants to fight," she continued after a short, tense pause, "and he wants to do it in his own way. I want to be there fighting alongside him."

"But you're leaping to conclusions I'm not sure are justified. How do you know he's alive and in Palestine? You haven't given me any answers yet."

Hala came in at this point with some coffee, excusing herself from sitting with us on the grounds that she was getting dinner ready. She went out again, but only after giving me a quick look that said something like "What's the matter?"

Wisal now started talking in a rambling, disjointed fashion. She told me how she'd contacted Issa Nasser in Amman and Khalid Abu Matar in Beirut, and Usama Hammad and Abd al-Rahman al-Nazir, and . . . and . . . a whole host of names I don't remember anymore. They almost all came to a single conclusion, that Walid had deliberately disappeared to throw his pursuers off the scent, so he'd be able to move freely behind enemy lines. "He wants revenge for the killing of Marwan, and in his own way, his own crazy, stubborn way. The day he feels his thirst for revenge has been slaked, he'll come back. You'll see, Jawad. He'll come back. One day, a while back, I had a feeling he'd been killed. I could see him before my very eyes with bullets searing their way into his body; he kept twisting and rolling over, but the bullets kept chasing him. But now I've come to the conclusion that he's conquered death. Don't smile, Dr. Jawad. I'm not crazy, nor am I as naïve as you may imagine. It's my hunch that he's alive. He thinks of you all and laughs. He thinks of me and laughs. And then he cries because he realizes how much I've been crying for his sake."

I wanted to call my wife in to make sure I wasn't dreaming. I'd lost control over my feelings. Either I was in some kind of trance and Wisal had used some sort of magic spell to draw it up from among all my books and papers, or else this poor, beautiful girl was the one in a trance, a trance now so intense that she'd managed to get me involved in her illusions. I started to be convinced, however much or little evidence there was. It was all to satisfy her wishes, and maybe my own as well. Why shouldn't Walid still be alive? Why shouldn't he go back to a cave as a hermit? He could be traveling under an assumed name, or be a monk in an Italian monastery, or some other monastery for that matter, one of the many he'd described to me. There are thousands of ways for a bird to return to its nest, and, from there, he could move on to action of whatever kind with some of his many friends. Let the heavens pour rain, let them pour fire; that won't scare a man who's traversed the waters without drowning and passed through the fire without burning. Or perhaps he wasn't afraid of drowning or burning anymore, wasn't a real being anymore, even to himself. But to Wisal, to Shahd, to the girl crossing the Euphrates on the back of her own painful imagination, Walid was the one true reality, keeping the faith across the vast expanses, calling from across the deserts and valleys and mountains. For several staggering moments she carried me with her on the back of her own painful imagination.

"Everything's possible with that man," I said. "Everything's possible."

Her cheeks began to flush in a strange way, so much so that I imagined I could actually see the blood as it spread beneath her translucent complexion, as though, before my very eyes, a white rose was changing its color to that of twilight. Her whole face looked like a large, unbelievable rose, with her lips, parted and perplexed, as its blazing center.

"You're with me then," she said, almost panting for breath. "You're with me!"

I didn't know what I was saying. This headlong torrent had swept me away. I forced my eyes to open wide, trying to resist the fall, clinging to the reality I could see all around me—the furniture, the books, and the garden visible through the window. But I failed. There I was still in the stream that swirled along according to its own inner impulse, the impulse of this girl who'd surrendered her will to a set of hurricane forces controlled only by their own secret logic.

"So you're with me, you're really with me!" Wisal repeated. "Don't say anything more, please!"

Suddenly, I stood up, overcome by a sudden feeling of fright that may have lasted for only a couple of seconds. I felt a huge shadow hovering over me like two vast black wings landing on top of my head, then taking flight again, and vanishing through the ceiling of the room into the sky above the garden. I found myself opening the window for no plausible reason, as though I were asking some rescuer from outside to save me. When I turned around again, it was to see Wisal looking at me in bewilderment, with her wonderful eyes and her lips parted; her breasts rose and fell to the beat of a deep and steady panting.

"I'm with you," I said. "I never imagined there was anyone else who knew Walid the way I do. But I was wrong. You know him more than me, better than me, more deeply than me . . ."

She stayed where she was, just looking at me, as though she hadn't heard what I'd said. I took a close look at the radiant face that gleamed from the middle of her jet-black hair, at her feline form as she sat there on the edge of the chair, at her black, open-necked shirt, at the Quran on her chest, at her bare golden arms, at her white leather handbag, her blue jeans, her red open-toed shoes . . . What could such a lovely creature, with her honey-colored eyes, want from a man who'd clutched her to his heart one day, then cast her aside as he did everything he owned or loved? The old thought came back to me: why hadn't Walid talked to me about her? But then there were plenty of things and people he hadn't talked to me about!

A few moments of an amazing, luminous blaze, then everything dies.

I offered her a cigarette and lit it for her, then went back to my seat opposite her and lit my pipe. She picked up her handbag with an air of decision, opened it, and tilted it toward me.

"Here are a lot of papers that may be of some interest to you," she said, "if you'd like to look at them someday . . ."

"Thank you," I said. "Thank you."

She took out several bundles of folded papers and a large collection of small blue pages all the same size. "Keep them with you," she said, "and promise me you won't read them for a long time. And if I ask you to give them back someday . . ."

"I quite understand, Wisal. I'll touch them only when it's absolutely necessary."

Her mascaraed eyes shot out a look of wonderful gratitude. Then she stubbed out her cigarette and stood up, and I called Hala to come and say good-bye.

"What's this, Wisal?" Hala exclaimed when she arrived. "Aren't you staying for dinner? What's the hurry? I'll be very upset if you don't stay!"

"I promise I'll be more sociable next time," Wisal replied with a laugh. "I'll stay for dinner then, and I'm sure it'll be delicious!"

My wife and I accompanied her to her car.

That was the last time I saw her. A few days later she took a plane to Beirut and never came back. I wasn't surprised; in fact, it's exactly what I'd been expecting. She joined the fedayeen and wrote me a letter telling me all about it. At the moment I'm waiting for more news of her and, may I say, of Walid, too.

So here I am today, after collecting my papers and preparing my notes. Now I'll begin my study in earnest. I wonder if I'll ever reach a definite conclusion about Walid. Can there ever be a definite conclusion about any event in life, let alone a man's life as a whole? I ought to sift through all the facts and data, eliminate the false trails and fabrications and delusions, then try to reach a conclusion that will entail the least degree of contradiction possible. But my sense of responsibility as a researcher won't let me do that. Even fabrications and delusions about a man have their own particular importance; why would they be invented otherwise, and where would they come from? Are events always material, palpable, and rationalizable? Don't some people have a power that can't be explained by these events, because it's a torrent of streams untrammeled by analysis, action, or place? The connecting parts don't always fit together exactly, and contradictions may show up in the tiniest elements. But who ever said that the different parts of life are all fitted together logically and harmoniously? Wherever life's a continuous struggle, a continuous challenge, continuous love, then all these things require the creation of conflicting relationships, so that the product of the parts is much greater than the mere whole. Walid was the product of his life, and the lives of those around him, the product of his own particular time and of our time in general, all this at once. And what time were they both, his time and ours?

So it's back to the forest and back to the sea.